# *a* PLACE *to* BELONG

## ABBIE WILLIAMS

central
avenue
publishing

2020

Published by Central Avenue Publishing, an imprint of Central Avenue Marketing Ltd.
www.centralavenuepublishing.com


Published in Canada
Printed in United States of America

1. FICTION/Romance     2. FICTION/Family Life

**A PLACE TO BELONG**

Trade Paperback: 978-1-77168-207-7
Epub: 978-1-77168-208-4
Mobi: 978-1-77168-209-1

For my sweet daughters.

# LANDON, MINNESOTA FAMILY TREES

Landon, Minnesota, 1930s/40s ~
*Myrtle Jean Davis
(Founder of the Shore Leave Café)
Minerva Jean "Minnie"
Louisa Rae "Lou"

*Louisa Rae Davis m. Aaron Owens
Ellen Jean
Joan Eileen "Joanie"

Landon, 1960s ~
*Joan Eileen Davis m. Mick Lawson Douglas
Joelle Anne "Jo"
Jillian Rae "Jilly"

Landon, 1980s/90s ~
*Joelle Anne Davis m. Jackson Gregory Gordon
Camille Anne
Patricia Joan "Tish"
Ruthann Marie "Ruthie"

*Jillian Rae Davis m. Christopher Isaiah Henriksen
Clint Daniel

Landon, 2000s ~
*Joelle Anne Davis m. Blythe Edward Tilson
Matthew Blythe "Matt"
Nathaniel Edward "Nate"

*Jillian Rae Davis m. Justin Daniel Miller
Louisa Rae "Rae"
Riley Justin
Zoe Joelle

*Camille Anne Gordon—Noah Patrick Utley
Millie Joelle "Millie Jo"

*Camille Anne Gordon m. Mathias James Carter
Henry Mathias
Brantley Malcolm
Lorie Anne
James Boyd

*Clint Daniel Henriksen m. Danielle Elaine Woll

# JALESVILLE, MONTANA FAMILY TREES

Jalesville, Montana, 1970s/90s ~
*Clark Thomas Rawley m. Faye Elizabeth Bridger
Garth Thomas
Marshall Augustus
Sean Harley
Quinn Bridger
Wyatt Zane

*Julianna Louise "Julie" Rawley *m.* Aaron Heller
(Owners of The Spoke)
Pamela Therese "Pam"
Netta Grace
Lee Louise

Jalesville, Montana, 2000s ~
*Patricia Joan "Tish" Gordon *m.* Charles Shea "Case" Spicer
Anne Marie "Annie"
Charles Shea "Shea"
Cady Louisa "Cady Lou"

*Ruthann Marie Gordon *m.* Marshall Augustus Rawley
Axton Clark "Ax"
Marshall Augustus, Jr. "Gus"
Celia Faye
Colin Miles
Luke Grantley

*Garth Thomas Rawley *m.* Rebecca May "Becky" Robinson
Thomas Clark "Tommy"
Isaac Jameson
Tansy Faye
Colt Alexander
Garrett Marston

*Sean Harley Rawley *m.* Jessica Rose "Jessie" Dahlen-James
James Bridger "Jamie"
Harleigh Faye
Michael Ulysses "Mikey"

# PROLOGUE

TIME ADVANCES AT A STEADY PACE, WHETHER you wish it did or not.

Memories, of course, are regulated by no such grounding.

That first winter, my thoughts seemed more frozen than the earth outside. An ice pick would have been required to chisel them free from the prison of remembrance. Despite the many and well-meaning assurances of those who loved me, passing months had done little to ease the ache. Images would assault me without warning, more immediate in those moments than reality; his face, his voice, the same ones I had known and cherished since my earliest memories.

*That layer of rocks out there, see that?* He indicated with an outstretched arm. *That's where my family first built a house on this land.*

My own voice next; how badly I craved his attention. *I know that. You told me the last time we were here. Can we ride out there?*

I knew he would say yes. As long as he deemed it safe, he never denied me a thing, and I loved riding beside him through the foothills surrounding his family's home, holding the reins as he had taught me, moving with my horse, feeling her strong, warm muscles against my legs.

*A good rider communicates with voice and body movements. And horses respond more to how you move, don't forget,* Wy had reminded me in the corral earlier that morning, while cinching his saddle strap. At fourteen, he knew more about horses than most adults did. Clark, his dad, once told me that Wy had learned to ride almost before he could walk, just like all four of his older brothers.

*I know,* I insisted. *I remember.*

*Do you need help with that?* He pointed to the cinch strap I was fastening beneath Sunny, my mare.

*No, I know how to do it,* I blurted, wanting him to be impressed with my memory. Wy had taught me to tack a horse the summer before, when I was seven. The only part I couldn't manage was settling the heavy saddle on Sunny's back.

He watched to make sure, without saying anything, and I finished saddling my horse, keeping the leather straps flat against Sunny's shiny, maple-colored hide, careful to avoid pulling her hair the wrong direction and to tighten the buckles just right. I concentrated so hard that sweat ran down the sides of my face in sticky trails and I almost chewed through my bottom lip.

*Good work, Mill,* he praised when I was finished.

*Can we ride out there?* I repeated, nudging Sunny's sides with the heels of both boots, easing her forward from a standstill. It felt so good to be outside, with the wild Montana air all around us and the bright sun beating down on our heads, and I wanted to ride fast and stay ahead of the rest of our families the way Wy let me—he knew I could handle a canter. He never nagged me to slow down. He just kept pace beside me.

*Sure,* was his cheerful response.

His gray cowboy hat, the one he always wore, made a shadow over his brown eyes, but I knew exactly what those eyes looked like, down to the smallest flecks of color. There was a gold splash in his right iris, like a sunbeam behind his pupil. He was riding Shadow, his horse. Wy had raised Shadow from a foal, and it was on Shadow's back that I had first learned to ride, during one of my family's summer visits to Montana. We drove from Minnesota nearly every July to visit my mom's younger sisters, Tish and Ruthie. Aunt Ruthie was married to Wy's older brother, Marshall Rawley.

*Race you there!* I yelled, startling Sunny, who snorted and swung her head, but she bounded ahead when I tapped her flanks with my heels.

The ground sailed past, a blurry rush of brown earth and green grass as Sunny flowed into a smooth canter. I held the reins exactly as Wy had taught me, gripping with my knees, bending forward over her neck to minimize drag. I saw Wy and Shadow catch up in the space of a breath, galloping into view about a dozen feet from my left side, Wy leaning low over Shadow's neck. They edged into the lead as the horses raced up a small rise in the dun-colored earth. I knew Wy would never let me win because I was younger, or a guest of his family—beating him required real skill. I heeled Sunny once more, screaming and laughing, exuberant sounds swept away in the wind we stirred up.

I shrieked to my horse, *C'mon, girl, go, go!*

The horses' hooves struck the ground with a steady, three-beat rhythm. We flew past the foundation of the Rawley family's old homestead, Wy and Shadow in the lead, and he drew on the reins to slow him before circling back around, whooping in victory.

*Next time!* I hollered, circling Sunny in the opposite direction.

*You wish!* He grinned as he added, *That was good riding, though.*

I felt sunlight glow inside my chest at the compliment; I never felt anything but joy around Wy. Since nearly the first time we met, I had loved him all the way down to the insides of my bones.

And once, I'd believed he felt the same.

# PART ONE

# CHAPTER ONE

## LANDON, MINNESOTA

"MILLIE, FIVE-TOP OUTSIDE!" RAE CALLED AS SHE breezed past me through the dining room, her arms loaded with empty baskets and beer mugs from her last porch table.

"I'm on it!" I yelled over my shoulder, hooking my pen behind my right ear so my hands remained free. I assured the young family whose order I'd just taken that their food would be right out, then hurried over to the bar to collect a tray of beer before pit-stopping at the ticket window to grab three baskets of fried clams. I deposited these items at two separate tables and still made it out to my newest customers in less than a minute.

Not only had I worked at Shore Leave almost every week since turning fifteen, two years ago now, I spent more time here at my family's café than at home. The first years of my life took place only steps away, in the house where my mother and I had lived after I was born. Since my many-times great-grandmother Myrtle Jean Davis first opened Shore Leave, each subsequent generation of Davis women had inhabited the lake house and worked in the café, raising children, wildflowers, vegetables, and, occasionally, some hell. My earliest memories revolved around women and the delectable food they made—fish fillets and thick-cut potatoes crackling in the deep fryer; soft dough in which I'd curled my toddler fingers and that I'd eventually learned to shape into biscuits and cinnamon twists; homemade raspberry ice cream decorated with fresh spearmint; chocolate buttercream frosting spooned in decadent swirls over cooled yellow cake.

The ever-present scent of coffee, brewed strong. Checkered blue tablecloths and dinner rush as the sun sank over Flickertail Lake; the sweet sigh of relief after the final ticket of the night was closed out and I could steal a moment with Rae Miller, my cousin and closest friend, to sit at a porch table to count our tips. I loved everything about Shore Leave, abundantly grateful I'd been raised in such a place, in proximity to family and friends and a crystalline expanse of water bordered by old-growth pine forest. Beauty knew no boundaries here in the north woods. I had learned to swim almost before I could walk and spent as many hours soaking in the lake as time and weather permitted. My great-grandmother, Joan

Davis, continued to occupy the lake house; her daughters—my grandma, Joelle Tilson; and my great-aunt, Jillian Miller—also lived nearby with their families; likewise, my parents had long ago made a home just around the lake road.

Spring was our only slow season at the café, that expectant, slushy lull while the ice was too thin for icehouses but had not completely melted away. "Ice out" was a big deal for all the local resorts; we marked the date on the calendar every spring, when winter's stranglehold on land and water ended and the spring tourist season officially began. Summer was currently in full swing, as our chaotic dining room attested. My mom, Camille, and her two younger sisters, Tish and Ruthie, were out on Flickertail just now, lounging atop inflatable rafts and drinking the lemon-infused beer they favored when it was hot; every so often one of them would swim to the dock to refresh their drinks from a packed cooler. I smiled at the sight, knowing how much Mom missed her sisters, who both lived many hundreds of miles away, in Jalesville, Montana. If we didn't visit them out west, Auntie Tish and Aunt Ruthie packed up their busy families in July and made the drive to Minnesota instead.

My good mood faded as I approached the newest table on the porch. Rae hadn't mentioned they were a group of frat-boy types, probably the sons of wealthy families staying at one of the fancier resorts on the lake. I'd waited on plenty of these sorts of guys during past summers, and experience had taught me that nine times out of ten they were jackasses. Fussy, entitled, and decked out in swimwear and hair products that cost more than I made in a month—in other words, the kind of guys I really detested.

I pasted on the impersonal smile I reserved for tourists and said brightly, "Hi there, what can I get you to drink?"

Hot noontime sun poured over us; they'd left their table's umbrella deflated, perhaps to work on their tans. Four of the five wore wraparound sunglasses and expensive short-john wetsuits which had left puddles beneath their sandaled feet, suggesting a morning spent wakeboarding; the fifth, to my immediate right, wore a sapphire-blue neoprene vest with matching trunks, showcasing muscular, sun-burned arms. Their conversation, loud and boisterous, ceased the minute I appeared. They all looked up at me; neoprene vest guy lifted his mirrored shades to the top of his head and leaned closer to read the nametag pinned above my left breast. At least, that's what I assumed he was doing.

With a growing smile, he slowly read aloud, "Millie Jo. That's so damn *cute*."

I tried not to grit my teeth as I muttered, "Thanks."

"This is Piers," announced the guy to his right, appearing lazily amused; both wore the presumptuous smirks of males who figure they can get you naked in less than twenty-four hours. "Isn't that a *cute* name too?"

But I was accustomed to this sort of exchange.

"Nowhere near as cute as the girls inside waiting for their margaritas." I spoke in a hushed voice, attempting to convey the sense of a juicy secret. Immediately the guys took the bait; this time, my smile was genuine.

They all spoke at once, craning their necks to peer toward the wide front windows, but the blinding sun blocked all hope of seeing inside the café.

"What girls?"

"Maybe the ones we saw on that skiff this morning!"

"Run in there, Graham, sniff 'em out."

"See what they're doing tonight."

"Yeah, like preferably *us*."

"Calm down, guys, don't be so fucking obvious."

The one called Piers returned his gaze to me after ordering them to calm down, and I realized he was beginning to smell a rat; his eyes narrowed as he ordered, "Buy them a round on us, will you, Millie Jo? Make it the most expensive tequila this place has. There *is* a top shelf in this place, right?"

If I'd been toting a pot of coffee, I would have upended it right over his shiny, neoprene crotch. I held his gaze as I said lightly, "You got it, Pierce."

I watched a scowl flicker across his brow but he didn't correct my mispronunciation of his name, instead adding, "And bring us a couple of pitchers of lager, whatever you have on tap."

"Then I'll need to see some ID."

They produced waterproof wallets without complaint; they were all mid-twenties, with addresses in suburbs of Minneapolis. I caught up with Rae at the bar.

She absorbed my expression and immediately said, "I'm sorry. I would have taken them, but I was too busy at that second. Are they really bad?"

"Just typical." I leaned on the bar counter to give my beer order to Barry, the daytime bartender.

"You got it, hon," he said over his shoulder.

I collected the pitchers and turned to head back to the porch when I noticed two of the wetsuit guys entering from outside and scanning the dining room.

*Shit*, I thought. *That was fast.*

I snagged Rae and requested, "Hey, drop these off for me. Pretty please."

"Sure thing."

"I owe you!" I promised.

I checked on my other tables, delivered food, and in general stalled, but Rae had been kind enough to take the frat-boys' order when she dropped off the pitchers.

"I can run it out for them too," she offered when we caught up again at the ticket window five minutes later. "They kept asking where you were and what we were doing later. The one guy just *loves* saying your name, doesn't he? I hate when guys do that, when they think they have something on you because they know your name."

"I told them there was a group of cute girls in here so they'd shut up, but it backfired," I explained, lining baskets of fish and onion rings along my left forearm. "Two of them checked and realized I was lying. No cute girls waiting for margaritas!"

Rae angled me a sly smile, her long ponytail swishing over her shoulder. I'd always been jealous of her silky, sunshine-gold hair. "Well, there's *us*."

"I meant girls who might actually be interested in guys like that." I blew a breath upward to redirect a strand hanging in my eye; sweat had collected along my forehead and beneath my arms. I cast a wishful glance toward town. "We should have gone to the beach with everyone this morning."

*With Wy*, I didn't say. Along with my aunts and their husbands and kids, Wy had arrived from Montana yesterday evening, which meant I had less than one week and six days left of this summer's chance for precious time around him.

But Rae knew me too well; she heard the longing in my voice.

"They'll be back soon. I don't think they took any food and it's already past noon. Are you helping me babysit tonight, or what?"

"Maybe," I hedged, not wanting to commit to anything until able to determine Wy's plans for the evening. A seedling of hope had taken root in my heart at the fortune of an unexpected opportunity—that Wy just might decide to stay behind at Shore Leave while all the other adults ventured around the lake to Eddie's Bar for the music, and then *I'd* stay behind, and then we could sit together at the end of the dock as the sun set . . .

"Look, there's the kids." Rae nodded toward the porch. "I bet everyone's back already."

I flew to the front windows for a better view of the parking lot; sure enough, everyone had returned from their trip to the Landon beach, toting inner tubes, sandy towels, and sunburns. My gaze sought and clung to Wy, and just that fast a vivid golden glow, like hot sun striking the lake, filled my chest. My reflection was faintly visible in the window glass, showcasing the beaming smile I could no more have contained than I could have stopped tomorrow's dawn from breaking.

*There he is, there he is!*

"You're a good liar," someone at my elbow said. Preoccupied by my absorption with Wy, I hadn't noticed his approach.

Irritated, I muttered without thinking, "They just didn't want your shitty tequila, that's all."

Amusement flickered over his features. Lowering his eyelids in a clear attempt to appear seductive, Piers murmured, "Well, then you *owe* us, Millie Jo. What are you and four of your close, personal friends doing later?"

It took sincere effort not to shudder; it was with satisfaction that I informed him, "I'm seventeen."

His gaze dropped to my breasts and then roved along my lower body with no sense of reservation or shame before returning to my face. "No fucking way are you only seventeen."

I forced myself to maintain eye contact despite the cold twinge in my gut. "I am. And no *fucking way* would I ever go anywhere with you."

All amusement vanished from his expression.

I turned away before he could reply, putting the crowded dining room between us, grateful to observe that he and his friends left within five minutes; Rae, who collected their checks, informed me that their collective tip had totaled around three dollars, mostly loose change.

"Assholes," she muttered.

"Typical," was all I had to say.

. . .

I struggled to concentrate after that, with Wy in proximity; I kept finding excuses to drift near the windows, peering outside to spy him helping the little kids stow their water toys and life jackets in the boat shed. He wore faded orange swim trunks and no shirt, offering a heavenly view of the lean, tanned muscles of his arms and torso, his chest covered in dark hair; a slim line of hair continued down the front of his stomach, disappearing into the top of his swim trunks. Heat concentrated in my lower belly as I imagined my fingertips following that line to its conclusion. A tattoo of a small black horse posed in galloping flight and with a wild mane graced his right bicep; that was new as of this summer.

Wy's shaggy, sun-streaked brown hair was slightly messy, as usual. I'd witnessed him "comb" it many times over the years; he used both hands, no comb. When we were in Montana, he perpetually wore his battered, much-loved gray cowboy hat; here in Landon he went hatless and let the lake dictate his appearance. Wy never seemed bothered by the overall state of his clothing or hair. He was the least fussy man I'd ever known and I found this unbelievably appealing. As I watched, he lifted my little cousin Celia, who was also his niece, and spun her in circles, both of them laughing.

He threw her over his shoulder, upside down; through the screen door I heard him demand, "Had enough yet?" as she shrieked with laughter and pounded her fists on his back.

"Miss, could we get our bill?" asked an elderly couple near the windows, and I startled to attention.

"Yes, of course." I hurried to riffle through the front pocket of my apron for their ticket, my final table of the afternoon. We did things the old-fashioned way at Shore Leave, no computers or digital screens in sight. I wrote out every order and clipped the small green sheets to the revolving metal wheel in the ticket window; later, I met each customer at the till, which chimed its cheery bell with every sale. I loved the way so many customers commented with appreciation on the outdated style of our café.

"You forgot to add our ice cream sodas." The man spoke politely, having donned a pair of glasses to scan the bill.

"They're on me," I offered at once.

"Well, isn't that nice," said the woman. "Thank you, dear."

I led the way to the front of the café, where the screen door was propped open by a twelve-pack of cola, allowing for a tempting glimpse of Flickertail basking beneath the afternoon sun. Mom and her sisters were headed up from the dock, wrapped in beach towels; Aunt Ruthie and Mom carried the beer cooler between them. Mom's long hair hung over her shoulders, the sun creating a bright halo around her curls as she walked with her arm linked through Auntie Tish's; they looked like teenagers. The elderly couple paid their bill and then ambled outside. The man placed a gentle hand on the woman's lower back as they navigated the porch steps, and I was somewhat stunned to feel tears prickle the bridge of my nose. Witnessing the sweetness of the gesture erased the lingering unpleasant chill Piers had left in my stomach.

"Hey, you done with work yet?"

And just that fast, Wy was striding up to the register from the opposite side of the café, gaze fixed on me like he couldn't wait to hear my response. He now wore a threadbare green T-shirt advertising his aunt's restaurant in their hometown, a bar and grill called The Spoke. His shoulders were slightly wet, creating damp patches on the shirt along the ridges of muscle extending from his neck. Tiny sand grains were visible in the dark hair on his forearms. The aroma of the lake clung to him, but beneath that was his own natural scent, which I could have singled out from a hundred others. Just like always, I battled the need to lean closer and inhale until my lungs filled to capacity.

"Did you guys have fun swimming?" I asked, embarrassed that I sounded winded. I couldn't help it; my heart was galloping as swiftly as the horse in his tattoo. It took effort to keep my expression neutral.

*I love you, I love you, I love you*, I thought as our eyes held, wishing he could read my mind.

"It would've been more fun if you'd been with," he said, as guileless and straightforward as usual. I'd known Wy since I was two years old and never read this type of statement as flirtatious. We'd been good friends since we were little and I knew he liked me just fine; an easy familiarity had always existed between us. Only in the past two years had I experienced such heady tension in his presence.

"I wish I would have come with." I indicated his right arm. "Is that Shadow? When did you get a tattoo?"

Wy's cheerful grin deepened as he shifted, rolling back his sleeve. "Isn't it great? A bunch of us got these in Pullman to celebrate the end of the semester, back in May. It was a toss-up between a horse and a longhorn skull, but I argued for horse. Luckily, I was in the majority. My friend Joey almost held out for the skull, but we talked him out of it."

"A skull wouldn't have conveyed the same message," I agreed, inspecting the tattoo, which was inked with a smooth blending of gray and deep navy, not flat black as it appeared from a distance. I traced my fingertips over the graceful, running shape and my heart thrust hotly at the direct contact with his skin.

"I had Shadow in mind, you're right," he explained. Shadow's mother had been Wy's beloved first horse, Oreo.

Two summers ago, during our last visit to Montana, I had climbed up on the lowest rung of the gate around Shadow's stall in the Rawleys' massive horse barn and combed my fingers through the gorgeous animal's thick, inky mane. Shadow's right ear cocked in my direction and I leaned close, patting his dapple-gray neck as I whispered, *I love him with all my heart. You keep him safe for me, okay?* Shadow had nickered in a companionable way and nudged my ribs with his long nose, and I'd indulged ever since in imagining that Wy's horse approved of my deepest secret.

"It's beautiful," I whispered, withdrawing my fingertips from the curve of his bicep; it almost hurt to stop touching him.

"You should see Scout these days, Mill, you wouldn't recognize him," Wy continued, and the sound of his longtime nickname for me sent giddy little thrills down my spine. "I know I showed you pictures last night, but I mean in person. Next summer, no excuses. Cider had twin foals this last spring, you should see them. And I'm thinking of getting a sow, did Ruthie tell you?"

"You are?" I asked, elated by his enthusiasm and tickled at the thought of a plump, grunting pig trotting between the sleek hooves of their numerous horses. The pig would be kept in a separate part of the barn, but still.

Wy returned my smile, leaning over the till counter on both elbows. "For one thing, I happen to like pigs. And for another, I'm hoping to eventually breed her.

There's a demand for organic pork in our area, so it's a bonus either way."

I knew him far too well to let this statement slide. "Yeah, *right*. You'd name every single baby pig and totally love all of them, and then you're telling me you'd sell them as organic bacon?"

His eyes glinted with teasing as he admitted, "I already have a few names picked out."

"Such as?" I demanded, my tension ebbing.

"Pork Rind and Chops, for sure."

"Petunia," I supplied.

"And maybe Ribsy . . ."

I cried gleefully, "Bacon Bits! For the runt of the litter."

"That's a good one, he'll be yours."

*Yours.*

I cherished the way he often said things like that. As though there really would come a time in which Wy's beloved pets would also belong to me; Wy, who loved animals even more than I did. To cover my fluster, I teased, "You're the one who famously stole a cat, remember?"

"Yeah, I can't deny that," he acknowledged as we studied each other in pure enjoyment. "And I would do it again, no questions."

Though I had not been present for the actual event, I knew every detail, thanks to Wy's family's fondness of the story; Clark, his dad, related it often. The summer Wy was twelve, he had seen another kid in their town holding a cat by the tail and whacking it with a stick. And so, without hesitation, Wy had stormed across the kid's lawn, shoved him aside, grabbed the cat, and then ran hell-for-leather. In the ensuing upset between the kid's parents and Clark, Wy's earnest insistence that he'd rescued the animal from abuse prevailed, and the cat—a shabby tom they renamed Otis Lee—had lived out its days in comfort with Wy's Aunt Julie.

"Of course you would. You're a hero," I said, with heartfelt sincerity.

His grin became almost bashful at my words, making him appear younger, as if he was my age rather than six years older. Just shy of six years; his birthday, February sixteenth, was only two days past mine.

*What would it take?*

*Oh God, what would it take for us to be together?*

*I'll be eighteen by next summer . . .*

Our gazes remained steady as silence held us in a temporary lull. His eyes were so incredibly beautiful, framed by spiky black lashes, irises a rich, smoky brown; my adoring gaze caressed his face, imbibing anew all the details I'd loved for so damn long I couldn't remember a time before that love—the gold sunburst in his right eye and his sensual lips, the upper sculpted with a crisp peak on the bow; the clean lines of his jaws and chin; his dark, expressive eyebrows and just-too-long, arrow-straight nose. A stubborn nose, Aunt Ruthie always said, possessed by all the Rawley men, to which Uncle Marshall would contradict, *Stubborn, yes, but not unreasonable.*

My pulse accelerated; the way Wy was leaning on his elbows over the counter put our faces only about eighteen inches apart. My smile slowly faded as I witnessed something in his expression change with hardly a shifting of his features—and sudden hope, almost painful in its intensity, swelled in my chest. My lips parted to ask about his plans for the evening but at that exact second he stood back to his full height, as though compelled to increase the distance between us, and confusion welled, diluting my hope.

Indicating the parking lot, Wy said, "I better help get the kids wrangled up." As though to minimize the sting of becoming suddenly aloof, he invited, "Head out as soon as you're done!"

And so saying, he loped down the porch steps into the hot afternoon sun, and I dragged my eyes away.

# CHAPTER TWO

MY YOUNGER BROTHER HENRY DARTED INSIDE
the café twenty minutes later, out of breath and soaking; he'd jumped or been
pushed into the lake since returning from the beach. Rae and I were sitting at
table three, counting our tips and rolling napkins around flatware in preparation
for tomorrow's shift. The parking lot had emptied of people; most of the little kids
had returned to the lake house for showers or naps. My parents, along with Aunt
Jilly, sat around a table on the porch, leaning on their elbows, fanning their faces
in the late-afternoon heat. Mom and Dad were sharing a beer and the sound of
their laughter as Aunt Jilly told a story could have been the soundtrack of every
past summer at Shore Leave. Low-slanting sun tinted the dining room the shade
of clover honey.

Wy and his dad, Clark, had disappeared around the bend in the lake road
ten minutes ago; the two of them typically rented a small suite at Angler's Inn
downtown since space was so scarce, what with all the cousins. In Wy's absence,
disappointment wedged its unwelcome self all around my heart; I hadn't ventured
outside to ask what he planned to do this evening, thereby wasting yet another
opportunity to spend time with him.

*It's your own fault. You hid out in here instead of joining them.*

*But he didn't even come inside to say good-bye.*

*Because he probably figured he would see you later.*

*But . . .*

"You're dripping all over the place!" Rae scolded Henry, interrupting my
woolgathering. She swept aside the green plastic tub of napkins.

In response Henry tipped forward over the table and shook his wet hair like
a puppy, sending droplets flying over us.

"Quit it!" I kicked his ankle.

"Mom, Millie's hitting me!" Henry hollered in the direction of the porch.

Mom leaned around Dad. "Is anyone bleeding in there?"

"I am!" Henry lied, hopping from one bare foot to another.

"There's bandages behind the counter!" Aunt Jilly called merrily.

"Just don't make the girls so angry they decide to break bones, son," Dad
added.

"What do you want?" I demanded of my brother.

"Hurry up!" Henry complained. "Mom said we can't go until you're done."

"You can go," Rae assured him. "I'll bring Millie home later."

"You better be nice to us tonight," Henry warned Rae; his voice had started changing last winter and it was especially amusing when it cracked just as he issued what was supposed to be a threat.

Rae laughed, snapping her gum. "Or what? You'll tell?"

Henry began bobbing his head in preparation to work up a loud belch.

"Don't you dare!"

He let loose with a rifle-shot of a burp, aiming for Rae's forehead, and then turned tail and ran back outside, bypassing the porch.

Mom yelled, "Henry Mathias Carter, I heard that!"

Dad only laughed. "The whole town probably heard that. No wonder my sisters always wanted to kick my ass when I was that age."

"This is why all children should be girls," Aunt Jilly said, vigorously fanning her chest with a corner of her beach towel. She leaned toward the open window. "Girls, whip up a pitcher of margaritas!"

"*Mom*," Rae scolded, teasing. "No hard liquor before five, you told me to remind you."

"It has to be close to five by now!" Aunt Jilly blew a kiss in our direction.

I studied my own mother through the window, as she sipped from her beer bottle. Dad rested a hand on Mom's back, just like the elderly couple from earlier, letting her damp, tangled curls twine around his fingers as he rubbed a tender path along her spine. For the second time today, tears caught me off guard; a stinging lump built in my throat.

*It would be like that between Wy and me, I know it.*

*If only Wy didn't see me as a child, a little tagalong girl.*

Rae finished the last set of flatware, flinging it in the green plastic tub with a sigh of relief, and I turned away so she wouldn't question why I appeared on the verge of tears. No such luck; I already felt her speculative gaze. Just like Aunt Jilly, Rae had always possessed high levels of intuition, which bordered on occasional precognition; the name our family had long ago assigned to these strange flashes of the future was "notion." No one bet against Aunt Jilly or Rae, regarding anything; it was best to assume they already knew.

Even though Rae's older brother, Clint, had just driven his truck into the parking lot, beeping his horn and directing everyone's attention his way, Rae kept her voice low as she informed me, "Wy said he was going out to Eddie's tonight. You could join them. I can handle the kids."

I loved that I never had to explain myself or justify anything to my cousin.

Knuckling my eyes, I muttered, "I'm not going to chase after him. It's humiliating."

I sensed her leaning over the table. "You're hardly chasing him. You guys are friends, you always have been."

"I fucking *hate* that word and you know it." I kept my gaze averted, not wanting to spy any stray pity on Rae's face.

Outside, the ruckus increased with the arrival of Rae's dad, Justin, and her grandfather, Dodge, who worked together at Miller Auto, their filling station and repair shop. Aunt Ruthie and Uncle Marshall were strolling toward the café from the lake house, holding hands, Uncle Marshall carrying a black guitar case. Aunt Ruthie wore a short green sundress that showed off her tan and clung softly to her curvy body, swinging their joined hands as they laughed about something together. Marshall was Wy's older brother and resembled Wy so much that it was like glimpsing the future—a thirtysomething Wy walking along holding hands with a beautiful wife.

Just imagining that wrenched my heart with such force I pressed a fist against my ribcage.

Rae lowered her voice another notch. "This has to stop."

I chewed my lower lip, hating my current lack of emotional control. Rae's tone was gentle and her words rang true, but I couldn't heed them. Not yet, anyway; my hope would persist until proven wrong. Rae was the only person who knew the true depth of my feelings for Wy. Mom and Aunt Ruthie called it a crush and assumed it would pass. I didn't resent this; they couldn't realize the strength of what I felt. I kept almost no secrets from my mother, but had never confided that I was in love with Wyatt Rawley; I already knew I couldn't bear the resultant conversation.

Rae rested her fingertips on my wrist, inspiring a small, electric tingle along the bones of my forearm, the same one I felt when Aunt Jilly touched me; a nonverbal recognition of their vibrant energy. Picking up the discarded threads of the conversation we'd started late last night, she murmured, "I get it, you know I do. Wy is great. He's funny, he's sexy as hell. If I was you, I'd want my first time to be with him too. But he's a *man*, Mills. A grown man. You know you can't ask him something like that."

We'd spent over an hour debating this topic last night and Rae had been ready to strangle me at several different moments. At one point, torn between hilarity and exasperation, she had demanded in a whisper, *Just exactly how do you plan to ask him? Straight out? Like, "Hey, Wy, I have a question. If you're not busy later tonight, would you mind taking my virginity? Yes, you heard me right, my virginity. You know, just the irretrievable symbol of my innocence, no big deal. You're not busy?*

*Okay, great! I'll call you around nine, then?"*

And we'd laughed until our stomachs ached, burying our faces in her bed pillows.

Despite the absurdity of Rae's version of the potential conversation, I had no intention of letting this summer pass without somehow asking Wy that very question.

*Wy, listen. I have a proposition for you . . .*

"I'm not a little kid. I know exactly what I want," I protested, fiddling with the pile of stacked napkins on the table.

"You don't look like one anymore, but in his eyes you are still *for sure* a kid." Rae abandoned tact and went right for the jugular. "I mean, if you were eighteen it would be one thing. At least Wy wouldn't go to jail for having sex with you."

The phrase *having sex with you* erupted like a volcano along my lower belly, hot and thrilling and ultimately forbidden. The thought of kissing Wy was enough to send my heart into a seizure, let alone the thought of having sex. I'd never had sex with anyone, had never come close. I'd kissed a few guys and once let Sam Mulvey get to second base, but none of the boys I attended school with compared to Wy.

"I'm just worried about you," Rae said softly, and I knew this was true; I trusted her. We watched out for each other as well as any two sisters would. She drummed her fingers lightly on my wrist bones, her gaze tipping upward and to the left as she considered for a moment. "Evan is coming over after work. Why don't I ask him to bring Sam along?"

"No," I said at once. "No *way.*"

"Come on!" she protested. "Sam's so cute, and he adores you, you know he does. He would be over the moon if you asked him what you want to ask Wy."

"Rae," I warned.

"Just saying." Her humor fizzled as she observed my intensity. "Your secret is safe with me, don't worry."

"I know." I drew another deep breath, gathering my resolve. "I'll head home and change, and see how I feel then."

"Feel about what?"

"About what I want to do tonight."

"Think about Sam, seriously. He's a good guy."

And I did think about Sam Mulvey as I rode around Flickertail in the back of my dad's pickup a few minutes later, the lake breeze ruffling my loose hair and drying the sheen of sweat from my forehead. Ignoring my siblings as they laughed and talked and bickered, I sat with my elbows resting on my thighs, cross-legged, facing the tailgate. Dust spiraled from the rear tires and lifted the scent of a recent rain. Sounds I'd heard a thousand times and more—the whine of outboard motors on the lake; the high-pitched chorus of frogs gliding among the cattails, punctuated by the deep, intermittent croak of bullfrogs; the soft, haunting coos of the mourning doves nesting among the pines—faded to a background murmur as I recalled a party Rae and I, in addition to most of our classmates, had attended last January.

Sam Mulvey, whose mouth slid wetly across mine when we kissed, his tongue tasting like stale beer as he fumbled with the hem of my sweater. There had been nothing arousing about our brief encounter; at least, not from my perspective. That I'd let Sam momentarily cup my breasts seemed ridiculous now, an extreme error in judgment. I wanted to wipe my lips and crunch a breath mint the moment we stopped kissing. By no one's estimation was I the most experienced person alive, but I knew the physical things leading to sex were *not* supposed to feel like that. Rae was my informant. She and Evan had come close in the past year, but Evan was too scared of Uncle Justin, Rae's dad, to risk going all the way. The point was Rae *liked* the things she and Evan did, liked them a whole lot; nothing like the embarrassment I felt about Sam after the party.

The notion of sex, let alone the reality of it, occupied a great deal of space in my thoughts these days, which I found both startling and intoxicating. My fantasies were not indiscriminate; only one man ever starred in them, and had for longer than I could remember. When I was younger, I had not imagined straddling Wy and holding him close as we kissed, or pictured the expression in his eyes as he untied my bikini top and slipped it from my shoulders, but since the summer I was fifteen my imaginings had become overwhelmingly erotic. I wanted to have sex with Wy, wanted it so much it was almost painful, a hunger rooted deep inside me; something I needed to survive. I wanted my first time to be with him.

*First, last, and every time in between.*

*You'll graduate high school next spring. You'll be eighteen by then.*

*And maybe, just maybe . . .*

I clung to a desperate sense of hope, like a gambler in the last round of high-stakes poker, that Wy would not only remain single until then but that he would be even remotely interested in pursuing a relationship with me. There were fleeting moments, like earlier today, when the expression in his eyes suggested that his feelings were more than simple friendship. A whole lot more.

*But if that was true, why wouldn't he tell me?*

*Think about it, Millie. Like he would dare risk telling you he liked you.*

*Not when you're only seventeen and he's close to finishing grad school.*

*I love him so much . . . how can he not realize?*

The logical part of my brain nagged that it was impossible to be in love with someone I had never dated, had never really touched beyond occasional rough-housing or the kind of friendly hug you'd give a family member. Wy was present in some of my earliest memories, very much *there*, and always sort of larger than life. I'd noticed him immediately, even as a little girl, had been drawn to him the way a compass needle is tugged instinctively north, beyond its control. There wasn't a logical explanation; I just knew what I felt. At age five I told my parents I meant to marry him someday, a story they'd related to the entire family numerous times since, not realizing I'd been dead-serious. I'd done my damnedest to capture Wy's attention from nearly the first moment we met, tagging along, asking endless questions, finding any excuse to be at his side. Being near him felt as natural to me as breathing.

*And here you are, wasting time feeling sorry for yourself when you should have gone outside and asked what he was doing tonight.*

"Millie, you okay?" Brantley crouched near me to ask the question and it took a moment to realize the truck was no longer in motion; we'd arrived home without my noticing. Henry, Lorie, and little James bounded over the tailgate to race for the house, intent on being the first to claim the shower stall, but Brant was worried about me. Gentle and observant, Brant was Henry's opposite in everything but looks. When Mom and Dad first brought the twins home from the hospital it had taken me months to tell them apart. Now, fourteen years and then some later, I found it impossible to imagine a time when I'd confused my brothers. Brant searched my face as he hunkered with his forearms braced on his thighs. His hair was a mess and dirt smudged his right cheek in stripes resembling fingers.

I nodded, conjuring up a smile; Brant would continue to worry if I didn't offer reassurance.

"Are you coming with tonight?" he asked. "It's gonna be fun. Uncle Justin set up the volleyball net and we're having pizza."

"I don't know yet, I kind of have a headache." I created the lie on the spot, feeling a small rush of guilt. "I think I might hang out here."

Mom overheard as she climbed down from the truck. "Babe, you have a headache? I thought you looked a little pale."

Dad reached to help me step over the tailgate. Once again on solid ground I tucked close to the warm familiarity of my dad's side, resting my forehead against his chest, and he kissed the top of my head as he teased, "Are you working too hard these days?"

"I like working at Shore Leave," I mumbled, embraced by the welcome simplicity of being my dad's girl. Dad smelled like aftershave, fish, and lake water, his perpetual summertime scent. His worn shirt was damp with sweat but I didn't care; he was always sweaty in the summer. Dad's chest was strong and barrel-shaped, and I remembered thinking when I was little that no one was stronger than him, the security of his arms a perfect place to seek and find reassurance.

Mom rubbed a palm over my back. "I'll get you some aspirin. See how you feel after you rest a little while. You don't want to miss the music at Eddie's."

Dad sent her a grin. "If I don't mistake the anticipation in your mother's voice, I think she and I just might get talked into singing a song or two."

My parents sang all the time but didn't usually get a chance to "perform" for anyone other than us. Many years ago, during a trip out west to Montana, they first met the Rawleys because the guys needed a lead singer on open-mic night. What force besides fate could have led Mom and Dad to dinner at The Spoke that particular summer evening?

"You better dust off your cowboy hat, honey," Mom told him.

I swallowed a dose of aspirin and lingered in a lukewarm shower, but by the time Dad hollered for us to load up the truck to head back around the lake, an actual headache banded my forehead.

*Serves you right.*

I drifted downstairs and then outside to tell everyone good-bye, compliment-ing Mom and Dad on their outfits—Dad wore faded jeans and a black shirt, with a matching hat and boots, while Mom had opted for a swishy white sundress, her hair loose, dangly silver earrings brushing her delicate jaw on either side.

"I did Mom's makeup," Lorie announced proudly, as Dad twirled Mom un-der his upraised arm, making her skirt swirl.

"You can do mine tomorrow," I promised, knowing how much my little sister loved experimenting with eyeliner and lip gloss and blush. She was toting her bright pink cosmetics case, almost as big as Dad's tacklebox; none of the cousins, male or female, would be safe from receiving a makeover this evening.

"C'mere, little butterfly, let's get you in the truck," Dad said, swinging Lorie into his arms while I snagged my baby brother, James, for a hug as he ran past, trying as always to keep up with Henry and Brant.

"No hugs, no hugs!" He twisted and struggled but I kissed his cheek anyway.

"Ha, ha!" I said as James swiped my kiss from his skin with the back of one hand.

"I'll call you later, love," Mom promised, and for a second her concerned gaze made me squirm; it was all but impossible to hide anything from her. "We won't be too late."

"I'm all right," I muttered. "Just tired."

I knew she wanted to ask what was truly wrong; I saw it in her eyes. But she said only, "Head over to Eddie's later if you feel better."

# CHAPTER THREE

RESTLESS AND ENERGIZED, I OPTED FOR A WALK.
Unable to bear the empty house but unwilling to join all the cousins at Rae's, I
slipped on my sandals and angled east around Flickertail, toward Shore Leave.
I had no destination in mind but did not intend to show up at Eddie's Bar; at
least, not yet. I stuck to the side of the road nearest the water, which lay as flat and
smooth as a length of pale silk beneath the setting sun, enjoying the calm of the
daily lull between the dinner hour and the evening pontoon cruisers.

My damp hair hung over my shoulders, ruffled by small tufts of lush air, almost as though the lake exhaled gentle, periodic breaths. I let my gaze skim out
across the water, its surface sparkling with golden droplets of fractured sunlight
on a downward slant; I traced the tops of the wildflowers growing tall in the
ditch, small, colorful petals tickling my right palm. Surrendering to need, I let the
familiar spell wash over my body as I allowed my imagination to fly along wild
paths. I was dying to touch Wy—to *be touched* by him. Just imagining it supercharged my nerves; the sensitive skin between my legs grew slippery in time with
my heartbeat. My nipples became rounded peaks and I cupped my left breast,
feeling the thrust of my pulse just beneath, shivering at the contact.

There wasn't a house in sight, let alone another person; even so, self-con-
sciousness overwhelmed my senses and I let my hand drift back to my side.

Earlier, standing naked while tepid water coursed over my skin, I'd lifted the
showerhead from its holder and brought it between my legs, bracing one bare
foot on the bathwater spout. The jetting spray was a sad substitute but fantasy
took over, as it so often did, and the shadow of Wy was at once in the shower
with me, caressing both inside and out, until my breath came in gasps and I bent
double to contain the bursting rush of pleasure that left my bones feeling like jelly. I released the showerhead and its spray splashed across my ankles as I cupped
the tingling flesh at the juncture of my thighs, hoping to prolong the sensation.

*That feeling, that's what I'm talking about,* Rae had said when I asked what it
felt like when Evan touched her. *It's like a current that runs between us, something
that builds and then . . . sort of overflows all through your body.*

*That's what sex is supposed to be like, right, that electric feeling?*

*Right. At least, it better be! Evan's willing to do everything else but he's terrified of Dad finding out we had sex and killing him.*

At the sobering reality of fathers, my own included, I drew a deep breath, inhaling the scents of musky shoreline and dewy grass as logic seized momentary hold of my thoughts.

*You know you can't possibly ask Wy to take your virginity. You're crazy if you think there's a chance in hell you could dredge up that kind of courage. And besides, you have no context for assuming he would be willing.*

I tilted my head in the direction of the treetops for a few steps, until I felt a mild rush of vertigo, aggravated by my lack of experience, the immaturity which led me to fantasize that I could ask Wy to make love to me. I may not have had sex yet but I realized there was no doubt Wy *had*; I couldn't pretend I believed otherwise. He was a twenty-three-year-old college student, sweet and funny and handsome. It hurt like a branding iron on bare flesh to imagine all the girls he'd likely been with.

*It's none of your business.*

*I know, but . . .*

*Maybe he's too busy with school.*

Earning his doctorate in veterinary medicine had always been Wy's ambition. How easily I could picture him as a vet, handling all animals—but especially horses—with ease and capability. I respected his drive, his passion for his future career; and on a deeper, much more personal level, I was grateful that his coursework kept him so occupied. Far too occupied for any serious girlfriends, or so I desperately hoped. I knew about at least one girl he'd dated in the past—*Hannah*, her name bitter as rust on my tongue—but Mom insisted that Aunt Ruthie said it wasn't serious between them. This did not negate the fact that Hannah had most certainly had sex with Wy, therefore earning her my unmitigated hatred.

*But Aunt Ruthie said it wasn't serious.*

*And I've never heard Wy mention Hannah, not even once.*

There were times I attempted to prepare myself, sweeping together all scraps of my rationality, for the news that Wy had found *the one* even as I recognized I would never be prepared for such devastation. I would truly rather die than attend his wedding to another woman. My steps faltered; I had reached the fork in the lake road that curved toward downtown Landon. Momentarily in proximity, I heard music and laughter and raised voices, most of the town no doubt headed to Eddie's Bar for a night out. Did Wy wonder where I was? Did he miss me this evening? I couldn't help but speculate. Maybe he didn't even notice I wasn't in attendance. But I refused to linger with those thoughts, and headed instead for Shore Leave.

The café appeared around the final bend in the lake road minutes later. On a typical Saturday night in June it would be packed with customers, in full tourist-season swing, but just now the familiar structure appeared tranquil in the gathering twilight, its wide front windows reflecting the sunset. The air had altered as I journeyed around Flickertail, becoming darker in tiny increments. The western horizon, moments ago glowing glossy yellow, was now the hue of worn denim. I could have headed to my great-grandmother's house, only a few dozen paces along the shoreline, where the kitchen lights glowed with warm welcome and a batch of snickerdoodles had no doubt been recently pulled from the oven, but a dismal, blue-gray mood had settled over me.

I skirted the café and ventured down the gentle slope leading to our small beach. I stepped out of my sandals at the edge of the water and curled my toes in the cool, gooey mud on the bank, leaving damp footprints on the dock boards. With a small sigh, I settled on the glider at the end, determined to shed this uncharacteristic bout of self-pity. Shore Leave never failed to possess a restorative power. This place had been my home since birth, since the summer my mom met Noah Utley and became pregnant at seventeen, my exact age. Hanging on the wall near one of the booths in the dining room was a framed picture of Mom, Auntie Tish, and Aunt Ruthie from Trout Days that particular summer. Grandma Joelle, their mother, had enlarged the original print and added it to the collection of family photos adorning the walls.

All three girls were dressed in swimsuits, jean shorts, sunglasses, and the silly foam-fish headbands they always sold at the town festival, standing with Aunt Ruthie in the middle. Wide, carefree smiles, their curly hair glowing with a bright rim of hot midday sun. The ongoing bustle of Trout Days captured at mid-stride; frozen forever in the background of the photograph, and yet still so vivid the laughter and chatter drifting through that long-ago summer afternoon was nearly audible. I could close my eyes and catch the scents of fried trout and cotton candy and bite-sized, sugar-caked donuts. In the picture my mother looked pretty and soft and impossibly young. Far too young for sex, let alone the responsibility of motherhood; and yet, here I sat, feeling more than ready for at least one of those things.

I'd spent hours of my childhood studying that photograph, searching my mother's teenage face for clues. Clues to what, exactly, I didn't know. Hints of her life before my entry into it, I supposed; traces of my features in hers. Everyone always said how much we looked alike. My great-grandma Joan, Grandma Joelle, and Aunt Jilly had also been young mothers; I knew the odds of breaking the cycle of teen motherhood were not exactly in my favor. Mom and I talked openly about most things, and therefore I knew that despite her initial shock and fear over an unexpected pregnancy, my arrival in her life was a blessing. I trusted her;

I'd never doubted her word. I knew my biological father, Noah Utley, but he was not my dad; I would always consider Mathias Carter my *real* father.

I clearly recalled a time before Noah Utley entered my life, but not my dad. My birth certificate read *Millie Joelle Gordon*, Mom's surname at the time, but in my heart I was a Carter, same as my siblings. I believed in fate, I believed in things working out as they were meant to, but lately I'd spent more time than ever pondering the ways in which Mom may have spun the tale of my birth in order to spare my feelings. For example—how did a mother implore her daughter to abstain from sex, and therefore the possibility of young parenthood, without indirectly admitting that her very existence was a mistake?

*"Mistake" is a really harsh word,* Rae had said during one of our late-night talks. *Your mom doesn't think of you as a mistake!*

*I know. But you have to admit it's ironic. "Don't have sex because you might get pregnant, just like I got pregnant with you! And meanwhile, my life went into a tailspin!"*

*Can you imagine having a baby right now?* Rae demanded. *You'd love your baby, no doubt, but think of how much your life would change. Talk about a tailspin. Good-bye, college! Good-bye, future plans! Your mom just wants you to have a chance to live your life on your own terms.*

*Just like she didn't get a chance to,* I threw back, determined to edge Rae toward my overall point.

*But that doesn't mean you were a mistake to her.* As usual, Rae would not be budged.

I rested my palms against the soft material of my T-shirt, splayed fingers creating a lopsided little circle with my belly button in its center. Mom had carried me inside her at age seventeen; a girl whose world had indeed been turned upside down, she abandoned her plans to attend Northwestern University in Chicago and instead moved in with Grandma Joan at the lake house to raise me as best she could on a limited budget. Noah had been no help; he struggled to accept my existence, not becoming an active part of my life until years later.

Studying the disappearing rim of sun, I thought, *I can't imagine Mom as a scared, pregnant teenager. And I can't imagine her being with Noah.*

I'd only ever known Mom in her capacity as my mother, a busy, happy woman whose family was her entire world. But she was many other things and always had been, whether I was aware of them or not. Had she sat on the dock in the mellow evening light that summer, exactly where I sat now, fantasizing about Noah Utley? Where in tiny, nosy Landon had they ever found a place to have sex? Shore Leave was always so busy and crowded; definitely not here. Maybe in Noah's car? Out to the clearing in the woods where kids from school went to drink?

Noah currently lived in St. Paul and I saw him once a year at most; I felt very little connection to him and no guilt over the fact. Sometimes, though, when I visited his mother, my paternal grandma, and then only if no one was looking, I picked up and held Noah's senior photo, a framed 8-by-10 of my biological father's younger self. He'd been good-looking; blond, tanned, confident. But his smile was just a little too smug, never failing to rouse my curiosity as to what had motivated that expression as the shutter clicked. Hadn't Mom noticed that icky little smirk lurking around Noah's mouth when they met? Hadn't it been a warning to her? I couldn't even conjure up an imaginary vision of my dad, Mathias, smirking.

*God, it's weird to think of Mom and Noah being teenagers and having sex. It seems so wrong on so many levels.*

*But they did have sex, more than once. Did Mom enjoy it? Is it what she wanted? Or just what she* thought *she wanted?*

As close and trusting as our relationship was, I had never asked my mother such questions; too personal, too close to the secret heart of her that wasn't my business. I would never dream of asking Noah such questions either. But I was still curious. Mom had clearly considered herself mature enough for sex at my age. And Noah had been older than her, definitely past eighteen; smug, smirking Noah, who had knocked her up almost two decades ago now.

*Mom obviously saw something in him, maybe even thought she loved him.*

But what occurred between them had not been love—at least, not like the love she and Dad had shared for many years now. And definitely not like what I felt for Wy. Wy would never smirk, would never think of smirking. It wasn't in his nature. Wy was the most honest and true man I'd ever known, other than my dad. If Wy made someone pregnant, he would never leave her behind, would never abandon her or their child because he wasn't "ready" for fatherhood.

*Jesus Christ, Millie, listen to yourself.*

*Is this some sick, subconscious way of saying you want to get pregnant? Just so Wy would have to stay with you?*

I cringed from the appalling thought.

*No; God, no. I want him to be with me because he loves me back, not because I'm pregnant.*

*I don't want to have Wy's baby . . . at least, not yet. Not for a long time, and only if we had already finished college and were married.*

The muted sound of the phone ringing up in the café startled me from my thoughts. Night had fully advanced while I sat stewing; mosquitoes whined near my ears, taking potshots at my face and neck. I shivered and brushed them aside, standing too abruptly; dizzy spots danced across my vision as I jogged up the incline. The screen door snapped back against my heel as I hurried inside Shore Leave and answered the landline on its fifth ring.

"Hello?" I inquired, only to hear a dial tone. No chance of identifying the caller; the café phone was an antique rotary box that Grandma Joelle and Aunt Jilly found at an auction a few summers ago. My cell phone was currently stranded somewhere unknown to me; I didn't usually tote it around. Figuring Rae had called, I dialed her cell from the dim, otherwise silent café, the dining room simultaneously familiar and eerie, cloaked as it was in tones of gray. The rotary dialer issued an elongated clicking sound with each subsequent number.

Rae answered by saying, "Your phone is on my dresser."

"How'd you know it was me?" I realized there was no point asking; Rae always knew.

"Who else would be calling from Shore Leave? Are you coming over soon?" Rae spoke loudly so I could hear over the background chaos, which sounded like a zoo at feeding time. Never one to waste an opportunity, Rae had demanded a high salary for watching the older cousins, and Uncle Justin paid in advance. She turned from the phone to bellow at her younger brother, "Riley, knock it off! I am going to *kick your ass!*"

I giggled, feeling only slightly guilty. Rae had made a pile of money this evening and I put up with my brothers all the time for no compensation. I joked, "Things seem to be under control."

"They're not. Henry and Riley are being as obnoxious as you-know-what."

"As 'fuck'?" I finished for her. "So what else is new?"

"Get over here! We're about to get Monopoly going. And Evan is on the way with pizza." She paused to tell someone, "Set the oven to three-seventy-five before I forget."

"He's not bringing Sam, is he?"

She hesitated a second too long.

"Rae!"

"They're both working tonight. I couldn't exactly tell Sam not to come with. It would be rude." Sam and Evan delivered pizza for Extra Anchovies, the little parlor attached to Angler's Inn. Rae added, "Besides, there's eight thousand kids here. I can't see Sam making a move under these circumstances." Humor flowed beneath her words.

And then in the background I heard Henry and Riley yell, in gleeful, sing-song unison, "Millie and Saaa-aaaam, sitting in a tree!"

"Just come over, it'll be fun. See you in a few!" Rae hung up fast, before I could protest.

*More than a few*, I thought grimly. I'd already lost time with Wy; the countdown to the end of this summer's visit was ticking away too fast, as always. Surely he was downtown at Eddie's Bar for the music. No chance he would magically appear at Shore Leave, seeking me, no matter how desperately I wished for it.

*Head over to Eddie's; at least you can see him then.*

I jogged down to the dock to retrieve my sandals. Hands buried in the pockets of my shorts, I angled back the way I'd come, the lake road so familiar beneath my feet I could have strolled its entire length with eyes closed. I let the balmy night surround me like an old friend, admiring the silvery glimpses of Flickertail through the pines, hearing crickets and gray peepers and an occasional pair of loons. I had walked about three-quarters of a mile when I heard an approaching vehicle. Almost immediately I recognized Aunt Ruthie and Uncle Marshall's giant 4-by-4 and waved, figuring they were headed home for the evening. The vehicle slowed, coming to a halt once it reached me, and to my tremendous surprise Wy occupied the driver's seat, window rolled down.

For a beat of complete silence, we stared at each other; he was alone, radio playing quietly. My heart landed a series of rapid punches against my breastbone.

"Hey there," he said easily, conveying a good mood, as usual. The dash lights accentuated the right side of his face. "I was just coming to get you. I figured you'd be at Justin and Jilly's place with everyone else."

Though elation flooded my senses, I forced a calm response. "You were coming to get me?"

"I figured you wouldn't want to miss the whole show. Camille said you had a headache. Are you feeling better?"

I nodded wordlessly.

"Don't you have your phone? We were all texting you to head over to Eddie's. You weren't answering so I told your mom I'd make sure you hadn't fallen in the lake or something."

He stepped down from the 4-by-4, leaving it idling, and walked around the hood just so he could open the passenger door for me. I studied him in the glow of the headlights, my eyes roving without reservation along his wide shoulders and lean hips, the back pockets of his faded jeans. He'd driven from town to pick me up.

*Oh my God, he came to pick me up!*

I passed so close to him to climb inside that my stomach was up beyond the clouds. He smelled so damn good, just faintly of cologne; I closed my eyes and inhaled until my nostrils compressed, slipping my hands beneath my thighs on the smooth leather of the seat, tightening my muscles to still their quaking. If only we had hundreds of miles to drive, just to prolong this blissful instance of time alone together. We would arrive at the bar in minutes.

Wy settled back into the driver's seat and asked, "So, where were you head-ed?"

"Headed?" I parroted.

"You were walking somewhere just now," he clarified, angling a tight U-turn to drive back to Landon. "Deep in thought, from the looks of it."

I flushed from hairline to toes, grateful for the darkness. Determined not to let my rioting nerves dictate our conversation, I explained, "I sat on the dock for a while but then I figured I'd walk over to Eddie's."

"Without your phone?"

"I never carry my phone."

"Even when walking alone at night?"

I shot him a sidelong look. "This is Landon, not Chicago."

"What about wildlife?"

I adopted the same teasing tone. "I don't think a phone would help in the event of a bear." The warm night air filled the space between us, thick with hu-midity; a loon wailed out on the lake, mournful and ululating, inspiring a small shudder between my shoulder blades. Moments later a second loon responded and I murmured, "Speaking of wildlife."

"I love that sound. No birds in Montana compare." Wy turned right, toward downtown, while I reflected how much *I* loved the sound of his deep, slightly throaty voice, letting it caress my skin as he continued speaking. "Although, not much beats a meadowlark in the early morning. They nest out in the foothills all spring and sort of serenade the sunrise."

I envisioned this scene, adding detail without restraint—a creamy pink dawn tinting the sky, Wy standing behind me on the back deck of his house, arms locked around my waist; as tall as he was, my head would be cradled against his chest. The sweet songs of meadowlarks would echo from the foothills beyond as he nuzzled my neck. We'd have spent the entire preceding night making love, and he would murmur my name and gently brush my hair to the side . . .

My spine jolted; damn my stupid fucking imagination. I babbled, "Is the mu-sic any good tonight? Who's playing? Untamed, right? That's Eddie's nephew's band."

Wy seemed amused but maybe I was just imagining that. "No, Eddie asked Case and Marsh to play, remember? Although there is a local guy on drums. He introduced himself as Zig."

"Zig Sorenson, he's one of Eddie's grandsons," I confirmed, smiling. "Rae thinks he's so hot."

"The place is packed. It's like The Spoke back home, but with a north woods spin."

I knew The Spoke well; it was a tradition to eat there at least three times whenever we visited them in Jalesville. I decided I couldn't let his description slide and repeated, "'North woods spin?' You guys are the ones with a moose head over your bar. Eddie doesn't even have any deer!"

"True," Wy conceded. "But there are about a dozen pheasants and wood ducks above his counter. Posed in flight, no less."

I admitted, "Eddie does the taxidermy himself."

Wy downshifted to second as we neared the little bar, a longtime fixture in downtown Landon; cars and trucks lined the usually quiet street. He added, "Like I should talk. I love the atmosphere at Eddie's. It's a place with character. Everyone knows everyone else. Blame it on my roots, but I couldn't imagine settling long term in a city."

"You plan to live in Jalesville, right, not Pullman? Once you're done with school?"

I was so proud of him; he was one of only about a dozen or so students from Montana to be accepted into the Doctorate of Veterinary Medicine program at Washington State, in Pullman. One of my most cherished memories was centered upon the last summer my family drove out to Jalesville, two years ago, when Wy let me watch while one of their mares gave birth. "Foaling" was what he called the process, and I'd stood in the barn alongside him through the entire experience. The foal had been a colt, a beautiful, perfectly formed baby horse that Wy had generously allowed me to name. In the years since, he never failed to keep me updated regarding Scout. Foolish or not, I'd always since considered Scout *ours*.

"I do, I couldn't imagine practicing medicine anywhere but home," he affirmed. "I'll be done with school in four more semesters, including residency. This next year is supposed to be the toughest in the program but I don't mind. I like the challenge."

His intellectual drive was one of a thousand things I loved about him; the mere thought of his hard work and stellar grades had compelled me to keep my GPA in the top range all through high school, and I intended no less for college.

"What's the focus this year?" I asked. "Last year it was diseases, right?"

"Yeah, talk about the power of suggestion. I thought I had some human form of just about every condition in the assigned reading. This year, third year, it's the principles of medicine and surgery. There's so much to learn I couldn't learn all of it if I had twenty years of school left. But the instructors say you learn more in your first year of practice than all of college combined."

"That makes sense. Will you perform surgery on both large and small animals?"

"This year, yes. When I'm in my residency, though, I'll shift toward a focus on large animals and agricultural medicine, since that's what I'll primarily practice once I'm licensed."

"How long is your residency?"

"Forty-three weeks, give or take. I'll start mine next May, right after spring semester, and if all goes well, I'll conclude and graduate the following May."

My hands were still tucked beneath my thighs and I relaxed the awkward position as Wy snagged a parking spot a few blocks from Eddie's.

"You're lucky to have so much certainty. I change my mind about careers about a dozen times a year."

"Last we talked, you were thinking biology," he reminded me.

Flattered that he remembered, I said, "That's still on the table. But lately I've been considering psychology."

"Oh yeah? What area?" Wy sounded truly interested, but then he always did; his sincerity was a foremost quality, one I counted on.

"It started because I was reading about equine therapy this past winter, it's *so* interesting, Wy, I thought of you right away. I'm sure you've heard about it." The bar was only a few blocks away but I was dying to remain isolated here, talking; there were so many things about which I craved his opinion.

"For sure I've heard about it. That's so funny, Mill, right before we left town Netta and Tuck were talking about opening a rehabilitation center outside Jalesville. You remember my cousin, Netta, right, and her boyfriend, Tuck Quillborrow? Well, they're married now and Tuck just finished up a degree in psychology. He's interested in equine therapy in particular. He inherited acreage from his grandparents and he and Netta are looking into what it would take to develop and build out there."

"That's incredible," I whispered. If only I was older, a college graduate. Wy's tone was one of deep anticipation and I ached with longing to be somehow involved.

"It's an idea with plenty of promise," Wy agreed. "Tuck offered me the chance to rent office space from him once the center opens and I'm up and running, with a degree hanging on the wall. I can hardly wait." Excitement lent his voice a boyish note and my yearning tripled; he couldn't know how badly I wished to be at his side, to share in the joy of these accomplishments with him.

To stall our departure from the conversation, I said, "If I went into that sort of field it would be a perfect excuse to learn more about horses." I tried for a note of teasing as I added, "I blame it on all those summers out in Montana. And you were always a good teacher; you're such a natural with horses."

Even though he'd killed the engine he didn't move from behind the wheel, studying me with less than an arm's length between us. He suddenly asked, "What are your plans next summer, once you're done with high school?"

I almost stuttered I was so eager to respond. "I don't know, college for sure, but that's not until fall . . ."

"There's a good psych program at the state university over in Billings. Or in Bozeman. I did all my undergrad work there, plus the first year of vet school before I transferred to Washington State. Maybe . . ."

Our gazes held tighter than banded wire; I hardly dared to breathe.

He finished quietly, "Maybe instead of the University of Minnesota, you'd consider Montana." A hint of a smile tugged at his mouth. "You're a natural yourself, and I happen to know an entire *barn* full of horses that would love to let you practice some therapy with them."

It didn't matter in that moment whether Wy was suggesting, in a roundabout way, what I thought he was—all that mattered was that he'd spoken the words.

I whispered, "I'd love to practice with them."

His smile became a grin and my heart accelerated further, happiness beating at my senses.

"That would be amazing," he said.

*It would be more amazing than anything I could even imagine*, I thought.

"Let's go listen to the music. Hang on, I'll get the door for you." And Wy shouldered his door open and rounded the hood to perform this simple courtesy.

My belly turned a slow, delighted somersault as I watched, linking my fingers beneath my chin. I had never, before this very moment, felt such bursting optimism in my chest.

Maybe there really was a chance he saw me as a woman.

# CHAPTER FOUR

COOL IT, WY. JESUS.

My guilty conscience thrummed a steady drumbeat against my skull, attempting to override other, less civilized parts of my mind. I clamped down on all thoughts of lifting Millie from the truck and straight into my arms, instead opening the passenger door and stepping to the side. But it did less than no good—her gaze held steady on mine as she climbed down and it would have required blindness combined with a critical head injury not to notice her.

*Next summer is the very earliest you can make any sort of move. And only if you're certain it's what she wants. Until then Millie is strictly off-limits. No-man's land, do you hear me?*

*I hear,* I thought, with grim severity.

*You're twenty-three. She's seventeen.* My conscience continued badgering, not about to let me off the hook. *No matter how you feel, you keep her age right at the forefront.*

But the straight-up truth was that Millie was no longer a kid, and hadn't been for the past two summers—at least, not in my eyes. I recognized the fact that to everyone else concerned she was a kid, I was an adult, and there was no middle ground. No gray area. End of story.

*Millie Joelle Gordon.*

*You have no idea what you do to my heart.*

Even though she was careful to hide it, I was pretty damn sure she liked me. It was something I'd sensed a long time ago but I couldn't let my happiness over this fact show any more than I could let on that I returned those feelings, and then some. I wouldn't, if it killed me. I couldn't risk such potential damage. She was so young, with so much ahead of her. One of us had to know better and I was already pushing my luck, suggesting she move out to Montana to attend college next year.

I prayed she'd consider it.

In my family she was referred to, almost without fail, as *sweet Millie Jo.* Mathias and Camille's oldest daughter, a pint-sized baby doll the first time I'd ever seen her, as the flower girl in her parents' wedding. There were six years between us but we were just kids in those days, enjoying summertime adventures. It didn't matter whether we were out in Montana exploring the foothills and hanging out in the horse barn, or here in Landon spending lazy days lounging in the lake; we always had fun in each other's company.

The July following their wedding, Mathias and Camille drove out to Jalesville to visit us for two weeks, hauling along Millie and her new twin brothers, creating a tradition that endured to this day. In that way, Millie and I had grown up together. My earliest memories of her revolved around our mutual love of horses; I remembered being impressed that she was never afraid, despite having no experience, and I'd been proud to show off for her. My family stabled between six and ten horses at any given time and I learned to ride around the time I learned to walk, the same as my older brothers. The first time Millie ever sat in a saddle was on the back of my horse, Shadow; I'd been the one to teach her the rudiments of saddling, mounting and dismounting, and handling the reins.

*You want to be a vet?* I heard her asking, deep in my memory. Nine years back. *A horse vet, right?*

I nodded confirmation, both of us with our sunburned arms dangling over the top beam of the fence; we'd climbed the lower rungs for a better view of the corral.

*Do horses get sick like people? Do they get the flu?*

*Horses get sick*, I responded. *But not like how you're thinking.*

Sweet Millie Jo, looking up at me that afternoon with such trust, at my side beneath a hot July sunbath, bits of prickly hay decorating her tangled curls. Her beautiful hazel eyes, with their endless golden depths and darker spokes radiating outward from each pupil, already seemed to see inside me. That was the first time I felt a distinct shift in my gut. Far too young and uncertain to understand such feelings, feelings that ran much deeper than friendship, let alone to consider acting on them, I felt that shift all the same, powerful as an incoming tide or a gravitational force.

And then for many years the gap in our ages was all but impassable, creating an unwanted gulf between us; even still, the summer she was fifteen Millie had pleaded to stay behind in the barn and watch Twyla, one of our mares, give birth. I'd been in my second year of college at the time and my focus was narrower than a train tunnel, pinned on the light at the end—earning my doctorate of veterinary medicine. Millie's persistence won out and I was reminded all over again how much I truly enjoyed her company. It seemed we could laugh about anything and everything. Millie was the oldest among her siblings while I was the youngest; she had always carried herself with self-possession and a maturity beyond her age . . . or maybe that was just my hopeful perception.

Twyla's laboring had extended into the evening and as we waited together,

Millie's elbow periodically bumping mine as she leaned over the stall beside me, the realization struck me like a dart—

*Someday our age difference won't matter at all.*

Immediately I recoiled from such thoughts, beyond ashamed of myself. For the love of God, she'd been fifteen to my twenty-one that summer. I'd tightly reined in all notions of Millie's then-distant eighteenth birthday, feeling guilty as hell, almost criminal. I deserved a preemptory ass-kicking, which Millie's dad, Mathias, would have been more than happy to deliver had he suspected the direction of my thoughts.

*Someday is still a long way off.*

The bulb above Twyla's stall created a cone of light, allowing us to observe the foaling as it unfolded. I'd observed or assisted with dozens of births before this one, but it was Millie's first and she was completely engrossed, full of questions.

"Is she hurting?" she wanted to know right away, concerned for Twyla, who by that point lay on her right side atop mounded hay, legs extended and occasionally twitching, issuing deep, periodic grunts.

"Well, it's damn hard work," I replied, with a touch of humor. I supposed that to someone unaccustomed to the sight of a laboring mare it seemed barbaric to watch without attempting to help or ease the pain. But I knew from long experience that a healthy mare needed no assistance to deliver her foal, just a clean stall, plenty of hay for bedding, and patience. A foaling was such a common occurrence in our barn that Dad and my brothers left us alone, trusting me to keep vigil once it was apparent it was Twyla's time.

I explained, "This is Twyla's fourth live birth and she knows what to do without any help from us. The foal is positioned properly, I checked earlier, so now we just wait and keep an eye out for any signs of trouble."

"What kind of trouble?" Millie demanded.

"At this point we should expect the birth to occur within thirty minutes or so, any longer could mean trouble. Or if the foal is positioned incorrectly, that's a real problem." I considered for a second before explaining, "The baby should present like he's doing a surface dive. We should see one hoof first, then the second about six inches behind, then the foal's head. The legs emerge separately so the foal's shoulders aren't squared and taking up too much space in the birth canal."

Millie nodded with all due seriousness, not quite able to contain a wince as Twyla's back legs jerked sharply; the mare issued a low-pitched snort, ribs heaving.

"Are you sure you want to stay out here?" I didn't want her witnessing more than she was ready for, but Millie stood straighter at once, determination replacing the concern on her face.

"Aunt Ruthie told me how amazing it is," she insisted. "Let me stay. *Please*, Wy, don't make me go back inside."

Gladness filled my heart; how could I refuse? I stole a look at her in my peripheral vision, standing just to my left; her long hair was arranged in a thick braid that hung over her shoulder. She was all arms and legs that summer, her nose sunburned and dusted with tiny freckles, her sensual prettiness still contained in innocence. A lone curl trailed along her jaw. Sweat created a faint shine along her hairline and her eyes were wide with wonder. A force field surged in my chest, inspiring intense protectiveness; I thought, *If anyone ever hurts this girl, I will kill him.*

Behind us, the open barn doors allowed the last of the long summer day's violet light to filter inside. Stars spangled the western sky, visible above the corral. Twyla's laboring had advanced to the point where I expected the emergence of the foal's first foreleg at any moment. Earlier in the afternoon the mare had displayed signs of imminent labor, growing anxious and restless in her stall, occasionally biting at her own flanks. She was now well into the second stage, sides periodically trembling, tail lifted to expose the birth canal. It was a natural process that would only get messier but Millie showed no further signs of squeamishness.

"Has a foal ever presented wrong while you were watching?" she asked, glancing my way with such an abundance of trust that I felt almost undeserving.

"We've been pretty lucky that our mares have had uncomplicated deliveries, as a whole. A few years back, Banjo had a foal that presented the wrong way." I paused, recalling that tense evening. Marshall had been adamant we do everything in our power to save Banjo and her foal; Banjo was Ruthie's mare and Marsh knew she would be devastated by her loss. "Dad knew how to help, thank God, because the closest vet was about seventy miles away at the time. Most of the local ranchers have a rudimentary knowledge of what to do in an emergency and Dad and Marsh were able to turn the foal in time."

I found myself talking to Millie like she was my age, a fellow veterinary student rather than a fifteen-year-old girl. But it felt entirely natural and she listened with silent attention. I indicated the stall to our immediate right, currently empty. "The colt was just fine and Ruthie named him Dusty."

"I remember Aunt Ruthie talking about him," Millie said. "That's part of why you want to be a vet, isn't it? Because there aren't many in the area."

"Yeah, that's definitely part of it. But also because I couldn't imagine any other line of work."

Millie glanced around at the additional stalls in the darkening barn, three of which were occupied by mares. She spoke with a tone of muted awe. "It's like they know Twyla is suffering. You can almost hear them worrying over her."

It struck me that she would notice; it was true, the other mares always seemed to murmur among themselves when one of their own was laboring, offering wordless encouragement and support. "I think they are. They care about each other and they can sense what's going on."

"Look!" Millie suddenly cried, leaning so far forward she was in danger of toppling into the stall.

A beat of excitement held us in suspension. I grinned at her enthusiasm. "See? Perfect presentation." To Twyla, I added, "There's a good girl. Good girl!"

I stood poised to intervene if the mare needed me but she was an old pro in the delivery room, long, heavy head tucked low as she strained to push. Amniotic fluid wet her back legs and the surrounding hay; her bulky body quivered with tremendous strength, her vulva red and swollen, stretching unimaginably far to allow new life to enter the world. The foal's shoulders cleared the birth canal, the most difficult step of labor.

"Is he all right? What the heck is he in?" Millie cried, astonished, lips dropping open at the spectacle of the foal easing free of his mother's womb in what appeared to be a slippery, bluish-white plastic bag.

"It's all right, it's just the amniotic sack, I should have told you it would look like that. Good girl, Twyla, there's a girl!"

Dad called from the outer corral fence, "How's everything, son?"

"Great!" I yelled back. "Twyla's almost delivered, Dad, come see!"

"There he is!" Millie yelped, trembling with excitement. "Oh, my gosh, Wy, look!"

I entered the stall to ease nearer to Twyla, speaking to her in low, comforting tones. The foal was roughly halfway free of her body, the birthing sack slick and wet, almost rubbery, the last physical link between the foal and his mother. Once completely free, it would be up to him to break the umbilical cord. The wonder of birth never failed to touch me, the miracle of a perfect little horse appearing as if by magic.

"Hey there, little guy," I murmured, even though I wasn't entirely sure yet if he was a colt. I crouched near his head and forelegs, making sure I left enough room for the full delivery.

Millie followed right on my bootheels. She knelt at my side in the trampled bedding, one fist curled at her lips. The hay was wet with fluid but Millie appeared not to notice, fixated on the foal.

Her fingertips rested like small, precious birds on my shoulder as she whispered with reverent awe, "Oh, wow . . ."

"He's almost out. He's a beauty, look at him."

"Oh, look, *oh my gosh* . . ."

"Here he comes!"

The foal slipped free, the thick white umbilical cord trailing over his narrow back. Twyla grunted and heaved and a last gush of fluid stained the hay while the colt—and it was a colt, I could now tell—rolled to his belly and attempted to find his footing. His unsteady legs resembled those of a grasshopper, long and slender and acutely bent.

Tears streamed down Millie's face. "Oh, he's so beautiful! Oh, my goodness."

Twyla repositioned to offer maternal assistance, licking her newest baby with long strokes of her tongue; now that he was delivered, you'd never guess at the mare's struggle. Twyla nosed his ribs and nuzzled his neck, licking his shiny hide as he tried again to rise to all four tiny, wobbly hooves.

"A colt," I confirmed, letting him nose my palm, grinning so wide I thought my jaw might bust. "Isn't he pretty? He's breathing normally, that's something you should always watch for after a foaling, but there's no concern with this little guy. He's a strong one, already trying to get up."

"Can I touch him?" Millie begged.

"Of course. Just move slow."

"Hi, sweetheart," she whispered, hushed with awe, stretching a hand palm-up toward the baby's long, velvety nose. His hide shone dark gold under the overhead light, gleaming with dampness; his mane and tail were as pale as whipped meringue. His little ears stood straight up, at attention, inquisitive eyes unblinking as he momentarily abandoned the attempt to stand and let his gangly legs fold awkwardly beneath him.

"His sire was a palomino," I explained. "This little guy inherited the same coloring."

"That means he'll be gold, with blond hair, right?" Millie asked, gently combing through his mane. "It's hard to keep all the different types straight."

"Yeah, palominos are gold with lighter manes and tails. His sire is named King and he's a show-off. It's actually hilarious to watch him in action."

Millie giggled. "What do you mean?"

Our hands rested on either side of the colt's sleek neck, our eyes on each other.

"You know how Arrow prances around the corral like he owns it?"

Millie nodded slowly and, as I watched, her gaze detoured to my mouth. Her lashes created spiky shadows along her cheekbones. There was the tiniest little indentation at the center of her chin. I imagined what it would feel like beneath my lips and immediately refocused, hardly aware of what I was saying.

"King is about ten times worse than Arrow. When he's offloaded in the corral with a breeding mare he paces around like a model, swishing his mane and high-stepping, the whole works. He thinks he's the best-looking horse in the pasture."

Millie smiled at the picture I'd described, returning her attention to the foal. "You're so sweet, little baby, you won't be a show-off like your dad, will you? Look at you, sweetheart, you're the cutest thing I ever saw."

I teased her, "Yeah, that's the way to keep him from being too full of himself."

The colt nosed her palm and she giggled. I was equally enraptured by Millie, my gaze eating up her enchanted expression, and my spine twitched when Dad said, right behind us, "Well, would you look at that. Good job, you-all."

"We didn't do anything! It was all Twyla," Millie contradicted, caressing the colt's nose, unable to tear her eyes from him. Twyla, accustomed to us and unconcerned, continued to clean her baby, concentrating her efforts on his flanks.

Dad held my gaze as I remained in a crouch, forearms on thighs, and I wondered, with sudden heart-pounding tension, if he somehow suspected what I felt for Millie. What a twenty-one-year-old college student felt for a girl six years his junior. Dad never missed a thing when it came to his sons. But my father only smiled, nodding toward Millie with fond amusement, tickled to see her lavishing such love on the colt. I allowed a small exhalation of relief.

"We'll need to treat this little guy's navel stump with iodine and Twyla needs to deliver the placenta within the next half hour or so," I said after a moment, hating to drag Millie's attention from the foal. "We have to get her up on all fours in about ten minutes, if she hasn't stood on her own by then."

Millie nodded at once, tipping forward to kiss the colt between his eyes, where a pale blotch stood out against his blond hide; a fist seemed to tighten around my heart.

I said immediately, "You name him."

Her gaze flew to mine. "Me?"

Dad rested a hand on the edge of the stall above his head, his long arm making a right angle. He agreed, "For sure, Miss Millie. The honor is yours."

Without hesitation, she announced, "Scout."

I nodded, eyeing the colt speculatively. "It suits him."

Millie bent to the colt and rubbed his ears, trying out his name as she murmured, "Hi, Scout. Don't forget me, all right? Because I plan to see you as often as I can, from here on out."

# CHAPTER FIVE

LATER THAT SAME NIGHT, AFTER TWYLA AND
Scout were clean and bedded down for the night, Millie and I stood side by side
at the corral fence beneath a dark canopy of night, as proud as any two parents.
Everyone else, her family and mine, had taken seats around the nearby bonfire
but their laughter and chatter, even the haunting notes from my older brothers'
fiddles, seemed distant. Millie and I were alone together in our accomplishment,
sheltered from direct view, our gazes uplifted at a sky thickly seeded with summer stars.

"Thank you for letting me stay and watch," she whispered, in keeping with
the mood of hushed reverence surrounding us.

I dared a glance her way. Her lips and lashes were highlighted by the three-
quarter moon's bright glow. She stood studying it, chin tipped upward.

"You stuck it out, that's impressive." My voice sounded hoarse. "Not everyone
would be willing."

A smile bowed her lips. "Thanks for explaining everything. You know so
much, Wy, you'll be such a good vet." She hugged herself around the waist,
squeezing hard, keeping her gaze on the heavens.

I stood in silence, my forearms resting on the top rung of the corral, caught
up in studying her face. I wanted to draw her close and kiss her mouth, gentle and
soft, taste her inch by sweet, lingering inch. I wanted to shelter her in my arms
and sink both hands in the wealth of her beautiful curly hair, now loose over her
shoulders, to inhale her scent until it filled my lungs. I wanted her arms around
my neck and my name on her lips, to be surrounded by the enthusiasm and happiness always radiating from her. I wanted these things so much a sharp ache
grew boulder-sized in my chest. But I couldn't dare; I would never risk offending
her, not for anything.

*Take your time. You can never, ever push Millie to feel something for you, you un-*
*derstand this. She's so young. Wait, be patient. Give her time. If you are luckier than a*
*man has a right to be, one day she'll return your feelings.*

I spent many hours that summer, after Millie and her family had returned to
Minnesota, pondering the fact that I didn't deserve her, and had no right to vie
for her heart. I was no saint. At twenty-one, neither was I a virgin; that ship had

sailed at age seventeen, when my girlfriend at the time, Hannah Jasper, had produced a condom from her purse and asked whether I wanted to have sex or not.

Hannah's exact words were, *Aren't you curious?*

I'd been too immature at the time—especially at that moment, both of us naked from the waist up, Hannah's breasts near my nose, and very little blood left in my brain—to realize this was not the most romantic or rational reason for lovemaking. My articulate reply had been something like, *Well . . . yeah.*

At that point Hannah and I had been together for just over two years, since the spring we were both fifteen and I'd tried to kiss her at a party; when she turned away at the last second, I accidentally landed the kiss on her ear. Our mutual embarrassment had eventually become laughter over a shared joke, and then, not long after, a relationship, the first of that sort in my life. Hannah and I went our separate ways after high school, to my unspoken relief, but in the years since then she had pressed for a return to our status as a couple. I refused. I couldn't pretend I loved her and she knew it; many of our fights had centered on that awkward topic.

I was honest with her, guilty over my lack of feelings, but I had long since recognized the distinct difference between love and lust. And loneliness, which sometimes gnawed at me like persistent hunger pains, and had since I was a kid. Even the thrill of acceptance into the DVM program at WSU did not appease the slowly-growing ache of loneliness, which scared me sometimes when I lay alone in bed, both forearms slung over my eyes. It wasn't until the summer of Scout's birth that realization struck.

*I'm in love with Millie. I love her and I can't even tell her because it would scare her away.*

*Millie deserves a thousand times better anyway, Wy, who are you kidding? You still have sex with Hannah even though you aren't dating. You use her.*

There was no way to sugarcoat this rotten truth, no way to make it something other than exactly what it was—me taking advantage of Hannah's continued feelings for me. It was shitty and lowdown, and I knew it. My dad would give me hell if he ever caught wind; it went against everything he had ever taught my brothers and me. Ruthie had been after me since last winter to end things with Hannah, once and for all; May was the last time we'd had sex, New Year's Eve the time before *that.*

The night last May was a flat-out mistake, Hannah and I both drunk; there was no excuse, I knew, but pints of beer atop shots of whiskey had contributed to the unfolding of events that evening. I'd been plastered, celebrating the end of the semester, and one thing led to another. But the next day I called Hannah first thing, apologizing for my behavior before telling her, in no uncertain terms, that it would never happen again. Then I apologized roughly a dozen more times. Hannah had been furious, calling me every name in the book.

I hadn't heard from her since.

And now here I stood, months later, on a dark sidewalk in Landon, Minnesota, surrounded by the warmth of a humid summer night, no more than a few steps from Millie, the woman who reduced me to shreds. Quivering, tight-in-the-chest shreds, her very presence like an arrow shot through my center.

"Thanks for coming to get me, Wy. I'm glad you did."

"Same here," I said. I loved how my name sounded on her lips.

*Next summer. Next summer, next summer . . .*

The words became a steady refrain. I wished for a year to pass in an instant.

The rowdy thump of my brother Marshall and his best friend, Case, making music met us a block away from the bar; laughter, cheering, clapping, and shrill whistles flooded our ears as I opened the door, letting Millie lead the way inside the familiar space. Eddie's was the type of place where it was impossible to feel unwelcome. The guys were jamming onstage, playing as though their lives depended on it, the entire crowd singing along, many with beer bottles lifted in salute. Millie's family, combined with mine, occupied over half the scattered tables and I grinned to see it, grateful to belong to them. I never took for granted the family we'd found in Landon, let alone took for granted my dad and brothers; a direct result of being raised without a mother. I'd always known how much I had to lose.

Millie paused to tell me something and I almost crashed into her. She tilted her head in my direction, toward her bare left shoulder, and I bent closer so I could hear her voice over the music.

"They got Mom and Dad up there." She indicated the stage.

"I'm surprised Ruthie isn't up there too." For an instant we were close enough that Millie's left side brushed against me and I smelled the sweetness of her hair, and I stood straight at once, praying it wasn't obvious I'd shivered.

Mathias and Camille were sharing a mic as they sang "It Ain't Me, Babe," a high-energy version of the Bob Dylan tune as covered by Johnny Cash and June Carter. Case was on fiddle tonight, Marsh on lead guitar, their combined talent infusing the bar with joyous abandon, an all-out true love of music flowing from their hands; I'd been raised in a household of musicians and knew the feeling well.

About two dozen people called greetings as Millie and I approached.

"Here," I said, spying a lone empty chair at one of our tables. I withdrew it for Millie, forcing my gaze not to follow the curve of her hips as she sat.

*Strength*, I reminded myself. Millie was so much more than her looks. But this did not alter the fact that she was so damn beautiful it was a blow to the chest, a five-hit combo delivered directly to my sternum. I indulged in imagining that we were a couple; that I was at liberty to tug her onto my lap in this crowded space. She would lean back against me and I would kiss the tops of her bare shoulders, one after the other, and she would laugh and sling an arm around my neck so we could kiss for real . . .

"Wy, honey, will you get us another couple of pitchers before you sit?" Ruthie asked, leaning my way to make the request.

Ruthie was Millie's aunt and my sister-in-law, not to mention the love of my brother's life, someone I'd known since she married Marshall back when I was just a kid. Ruthie had been such an important part of our lives for so long now that I considered her as close to a mother as I would ever have; she certainly worried about me like one. Ruthie and Camille resembled each other enough that Ruthie could have been Millie's youthful mom just as easily; golden-hazel eyes and tiny freckles and the soft shape of their mouths. I'd grown up admiring the Davis girls; first Camille that long-ago summer when she and Mathias met our family, then Tish years later, when she moved to Jalesville for what was meant to be a three-month internship. Long story short, Tish fell hard in love with Case—who was already crazy in love with her—and never left. Ruthie came to visit Tish in Jalesville later that same summer and I had a front row seat to observe as Marshall did his damnedest to win her heart.

*There's no one for me but Ruthann,* I heard Marsh say in my memory, his voice rough with certainty, all those summers ago when he didn't yet know if Ruthie would stay in Montana, before he realized she loved him just as deeply. *I will die alone without her, do you hear me?*

Marsh had been despondent that afternoon, sitting with his face buried behind both hands in a chilly hospital waiting room; at that point we didn't know if Case would recover from injuries sustained in a barn fire, and Tish was an all-out emotional wreck. I remembered standing near Marshall's bent knees; Dad had told me to convince him to come home for a few hours and get a little rest, not that I had any effect on his state of mind just then. There was no good response to Marshall's pained words and so I remained silent, recognizing my brother's sincerity as I thought, *Just like Dad.*

Dad's love for our mother had never wavered in conviction or strength. Even now, nearly two decades after Mom's death, Dad had never dated, let alone considered remarrying.

The Rawleys tended to be one-woman men.

I realized Ruthie was waiting for me to respond about the beer. "Sure. What kind are you drinking?"

"Another two pitchers of Leinie's, right, guys?" Ruthie addressed the crowded table, which included my dad and Millie's grandparents, Joelle and Blythe Tilson.

"Make it three, we're thirsty," said Joelle, offering me her lovely smile. "Thanks, Wy, you're such a sweetheart."

I was about to ask Millie what she wanted to drink when she stood in a rush and offered, "I'll help."

The song ended with a final flourish from Marsh on the guitar, the crowd cheering and whistling, revved up beyond belief, and, maybe emboldened by the mild chaos, Millie grasped my forearm and tugged me in the direction of the bar. She let go almost immediately as I followed. Unable to see her face, I studied the graceful lines of her arms and shoulders, the way her thick, curling hair rippled down her back. I refused to let my gaze stray further south on her body for longer than a second. Her white jean shorts were faded, almost threadbare, and very short. Sweat beaded on my spine as I kept my eyes away.

We reached the gleaming bar counter, where Eddie Sorenson, proprietor, stood with arms folded over his chest, grinning in the direction of the stage, enjoying the show as well as anyone. A cheerful elderly man with a sunburned face and many dozens of busted capillaries in his nose, in the fashion of a longtime drinker, Eddie regarded us with a fatherly smile. Even though she wasn't twenty-one, Eddie made allowances for Millie; it was obvious he adored her as much as the rest of the women in her family.

"Hi, doll, what'll you have?" he asked her.

"We need three pitchers of the Honey Weiss and I'll have a root beer."

"You want ice cream in that?" Eddie asked as he lifted a pitcher to the tap.

"Do you have vanilla tonight?" Millie leaned over the counter on both elbows, returning greetings from everyone seated along its length.

"Sure do," Eddie said, already filling the second pitcher.

I stood to Millie's right and rested my left hand on the edge of the bar, close but not too close.

A guy about my age, with stoned-looking eyes, openly checked her out, leaning around the couple sitting next to him to say, "Hey there, Millie Jo."

"Hi, Jere," she said distractedly, edging closer to me.

Up on the stage, Marshall said into his mic, "You-all are the best crowd we've played for in a long damn time. Anybody mind if I take a breather and dance a couple with my baby?"

He passed the guitar to Case and jumped from the stage, the crowd cheering and laughing, and swept Ruthie into his arms, twirling her among the couples on the floor. Case grasped the mic, holding the guitar to one side, and promised Tish, "Honey, I get the next couple dances," and she giggled and blew him a kiss from their table as he strummed out the first few liquid notes of "The Dance," in keeping with the classic country they'd been playing all evening.

Eddie set a tall glass in front of Millie and handed her a spoon. "Enjoy!"

She angled in my direction, stirring her root beer float. "You know what I just realized? I don't know if you can sing. I mean, I've heard you sing around the campfire, but can you *really* sing?"

I allowed myself the sweet indulgence of studying her eyes at close range as I admitted, "I can't. The musical gene skipped over me."

"I can't either! Mom and Aunt Ruthie are such good singers, I always wished I could."

The words flew from my mouth before I could think. "Let's drop off these pitchers and then go dance."

My heart sped up as her brows arched in surprise. I tried to sound like I was just kidding around as I added, "I mean, if you *can* dance. I can't really either, but it's a good song . . ."

I watched heat warm her cheeks. She was flustered but her gaze did not waver.

"Let's," she agreed.

. . .

Wy carried the pitchers to the table, leading the way this time. I followed a few steps behind, hope rioting through me with such force I could barely manage the act of walking. My thoughts exploded like miniature firecrackers, each one more exhilarated and speculatively frantic than the next.

*He asked me to dance!*

*Is he just being nice?*

*How close can we dance before Mom gets suspicious?*

*His arms will be around me!*

*I'm never washing this shirt again because it will smell like him afterward.*

*Oh God, he asked me to dance!*

Wy delivered the beer to much gratitude; his dad offered him a glass but Wy shook his head. It was too noisy to hear exact words but I saw his lips move.

*Not yet*, he said.

And then he turned my way and extended his right arm.

*It's just a dance, Millie. Calm down! Almost your entire family is here.*

My parents had been lured off the stage by the slow song, holding each other close as they laughed about something Dad was saying. I smiled to observe their characteristic affection; they always danced the same way, with their joined hands tucked close to Dad's heart. Grandma Joelle and Grandpa Blythe were also dancing, along with Aunt Ruthie and Uncle Marshall, while Uncle Case sang the

Garth Brooks song in his deep, rich voice, accompanied by Zig Sorenson on the drums.

I slipped my arm around Wy's, letting him lead us to the outer edge of the dancers, and I should have known better than to be nervous because he made me laugh right away, clasping my right hand and twirling me under his uplifted arm, then dipping me backward like someone showing off at a ballroom competition. Upside down over his forearm, my hair dangling toward the floor, I was laughing so hard I couldn't breathe as he righted me and then situated us in a traditional waltzing stance, his right hand gently bracketing my waist and a proper twelve or so inches between our bodies.

*Well, what did you expect? For him to scoop you close, no distance between you? And then maybe you could start grinding on him, wouldn't that be classy as hell?*

"Do you two-step?" he demanded, grinning down at me, and I was enveloped in heady scent; his breath, his skin. *Him.* He was Wyatt Rawley, the man of my waking and sleeping dreams.

"I don't two-step," I admitted, so focused on his eyes I almost stumbled.

"Then we'll start slow," he promised, holding my right hand in his left, our arms extended. He directed his gaze toward our feet and nodded once. "Okay. I'll lead you. This is a good song to start with. I'll step forward with my right foot and you'll step back with your left, like so." He moved us accordingly. "Then we take two steps like that, you moving backward, sort of gliding." He lifted his eyes briefly to mine, smiling with such boyish happiness that I glowed in response, firefly-like. He gently squeezed my hand and then returned his gaze to our feet. "Then we do a shuffle step, side to side, like this, before going back to the original step."

"This isn't so tough," I murmured, very conscious of his right hand on the notch of my waist, his touch so careful, as if he feared I might break; my palm cupped the hard curve of his shoulder, the heat of his body flush against my skin. I let my thumb stray so that it came to rest on the outer edge of his collarbone. Wy led me effortlessly, keeping the pace slow for my sake; I had never been so close to him for such a prolonged period.

Something occurred to me. "Hey, you said you couldn't dance."

This time his smile was half-wicked as he admitted, "I can dance. I learned when I was a kid. Dad made us all learn."

"Can you waltz and tango, all of that?"

"Waltz, yes; tango, no."

One of Eddie's sons and his wife bumped us as they danced past, with laughing apology; Wy's hold on my waist tightened and I seized the chance to move closer. He acknowledged this with just the slightest shifting of his dark eyebrows, mouth suddenly somber; I watched him swallow. His right hand resettled on my lower back, again with the gentlest of touches. My stomach was less than three inches from his and I gripped both his shoulder and left hand more firmly. And then, with slow, deliberate movements, Wy threaded the fingers of our joined hands and returned the subtle pressure I'd just applied—this simple gesture the most poignant and endearing I'd ever experienced.

"You ready to try a spin?" he asked, attempting levity, but the air had altered between us; an unspoken recognition of our mutual attraction. My lungs were empty of all but astonishment.

I shook my head in response, not wanting him to let go. Up on the stage, Uncle Case was strumming his guitar, singing the chorus for the final time—and this beautiful moment would come to an end along with the song. Wy's arm tightened around my waist. His breath grazed my cheek. Our eyes held steady, his expression as dead-serious as I'd ever witnessed it.

*Oh God, please . . .*

And then the song was over, couples all around us separating to clap and cheer and whistle. We couldn't keep touching this way and we both knew it; Wy released his hold, grasped the fingertips of my left hand, and then bent to touch his lips to my knuckles.

Standing straight once again, he said solemnly, "Thank you for the dance."

# CHAPTER SIX

"AND THEN WHAT?" RAE SHRIEKED IN A WHISPER, leaning on her elbow above me in the dimness of her midnight bedroom. I filled in all the shades of her features, which I knew as well as my own. I lay on my back, wallowing in ecstatic remembrance of Wy's arms around me, his body so deliciously close; his lips on my skin when he kissed my hand. Even that brief, very proper contact sent my nerves screaming with the need for more. When he told me good-bye he said *good night*, which seemed far more intimate, as our gazes held a second longer.

It stunned me how often, how effortlessly I fell in love with Wy all over again, tumbling headfirst over a steep cliff while my stomach soared with joy.

"And then Grandpa asked me to dance and Grandma danced with Wy, and not too long later things were already winding down." It didn't escape my notice that Mom seemed far more concerned than usual about where I intended to spend the night. She insisted I ride over to Rae's with her and Dad after we left the bar, all but walking me to the front door. I bit back a sigh. "And now Mom suspects something is up."

"How come? Just how close were the two of you dancing?" Rae's eyes gleamed through the dimness as she poked my bare leg with her toes, the two of us lying on the sheets rather than beneath them, courtesy of the humid air.

I hugged my ribcage, rocking side to side. "Close enough that my shirt smells like him." Immediately I tugged the collar over my nose, inhaling deeply, catching the faint but unmistakable scent of Wy on the material. My voice emerged slightly muffled as I babbled on, "This is the first time I've ever felt like he might actually like me back. Like there's a chance. He said I should consider college in Montana. He wants me to move out there next summer, *to live near him.*"

"You'll be eighteen then; it's not so farfetched to think it could work out." Rae leaned near to land a fond smooch on my forehead. "Aw, Mills, this is awesome. I'm so happy for you. It seems right, you and Wy, you know? Like it was meant to be all along."

I gripped her wrist. "Did you see it?"

"I would tell you if I had, you know that. I can't force a notion," Rae reminded me.

"I know," I whispered reluctantly; since we were little girls, I'd known this truth.

Just like her mother before her, and many other Davis ancestors, all of them women, the strange ability flowed strongly through Rae. Though they happened rarely and without warning, notions never failed to accurately predict some future event. It was a family secret that stretched back many generations, a gift or a curse, dictated by circumstance. When Rae and I were twelve years old she saw her brother Clint's wife in a notion. I'd been at Rae's side that summer afternoon and recalled, to the smallest detail, the terror that pumped through my heart simply observing the notion grip her; without warning she went motionless, gaze fixed on the distance, her tanned face sliding to fish-belly white before my fearful eyes.

*What is it, what's wrong?* I could still hear my pleading voice.

She couldn't answer—not until it passed.

I had never, before or since, witnessed her experience a notion of such force.

Later, we ran together into the woods beyond the café, safe there from any prying ears or eyes, and I held Rae as she sobbed, drenching my shirt.

*Dani, it's Dani,* she kept repeating. Minutes passed before she regained enough control to tell me what she'd seen.

*You have to tell Aunt Jilly,* I said when she was done explaining.

*No,* she said at once, gripping my elbows, her brown eyes severe with insistence. *Not unless Mom already saw it. We can't tell anyone, Millie, this has to be our secret. Maybe I was wrong.*

And so we remained mute, carrying the terrible knowledge between us, a shared burden. At the time, Dani was in perfect health and, as two years passed, Rae and I became convinced that the notion was some sort of ugly misunderstanding. When Dani was diagnosed with breast cancer the summer we were fourteen, the weight of guilt dragged at both of our souls. To this day, neither of us had ever confessed to anyone that we had already known Dani was going to die.

I whispered, "What if I'm just reading too much into it? Maybe he was just being nice."

"You're not. I don't need a notion to know that." Rae lifted her hair and fanned the back of her neck, and even with my eyes directed at the ceiling I felt the sudden sharpening of her gaze. "But don't have sex this summer, *promise* me. Wait until next year, when you're a legal adult."

Next summer might as well have been a century away from my current perspective, as distant as Venus. Where logic continued to claim a small handhold, I knew Rae was right. I *knew* this and yet it required monumental effort to keep from racing outside, into the warm caress of the darkness, all the way around Flickertail to the inn downtown where Wy spent the night hours. Was he asleep? Or was he lying awake in the dim little room in an unfamiliar bed, staring at the ceiling fan with both forearms tucked beneath his head, reliving every moment of the past few hours? I could picture him exactly—shirtless, solemn, his lips soft and his hair messy, long nose casting a shadow along the lean angle of his cheek. One knee bent, his feet bare.

Longing expanded beneath my skin until I felt feverish.

*Lovesick*, I thought. *This is what it means to be lovesick.*

"God, Rae, I just *crave* him. I can't wait until next summer. It's impossible." I rolled to face her, drawing both knees to my chest, hugging them to calm the shivers.

She heaved a long-suffering sigh and drew upon my oldest nickname. "Millie Jo-Jo. You're impossible." But she spoke with affection. "How is it that I'm the voice of reason here? Nine times out of ten you make the responsible decision while I say 'fuck it.' It's not like I don't understand all this, I just worry for you."

"I've loved Wy since I was a little girl." I covered my eyes, pressing until a blotchy checkerboard pattern appeared on the backs of my eyelids. Dark purple and murky yellow, like too-ripe sliced plums. "I'll never love anyone *but* him."

There were many responses Rae could have chosen; instead, she only murmured, "I know."

...

From the bar, I hitched a ride back to Shore Leave with Millie's grandparents, Joelle and Blythe, which meant Millie was only a short walk through the woods from the lake house, where I stretched out for the night on a twin bed in the attic bedroom, atop a mattress much too small for a grown man. My legs extended far past the end and I shifted to my right side, drawing my knees up, attempting to find a more comfortable position. I was no complainer, recognizing the humor in the situation—trying to sleep in a bed sized and decorated for a preteen girl, the only available space left in Millie's great-grandma's house. I'd considered throwing a sleeping bag among the little kids on the living room floor, but there wasn't a spare inch between them.

Earlier in the evening Marshall had begged Dad to let him and Ruthie have the suite at the inn—and therefore privacy—for the night, and Dad generously agreed. I realized my brother and Ruthie, as the parents of five kids, deserved a night alone but I was jealous as hell at the same time, wishing for things I knew I had no right to wish for. Like Millie and I alone in my room at the inn instead, with its big brass bed and the entire night stretching before us, sweeter than the promise of heaven. I was harder than an I-beam just imagining it and muffled a half-groaning laugh into the nearest pink, ruffled pillow. It was either laugh or cry.

*Yeah, that's great, Wy, jerk off in this tiny little twin bed with pink ruffles and polka-dot sheets that smell like flowers. You dumbass.*

I knuckled my closed eyes, finding the humor in torturing myself; guilt pangs struck for even *being* hard while lying on this small, narrow mattress in which each of the Davis girls had at one time or another slept. Astonishment continued to beat my senses as I rolled to my back, slinging an arm over my forehead. The light fixture on the wooden ceiling disappeared before my continued steady gaze; I was already back at Eddie's Bar, holding Millie in my arms.

Nothing had ever felt more right. Or so good, so damn good it was almost pain.

*You're moving too fast. You'll scare her off.*

But even as I reprimanded myself, I knew the words weren't true. Based on the look in Millie's eyes as we danced, I wasn't moving fast *enough*.

*She likes you. A lot.*

*That doesn't change anything and you know it!*

*You still have to wait until next summer, no exceptions.*

*Do you hear me?*

But all I heard was the wonder building in my blood, filling my chest cavity with light. Clear, yellow-green light that glowed on the backs of my eyelids when I blinked; light that annihilated doubt and hesitation and loneliness. Images whirled across my mind, rapid-fire—Millie moving to Montana next summer, living within a few miles rather than hundreds. The two of us finally together, an actual couple, allowed to touch without reservation. All of the romantic things I would do for her to show her I loved her and was worthy of her love in return, every last touch and kiss and word. Picking her wildflowers, making us dinner, taking her riding toward the mountains like we always used to as kids. Working together with the horses, listening to her tell me about her day, telling her about mine in turn, making love way out in the foothills beneath the setting sun.

*Oh God . . .*

I rolled the other way yet again, bedsprings creaking under my weight, guilty as hell but unable to keep from picturing us making repeated, uninhibited love—anywhere, everywhere, unending. The bedroom seemed about two hundred degrees, the sheet bunched under my legs, sweat sliding down my chest. I spent minutes inhaling and releasing deep breaths but was unable to stop thinking about holding Millie close as we danced; there had been an electric current surrounding us, alive and all but crackling between our bodies.

*It's because you love her.*

*This is how it's supposed to be, it's what love creates between two people.*

My parents had been in love. Clark and Faye Rawley, married back in the late 1970s in a simple ceremony in our hometown of Jalesville, Montana. My dad, the third of four children, had inherited the family homestead after his parents' deaths; his two older brothers had moved east for college by then and to this day resided on the Atlantic coast, with little interest in returning to Montana. Aunt Julie, my dad's little sister, married young to a local rancher's son; none of the siblings besides my dad wanted to deal with the original homestead. And so together my parents had worked tirelessly to renovate the old house and proceeded to raise five boys there—four boys, really, because Mom died when I was a little kid.

I remembered her only in patches, like a beloved story missing key pages, or a television show with fuzzy reception. I had long since given up wishing for a firmer grip on my memories of my mother. I knew I was lucky; I had been raised by a kind and devoted father, and had never lacked for parental love. But deep inside was the ancient ache of missing the mother I'd never really known. I still dreamed about her sometimes. I remembered telling people back then that she'd been too young to die, and demanding an explanation. To date, no one had ever delivered a satisfactory one. My brothers' collective memories of her were far more detailed. They'd all been teenagers that autumn, when a truck crossed the yellow line on Interstate 94 and hit my mom's car.

My father had never remarried and he never would, we all knew. Of all the many important lessons I'd learned from Dad, the foremost was that your wife and children were to be cherished above all else. He taught the same lesson to my brothers—Garth, Marsh, and Sean were each wed to women they loved and cherished; Quinn hadn't yet married. One of the major reasons Ruthie had been on my case about Hannah for the past year related directly to this truth; I knew I'd done wrong regarding my old girlfriend, and I was not proud of myself.

*It's all right, you ended things with Hannah for good.*

*Hannah knows you don't love her and that it's over, as it should have been a long time ago.*

*Everything's all right now.*

*Millie likes you! Maybe someday she'll even love you.*

*Just take it slow.*

In the dark, silent house below, I heard the front screen door ease open.

. . .

I made my way through the woods, following the familiar trail leading between Rae's cabin and the lake house. It was a good three hours past midnight by now, the stars riotous in an inky sky, deep enough into the night that even the frogs had quieted. I crept barefoot, avoiding low-hanging branches, knowing the way well enough that I hadn't toted along a flashlight. I had no real purpose for venturing to the house where I'd lived as a little girl other than sheer restless energy. Sleep remained a stranger long after Rae drifted off and so I finally slipped from bed and tugged on my shorts. No bra, but that didn't matter in the darkness. I knew I wouldn't encounter anyone; all my little cousins would be asleep. Even if my great-grandmother caught me sneaking into the house, she'd only give me a hug and fix me a plate of cookies; in her eyes, I was eternally five years old.

I smiled at the comforting thought, spying the house just ahead, its peaked roof slightly darker than the surrounding sky. I sat on the top step of the front porch for a little while, staring out at the yard, seeing nothing but Wy's face. Morning was mere hours away and then I would be near him again, at breakfast. I imagined what we would say to each other. I wanted to talk about equine therapy, about his veterinary studies, about horses. I wanted to talk about the future, the incredible one in which he'd suggested I move to Montana for college, a future that involved the two of us together. Maybe tomorrow we could take a walk. If we were alone, we could acknowledge what existed between us, something beautiful and wild and tremendous. Something beyond us both.

*This is what love is all about, this is how love affects two people.*

I hugged my torso, shivery with exhilaration at the possibility that Wy could love me as much as I loved him. An entire world had all at once flung open its doors, granting me determination and purpose.

*Next summer we can be together, that's what he meant.*

I imagined us riding far out into the foothills on Shadow and Scout, like we always used to as kids, or hanging out with the horses in his family's stable, a space I dearly loved. Wy knew horses better than anyone; his connection with all animals was extraordinary, but especially horses. He had taught me everything I knew about them and I knew he would, in turn, show me the things he learned in school—and one day, once I graduated college, we could work side by side, caring for animals, raising horses, raising children . . .

*Wyatt and Millie Jo Rawley*, I thought, unable to resist.

*Our names sound so right together.*

*It's like Rae just said, it's not so far-fetched to think it could happen.*

Mosquitoes were gathering near my temples and ankles and I couldn't continue to sit here woolgathering, as lovely as it was to daydream about a future with Wy. I stood to venture inside, opening the unlocked screen door with care so it wouldn't sing on its hinges. The living room carpet was lined with sleeping bags containing my youngest cousins. I tiptoed past them, smiling at their little snoring sounds, and filched a big handful of cookies from the stoneware jar on the counter. I was back outside on the porch less than a minute later, my mouth crammed full with an entire snickerdoodle, when I heard the screen door open behind me. But the whispered voice speaking my name was definitely not my great-grandmother's.

"Millie?"

I spun around so fast I dropped the rest of the cookies and half-choked on the one in my mouth. Wy was at my side in a heartbeat, concerned as I bent forward, unable to keep from coughing. My eyes watered with both surprised embarrassment and the effort to dislodge snickerdoodle bits from my throat. He gripped my elbow and patted firmly between my shoulder blades until I stopped hacking. Amazingly, no one else appeared on the porch behind him, wondering what was happening out here.

I managed to draw enough breath to whisper, "Thank you."

"I heard the door open, so I came down here to see who it was," Wy explained. He removed his hand from my elbow but my heart was still on overload, pumping blood at twice its usual speed. He was so near I could have leaned forward about six inches and kissed his collarbones. He wore jeans and nothing else. Not one thing, except maybe underwear. His chest hair stood out against his skin, darker than his tan.

"What are *you* doing here?" I whispered instead of offering an explanation, attempting to sound unrattled, terribly conscious of my breasts, bare and wobbly beneath my T-shirt; my nipples had become hard pearls. Thank goodness it was dark. "Aren't you and your dad staying at the inn?"

His teeth flashed in a quick grin. "Marsh and Ruthie begged to stay there tonight."

A hot beat of silence passed between us.

*So they could have sex all night*, Wy didn't have to say.

"They probably don't get much time alone." My voice sounded thin and reedy.

"That's the truth," Wy agreed. We hadn't budged an inch apart. I could smell his breath and it made me ache to kiss him, if only to taste that scent against my tongue. His voice was quietly amused as he observed, "You're out walking alone for the second time tonight. Is this something you do often?"

"No. I couldn't sleep." Awareness burned as bright as noonday sun; I thought of how he'd threaded our fingers with such tenderness, of the way we held each other tighter at the very end of the song. I swallowed hard, dragging my eyes away and gesturing lamely at the cookies underfoot. "I better clean these up."

"I'll help you." He dropped to a crouch to do so; we worked alongside each other, collecting cookie pieces in our cupped hands with unusual intensity. But then our elbows bumped and we both started laughing, shattering the tension.

"You scared the shit out of me!" I yelled in a giggling whisper. "No wonder I started choking!"

"What if you'd been an intruder? I was just keeping your grandma's house safe." He nudged my shoulder with his.

We paused with full hands, studying each other, our faces cloaked in shadow. I said in a rush, "I'm so glad you asked me to dance."

"I'm so glad too," he whispered without hesitation.

The bits of cookie in my cupped hand fell back to the floorboards. I thought my heart would crack with the force of its beating as I did what I'd longed to do for the past decade, let alone the past few hours. I shifted to my knees and touched his face, his jaws lean and warm beneath my palms, rough with un-shaven stubble. I sensed the jolting of emotion pass through him, surprise and mild shock, but then he caught my waist in both strong hands, drew me in close, and kissed me. Like he knew exactly how much I wanted him, like he'd known all along. Joy thrashed my senses. His lips parted to deepen the kiss, encourag-ing mine to do the same, and his tongue swept gently inside as he held us steady while remaining in a crouch, his thighs bracketing my hips.

Nothing so far in life had prepared me for kissing the man I loved. Not one damn thing. It was beyond words. There was only awareness. And an immediate, unbridled sense of possession. I couldn't get enough, curling my fingers through his hair, sliding my hands over the sides of his neck and his strong bare shoul-ders. Arousal pelted me like swinging fists. Our heads slanted one way and then the other as we kissed with an increasing lack of restraint, exploring, tasting each other, as soft, throaty sounds meshed between our lips. My touch skimmed lower, down along his ribcage, and immediately he broke the contact of our mouths.

"I'm sorry," I whispered inanely, stunned by his unexpected withdrawal. Apologizing seemed ridiculous but I didn't know what else to say.

"Don't be sorry." He held my waist in a careful grip, his breath warm on my cheek.

"You don't want to . . ." I broke off the sentence, afire with embarrassment.

"That's not it at all. I want you so much I feel like a criminal." He spoke in a low, serious voice. "But I *can't* want you, not this way, not yet. Your dad would kill me. *My* dad would kill me. Shit, *I* would kill me if you were my daughter."

Relief, and the urge to giggle at his explanations, washed over me. "That's not true. We're not doing anything wrong."

A grudging smile elongated his mouth. "I'm twenty-three. You're seventeen. In the eyes of just about anyone you'd care to ask, that's wrong."

"I don't care what anyone else thinks," I argued. Despite his words he had not released me, and I was emboldened.

He said quietly, "I can't let this happen yet."

And then I spoke, without intending, without thinking twice; I could no longer hold down what was in my heart. "I love you, Wy. I've loved you since I was a little girl."

A profound silence throbbed between us as he stared at me without blinking.

"Did you hear me?" I insisted in a whisper.

He took my face in his hands, cradling it. "Millie Jo. You have to know you've been in my heart for as long as I can remember, even when I was too dense to realize what I felt for what it was."

Emotion pulsed in my throat, the longtime ache of waiting for such words. "Are you saying . . ."

Here we knelt on my great-grandma's porch in the middle of the night, broken cookies scattered beneath our knees, tears blurring my vision. This would be the place Wy told me he loved me.

"I'm saying things I have no right to say," he whispered, resting his forehead briefly against mine. "I told myself I would wait until next summer after you graduated, when . . . *if* . . . you moved out to Montana. I wasn't going to rush you into anything."

"*You love me* . . ." Tears and laughter tangled together in my throat.

"Of course I do." He spoke with tender sincerity. "I can't imagine loving anyone but you."

# CHAPTER SEVEN

THE KITCHEN LIGHT GLOWED TO SUDDEN LIFE, maybe a dozen steps from us, and we sprang apart as if electrocuted.

"Come on!" I whispered, keeping low, tugging his arm to follow.

We remained bent over until we cleared sight of the porch; I didn't hear anyone calling after us or opening the screen door, so maybe one of the little kids had simply been headed for the bathroom. Breathless and laughing, we ran with bare feet toward Shore Leave; if we kept the lights off, we could sit undisturbed in the dining room.

"We can talk more in here," I explained as we reached the front entrance, unlocked as usual. I led the way to one of the booths, where we slid atop the bench seats, facing each other in the dark, silent space. The window boasted an unencumbered view of the lake and lent the opposite sides of our heads—my left, his right—a bluish glow from the streetlight in the parking lot. We reached instantly for each other, grasping hands on the checkered tablecloth, leaning forward. If anyone happened upon us, we'd be hard-pressed to maintain innocence, hiding out in the empty café in the middle of the night, but I didn't care about getting caught.

Nothing mattered more than this moment.

"Your hands are so delicate." Wy lifted our linked fingers and kissed my knuckles, one after the other in a row. "They feel so good in mine, like I'm protecting you somehow. It's so crazy, just earlier tonight I was thinking about how amazing it would be if we were an actual couple. I was thinking that when we first got to Eddie's. I wanted to pull you onto my lap."

I knew he could feel the way I was trembling, in both disbelief and joy.

"You did?" I whispered.

"Heck yes, I did." His smile became a grin, slow and sexy. "I can't believe this is where we ended up tonight. Before you showed up, I was upstairs in one of those little pink twin beds, thinking about you. I thought I was seeing things, like maybe I was hallucinating the sight of you on the porch because I wanted to see you so much."

I loved the way he always spoke what he was thinking, therefore allowing himself to be vulnerable.

"You were the last person I expected to see just now," I admitted. "I was at

Rae's, telling her all about us dancing, and I figured you were over at the inn. But we must have sensed each other so close."

"I could hardly wait for morning so I could see you again." He stroked his thumbs over the backs of my hands in gentle, repeated arcs.

I touched him in return, reveling in the ability to do so; our joined hands had become a language unto themselves, a communication beyond words. His were hard and warm, long-fingered and wiry with strength—sexy, capable hands I had observed so many times, handling horses, straightening a rein, adjusting a saddle—and at long last, caressing me. Bombarded by a sense of resolve, I explored his knuckles, the broad sweep of his palms, the ridges of bone along his wrists. We had missed so much of each other's lives already, forced by circumstance to limited time together; every July, nothing more. But that, I vowed right now, was going to change.

"I remember the first time I met you, at my parents' wedding. You were wearing your gray cowboy hat. I smacked you with my flower girl bouquet to get your attention, do you remember?"

He nodded and I could see the warm humor in his eyes. "Oh, I remember, believe me. There were rosebuds rolling all over the place. I remember the first time I ever heard about you, even before the wedding. Your mom and I were riding horses, back during that first summer we all met. She told me she had a little girl named Millie who was two years old. I told her that was a pretty name. It's still the prettiest name I know."

The lump in my throat swelled. "I can't remember a time when I haven't loved you, Wy, you think I'm exaggerating but I'm not."

He squeezed my hands. "That evening we watched Twyla deliver Scout, I wanted to tell you I loved you then. I wanted to kiss you when we were standing out by the corral afterward but I knew I couldn't. I would never have dared. You were so young, you're *still* so young. The last thing I would ever do is rush you, or push you into feeling something you don't. That's why I told you I can't let this happen, not this summer."

"But it's already happening and I'm not sorry. You're not rushing me, not one bit. I'm not as young as you think. I know what I want." Earnest warmth climbed my neck as I insisted, "I want *you*. I want us to be together, I want to know what it's like to be your girlfriend."

"I want all that too, you have no idea how much. I just don't want any of your plans to get set aside. Mathias and Camille would never support us dating right now, not when you're still in high school, with college ahead of you. They'd see it as me taking advantage of you."

I wanted him to say it didn't matter what my parents thought, but I knew well it mattered. I loved them and I knew Wy loved them in his own way, just like I cared for his dad. Our families had been connected for over a decade and a half.

He continued, with conviction, "I know your parents would approve of us being together, at least down the road they'd approve. School has been my whole world for the past five years. I would move to Landon to be close to you but I couldn't quit school now, not when I'm only two years from finishing."

"I would never let you do that," I interrupted. "I know how important it is to you, I've always known."

"Would you consider Montana for college? I don't want you to give up anything for me, do you understand?" Solemn and unsmiling, dark eyebrows drawn inward, he appeared almost stern. Shadows played over his nose and cheekbones, sharpening and elongating his face.

I said softly, "I know that. You are the one of the most honorable men I know, Wy."

"Thank you," he whispered. And then, with more urgency, "You'll consider it, then?"

"I would move out there next week if I could, are you kidding? When you were telling me about the rehabilitation center, all I could think was that I wanted to be there, working with you, making it happen. A year seems so long to wait." Sudden fear sliced across my gut and I admitted, "I'm scared you'll get sick of waiting for me."

"Sick of waiting for you?" Surprise overtook his features. "You have to know there's no chance of that. I would wait forever for you."

With every passing second I fell all the more in love with him, a swelling agony of love, something from which I could not recover. It was love inscribed on my very bones. Next year was far away from the perspective of this moment but this moment was what we had—and I was not about to waste one second.

"We have tonight. And tomorrow, and next week. We can write letters all winter." I found this prospect unexpectedly appealing. I clarified, "*Real* letters, I mean, the way people used to. I'm not really into social media."

"I'm not either. We could text too, in between letters. I'll call you every night. And I'll drive to Landon whenever I get a chance." His thumbs curled possessively over mine. "You're so beautiful, Mill. Inside and out, you're beautiful. You have no idea. And I'm sitting here terrified that I'm rushing you, that I'm moving too fast . . ."

"You're not rushing me." Desire blazed beneath my skin, overriding basic sense; more than that, I wanted him to know the truth. I gathered all my courage and implored, "I want my first time to be with you, this summer."

Motionless, almost statue-like, he studied my face; I'd rendered him speechless. When he spoke at last his voice was low and hoarse. "You say that like I have a choice in the matter and I don't. I'd be taking advantage of you and I would never do that."

I understood his hesitation but refused to accept it.

"It's no one's business but *ours*."

"You're seventeen. I swore to myself I'd wait until next summer before even considering—"

"It's only six years, that's not so much," I interrupted, sensing his resolve weakening. "Uncle Marshall is six years older than Aunt Ruthie."

"But Ruthie was twenty-two when they started dating, not seventeen."

Darkness masked exact colors but I pictured the gold sunburst in his right iris, his long, spiky eyelashes; his pupils were wide with the lack of light. His logic was difficult to deny but I was not about to give up. I insisted, "No one has to know."

"You don't deserve sneaking around, which is what we'd have to do this summer." He was quiet but adamant. "I won't take advantage of you, not for anything."

"*Wy*," I groaned, exasperated even as I laughed, thumping our joined hands against the tabletop. For emphasis, and because I simply liked the sound of his full name, I added, "Wyatt Zane. Stop saying you're taking advantage of me! You think I don't know you better than that? You'd never take advantage of me. Just like I know you'd save any animal you could, just like you'd never have the heart to sell your baby pigs for organic bacon!"

Humor won out at my words and the way I was almost yelling.

He promised, "I won't say it again, but the principle of the matter doesn't change."

I stared hard into his eyes, squeezing his hands, feeling the length of his fingers. Hair grew along the backs of his wrists, which were narrow, emphasizing the lithe strength of his forearms. I whispered, "Please don't make us wait until next summer."

He returned the pressure, stroking up and down along the undersides of my wrists in a way that sent an electric current buzzing straight between my legs. He muttered, "This is like being granted a wish I can't make."

Hardly more than a breath emerged as I repeated, *Please . . .*

I watched his shoulders rise and then lower as he drew a deep breath. "I've barely let myself *fantasize* about being with you because I feel guilty as hell."

"Why would you feel guilty? I don't." An unexpected burst of anger detonated in my chest and I yanked my hands free, jamming them beneath my thighs. "Is it because you have a girlfriend?"

"I don't have a girlfriend."

"What about Hannah?" Her name emerged like something acidic I'd spit out.

"Hannah and I are not together. I ended things with her last spring, once and for all."

"But she *was* your girlfriend. You've had sex with her." I was aware I sounded petty and immature, and further, that it wasn't exactly my business.

"I have," he agreed calmly. "Hannah is the first and only girl I've ever had sex with."

I steeled my soul against the inevitable truth, but I couldn't deny it hurt to hear, hurt a whole fucking lot. I said stubbornly, "I've never had sex with anyone. I've never even come close."

Wy kept quiet at this remark, his gaze unwavering. His hands remained in the middle of the table as though awaiting mine to return.

I made fists to keep from reaching for him, hearing myself ask, "When was the last time you had sex with her?"

For a second I thought he wouldn't answer, but I should have known better; he was no liar, he would tell me the truth even if I didn't want to hear it. He admitted, "In May, at the end of the semester. Hannah and I met up at a local bar and it . . . just happened."

Jealousy swarmed over me like threatened hornets. "How does sex just 'happen'? Like, you just bent her over a barstool? Or what, met up in an alley?"

"It's over between Hannah and me. I've never loved her, even if that seems shitty because of the fact that we've had sex, but it's true. She knows it and she could never get over it, and I always felt like shit because I couldn't love her." He spoke with an edge now, unwilling to let me take unfair potshots. "We've occasionally had sex over the years, yes. I'm not proud of it, all right?"

"Because you love me? Is that why you couldn't love her? If you love me so much, you shouldn't have been *screwing another girl!*" My voice oscillated close to a shriek on those last few words and I clenched my jaws, tears forming before I could stop them.

"It's not fair to throw that in my face," he said tightly.

I knew he was right but I steamrolled ahead anyway; maybe somewhere inside I recognized the necessity of clearing the air regarding these issues. "And now you won't have sex with me because you feel guilty, even though we love each other? That's the *stupidest thing* I've ever heard!"

Hot with fury, I darted from the booth and headed for the door.

Wy followed directly after me. "Wait. Please, wait."

I stopped but refused to look at him, using one hand to swipe almost viciously at my tears.

He implored, "I'm trying my damnedest to do what's right here. No matter what we think, to anyone else involved *I'm* the adult and there's no way around that. You can't possibly think I'd ever touch anyone else after this. There's no one but you."

When I didn't respond, he took my face between his hands.

"Do you hear me?" he insisted softly, his thumb caressing the shape of my mouth again and again, until the trembling in my knees almost took me to the floor.

I nodded reluctant agreement, knowing he was right even if I wouldn't admit it. I let my palms come to rest against the hair on his chest, a dark, thick patch where I wanted to press my nose, my mouth; my bare nipples. His thumb made another pass across my mouth and then he bent and kissed me, as softly as a petal brushing my skin.

"*Please*," I begged, feverish with need.

With one smooth motion, he grasped my waist and set me atop the nearby diner counter, which ran half the length of the room. A stool toppled over but we didn't care.

I slid my arms around his neck, pleading, "Touch me, please, *touch me* . . ."

He obliged without hesitation, slipping both hands beneath the hem of my T-shirt, caressing my ribcage with gentle movements, as though concerned I might shove him away. His hands were warmer than embers and felt better than anything I could have conjured even in my most vivid fantasies of him. We kissed with a singular intensity, tasting deeply, savoring every drop.

"*I want . . .*"

My plea was lost between our mouths but he understood without further words, his touch moving carefully upward, wide palms engulfing the fullness of my breasts at last. The length of my spine bowed toward him; I clung to his neck as a live wire arced straight downward, exploding between my legs.

"*Millie*," he murmured, husky sweetness and urgency all tangled together in his voice as he stroked my nipples, making slow, sensual circles with his thumbs. The sensation was overwhelming, heat that flowed in powerful, escalating waves toward my belly and then sharply lower. I clutched his wrist and directed his touch where I needed it most, and he cupped the soft curve where my thighs parted, using two fingers to trace a path along the wet slit separated from him by nothing more than my threadbare jean shorts.

I pressed my forehead to his neck, shaking hard and overcome; he wrapped me tenderly in his arms, our hearts slamming against each other. I felt the trembling in his muscles and hugged him all the harder, stunned by the strength of what we released in one another.

He whispered hoarsely, "Our first time making love can't be here, on this counter."

"Yes, it can," I insisted in a whisper, and then we were laughing and shivering and kissing again, unable to get enough.

"You feel so good in my arms." He buried his nose in my tangled hair. "So damn right. I don't want to let go."

"Don't ever let go," I agreed, inhaling against his neck until my nostrils compressed, then moved to his chest, rubbing my cheek there as my hands glided all over his bare torso.

Wy combed through my hair with both hands, roots to ends, letting it fall in great sweeps of curl as he marveled, "Your hair is so gorgeous, and thick, it's like a horse's mane . . ."

"I suppose you mean that as a compliment," I murmured, even though I knew he did.

"Of course I do. Holy God, I've wanted to touch you like this for so long . . ."

I muffled a giggle against his neck. "You sound like you're praying."

He nipped my earlobe, then kissed the same spot. "Damn right, I'm praying. You feel like heaven."

I commandeered his hands and brought them again to my breasts.

"Oh Jesus, *you feel so good . . .*"

"You're praying again."

"Hell yes, I am." He kissed with such sweetness and skill, his tongue circling mine, tracing the inner skin of my lips, the hollows of my cheeks. As always, since my earliest memories of him, everything with Wy felt right. This was how kissing was supposed to be—something I wanted never to end. He stroked downward along my waist and around my hips to cup my backside, squeezing gently as he asked, "Have you ever had an orgasm before?"

"I think I've given myself one," I whispered in response; our faces were so close his eyes had melded into one, our noses brushing.

"You're not sure?" Tenderness and slight amusement mingled in his voice.

"I *told* you I've never had sex." I heard a defensive note in my tone. "But I'm pretty sure I've had an orgasm in the shower." I flushed, squirming closer. "I use the showerhead and . . . you know . . ."

He exhaled a low groan, his grip tightening as he confessed, "I'm so hard I think I could saw through a tree trunk."

I admitted, "I've never seen one before."

His grin widened. "What, a tree trunk?"

Laughter rolled between us and I found room to be amazed by the fact that we could sit here blazing with desire and laugh this way.

"Let me see you," I begged, not to be deterred, reaching for him before he could say otherwise, unfastening the metal button on his jeans and tugging down his zipper. He exhaled a half-gasp as I curled my touch around the hot, smooth column of his flesh, using both hands. There were so many things I was dying to know and the darkness cloaked exact details, including color. My fingertips brushed over his coarse pubic hair and explored the bulging helmet shape at the top of his hard-on; there was an indentation along the center of this, slippery beneath my questing thumbs. Wy braced his hands on the diner counter on either side of my hips, his breath coming fast now as my intense concentration was directed south of his waist.

I was beyond fascinated. "When you come, does it shoot out in a jet?"

"It depends . . . on how long it's been . . . since you came last."

His breathlessness delighted me and I bent closer, rubbing the tip in firm circles as I demanded, "When did you come last?"

His voice was overtly hoarse as he admitted, "This morning, in the shower. And any second, if you keep touching me like that."

"Did some already come out? You feel all slippery." I was throbbing inside, right where this hard-on was intended to fit.

"A little comes out while you make love . . . before you finish."

Arousal all but swallowed me whole as I caressed up and down; Wy appeared lean and sleek, almost predatory—but so very much at my mercy—standing half-naked here before me, wide shoulders arched forward, biceps tense and bulging. His face was in shadow, mine cast in an otherworldly blue from the streetlamp.

He released a sudden, harsh breath.

I refused to let go and wet heat cascaded between my fingers.

We were overwhelmed in hushed, disbelieving laughter yet again, Wy tugging his jeans back into place, both of us attempting to find a napkin in the dimness, this progress impeded by the need to kiss. He took care to wipe my hands clean, one finger at a time. I couldn't stop smiling, giddy with pleasure at what we'd just done.

"This is crazy," he murmured against my lips, anchoring me between his thighs as he straddled a stool while I remained standing; he was so much taller than me this position put our faces closer to the same level. "We were just talking about giving you an orgasm and here I am coming in your hands. That's not exactly fair."

Drunk on the bliss of intimacy, I murmured, "No way are you getting out of giving me an orgasm."

He smoothed his palms up and down along my waist as he said, with teasing formality, "I promise to give you countless orgasms, my sweet, sexy baby."

I linked my arms around his neck, immeasurably pleased by the endearment. "I guess this means we can make love this summer."

"Some testament to willpower, I am. Oh God, Mill, I'm—"

"You're not taking advantage of me!" I cried, pressing both thumbs to his lips to stifle the words.

He gently bit my right thumb. "But I am, God forgive me, let alone any trust your parents have in me. Mathias would beat me to a pulp if he knew what we were doing in here."

An uncomfortable twinge ricocheted through my gut, realizing this statement was likely true. "He'll never know."

"What about tomorrow at breakfast, when we're sitting at this counter and all I can think about is this moment?"

I giggled, mollified but far from ashamed. I did not believe anything we were doing was wrong, no matter what opinions to the contrary my parents might harbor. The front entrance remained in my peripheral vision and it was at that exact second a figure appeared there, silhouetted against the screen.

I choked on a shriek.

Wy rose without hesitation and stepped in front of me, shielding me from view. Sudden, agonizing tension buzzed in my ears and I hunched forward, expecting to hear my mother's reprimanding voice at any second.

The screen door creaked inward and Rae whispered, "Millie, are you in here?"

I nearly crumpled with relief. "Yes, I'll be right out!"

She slipped inside, letting the door ease shut behind her, but hadn't taken more than two steps before Wy admitted, "I'm here too."

Rae stopped walking but I felt her thoughts continue advancing like a bright arc of droplets kicked up from the lake. She finally said, "Shit. I'm sorry, you guys."

I hurried to say, "It's all right, were you worried? Oh God, is Mom at your house?"

"No, no, nothing that extreme. I woke up about fifteen minutes ago and you were nowhere. I just came up from the dock. I figured you'd be down there stargazing."

"We've been in here, talking," I said lamely, but my obvious downplaying was too preposterous for Rae to let slide. Even Wy bit his lower lip to contain a smile.

"Talking, right." Rae sounded exactly like her mother. I heard the restrained laughter in her voice. "What a great thing to do in the dark."

"Rae, come on," I moaned. "Give me a sec and then I'll walk home with you."

"I'll be right outside," she said cheerily.

Alone again, Wy drew me back into his arms. "Well, at least someone in your family knows and approves of us."

"I'm not forgetting what you promised." I rested my chin on his chest.

"Me neither," he whispered, and we stole one last deep, sweet, delicious kiss.

# CHAPTER EIGHT

I WOKE TO AN INSISTENT, REPETITIVE SOUND. Momentarily disoriented, I blinked and then blinked again, and just like that, last night rushed back with the crackling force of an avalanche. A grin split my face as I stared up at the wooden ceiling, my lower legs hanging from the end of the tiny pink bed I'd crept back into before sunrise. It was still early, the room only just beginning to warm with light. I crossed both arms over my chest and gripped my shoulders, my heart already pumping like crazy.

*Millie Jo, my sweet Millie Jo.*

The words, her name, flowed like the refrain of a song I wanted to spend the rest of my life singing.

*Millie Joelle Rawley*, I thought, attaching my name to hers, somewhere between a plea and a prayer. *Someday, God, please let her be my wife someday. When she's ready, when enough time has passed that everyone sees how serious we are, how much we love each other. We can get married when she's done with college. Or before that, maybe once she starts college . . .*

A shrill vibration cut through my wishful thinking, the same sound that had woken me a minute earlier. This time I placed it in context, rolling to my belly and leaning toward the floor, riffling through discarded clothing and a pink flannel blanket to locate my phone. I saw before even picking it up that Hannah was calling, her number flashing across the screen like an accusation.

*What the hell? It's even earlier in Jalesville than it is here.*

I lowered the volume to stifle the vibrations, letting the call go to voicemail, unwilling to get drawn into what was surely the tail end of a rough night; Hannah was probably still drunk. Before we left Jalesville, I'd heard from my cousins during one of our weekly family dinners that lately when Hannah drank at The Spoke, she drank hardcore.

*It's not your fault. It's not up to you to fix anything here.*

*You were honest with her. You ended it.*

*There's nothing else you can do.*

Hannah left no message, to my relief, and I decided to write off the call as accidental.

Without intending it I fell asleep again, waking this time to the sounds of

Axton, Gus, and Celia—Marsh and Ruthie's three oldest; they were taking turns bouncing from my twin bed to the other. The sun was at full morning tilt, the house smelling like a bakery, yeast and sugar and flour. Syrup and bacon too, somewhere in the mix of aromas. I heard my brother and Ruthie downstairs, chatting with Millie's great-grandma. My pulse sped up as I listened for Millie's voice among them but she was probably still over at Rae's.

The sooner I got up, the sooner I could see her.

"Watch out below!" bellowed Axton, poised near my knees with arms extended. He leaped, belly-flopping on the opposite bed while Celia scrambled to be the next to jump.

I grabbed my niece around the waist and stuffed her under a nearby blanket while she laughed and shrieked and struggled. Between my three married brothers there were thirteen kids; I loved my nieces and nephews dearly and they knew it. They were at our house in Jalesville all the time, since Dad was the default babysitter for his many grandkids. Besides, there were only about twenty steps between Marsh and Ruthie's back porch and my dad's. My torturing of Celia drew Ax and Gus like magnets and they leaped onto the twin bed, bouncing and laughing, always more wild than usual when we visited Landon.

"Are those my naughty kids I hear?" Marshall hollered from the stairwell.

"Daddy!" Celia rolled out from under the blanket and ran headlong, trailed by her brothers.

"Sorry, little bro!" Marshall called, herding the kids toward the kitchen.

I sat up and knuckled my eyes, wearing nothing but the same jeans from last night. I rested one hand lightly on the faded denim across my zipper, thinking of the way Millie had touched me, her curiosity and questions and the straight-up heat between us—her sweetness combined with a level of passionate hunger that blew me away. I'd never experienced anything like what I felt with her, not even close. Dying to hear her voice, I grabbed for my phone and saw that she'd texted me already this morning. My heart went light as a dandelion gone to seed as I read her words from an hour ago.

*Good morning! Remember your promise.*

I wrote back immediately—*Hi baby, just woke up. That promise is all I can think about.*

She replied almost at once—*I love when you call me your baby.*

She'd told me so last night and it was one of the many small things I already knew she liked, the list accumulating.

*Where are you, still at Rae's?*

*No, I'm home. About to shower.*

My heart thudded and I was hard just that fast. I rolled toward the wall, stretching full length on the twin bed, thinking of what we'd done together last night as I typed a reply—*I'm jealous of the showerhead, wish I was there.*

No sooner had I sent this message when, from the doorway, my brother asked, "Hey, you have a minute?"

A younger version of me would have appeared as guilty as I felt, but I was no longer a kid, or intimidated by my older brothers. My phone buzzed with a return message I wanted badly to read but I stashed it under the covers and looked over my shoulder at Marshall, who stood gripping the doorframe with one hand. Sleepless smudges bordered his eyes and he hadn't shaved in about a week, but there was an aura of lazy contentment surrounding him.

I said, "Hope you enjoyed the suite."

"We did, indeed," he drawled, exactly matching my sardonic tone. "Don't worry, Ruthie made me strip the bed so you won't get pregnant or anything when you sleep there tonight."

I grabbed a round, ruffled pillow and flung it at him like a Frisbee; he caught it in one hand and threw it back, sinking to sit on the twin bed opposite, fixing me with a look that I knew from experience meant he had something of substance to relate. He stretched his left leg and tapped the door so it swung closed.

*Oh, shit.*

I sat straighter at once. "What is it?"

Marshall was not one to mince words; he never had been. But I knew him well enough to sense he was at something of a loss. Holding my gaze, he finally asked, "Wyatt, do you care for Millie Jo?"

My brain clicked with surprise but I was not about to pretend I didn't know what he meant. I said immediately, "I do. I always have."

Marsh nodded slowly, absorbing this information. I figured he hadn't anticipated getting so quickly to the heart of the matter.

I trusted my brothers without question, Marsh maybe even most of all. Beneath all his layers, he was a person of extraordinary understanding and insight. I leaned toward him as I explained, "Millie and I talked for a long time last night after we left Eddie's, about our feelings for each other. We talked about the future and what everyone would think about us being together as a couple."

"Please tell me when you say 'talk,' you really mean talk," Marsh interrupted.

I thought of Millie saying, *It's no one's business.*

"We just talked." I spoke levelly, praying he wouldn't call out the lie.

"Go on," Marsh invited, and my shoulders relaxed.

"We sat over at the café and talked about next summer. Millie will be eighteen then and she wants to move out to Montana for college. I pretty much begged her to consider it." I plunged both hands through my hair, in momentary agony at the length of time separating then and now.

Marsh stayed silent, his expression neutral, but I knew him well enough to detect sympathy in the angle of his eyebrows.

I kept my voice low as I continued, "Both of us know how Mathias and Camille would react right now. I get it, and I understand that. But by next summer, we figured it would be all right if we started seeing each other openly."

"You two care for each other, this is what you're telling me?"

"We do. I know she's young and I know what everyone would think, that I'm taking advantage, but I'm not, I swear I'm not." I held his unwavering gaze. "I love her, Marsh."

It was a word never spoken lightly in our family; my brother recognized this.

I heard only sincerity in his tone as he murmured, "I'm glad to hear that." He paused for a moment, glancing toward the ceiling. "You know I first met Ruthie when she was only fifteen. I knew even then that someday we'd be together, but I didn't dare make any sort of move that autumn because she was so young." His eyes lowered again, piercing mine. "What I'm trying to say is be smart, little bro. I know about strong feelings, believe me, but you're the adult here. You can't let those feelings overpower your judgment."

"I know," I whispered, guilt striking like hailstones. It would be useless to attempt to justify last night's behavior. I implored, "Hey, please don't say anything to anyone. And can you ask Ruthie not to either? I know she knows because it's the only way *you* would know."

"Of course she knows. We talked about it last night after we saw the way you and Millie were dancing at the bar. Ruthie's concerned. She offered to talk to Millie but she doesn't want Camille to be upset about that. So here I am, talking to you instead."

"Lucky me." I dropped the sarcasm as I admitted, "I'm glad that you know. It's not like I want to hide how I feel. Shit, I want to tell everyone. Next summer can't come fast enough."

Marsh avoided the tone of a father administering a sex talk to his eldest son, speaking instead with subtle humor. "Just keep your pants on *this* summer, okay? Buttoned. And zipped."

I felt the tingle of a blush start behind my ears, like I was about thirteen; man, had my pants been neither last night. I muttered, "Jesus *Christ*."

"And her pants on. Buttoned and zipped."

"Marshall Rawley, the moral compass," I intoned, unable to keep from giving him shit. "I remember that summer you and Ruthie started dating like it was yesterday, you know; I wasn't exactly blind or deaf. Ruthie and those tiny little shorts she always wore. You couldn't keep your hands off of her. Were *your* pants zipped and buttoned at all times . . ."

Marsh jumped up and snaked out an arm, catching me in a tight headlock, knuckling my scalp as though I wasn't two inches taller than him these days. Grunting with the effort to restrain and escape, respectively, we couldn't help but laugh.

"You little shit . . ." Marsh flicked my ear and I yelped, jabbing his thigh with a closed fist.

"Boys, breakfast!" Dad called from the stairwell.

Marshall released hold of my neck but gripped my right shoulder in an iron clamp, speaking low, slightly out of breath. "Hey, I want you to know I'm happy about you and Millie Jo. I know Mathias and Camille would approve. Camille spent half the night at Eddie's talking about how she's proud of you. They'd pick you to be with their daughter in a heartbeat." He paused, letting that sink in before concluding firmly, "When she's old enough."

I nodded, grateful for his supportive words.

"Thanks, Marsh."

"What else are brothers for?" he replied, smacking the back of my head in a gesture caught somewhere between affection and exasperation.

. . .

I left my hair loose over my shoulders after I showered, thinking of Wy's heartfelt compliments, so lightheaded with happiness my trembling hands could barely perform normal morning tasks like brushing my teeth and applying a little mascara. I had awoken to the splendor of a world in which Wyatt Rawley loved me in return.

"Honey, are you coming?" Mom called up the stairs. "We're leaving for the café in a few minutes."

"I'll be right down!" I pressed both palms against my belly, which was home to a sudden flock of fluttering birds. Because it was a vehicle through which I could contact Wy, my phone had not been more than a few inches from my grasp since last night. I scrolled through the texts we'd already exchanged this morning, reading his words for probably the fiftieth time. I'd used "Scout," our horse's name, for Wy's contact, in the unlikely event that my phone fell into the wrong hands—i.e., Henry's or Mom's or Dad's. Though I intended to delete the messages for the very same reason, I had not yet mustered the strength to do so.

*Doesn't this just prove Wy's point? If you aren't doing anything wrong, why would you take the time to hide it?*

*You know damn well why you're hiding it. Because your parents would kill you. And, way worse, they'd kill him.*

I owned no sexy, let alone matching, lingerie, a fact over which I momentarily despaired; in the summer months, I usually wore a swimsuit in place of a bra and underwear. I settled on a simple nude bra beneath a white tank top, then located a clean pair of jean shorts and skipped underwear altogether, grateful that my period wasn't due for at least two more weeks. I spared a moment to clasp my favorite earrings into place, small turquoise droplets set in silver. I dabbed mango-scented lotion on either wrist and at the hollow of my throat, feeling the slam dance of blood beneath my fingertip as a single thought spun on repeat in my head.

*By tonight. We could have sex by tonight.*

"Any big plans for the day, girls?" Mom asked as she drove Lorie and me around the lake.

Dad had left earlier, headed for a fishing trip which included most of the menfolk—Wy purposely *not* among them—and any kid who wanted to spend the day cruising in the pontoon, slapping at mosquitoes and dealing with night-crawlers and bait minnows and tangled fishing line.

"I'm just working lunch, then nothing definite," I mumbled, fiddling with my hair—a dead giveaway, had Mom been on the alert for any hint of deceit. But she continued humming along with the radio station as she followed the lake road, oblivious to my lie. I'd been concerned she would start posing questions about last night, but so far nothing seemed out of the ordinary; Mom was in a good mood, excited to spend the day with her sisters.

"We're having a wedding today," Lorie announced from the backseat.

"A wedding?" I parroted, smiling, turning to look at her over my left shoulder. She wore a green tutu over a sequined swimsuit, her little forearms hidden beneath a colorful array of stacked jelly bracelets, old ones of mine I'd given her. Her fingernails were painted with meticulous daisies, which she'd created using polish and toothpicks. "You look so pretty, Lor. I love your nails."

"I did everyone's last night!" She beamed with modest pride. "Even Brant let me do his."

"That's awesome. Who's getting married today?" I reached to wiggle her knee.

"Annie and Zoe," she explained. "None of the boys wanted to get married; they wanted to go fishing. I'm doing their hair and makeup and their dresses are going to be seaweed and flowers."

"That's cool!"

"What time is the ceremony? Are we all invited?" Mom asked, slowing to make the right turn into the parking lot.

I lost all track of the conversation, scanning the café for my first sight of Wy. I knew he was already here, thanks to our texting; he'd eaten breakfast earlier. It was midmorning by now, the sun pouring liquid gold over the lake, heating my shoulders as I hurried from the car. I couldn't fill my lungs as I climbed the steps to the side porch, the tables there resembling immense sky-blue flowers in full bloom, their sun umbrellas all propped open. I heard laughter and about five different conversations from inside, and a second later Wy appeared, propping the screen door open against his forearm and offering me a grin for which I would have walked the circumference of the earth atop burning coals.

"Hey," he said softly, then immediately directed the focus of his attention toward Mom and Lorie, only steps behind me. "I heard there's a wedding here today. Lorie, you're dressed up for it, I see."

My little sister giggled as she darted around us toward the kids while Wy held the door for Mom and me. The women were gathered at the diner counter; other than Wy and baby Luke, all of the men and boys were absent. Mom grabbed her coffee cup and ventured behind the counter to fill it, while I basked in the warmth of Wy's attention, both of us radiating with awareness of each other. Rae wasn't here, probably still at home getting ready for work; it was edging toward eleven, when Shore Leave opened for lunch.

Wy tilted his head toward the booth near the window, where we'd talked last night, and we took the same positions as before, only this time my hands remained in my lap while Wy sat with his forearms lining the table's edge, both of us slanting forward, longing to touch. His posture emphasized the width of his shoulders, our proximity inspiring a woozy rush of delight across my lower belly. His hair was still damp from a recent shower and our conversation regarding showerheads took precedence in my thoughts. I imagined warm water coursing over his lean, naked muscles, his strong hands lathering soap and gliding all over his skin . . .

A grin spread across his mouth as we sat staring at each other in mute, escalating awe.

"What?" I murmured, grateful for the noise and chaos of the little kids. I dug my nails into the vinyl of the seat to keep from reaching across the table.

"I'm just glad to see you." His nose was sunburned, his cheekbones slightly flushed, eyes fixed on mine. The thought of being kept apart until next summer hurt like sharp rocks wedged behind my breastbone. I could hardly sit still.

I admitted, "I kept my phone at my side all night. I never do that. Every time I got a new message my heart just about quit beating because I couldn't wait to see what you'd written."

"Same here." He lowered his voice a notch. "You look so pretty. God, you're beautiful, Mill."

All shivery and delighted at his words, I kicked his ankle beneath the table. "Shhh!"

His grin intensified. "What time will you be done with work?"

"By two."

"Can I help out around here until then? I tend bar at The Spoke sometimes, when one of my cousins needs a night off."

The idea grew in appeal. "Have you ever waited tables? It'll be busy all day, since it's Saturday *and* tourist season."

"I haven't but I'm a fast learner." His gaze detoured to my mouth. "I want to kiss you. I'm dying."

"Meet me at the shed in about a minute. Just give me a head start."

I slipped casually from the booth, taking careful note of my mom; the women were debating where to spend the day shopping for antiques. No one glanced my way as I walked slowly outside, as if headed to check something on the porch. Fifteen seconds later I had skirted the café, hurrying down the incline toward the ancient wooden shed where we kept canoe paddles, water toys, and life jackets. I let the shed door ease shut behind me, pressing both palms against my belly, all but vibrating with anticipation; sunlight streaming through the solo window created a bright, slanted square on the wooden floorboards, bisected into four equal parts. The shed smelled musty, of dampness and dust; intricate cobwebs decorated the eaves.

The door creaked as it opened behind me and a second later I was in Wy's arms and his mouth was on mine. He grasped my hips, my waist, my ribcage; each in turn, his touch roving up and down as I held fast to his shoulders. Amazement swelled between us as we drew slightly apart, to study each other.

"This is so . . ."

"Incredible," he finished for me.

I nodded, touching his lips with my thumbs as he had touched mine last night, tracing their shape, until he shivered and reclaimed my mouth, a sensual tasting that I felt all the way to my tailbone. I slid my palms beneath his T-shirt, gorging on the texture of his skin, spreading my fingers in the hair on his chest before running both hands around to his back, feeling his muscles shift as he touched me in return. My shorts grew wet along the seam and I grasped his wrist, just as I had last night; he immediately encountered bare flesh on either side of the damp denim.

"Holy shit, baby, you're not wearing any—"

"Panties," I finished against his lips, pressing closer, thrilled by his tone.

I felt his heart thrusting. He deepened our kiss at once, bracketing my hips with both hands. His thumbs made sweeping arcs over my pelvis and small pleading sounds rose in my throat. Wy squeezed my waist and forced himself to withdraw enough to see my eyes. His pupils were dilated, brows drawn inward and nostrils flared, hair falling over his forehead.

"Don't stop," I begged.

He drew a slow, deliberate inhalation. "I meant to tell you before I got carried away. Ruthie and Marshall know about us."

"They do?" Surprise wrinkled my forehead. "How?"

Wy smoothed hair from my temples, letting his touch linger in my curls. "I talked to Marsh this morning. He asked if I had feelings for you and I told him the truth."

"But how did . . ." I was mystified, thoughts whirling.

"Ruthie knows. It's the only way my brother could know."

Alarm bells clanged in my head. "I have to talk to her right away. Oh God, what if she talks to my mom . . ."

"Marshall promised not to say anything. Ruthie wanted to talk to you but she didn't want to upset Camille. Ruthie always knows everything, I can't believe I've ever tried to hide anything from her."

"Just like Rae," I muttered, before asking, "You're not upset that they know?"

"Not at all. It was actually a relief telling Marsh the truth." A smile lit his eyes before traveling to his lips. "I told him that I love you."

"You did?" I melted all over again. "Oh, Wyatt . . ."

"I love hearing you say my name like that, you have no idea." He rested one hand lengthwise against my lower back, hauling me closer, briefly touching his forehead to mine. It struck me how he often chose this sweet way to communicate his feelings; further, it reminded me of the way a horse showed affection. He spoke with quiet conviction. "I haven't forgotten my promise, I swear, but we can't stay in here. And I sure as hell won't be able to forget that you're not wearing panties."

"I want to be alone with you later," I insisted. "Later *today*."

"Mill . . ."

I cried, "If you say one more time that you're taking advantage of me . . ."

"I'm not, I promise." He hesitated, torn somewhere between responsibility and subtle amusement. "It's just that I promised Marsh we would . . ."

I demanded, "Would what?"

Humor won out in Wy's expression. "That this summer we'd keep our pants buttoned and zipped."

I giggled in spite of myself, mild embarrassment mixing with a grudging understanding; Aunt Ruthie, not to mention Mom, would have insisted on exacting the very same promise.

I whispered, "But next summer is so far away."

"An eternity," he agreed.

"What if I just wear sundresses? Then there's no buttons or zippers to worry about."

He kissed me in response, laughter caught between our lips.

"It's no one's business," I reminded him, pointing my index finger at his long nose. "No one's but ours."

"I know, I really do. But my better judgment isn't functioning at full capacity just now. Besides, our first time together should be someplace where we don't have to rush. Where I can take time to get you there." To my delight, a hint of bashfulness crossed his face. Studying my eyes, he finished softly, "I want to make it amazing for you."

"Everything that's happened since last night has been amazing."

He lifted my chin. "C'mere, let me kiss you one more time before we have to go back out there."

He proceeded to work the bustling lunch crowd with Rae and me. The customers loved him. Distracted and smiley and all but bumping into walls, I could hardly keep my eyes away as he hustled around the dining room, brimming with characteristic enthusiasm. Rae and I outfitted him with a server apron, an order pad, and a couple of pens, which he kept setting down and subsequently losing.

"This is fun," he said as we caught up at the ticket window about an hour into the shift, ducking his head to ask Grandpa Blythe, "Can you throw some parmesan cheese on these fried mushrooms, please?"

"It's for the Allens," I called to Grandpa. "Their usual."

"No problem." Grandpa grabbed a towel and dried his hands, sending us a fond grin. "Wyatt, you're a good kid, helping out with lunch. I hope the girls let you keep your tips."

"We haven't settled that yet," I said.

"No way, I've already made like fifty bucks," Wy shot back, digging an elbow in my ribs, tickling me.

I squirreled around him so I could clip my next two orders on the ticket wheel. Wy's hair was wilder than normal, falling over his forehead; his T-shirt and server apron were smeared with grease, and three ink pens listed at cock-eyed angles from his back pocket. I wanted to jump into his arms, latch my legs around his waist, and kiss him until my jaws ached. I thought I might die waiting for later.

"That's a conflict of interest." I indicated his shirt, which advertised The Spoke.

"You *just* noticed that?" He tugged on the back of my apron, neatly untying it.

"Hey!" I set down three orders of cheese curds to retie the dangling strings.

"It's all right, you can wear a Shore Leave shirt when you help out at The Spoke next summer."

Our gazes held, exchanging promises for later—later tonight and beyond; the whole world suddenly ours.

My naiveté knew no limits that summer.

Rae joined us. "You two are damn lucky Mom and Aunt Camille aren't around."

The women returned an hour later, just after Wy, Rae, and I had settled at table three to roll napkins around silverware for tomorrow. We looked toward the parking lot at the sudden commotion of returning vehicles, watching as the female members of our families descended into the heat of late afternoon. The humidity was almost unbearable and even the whirring counter fan we had strategically positioned toward our table allowed for little relief; Shore Leave had never been equipped with air conditioning. The little girls, conducting their wedding ceremony down on the shore, came running to greet their mothers and aunties, trailing lakeweed, colorful feather boas, and a pale, filmy length of what appeared to be draperies.

"They'll want margaritas, first thing," Rae predicted, jumping up and heading for the blender.

Left relatively alone with Wy, our attention was at once fixed upon each other. Perspiration gleamed along his hairline and the collar of his T-shirt, which I found irresistibly sexy. I wanted to rip the shirt off his body and lick the sweat from his muscles—and that was only the very beginning of what I wanted, the merest tendril of flame. My insides throbbed with the old, familiar ache of longing for him. Wy held my steady gaze, his happy amusement replaced by a growing sense of intensity, and an entirely new idea struck me, far better than the walk I'd spent the entire lunch shift imagining.

I stood in a rush. "Let's take out a canoe, come on!"

Rae called from behind the bar, "Hurry if you don't want to explain. I'll cover for you guys."

"I owe you!" I called over my shoulder as we flew from the table without further prompting and raced outside.

# CHAPTER NINE

WE NEARLY TRIPPED OVER EACH OTHER IN OUR haste to make a beeline for the shed, against which leaned all five canoes my family used in the summer months. We grabbed the first one we saw, an ancient boat with shiny, sheet-metal sides pockmarked by dents. Wy hauled it to the water while I grabbed two life jackets and an oar, hopped up on pure exhilaration. He held the craft steady while I clambered aboard and claimed the bow seat; I stashed the life jackets, balancing the oar in one hand like someone walking a tightrope, as Wy shoved off from the lake bottom. The boat rocked wildly as he jumped aboard and we cut through the moss-green shallows.

"Hurry, head to the left!" I ordered, flushed and giggling as I passed him the oar.

"I'm hurrying," he promised, accepting the oar and strong-arming us quickly away from the café; he was in a better position to row, stationed as he was in back.

I gripped the rounded aluminum edge of the canoe and peered behind him until the dock was safely out of sight.

"We made it!"

"And we're still wearing our aprons," he noticed, nodding toward mine as he rowed like a gladiator, biceps bulging, wide shoulders shifting repetitively. Water droplets flecked his faded jeans with each pass of the oar across his lap, from one side to the other.

My smile was one of sincere joy; I had achieved exactly what I wanted—time alone with Wy. I slowly pulled the rubber band from my hair, its messy, uncombed length tumbling down my back. Loving the heat of his undivided attention, I next removed my apron, letting it glide between my feet. I didn't stop there, cheeks scorching as I finished my "striptease" by removing my bra, one strap at a time, at last easing it from the bottom hem of my white tank top—the most daring article of clothing I risked removing in the middle of the day.

The canoe listed toward shore; Wy had ceased rowing altogether, the tip of the oar trailing forgotten in the water on the starboard side.

"You're next," I demanded. My nipples stood out like gemstones against the thin material of my shirt.

He grinned like the sun bursting from behind a cloudbank, resting the oar across his lap before gamely untying his apron, tossing it aside and then removing his T-shirt with a flourish, spinning it in the air above his head, both of us dying with hilarity when it sailed from his index finger and landed in the water twenty feet away.

"I'll get it," I offered between huge, rolling gasps of laughter. "Head that way!"

Wy angled the bow toward the floating shirt, aiming for the northern part of Flickertail, the least crowded section of the lake on any given day; its shoreline was bordered by thick stands of tall, clicking cattails and teeming clusters of water lilies, whose tangled roots quickly choked up outboard motors, therefore keeping the boat traffic to a minimum. The sky had grown overcast along the western horizon. Silver coins of light spangled Flickertail's opal-smooth surface as the canoe glided soundlessly, the damp air hushed and static; a thunderstorm was no doubt advancing.

I was breathless now for other reasons, watching as he rowed us into deeper water.

Concerned that I might relent to my desperate urge to leap across the boat and straddle his lap, I leaned over the side of the canoe and scooped a handful of water instead, gratified when he gasped at the sudden shock of water splashing his bare torso.

"Now you're in for it," he warned, using the oar to splash me back; it may or may not have been his intent to douse the front of my tank top.

"You are in *so much* trouble!" I yelped, water dripping from my nose and chin.

"I didn't mean to do that!" he cried, barely restraining laughter as I plucked at my inundated shirt, now as transparent as plastic wrap. His grin grew wicked as he teased, "You look like the winner in a wet T-shirt contest."

The canoe teetered as I stood and climbed on the bow seat, with care; only years of performing the exact maneuver allowed me to make a shallow dive with barely a splash. I surfaced, smoothing wet hair from my forehead as I circled back and curled my hands around the aluminum edge nearest Wy's right hip. The water rippled like silk against my overheated skin, cool and sleek.

"You wouldn't," he said, clearly recognizing my intent.

"Oh, I would."

"Not if I jump in first!" Before I could capsize the canoe, he stood, cast aside the oar, and cannonballed over the side, displacing about half the lake and sending the boat rocking like a bobber in heavy waves.

I shrieked as he swam underwater straight in my direction and grabbed my waist, flipping me effortlessly over one shoulder as he broke the surface. Water flooded my nostrils as I rolled in a clumsy backward somersault; I came up sputtering, wet hair painting stripes across my face, lunging to latch hold of his neck from behind. Wy clutched my forearms, creating an unbreakable anchor, and then dunked us both. To get even, I grasped his jeans and tugged downward, hoping to render him half-naked, but the soaking denim wouldn't budge.

"Ha, ha!" he teased as we wrestled, finally managing to get his arms hooked behind my knees; without further ado, he chucked me high into open air. My arms windmilled as I shrieked again, the sound echoing across the quiet water-scape, as though the two of us were the last people on earth. I landed butt-first in the lake with an ungraceful *plonk.*

Wy swam fast, closing the distance between us in a few strokes. His hair appeared shades darker from the water; inundated, it hung nearly to his bare shoulders. I changed my mind about kicking a tidal wave his way—almost before I knew I'd moved, my arms encircled his neck and my legs, his waist. Wet kisses, our fingers gliding over each other's tangled hair and sleek skin as we explored with increasing abandon; I held fast to the firm edges of his shoulder blades as Wy carefully unzipped my shorts, seeking my bare flesh.

I gasped, breathless sounds caught between our kisses as he caressed with gentle pressure, exploring the soft, wet folds. My hips jerked toward him, a word-less invitation; in response, he slid two fingers within my body, intensifying his rhythmic touch. From a distant horizon, thunder grumbled a low warning. Feath-ery plips of light rain spattered Flickertail's surface as a sharp and pulsing plea-sure stemmed outward from between my legs. The scent of the oncoming storm blended seamlessly with the storm occurring inside me; forever after, the one would never fail to call the other to mind. My hips moved against his hand in a steady rhythm as he plundered my mouth with hungry kisses. At last I clamped hold of his wrist, digging my nails, anchoring his touch as I shuddered violently.

"That was . . . *that was* . . ." I couldn't catch my breath or find the right words, and pressed my forehead against his neck; the rain had increased, cascading over us.

Wy held me like he never meant to let go; sheltered against his body, I want-ed to remain here with him in the downpour, letting eternity slide past us like a silent, endless current of air.

"Is that what sex is like?" I whispered against his drenched skin. Rain all but obscured the shore from view.

"Sex is even better." He drew away just enough so I could see the promise burning in his eyes.

Water washed over our faces, leaching through our eyelashes and dripping from our chins. The lake was shoulder-high on Wy; I knew if I put my feet down, the marshy ground would be far beneath my toes. We clung, shivering, heated only by proximity to one another—and by our very words, spoken with the utmost sincerity of the unscathed. Thunder exploded in the purple-gray mass of clouds above our heads, followed by a jagged bolt of pure energy, and Wy moved fast, carrying me out of the water. Once on shore we scurried through boggy clumps of weeds and wild iris, seeking shelter deeper in the woods. The rain slackened as we ducked under the cover of the dense pines, walking until we found a patch of grass to wait out the storm.

"It's because . . . it was so . . . humid," I managed to say, teeth chattering as moisture swiftly evaporated from my chilled skin. Mud covered our shoes and dappled Wy's jeans and my bare calves.

He sat and enfolded me on his lap. Even without a shirt he was by far warmer than me and I snuggled close. He pressed a kiss on my ear, tucking aside snarled curls to do so.

"The strength of the storm, you mean?"

I nodded, eyes drifting closed, my cheek resting on his chest as I murmured, "Tell me more about sex."

His torso rumbled with a laugh. "There's so much I want to *show* you."

"Like what?" I whispered, drowsy and content in his embrace.

"Like going down on you," he murmured, gently stroking my face, repeatedly following the curve of my jaw, as though sculpting clay.

"Oral sex?" I whispered, opening my eyes to his crooked, teasing smile.

"Yes, that's it exactly." He cast a speculative gaze around the clearing, the air as dim as ash beneath the trees and heavy cloud cover. "I wish we had a tent, even a little tent."

"A tent," I repeated, wondering why I hadn't stumbled to this conclusion already. "Of course. There are a dozen tents in the garage. It would be easy to sneak one out of there."

"How would we manage a night alone? I don't even have my truck here . . ."

"Leave that to me." My thoughts whirled. "I'll tell Mom I'm staying over with a friend from Landon. That way, I'll have an excuse to stay out all night. You can meet me. I'll borrow my mom's car and we can drive out to . . ." I considered the chances of running into a familiar face at the local campgrounds; the odds didn't exactly stack up in my favor. At last I decided, "We can drive out to Itasca. It's a huge state park, over thirty miles away. We won't run into anyone I know there."

"Wait," Wy said, and I heard the notes of resolve rising in his tone.

"No!" I cried, shifting to straddle his thighs, briefly covering his mouth with one hand. "Don't you *dare* say we shouldn't."

Our faces were so close our noses touched; Wy's breath was warm on my lips, his hands curving to fit around my hips. He pulled my lap flush against his as thunder shook the pines, rumbling along the ground like a reprimand.

"I don't want to rush you," he whispered. "Or pressure you. That's the last thing I want."

I licked his lower lip, lingering there, delighting in our proximity and my ability to touch him as I chose.

"You're not rushing *or* pressuring me, you *know* you're not." I caressed the damp hair along the back of his neck, where slight curls had formed, exploring the warm hollow at the center of his nape. Tenderness and love rushed my senses, overflowing as impassioned words. "Please don't make me wait until next summer to know what it means to make love with you. I don't want to be apart. Just the thought of you leaving hurts like someone stabbed my heart."

He cradled my face, his eyes dark with passionate resolve. "I don't want to be apart either. This year will go fast, we'll *make* it go fast."

"I know, but I want something to remember *this* year, something to hold onto. Please, Wy, *please* don't say no. You're not rushing me, *I want you so much . . .*"

"I can't resist you, not for a thing, especially when you say 'please' . . ."

We were kissing before he finished speaking, hot and ravenous. My wet shirt hampered its removal from my body, but Wy made short work of it and I curved toward him, quivering at the heat of his tongue on my chilled nipples. He spread both hands wide, spanning my back as he bent over me, murmuring throaty words of love that echoed in my gasping breaths.

"You taste so good, sweetheart . . . your skin smells like heaven . . ."

"That feels so good . . . *oh God, Wy* . . ."

I unzipped his jeans as I had last night and took him in hand, stroking with a firm, unceasing motion. I felt the same wetness at the tip and instinct propelled me to shift position, bending to take him in my mouth, mindful of my teeth. His cock was warm and smooth, harder than a shaft of fresh-cut wood between my lips, tasting of lake water and salt and . . . man. *My* man, the only person I ever wanted to share these secret, beautiful things with.

Wy uttered a low gasp, lightly bracketing the back of my head as I tasted him, exploring as much as anything else, fascinated by the ridges and textures of this ever-changing part of his body. I concentrated my efforts on the top half, knowing I would never be able to take his entire length down my throat without choking. Bent forward above me in the ashen light, his breath grew increasingly harsh and I reveled in my ability to arouse such pleasure. In all my fantasies of being with him, I had never imagined the joy of such a feeling.

"*Stop,*" he suddenly gasped.

Instead of lifting my head I continued industriously applying my tongue, caught off guard by the hot burst of what tasted like liquid salt jetting down my throat. I coughed and then covered my mouth, trying valiantly not to gag. My stomach lurched in immediate response and I inhaled hard through my nose, thinking of Rae's past giggled warnings.

*Don't ever swallow, it's so gross, I'm telling you.*

It was no use; I spit the remainder of the mouthful behind the tree, embarrassed but laughing, swiping at my sticky chin with the back of one hand. Wy rolled to his knees, simultaneously tugging his jeans into place, and rested a hand on my back.

"I'm so sorry, I didn't expect you to swallow . . . you kinda took me by surprise there."

"I wanted to . . . I really did . . ." I tucked hair behind my ears, laughter rising from my belly in great gulps as I declared, "But I'm *never* swallowing that much again. Oh, *my God* . . ."

"C'mere, crazy woman." He engulfed me in his arms, nuzzling his nose into my hair. "I *tried* to warn you."

"I just wanted to see what it was like," I defended, closing my teeth gently over one of his nipples just as he'd done earlier to mine, gratified when he shivered.

"Thank you," he added, in all seriousness. "I didn't expect you to do that."

"I wanted to," I repeated, shifting so I could see his eyes. "Everything with you feels natural. It feels the way it's *supposed* to, like something I never want to stop. The only other time I was with a guy, it definitely didn't feel that way."

I felt his muscles tense. "Some guy made you do something you didn't want to do?"

He sounded as though his next move would include finding said guy and dismembering him, and I hurried to explain, "No, no. Nothing like that at all. I just meant when I kissed someone from my class, at a party last winter, it felt all wrong."

The rigidity in Wy's posture ebbed and his tone grew confessional, laced with subtle humor. "The first time I ever tried to kiss a girl, she turned her head at the last second and I ended up kissing her ear."

It took effort, but I stifled my jealousy. "Was that Hannah?"

He nodded, twining one of my curls around his index finger, winding and unwinding its length. "Yeah, we were both fifteen. I was about as smooth as a gravel road, I tell you. My brothers never let me hear the end of it when I was stupid enough to tell them."

"You and Hannah started dating in high school?" I was determined to retain my composure; nothing would highlight our age difference more than my inability to hear these basic facts about his past.

"We did. But it's like I told you last night, I knew even back then that I didn't love her. I care for her, don't get me wrong, and I want her to be happy, but I was never in love with her."

"But she must love you." I spoke softly, as though thinking aloud.

"And that's why I ended things with her last spring. I know that how I've treated her over the years, occasionally hooking up, I mean, is unforgiveable. I don't have an excuse for it. If I try to explain, it just sounds like bullshit."

"Tell me," I whispered.

Wy studied my face, again caressing it like an artist shaping a sculpture. He finally said, "When I left to go to college, I was the last son in the house. I hated leaving Dad there all alone, to the point that I almost turned down the chance to join the program in Pullman, but Dad would never have let me do that. After Quinn moved out, it was just Dad and me. We really count on each other. I mean, he's the only parent I've ever known, my memories of my mom are all blurry. And I knew Dad would be lonely after I left, even if he wouldn't admit it. I hated to think of him like that."

I watched his throat bob as he swallowed before continuing.

"And I *know* loneliness, because I feel it so often too . . . it's hard to explain. I have no reason to feel lonely because I have Dad, and my brothers, and Aunt Julie, and my cousins and friends in Jalesville. Plenty of people who care for me. I know how goddamn lucky I am. But it's there all the same, deep inside. And that's why, over the years when I'd see Hannah and she was up for sex, I never turned her down."

I repositioned so I could wrap my arms more securely around him, hugging for all I was worth, resting my cheek against his chest.

He returned the strength of the embrace. "You crush out all that loneliness, Mill, that's what I'm trying to tell you. Just the thought of you sweeps it away. It's like you are pure joy and light, and you fill me up. It's how being in love makes you feel, I truly believe that. It's how my dad felt about my mom, how Marsh feels about Ruthie." He kissed my temple, letting his words brush my ear as he whispered, "We're together now. It's just the beginning of our lives together."

"Yes," I whispered, tears spilling from the corners of my eyes. "We can raise horses out in Montana. And we'll live near your dad so we can visit him all the time, and Aunt Ruthie and Uncle Marsh, and all your brothers and their families. You'll be a vet and I'll get my degree in psychology, and we can help run the rehabilitation center. When you were talking about that yesterday, all I could think was that I wanted to be there with you."

The storm had receded in the past fifteen minutes, the clouds shredding apart, leaving the pines dripping in a steady cadence all around us. As I spoke, a clear shaft of late-afternoon sunlight cut between the trees and fell across the clearing, an auburn benediction to highlight the promise in his eyes.

"Yes, that's just the way of it," Wy agreed. "I'll come get you next June. I'll come for your graduation and we can drive out to Montana together. Scout will be all yours, he's missed you."

"I miss him too! He must be huge now, I can't wait to see him. And Shadow too."

"There are so many things I want to show you, so much I want us to do together." His expression grew severe with emotion. "I love you so goddamn much, Millie Jo. I can't tell you enough."

The sun heightened other awareness, namely that of our long absence from Shore Leave. I had no idea what excuse Rae had offered up, but no doubt we'd soon be missed, if we weren't already.

"Tomorrow," I whispered, seized by sudden urgency. "I'll get us a tent and we'll go camping at Itasca."

Wy combed his fingers through my hair, something I'd already realized he loved to do; I sensed he felt as though he should disagree with this plan.

"Tomorrow," I insisted, before he could conjure up a contradiction. "We have less than two weeks left this summer. We can't waste a second."

"Tomorrow," he agreed at last.

# CHAPTER TEN

NECESSITY WOULD NOT ALLOW US TO LINGER, AS much as we wished to stay. I wriggled back into my dirty tank top, experiencing the first real pangs of concern about how we would explain this level of dishevelment.

"The canoe!" I cried; I hadn't given it a second thought until now. "Shit! It's probably long gone. Oh God, and your shirt . . ."

"C'mon, we better go see." Wy maintained calm, grasping my hand and leading the way.

We reached the shore within five minutes; to my extreme relief the canoe had grounded only about twenty paces away, lolling on its side and reflecting patches of the sinking sun in its gunmetal-gray surface.

"Thank goodness," I breathed, pressing my free hand to my heart. "I am never this irresponsible, I swear."

"I think my shirt's a goner," Wy decided, scanning the lake.

Flickertail was empty of watercraft, all recreational boaters chased away by the rough weather. A lavender tint lit the air in the aftermath of the storm, which had sailed east, the last traces visible in the receding cloud ridge. The western sky was ablaze with rich, peachy light, rippling over the lake in a stunning display of warm color.

"It's gorgeous here." Wy rested a forearm momentarily atop his head, taking in the western view as we stood side by side in ankle-deep water. "It's a different gorgeous than the mountains, but no less spectacular."

"I do love it in Landon," I agreed softly, drawing a slow breath, inhaling the scents of my earliest memories, that of lakeshore weeds and damp mud.

"I hope your bra decided to stay put in that canoe." Wy turned my way with a lopsided grin. "I don't know exactly how we'd explain why it was missing, otherwise."

I flushed. "Good point."

"I would take an ass-whupping every day of my life if it meant I got to be with you. If anyone's waiting to whup our asses back at Shore Leave, I mean," Wy clarified, running his fingers through his hair in a familiar gesture. "I say we stick as close to the truth as possible. We took a canoe ride and waited out the storm in the woods."

I nodded agreement, attempting to finger-comb my own hair; no use. Only a hot shower and a bottle of conditioner would alleviate snarls of this level.

"Come here," he said, humor softening his mouth. "You have something on your nose."

I lifted my face, closing my eyes as though anticipating a kiss, which Wy delivered—a gentle touch of his lips, flush against mine. Then he scrubbed the smudge from my nose and perused me at close range.

"All good?" I whispered.

"A million times better than good, my sweet baby."

My bra had indeed remained wedged beneath the bow seat of the canoe but we were missing the oar—a truly rookie mistake I was embarrassed over.

"It's floated way beyond reach by now." I scanned the water in the direction of Shore Leave.

"We can't be that far from the café. Should we swim the canoe back?"

"We'll have to. You're right, it's not too far." I blew a breath from pursed lips. "Well, at least that will explain why we're so dirty and wet." I giggled then, unable to fasten my damp, twisted-up bra straps. "Will you help me?"

Wy managed the delicate little clasp on the undergarment. Standing behind me, he was so tall and immediate and irresistible. Shivers cascaded like sparks across my skin as he cupped my breasts and bent to kiss the side of my neck, murmuring, "There."

"I don't want to go back," I mourned, slanting into his embrace. "I want to shower with you. Can we sneak over to the inn, do you think? Will your dad be there?" I was desperate to prolong our time together.

"We'd be caught for sure. I couldn't let that happen." His forearms were as tan as saddle leather against the pale skin of my belly.

"I know," I groaned.

Wy kissed my ear, promising, "Tomorrow. Unless it's too risky. Let's get a read on everyone once we get back. The last thing I want is for Mathias and Camille to be suspicious."

The simple thought of my parents was as effective as a bucket of ice chips dumped over my head. Resigned, I finished dressing, wriggling into my shirt. Because it was easier to swim without shoes, we stashed ours in the canoe and waded into the lake, guiding it between us.

"Front or back?" I asked Wy.

"Which is easier for you?"

"Front."

"Then I'll take the back."

Working together, we swam alongside the craft, aiding its progress, paddling like puppies. I grew quickly short of breath but Wy kept me entertained, telling a story about a memorable camping trip with his brothers, during which they dared him to sit alone in the midnight darkness of the foothills for what they dubbed his "manhood test."

"How old were you?" I panted, stealing a moment's respite from kicking. I couldn't see Wy from his position on the opposite side of the canoe, but pictured his expression.

"Nine," he said; grinning for sure, I could tell. "It was Sean's idea and I couldn't refuse when they dared me. I was always trying to prove how brave I was. Youngest child complex, and all that. I was scared shitless, I'm not gonna lie. The foothills had never seemed so huge or frightening. Every tiny sound made me hunch up. And then, those assholes," but he was laughing as he spoke, "crept out where I was sitting and pretended to be a grizzly. They just about pissed themselves laughing over it, later."

"They're so mean!" But I was laughing too, clearly picturing Wy at age nine. Nine, ten, fifteen . . . a summer had never passed when I hadn't seen him. I considered our future, all the new memories he and I would make together—a future of blissful summers, and every season in between.

"Nah, they just helped toughen me up. I needed it. I was a daddy's boy," Wy admitted. "I really was. And a tattletale."

"Well, you *are* the baby of your family," I reasoned. The water lapped my chin as I resumed dog-paddling. "And your dad is so great. I've always loved him."

"Dad's the best," Wy agreed. "He's exactly the kind of father I want to be. My childhood would not have been the same without him."

I slid a palm across my belly at his words, thrilled by a sacred, unspoken thought.

*Someday.*

*But many years from now.*

"We're almost there!" I called a few minutes later, spying White Oaks Lodge, my grandparents' resort, on the far side of the lake; I knew the contours of Flickertail as well as I knew the rooms of my childhood home.

I strained to listen for sounds of activity as we approached and heard nothing out of the ordinary. Within a few dozen yards the dock appeared around the bend; the paddleboats were both moored alongside Uncle Justin's speedboat, no one in sight in either the lake or on the grassy incline leading down to the water from the porches. Shore Leave appeared closed, empty of my family and any hint of customers. Muddy weeds brushed my ankles and I stood, grasping the bow and wading to shore, Wy toting the stern. Together, we hauled the canoe back to the shed and hung up our life jackets.

"Where is everyone?" I wondered aloud; fluttery tension continued to dominate my nerves. I'd been expecting to find Mom standing on the end of the dock, scanning the lake as though I'd missed my curfew. But we appeared to be entirely alone; the only vehicle in the parking lot was the rusty old service truck we used for chores around the café.

"I think we just got lucky, that's what," Wy said. "This gives us a chance to clean up. I figured Marsh would be here waiting, or Mathias, and we'd have to do some fast talking."

I tugged him inside the shed for a last kiss, safely hidden from view.

"I'll head over to the inn. I'll text you once I get cleaned up," he promised.

"I'll be at my grandma's," I said. "Grandma Joan's, I mean, right up the hill. Where you slept last night."

"Think of me when you're showering." His eyes glinted with teasing.

Five minutes later we had parted ways, Wy disappearing around the curve in the lake road, headed for town. I found an old sweatshirt of Grandpa Blythe's in the café, insisting Wy borrow it so he wouldn't freeze walking to Landon in damp jeans; the air had cooled in the wake of the thunderstorm, the humidity washed away.

"Gram?" I called upon entering my great-grandmother's house, the unlocked screen door creaking as I entered the familiar space. The light fixture above the stove glowed a warm welcome, but the kitchen was empty of people. "Anyone home?"

I heard no response other than the muted chirp of crickets through the window screens.

Before showering, I used the landline to call Rae's cell.

"Where have you been?" Rae demanded upon answering.

"We just got back from canoeing. Where is everyone? Do they know we were out on the lake?"

"Clint has a game tonight, remember? Everyone's tailgating over at the ballfield now that it quit raining. I told your mom that you guys took out a canoe, no one seemed to think it was a big deal. You're welcome," she added pointedly.

I made a mental note to prepare for questions later; Mom would never let me off the hook so easily. I heard noise and bustle in Rae's background and asked, "Where are you, out at the field?"

"Waiting for Evan to get done with work."

"Then you'll see Wy in a sec. He's heading that way now."

"Tell me more," Rae insisted. "Did you guys . . ."

"No. At least, not yet."

*"Millie . . ."*

"Please don't scold me," I begged. "I'm so happy, I can't even put it in words. Wy *loves me*. He told me so last night. There's so much I need to tell you."

"Wait, *what?* Why didn't you tell me today at lunch?"

"There wasn't a free second!"

"He told you last night? While you were talking at Shore Leave?"

"Yes, oh God, it was so beautiful. I finally told him how much I love him, that I've *always* loved him, and he loves me back, Rae." Tears spurted from my eyes, beyond my control. I babbled, "I'm so happy, I've never been so happy."

"There he is," she suddenly said. "I can see him out the window."

Seconds later she rapped on the glass; I heard it through the phone.

"I'm waving at him," she explained. "Here he comes. I'm talking to Millie," she said a moment later.

"You are?" I heard Wy ask, sounding full of typical good humor; my heart soared as he added, "Can I have the phone for just a sec?" And then his deep voice was in my ear. "Hey there."

"We could have showered together here!" I cried, simultaneously laughing and lamenting. "Everyone's over at the ballfield!"

"It's probably better to be safe than sorry."

"Says you! Hurry and get ready, I already miss you."

"Same here. I'll hurry," he promised.

"I'll meet you at the field," I told him. "You can head over with Rae and Evan."

I showered fast, leaving my wet clothes draped over the towel bar, next rooting through the shorts and tops in the narrow closet in my mom's old bedroom. I ran my fingertips over the row of sweaters on wooden hangers, selecting one the creamy white of daisy petals; I brought the garment to my nose and inhaled, engulfed by the sweet, lightly floral scent of my mother.

*Mom will understand,* I thought, with the warmth of certainty. *She and Dad are in love, they will both understand my decision to move to Montana next summer.*

I found one of my old swimsuits in a drawer and slipped a pair of jean shorts and the cream-colored sweater over it. My hair was shiny-clean but wild with disarray, not that Wy would mind.

*Wyatt Rawley is in love with me,* I thought for the countless time since last night.

I floated to town on a cloud, my feet hardly touching the ground. The evening was as clear as a crystal prism, fading golden light dancing between the familiar structures of my hometown. I headed south along Fisherman's Street, past Eddie's Bar and the post office, angling toward the baseball field where the summer leagues played. My dad's team played on Tuesdays, but no doubt the entire family would be there to root for Miller Auto, Clint's team. I skirted the thick stand of red pines guarding the edge of the field and spied the crowd sprawled all over the bleachers and lining the edge of the baseball diamond adjacent to home plate. My family occupied nearly half the available space; there were all the little kids, playing tag; I saw my mom, seated in a lawn chair near Aunt Ruthie and Auntie Tish, the three of them discussing something with their heads close together.

And then a beaming smile overtook my face as I saw Wy, sitting on a flannel blanket holding Aunt Ruthie's youngest, baby Luke, on his lap. He had been watching for me, I could tell; his grin radiated like a sunrise as our eyes held. No one paid any attention to my approach in the bustle of activity—the guys on the field were tossing baseballs around, running sprints between bases as they warmed up, the crowd noisy and excited, enjoying the golden tranquility of the setting sun in the wake of the storm. Most of the adults were drinking beer from cans encased in colorful, personalized coolies; a typical Landon summer evening.

Wy scooted over, making room for me on the blanket spread across the grass. He gently nudged aside Ace, one of our collies. All three of our dogs had found their way to his side, as animals always did.

"Hey there," he murmured as I joined him, our gazes clinging because we couldn't otherwise touch—but we didn't dare risk it, not with our families in immediate proximity. As I took a seat on the blanket, Wy's dad leaned from a nearby chair to offer me a kind hello. The men were seated in a loose semicircle of lawn chairs, listening and laughing as my dad told a story, gesturing with his beer can. I left a discreet twelve or so inches between Wy and me, but he moved just slightly closer, transferring baby Luke to the opposite arm. Ace poked his long, furry nose against Wy's leg, hoping to encourage further attention.

The low-slanting sun cast Wy's face in pure copper light, highlighting the golden tints in his brown eyes, his long nose creating a shadow on the angle of his cheekbone. My heart thumped with happiness so profound my ribs ached in response. He'd showered since we parted at Shore Leave, his hair still damp, and changed into jeans and a long-sleeved black T-shirt; how safe little Luke appeared, wrapped in Wy's left arm and held close to his chest—how badly I longed to commandeer his free arm and curl against him in the exact same way.

It was a perfect excuse to lean closer as I stroked Luke's round peach of a cheek and murmured, "Hi, sweetie."

Luke, my youngest cousin, was about ten months old, so chubby he appeared to have no neck, his green eyes wide as he absorbed the mild chaos surrounding us; the baby smiled for me, showcasing four little teeth, giggling as I tickled his stack of chins. Wy's jaw was less than three inches from my temple, and he held perfectly still while I leaned over his lap, focusing momentarily on Luke.

Wy murmured, "Your hair smells so damn good."

The urge to giggle washed over me as I purposely kept my gaze directed at the baby.

"Thank you," I whispered, basking in the undiluted joy of his attention.

It was with extreme reluctance that I sat back, bending my legs and wrapping both arms around my knees. This was in part because I was chilly as twilight advanced and also because I was trembling just slightly, overwhelmed by emotion.

Wy asked quietly, "Are you cold? You're shivering."

"A little," I admitted.

The game had started, whistles blowing and guys yelling; the crowd shouted encouragement. Wy leaned behind me, his shoulder brushing my back, and caught up the far edge of the blanket, tucking it carefully over my knees.

"There," he murmured. "Since I can't put my arms around you just now."

Another shiver rolled up my spine at his sweet words. Our eyes held and I squeezed my bent legs to my chest with all my strength.

"Thank you," I whispered for the second time, finding humor in my excessive fluster, considering what had happened between us in the woods as the storm passed over. Despite the activity from the ballfield, we didn't peel our gazes from each other.

"You're still cold, aren't you?" he realized. "Your hair is damp, no wonder. Here, take Lukey, he's about two hundred degrees."

With Luke stationed on my lap and Wy at my side, the shivers abated. Close enough to lean about eight inches and kiss, we remained dutifully on our respective sides of an imaginary line, talking without letup as the game progressed; I wanted to know every available detail about the rehabilitation center Wy's cousin Netta Quillborrow and her husband, Tuck, intended to build in Jalesville. Though the center was still in the blueprint stage, it seemed as though many a planning session had been conducted at both The Spoke and during Sunday dinners, which took place weekly at either Clark's house or Wy's Aunt Julie's; Julie was Clark's little sister, and her daughters, Pam, Netta, and Lee, ran operations at The Spoke. I was familiar with all of them from past summer visits.

"I love how you guys still have Sunday dinners," I said. In many ways, the Rawleys had always reminded me of my own family; every Sunday, as far back as I could remember, we'd gone to Dad's parents' house for dinner. All the Carters were expected, including Dad's three older sisters and their husbands and kids. Shore Leave was the perennial gathering spot for Mom's side, and had been since time immemorial; just like Wy, I was accustomed to large, raucous family events. I'd imagined being a part of Wy's family for so long now it almost seemed as though I always had been.

"Dad and Aunt Julie wouldn't have it any other way," Wy said; neither of us could stop smiling as we studied each other with both fascination and pure enjoyment. "It's a family tradition. And Aunt Julie loves the opportunity to boss us all around and complain that she doesn't have any of her own grandkids yet. She has to steal Dad's."

"Pam and Netta are both married now, right? What about Lee?" I pictured Julie's daughters, remembering them as no-nonsense women with plenty of attitude.

"Not yet. She always claims there's no good prospects in Jalesville."

"Will Netta quit at The Spoke, then?"

"That's the plan. They're about a year out from construction, give or take. Tuck is hoping to break ground by next spring. He's planning at least four barns, one with an indoor training arena, in addition to the main offices." Naming his oldest brother, Wy added, "Garth is a contractor, so his help will be invaluable."

"And that's where you'll set up your vet office?" My anticipation was so heightened it was like a drug in my bloodstream as I envisioned myself working there, at Wy's side, as early as next summer.

He nodded enthusiastic affirmation. "Most rural vets work a few days onsite and then spend the rest of the week out on call. There's so much territory in Montana, ranches spread far and wide, so I'll have to get a new truck, a bigger one, to make rounds carrying all my equipment."

"And you'll work with horses and cattle, mainly?"

"Likely for the most part, but I'll be licensed for the care of any sort of agricultural animal, from mules to swine to goats and sheep. I'm excited for the residencies I'll have next spring, because that means mostly hands-on experience."

The words *hands-on* sent a pulse through my belly and I was grateful for the indigo tint to the air, which hid my immediate blush.

"What will you spend your days doing, once you're licensed?" I asked, adjusting Luke on my lap; the baby had dozed off, snuggled against my breasts.

Wy considered for a moment. "I know everyone associates veterinary work with sterilizing dogs and cats, but I'll probably spend a fair amount of time doing things like preg-checks for cattle herds."

"Is that what it sounds like?"

"Confirming pregnancies, yep. It's so different these days than in, say, my dad's time. When Dad was still ranching sheep they mated naturally, one ram and his herd, and all that." Wy acknowledged my amusement by nudging my shoulder with his. "But these days it's almost all artificial. There are ranchers who breed these massive, genetically superior bulls and then teams travel to inseminate herds all across the state, via injector kit."

"*Eww.*" I giggled, unable to help it, nudging him right back. "I hope they wear big gloves."

Wy was laughing now too. "I think they're part of the kit."

"How do you confirm that a cow is pregnant?"

"Same way you do with humans, with an ultrasound machine. Ideally, you're hoping for at least a sixty-five to seventy percent success rate with artificial insemination. That's considered pretty decent. But there are no guarantees; it's always a gamble."

"You were saying that the center will also be for rescued animals, not just therapy for people," I prompted, curious to know more about this angle.

"We're going to try our best. Tuck wants to focus on horses, for now. There are so many mistreated animals out there, it makes me sick, but you do what you can and try to make peace with the rest. The racing industry, for example . . ." Wy trailed to silence, as though uncertain I was prepared to hear these details.

"Tell me," I insisted.

"It's pretty bad."

I searched his eyes in the gloaming. "Do you mean like saving them from getting sent to factories, that sort of thing?"

"Yes, that's definitely part of it. Most horses that go to slaughter are under age five, when horses can live for thirty or more years."

"Age five?!"

Wy's expression grew ever more earnest. "Thousands of racehorses are born in this country every year. Once they're no longer winning, or get injured, and therefore not earning for their owners, they're disposed of, sent to get processed into dog food. Or if foals bred for racing don't meet certain standards, they're killed almost immediately after birth. If they stand and begin to nurse, the stud fee has to be paid."

I flinched without intending it, biting down on my lower lip.

"I know, it's awful . . ." He sounded apologetic.

"No, I want to know these things. It makes what you're doing all the more important." Love clouted my senses all over again, striking like fists. I whispered emotionally, "You're such a good man, Wy."

He gathered my left hand in the darkness, closest to him between us, and entwined our fingers, squeezing as he said, "I want to be that man for you, Mill, for always."

It was by no means a marriage proposal, but even had he swept to one knee and presented me with a ring, I could not have been more moved. Tears burned the bridge of my nose.

"For always," I whispered.

# CHAPTER ELEVEN

"MILLIE JO! COME HELP WITH THE LAWN CHAIRS," Mom called once the game was over.

"I'll text you later," I murmured to Wy in the bustle of everyone sorting belongings in an effort to pack up.

"I'll be up," he promised, rising with his usual grace, reaching to help me to my feet.

Uncle Marshall, toting Celia piggyback, joined us, saying, "There's my little Lukey."

I transferred the baby to Uncle Marshall, who tucked him close in the fashion of someone holding a football, keeping his other arm under Celia, on his back. I supposed that, as a father to five children, Uncle Marshall was pretty expert at carrying more than one at a time. His and Aunt Ruthie's other kids, Axton, Gus, and Colin, were still playing tag with all the cousins. There was no good excuse to linger with Wy, so I ventured across the dewy grass to join Mom and my aunts, all three busy folding lawn chairs and yelling after the little kids, who were determined to continue playing despite the late hour and the mounting threat of mosquitoes.

"Ride home with me." Mom spoke lightly as I bent to grab blankets from the grass, but I recognized an order when I heard one; I bit back the protest rising in my throat.

I noticed the way that Aunt Ruthie's gaze lingered on me; I was dying for a few minutes alone with her, recalling my conversation with Wy this morning in the shed, but there was no chance of evading Mom. Henry, Brant, Lorie, and James all climbed into the bed of Dad's pickup for the short drive home, along with our dogs. I helped load the last two coolers in Mom's car, exerting true effort to keep my obsessive gaze from following Wy as he joked around with Uncle Marshall and their dad on the other side of the parking lot. I'd found it difficult to be separated from him even before we confessed our feelings; now it was an agony I'd never known.

Instead of heading straight for home, Mom drove past the turn for our driveway and continued around the north side of Flickertail, where the road gave way to gravel and meandered in lazy curves running parallel to the lake. I sat with indrawn breath, tense in the escalating silence surrounding us; Mom hadn't even turned on the radio, a sure sign that something weighed heavily on her mind. But I was determined to let her initiate the conversation. At last the headlights beamed across the small rocky beach where Dad and my brothers staked out their traplines in the winter months. Mom drove a few dozen yards down the beach and put the car in park before turning my way; the pale dash lights cast a blue tint over her familiar features and created pinpricks of light along the length of her braided hair.

"Mom . . ." I began.

"You're not in trouble," she interrupted, studying my face as though we'd been apart for the past year.

"Then what . . ." Sweat collected along my hairline and beneath my arms as I imagined her grilling me regarding my whereabouts this afternoon.

She said softly, "You really like Wy, don't you?"

"I do," I admitted, thinking of the way Wy had described his relief in sharing the truth with Marshall.

Mom cupped my cheek, a brief, gentle touch. "Unless my radar for such things is all out of whack, I'd say Wy returns those feelings."

"He does." My pulse escalated.

"He told you he cares for you?" Mom's tone changed, growing censuring.

*Careful, Millie,* I thought. *Proceed with caution.*

"We've always liked each other," I said, sidestepping her question and trying for a reasonable tone. "Since we were little kids. Don't you remember, I told you and Dad I was going to marry him someday?"

"Marry him?" Mom repeated, as though she hadn't related that anecdote about a dozen times over the years. "For heaven's sake, Millie, you're only seventeen years old."

"I didn't say we were getting married *next month*. We've just been talking about college and how maybe I'd consider Montana State instead of the U of M next year. I'll be eighteen by then and the difference in our ages won't seem so extreme. Wy is very concerned about what everyone would think about that." I braided my fingers together on my lap, guilt pumping along my nerves.

*It's no one's business if we make love this summer. No one needs to know, only the two of us.*

"I'm glad to hear he's concerned about it, that's very responsible of him. Wy is a wonderful young man; you know I think so. Your dad and I have adored him since he was a little boy. If, one day down the road, you were to have a more serious relationship with him, we would be thrilled." Mom paused, her gaze penetrating through all layers of my defenses. "But this summer is *not* that time. I know you understand this, honey. No matter what the two of you think, Wy is in a different part of his life than you." Even more softly, "If it's meant to be, it will be. There is no need to rush things."

"Like what, like the way you 'rushed things' with Noah?" The accusatory words exploded from my mouth with no warning, like small bombs. Immediately I backpedaled. "I'm sorry . . ."

"No, it's a fair question." Mom turned her gaze toward the windshield, though I knew she wasn't seeing the quiet expanse of dark water. The headlights created eerie tunnels of radiance over the lake's shrouded surface and her voice emerged almost like a stranger's as she said, "I know you wonder about Noah and me. I guess it only seems fitting that you'd ask about him this summer, when you're seventeen."

She paused, and I had the fleeting impression that she was no older than me; a weird ripple in the passage of time that momentarily stripped my mother of the years separating us. The sensation was so odd I shivered, clutching my upper arms and squeezing inward.

"I thought I knew everything at seventeen, you have no idea. I was so angry at my parents for messing up their marriage, furious at my dad for cheating and at my mom for covering it up. I thought I knew better than her, better than my grandmother, even my great-grandmother."

"Did you love Noah?" I whispered, reluctant to intrude on the flow of her words. But I truly wanted to know.

"Briefly, before I really knew him, I thought I did. I was attracted to him; he was very handsome and charming. I'd never really had a boyfriend before then." She drew a deep lungful of air. "But I never knew what love really was until I met—"

"Dad?" I interrupted.

Mom turned to face me. "*You*, Millie Jo. You showed me what it meant to truly love someone. You taught me so many things, without even knowing it."

Sudden tears throbbed in my eyes and throat, closing off my vocal cords.

Mom said, "I love Mathias dearly, he is the love of my life in many ways, but the love I have for my children is a different thing altogether. It's the purest love that exists, honey, and someday, many years from now, you'll understand that." She smoothed hair from my forehead. "Maybe with Wy, maybe with someone else. It's fine if you talk about things with Wy, acknowledge your feelings for him, but the point is, you have plenty of time to figure it all out."

I began sobbing without warning; the words "maybe with someone else" seemed branded on the insides of my eyelids, ugly and so very unwanted. Mom gathered me close and cupped the back of my head, rocking us side to side as if unaware of doing so. I'd never been in her embrace when she hadn't gently rocked me as though I was still a little girl. I both resented and found comfort in the familiar motion.

"What if Wy doesn't wait for me, what if he marries someone else?" The half-hysterical words shocked me almost as much as they did my mother.

*You know Wy would never marry someone else, what's the matter with you? Why are you freaking out?*

I sensed Mom's desire to choose the right words; at last she whispered, "I don't think he'll be ready to marry anyone for a long time, if you want to know the truth. He still has years of vet school ahead of him and he's a dedicated student. And I know how much college also means to you. It may not seem like it just now, but you have so much time to make important decisions and discover new things about yourself. Marriage should be the last thing you're thinking of at this point in your life."

Just that fast, I didn't want to hear another word. I didn't want her telling me that I would eventually meet someone new and move beyond my love for Wy; even the thought of that inspired a deep-seated pulse of nausea. Mom couldn't realize the depth of my feelings—and who could blame her?—but *I* realized.

"I know," I whispered, mostly to keep her from continuing the conversation. I rested my nose against her shoulder, inhaling the timeless, comforting scent of her clothes and skin. "Thanks for being here, Mom."

"Anytime," she whispered. "Anytime at all."

. . .

Thirty minutes later I curled up on my bed, facing the wall as I clutched my phone. My bedroom was draped in darkness, the only illumination the small, dimly-lit screen by which I could contact Wy. I had used my phone more in the past two days than in the entire preceding year.

*I talked with Ruthie about us*, he had written earlier. *She gave me an earful about keeping our hands to ourselves.*

I smiled at this phrasing, wishing I could call him without waking Lorie; by default, she and I shared a room while the boys bunked together in the bigger attic bedroom.

*I talked with Mom*, I wrote back. *She gave me the same message, about how we have plenty of time to figure things out.*

Wy responded at once—*She wasn't upset about anything? She's not going to keep you locked up for the rest of the summer, right?*

*She's not upset. She and my dad adore you, they always have.*

*I want their approval, it means a lot to me.*

*You have it.*

*Thank you for everything today. I loved being with you all day.*

*Same here. I'm trying not to think about you leaving but sometimes it's all I can think about. I already miss you.*

*We'll talk all the time. I'll call you every night, I promise.*

*And write me letters?*

*Hell yes. I can't wait to write you love letters.*

*I'd call you right now but I'd wake up Lorie. Our house is so crowded!*

*I know the feeling. Never any privacy with four brothers.*

*Are you at the inn?*

*Yeah, Dad's already sleeping. I wish you were here tucked beside me.*

*I wish so too. I love how I feel when I'm around you. I always have.*

*A lifetime doesn't seem long enough to be around you as much as I want to.*

His words were sweeter than anything I'd ever dreamed of; they filled me to the brim and beyond. I brought the phone to my lips and briefly closed my eyes before responding.

*I want to know everything about you. Start at the beginning, tell me something I don't know.*

I woke to a bright river of sunlight flowing over my legs, serenaded by a birdsong chorus; my phone remained clutched in my right hand, held close to my heart. Still clad in last night's clothes, I shifted to an elbow and immediately scrolled to my last text message. I could not remember ending the conversation with Wy, let alone drifting off.

*Good night, sweetheart, I think you must have fallen asleep. I'll see you tomorrow,* he'd written at 3:04 in the morning.

We had exchanged probably three hundred messages prior to that last one, discussing everything from favorite movies and songs to dreams for the future. By morning's pure light, I felt renewed, awash in love and hope. And anticipation— I had not forgotten for a moment that we planned to spend tonight at the state park. Exactly how we would manage this, I hadn't yet figured out; the first step was creating a believable alibi. I squashed a fluttering of guilt, considering last night's conversation with Mom; a thousand justifications clattered through my head, each more insistent than the last.

*No one will ever know.*

*We'll use protection, of course, and it will be our secret.*

*I want this so much. I can't wait until next summer.*

*The memory of tonight will sustain me through the next year.*

It was Monday, which worked both for and against my plans; it might seem strange to my parents, especially Mom, if I told them I planned to stay overnight at a friend's house on a weekday, but the state park campground would be much less crowded. I rolled to my back, staring up at the ceiling beams as I plotted. Lorie's bed was empty and breakfast was underway downstairs, just like any other normal summer day. Except that it wasn't; from here on out, this date would be one for Wy and me to cherish—July twelfth, our own private anniversary.

As though the heat of my thoughts had flowed across town straight to him, my phone buzzed with an incoming text.

*Good morning. I can't wait to see you.*

I almost dropped the phone in my excitement to respond.

*Good morning! I just woke up and was lying here thinking about you.*

*I'm thinking about you too. Do you work today?*

*Yes. You want to join us again?*

*I do, but your dad invited Marsh and Dad and me to go fourwheeling. I think all the guys are going. I don't know how to get out of it.*

*It's ok, it gives me time to figure out tonight.*

*I love you and nothing can change that. No matter what we do or don't do tonight, I want you to know it.*

*Don't you dare start feeling guilty!!!!!*

"Millie Jo, breakfast!" Mom called.

"Coming!" I yelled, sending Wy a final text before joining my family—*Have fun fourwheeling, I love you too.*

...

Luck was with me that day; in retrospect, I supposed it was the universe balancing itself out in some tiny way, allowing me a bout of unusual good fortune before annihilating everything. The afternoon passed uneventfully; Rae and I worked the lunch rush with Auntie Tish, who was excited to resume her former role as a server.

"God, it's like no time has passed when I'm standing here," Auntie Tish said to Grandpa Blythe, spinning the ticket wheel with a fond smile. "Nothing changes at Shore Leave, does it?"

"It's what I love most about this place," Grandpa said. "It's good to see you and Ruthie back here. I know it makes Joelle so happy."

About an hour into our lunch shift, Rae caught me at the bar; aware of my plans thanks to an impassioned conversation earlier in the day, she disagreed with my intentions but had loyally agreed to help.

"Kate and Kari Johnson are out on the porch, asking if we want to come to a bonfire at their place tonight. It's just a last-minute thing, but pretty much our whole class is going." Rae's tone was neutral but her dark eyes held steady on mine. She added, "It's a campout," as though I hadn't understood her meaning.

The Johnson twins were in our grade and lived out of town; better yet, their place was on the highway toward the state park. Excitement flared along my nerves, strong enough that my breath emerged as a little huffing squeak.

Rae studied my face, her own unreadable. "Are you sure this is what you want?"

"Are you kidding? This is *perfect*."

After such news, I could hardly contain my jittering anticipation; I texted Wy first thing, explaining the invitation and how we would accomplish the trickier aspects of our night, such as arranging a place to meet once I left the bonfire. Rae had her own car, so she and I would leave for the Johnsons' in the late afternoon; it was important that I made an appearance there, at least for a little while. After several hours, I would drive Rae's car back to Landon and collect Wy, who planned to meet me under cover of darkness. I considered every angle, texting Wy every time I thought of something new.

*How will you explain to Clark where you are all night?*

*I'll just hang out around the fire at Clint's place. Dad won't check up on me. I can always say I fell asleep in a chair by the fire pit.*

It finally seemed every base was covered; we would leave the state park before dawn, collect Rae from the Johnsons' house, and then the three of us would return to Landon, dropping Wy close enough to the inn downtown that his story of walking home after waking up beside the campfire seemed plausible. The last hurdle was convincing Mom. I opted for texting, fearing she might hear something suspicious in my voice.

*Hey Mom! Do you care if I go with Rae to a campout at Kate and Kari's tonight?*

No more than five minutes later, Mom responded, *That's funny, we just ran into Karen Johnson here at the craft fair. She mentioned that the twins were having a get-together. Sure, that's fine, honey.*

I sent a final text to Wy—*We're good to go!!!!!*

. . .

The sun had set at long last, leaving behind a clear, star-studded sky to accompany me on my solo drive back to Landon to collect Wy. A slender sliver of a waxing moon rode the sun's wake in the western horizon, seeming to offer me a blessing; each revolution of the tires echoed my escalating heartbeat. In less than an hour, we would be on the way to Itasca; a tent and camping supplies were stashed in the trunk of Rae's little car. And in my purse, crammed beneath my wallet, was an unopened box of condoms.

"Here, I got these for you," Rae had told me during our drive out to the bonfire. "They're Evan's. I know you were worried about where to get some, earlier. And it's not like Evan and I will be using these anytime soon."

"Thank you." Just holding the small, dark blue box made my fingers tingle. "Wy said he would take care of it when we drove through Bemidji, but just in case."

Rae angled me a look, clutching the steering wheel with both hands in the correct position, as though I was a driving instructor. "This is such a huge deal! Call me if you need anything and I'll call *you* right away if something is up, all right?"

"Don't be worried." At that point, my nerves remained level; the sort of preternatural calm that precedes a tornado. "Besides, I doubt we'll have reception at the campground."

Rae reached to squeeze my knee. "Check your phone a few times tonight, all right? I don't want you guys to get caught, that would be *such* a shit show. Do you hear me?"

"I hear you," I had assured, touched by her concern.

Wy called just before sunset to let me know he'd spent time hanging out at Clint's place, sitting around the barbeque grill with Clint and a few of his friends from the fire station. Exhausted by the busy weekend, most everyone else had begged off early, retiring to wherever they intended to spend the night. I quietly left the Johnsons' bonfire after Wy called; in the mix of almost our entire senior class, I knew I wouldn't be missed.

As I approached the outskirts of my hometown, my kneecaps were trembling. The dashboard clock read 10:24 as I angled around the lake road, heading for the small public beach where Wy was waiting in the darkness. The nervous excitement of all this was almost too much to bear; by the time I parked on the edge of the road near the beach, immediately killing the headlights, my heart was firing so hard it seemed to skip over every other beat. In daylight hours, Shore Leave was in partial view across Flickertail to the left, no more than a half-mile away.

*This is all worth it, and then some,* I thought, slipping from the car and easing shut the driver's side door, peering into the night-cloaked trees in search of Wy. *You aren't going to get caught, so quit worrying!*

"Wy?" I called in a whisper.

"I'm here." He appeared from the pines to my left with the suddenness of a ghost.

I jumped, swallowing a shriek, and dove for his open arms. He wore a sweatshirt and jeans, and smelled like soap and woodsmoke and himself, the indefinable aroma that was simply Wyatt Rawley, and no other. I pressed kitten-kisses along his jaw, which was freshly shaved, I could tell, and then he tilted his head to catch my mouth, kissing me deep and sweet as he squeezed me close.

"Hi," I whispered, shivering, clinging to him. "We better get out of here!"

Wy drove, following my directions to the interstate, where we headed north, toward Bemidji and, eventually, Itasca State Park.

"We made it!" I could hardly believe the immeasurable fortune of this time alone together; my blood refused to settle as I sat clutching Wy's right hand between both of mine.

He looked my way, driving with his left hand at the bottom of the wheel. "I've been torn up all day, I can't lie. Are you sure you're ready for this, that this is what you want?"

I understood his apprehension, and for the first time, I didn't fly off the handle in regards to it. I knew he was deeply concerned that he was rushing me into something for which I was unprepared, inadvertently pressuring my decision; further, I knew it was up to me to prove otherwise.

I lifted his hand to my heart. There, I pressed his palm to the thrusting rhythm behind my ribs, speaking with quiet conviction. "I'm ready for this, more than you could ever know. You know that, don't you?"

"I do," he whispered in response. "I love you beyond words, Millie Joelle Gordon, beyond anything. I want to make tonight beautiful for you, you have no idea how much."

"Then hurry and get us there," I whispered, my smile as wide as the night sky.

# CHAPTER TWELVE

WE REACHED THE STATE PARK ROUGHLY FORTY minutes later, driving beneath the dense canopy of white pines along the winding entrance road. I'd camped here with my family since I was a little girl, but felt in no danger of running across anyone I knew from Landon; the park was massive, most of the campsites secluded. Besides, it was a Monday night and the bulk of the weekend campers had packed up and headed out yesterday. Small wooden signs with yellow lettering directed our way through the hushed obscurity of night.

"I still have a little reception," I murmured, messing around with my phone's screen as Wy turned right, driving slowly, following a path through the forest toward available sites. "I told Rae I'd let her know exactly where we are."

"Any of these would be good," Wy said, watching as the headlights roved across small, intermittent clearings; the only indication of human inhabitance were the round iron fire pits centered in each, most containing the remnants of weekend cookfires. The car inched deeper into the otherwise empty woods; again, it seemed we were the last two people left on the earth.

"There," I finally murmured, satisfied that we were, for tonight, safely beyond anyone's reach. Wy parked while I sent Rae a quick text, letting her know we'd arrived and giving her our site number before stashing my phone in the central cupholder.

We stepped from the car and were immediately surrounded by the noisy resonance of wildlife; this early in the night, the harmonious cadence of toads, frogs, crickets, nighthawks, owls, and coyotes was in full swing, echoing through the tall trees.

"It sounds like we're in a jungle," Wy observed, chin tilted upward as he surveyed the impressive spectacle of old-growth white pines and towering oaks. The sky appeared in patches between the interlaced branches many dozens of feet above our heads, spangled with jewel-bright stars. The slender crescent moon had long since disappeared beneath the horizon.

"A north woods jungle," I agreed.

Wy opened the trunk and we unloaded the camping supplies, first lighting a small propane lantern and then working together to locate the most level ground in our clearing to stake out the tent I'd pilfered from the garage at Shore Leave earlier today, knowing it would not be missed. I was grateful for the darkness, which provided a measure of cover for my trembling hands and quivering knee-caps; the reality of making love with Wy had taken precedence over all else in my mind. Less than fifteen minutes after our arrival the little orange tent was erect, rain cover in place, sleeping bags unfurled inside. I retrieved two pillows from the trunk and carefully closed it, my knees so weak I wasn't sure I could manage the seven or so steps to the tent.

"My heart is beating about a hundred miles an hour," Wy confessed.

He finished adjusting a final cord, a tall, lanky silhouette backlit by the warmth of the lantern light. His words served to comfort, if not exactly calm; I squeezed the pillows against my belly, immersed in a near-agony of anticipation.

"Mine too," I whispered.

Wy closed the distance between us and scooped me into his arms, pillows and all.

"You're shaking," he murmured, brows drawing inward with concern. "We don't have to do this. We don't have to do anything you're not ready for."

"You're shaking too." I cupped his face, tracing a soft path over his lips, delighted that he was equally overwhelmed by emotion. "Besides, it's because I'm so happy."

Beneath my questing fingertips, he smiled with characteristic sweetness. "Same here. I've never been happier in my life."

Later, the remembrance of those words hurt almost more than anything else.

"Let's go inside," I murmured.

I crawled in first, Wy directly behind; we shed our shoes and he took care to zip the entrance, enclosing us in our small, orange-tinted heaven. The tent was constructed so that its ceiling angled backward to its highest point; neither of us could stand straight and so we knelt facing each other instead, the two sleeping bags rumpled beneath our knees. I set aside the pillows, breathless and palpitating and so flushed my face was up in flames, but gladness overwhelmed all feelings of anxiety. Nothing mattered as much as the promise of tonight with Wy.

"Come here," he murmured, and we met halfway, sliding our arms around each other, letting our bodies press full-length. He gathered my loose hair in one hand, bundling it at my nape to touch a soft kiss to my neck. "I want tonight to be incredible for you."

Giggly elation rose in my chest. "How polite of you."

Humor crinkled the outer corners of his eyes, though I knew he was serious. "I mean it. It's important to me. This is your first time."

The thought would have brought me to my knees if I wasn't already on them.

He took charge, but carefully, as though I might bolt if he moved too quickly. Clasping my face between both hands, he kissed my mouth like someone offering a sacrament, with tender devotion, letting our breath mingle. I clung to his neck, the heat and immediacy of him bombarding my senses. I knew without words that he intended to prolong every touch, every kiss; that he would take his time to make certain I loved everything we did.

"I want you to love it too," I whispered against his lips, arousal pounding in my blood, overflowing at all points of contact.

He released an exhalation, not quite a laugh. "Are you kidding? I'll love it so much I feel like I must be in a dream."

He shifted us, lowering me to one of the sleeping bags and stretching full-length at my side, bracing on an elbow as we studied each other.

"Your eyes are so pretty. There's so many different colors in them," he marveled, outlining the shapes of my eyebrows with his index finger. "About a thousand shades of green and gold."

"You have that sunburst in yours." I pressed my thumb beneath his right eye. "I've always thought that was so cool."

"Yeah, my eyes don't match."

"And you have a stubborn nose." I traced its contours in the fashion of a blind person. "The Rawley nose, like Aunt Ruthie always says."

"Damn right." He smiled wider at my continued exploration of his face. "You have freckles on yours."

"Only a *few*," I contradicted.

"And a tiny one right here." He leaned to press a soft kiss to my upper lip, sinking both hands in my hair, gently fanning it outward around my head. "Remember that night we stood by the corral, after Scout?"

"Of course."

"You'd had your hair braided all day but it was loose then, all over your shoulders. I wanted to touch it so bad, I wanted to feel it in my hands while we kissed."

I brushed aside the hair falling over his forehead, undone by his sincerity. "I love how you always tell me what you're thinking, how you show your feelings in such affectionate ways."

"I'll spend my life showing you, in every way I can think of."

Our bodies blended seamlessly as we lay side by side, the lanky heat of his lean muscles and long bones melting into the softer curves of my breasts and hips; need swelled like a springtime river and I begged, "Take your shirt off, I want to see you."

He shifted position and shed it at once, the lantern light playing over the dips in his biceps and along the ridges of his torso. I sat, gliding my palms around his ribs as I leaned close and pressed my nose to the thick patch of hair on his chest; his skin was warm and his muscles hard, and I could barely breathe as he gently grasped the bottom hem of my T-shirt, letting his thumbs graze the bare skin underneath. His lashes were long enough to cast shadows across his cheekbones as he eased the shirt over my head and reclaimed my mouth, our tongues making voluptuous circles. With deft movements he unhooked my bra, slipped the straps from my arms, and cupped my breasts, gently shaping them, stroking my nipples with his thumbs.

"Come closer." His voice was a husky command as he grasped my knees and drew my thighs around his hips, positioning me atop his lap.

I threaded my fingers in his hair, the curve of my back bowing toward him as he bent his head and lavished attention on my breasts.

"That feels so good . . ." Overcome, my voice shook on the words.

His lips were at my ear as he clutched my hips, anchoring me flush against him. "I want this to be so good for you. I want you to come again and again."

His words were nearly as stimulating as his touch. I quivered, ablaze with desire as he continued plying his tongue on my nipples, his firm grip guiding my hips as I moved with increasing intensity against the hard ridge separated from me by our jeans.

"*Touch me*," I begged, and he knew what I meant, taking me at once to my back.

He wasted no time sliding jeans and panties down my legs before gently drawing my knees around his hips, effectively parting my thighs. The orange walls of our tent seemed to pulse with energy, alive of their own accord; though I'd not consumed a drop of alcohol I felt intoxicated, my blood surging with lust and love, in nearly equal measure. I may have been a virgin but Wy was not; he knew exactly what to do, caressing between my legs both shallow and deep as we kissed, reveling in his ability to bring me pleasure, just as I had yesterday during the thunderstorm. Slowly, he worked his way downward on my body, pressing lingering kisses on my neck and between my breasts, tasting my nipples and the sensitive flesh of my lower belly, at last letting his nose brush my pubic hair.

"Can I go down on you?" he whispered, eyes hotter than coals.

"*Yes* . . . " I moaned, sweating and quivering, as though struck by a spiking fever.

I gripped the sleeping bag beneath my body, clutching hard, shock waves incinerating my skin as I felt his tongue explore and enter my sensitive flesh. By the time Wy lifted his head, we were both panting; his lips and chin were shiny. I could not catch my breath, aftershocks still firing along my nerves. Wy used one of the sleeping bags to wipe his face, grinning all over again, proud of himself.

"Did you like that?" He shifted gracefully, moving back above me. His jeans were unzipped, riding low on his hips, and he was harder than a marble statue.

I wrapped around him, quaking and fluid against his boxers, the final barrier separating us.

"You couldn't tell?!"

"I could tell," he admitted, smoothing hair from my sweating forehead, studying my eyes. "This is about as close to heaven as I can imagine. I swear you are so beautiful I could come just looking at you."

I traced the outline of his lips. "Show me more . . ."

He kissed me in response, ripe and wet. I tasted my own scent on his tongue but somehow this only increased the intimacy flowing between us. The box of condoms lay near our shoes and Wy made short work of shedding his jeans and unrolling one over his hard length while I watched, fascinated. And then we were back in each other's arms. He remained motionless for the span of several heartbeats and time hung suspended, on the brink of something beyond both of us; something beyond reckoning.

"I love you," he whispered, his voice taut with restraint. He was already primed at the point of entry and I felt the careful tension in his limbs as he held himself in check. A pulse thundered at the base of his throat.

"I love you too, I'm ready for this . . ."

"I'll go slow," he promised.

Oral sex had been so incredible I was unprepared for the first twinges of pain as he eased inside. I winced and he froze immediately, as though someone had aimed a gun at us.

"Does that hurt?"

I shook my head, afraid he would stop.

He resumed course and was maybe halfway when I cried out, unable to help it. I bit down on additional sounds as he halted all forward motion once again.

"I'll stop . . ."

"No!" The last thing I wanted was for him to stop.

"I don't want to hurt you. I would rather die than hurt you." Sweat shone on his brow, gliding down his temples on either side.

"It doesn't hurt," I lied, gripping his biceps as anchors. "Keep going."

Wy kissed me first, a soft joining of our mouths, as if tasting each other for the first time. When he felt I was ready he slid fully inside and I pressed my face against his shoulder, clenching my teeth. Every nerve ending seemed centered where our bodies joined, sizzling with an acute ache. I didn't dare move my hips, afraid I would tear apart; he felt more solid than a battering ram, and twice as long.

"*Millie*..." He exhaled a slow breath near my right ear.

I ran my palms down his strong, perspiring back, coming to rest on the lean muscles of his backside, my breath shallow.

"Are you all right?" he whispered.

I nodded in response, considering how wonderful it felt when his tongue and fingers had stroked me in the same place, and knew without being told that the amazing sensation would occur once I grew accustomed to lovemaking—but just now it was beyond reach.

"I won't move until you say." His voice was raspy with the effort to restrain.

I shifted again, attempting to find an angle that wasn't so painful. When I felt I could manage it, I tilted my hips upward, surprised when he issued a low, hoarse groan. For a split second, I wondered wildly if I'd somehow hurt him.

"I'm about to come," he confessed. "You feel so good, I can't hold back anymore."

"Come inside me." I latched my wrists around his neck.

At my whispered invitation, he plunged deep and I muffled a moaning cry against his chest.

"Oh God, did I hurt you? I'm so sorry, I didn't mean to hurt you." He drew carefully out, concerned gaze flickering downward. Bright red blood streaked my inner thighs, as though my period had just started; without hesitation, Wy grabbed his discarded sweatshirt from the edge of the tent. "Here, we can use this. It's all right, it's normal to bleed the first time."

He worked with care, grasping my leg and cleaning away the blood, and something about his tender, focused ministrations reminded me of the evening we had watched Twyla give birth to Scout in the Rawleys' horse barn. A glowing, vibrating cord seemed to connect that moment with this one; we had shared a birth and now we had shared lovemaking, earthy, sacred milestones of life, albeit in reverse order. Emotion rose in my chest and bloomed as moisture in my eyes, and Wy's expression grew stricken, his hands falling still.

"It's all right, I promise, don't cry, sweetheart..."

Tears poured down my cheeks like springtime rain, like life itself; I swiped at them, sniffling against the back of my hand, determined to explain. "I'm not hurting, not at all. I was just thinking about the night we watched Scout's birth. You were so calm that night, I remember thinking that everything would be all right because you were there. I was so happy to share that with you, Wy, and now ...we've shared this too."

Understanding and relief crossed paths on his face. "I'm so grateful to have shared these things with you. Thank you for letting me make love with you, I couldn't have loved it more."

"Thank you for making it so beautiful."

"You swear you're not hurting?"

"I swear," I assured him, oddly unselfconscious as he continued removing blood from my inner thighs, kneeling beside my bent legs with his sweatshirt in hand. I added, "I think it looks worse than it is. I guess it's true that you bleed the first time. I always wondered."

At last he bent and kissed my knee; my legs were free of all traces of blood. He murmured, "There. It won't so much hurt next time."

A flutter danced across my belly; I teased, "Next time?"

He encircled my calf with both hands, lightly rubbing his jaw on my skin. "A whole lot of next times. A lifetime of them. Come here, come lay beside me."

We snuggled close atop the rumpled sleeping bags, facing one another, my right thigh hooked over his hips. We were unable to stop touching, our fingertips moving over one another's features as though committing each detail to deepest memory. Lovemaking had washed away any remaining traces of inhibition and I reveled in the simple joy of stroking his body, no place left unexplored as we whispered about anything and everything.

At one point I admitted, "I didn't expect you to have so much hair down here."

I loved the way I could make him laugh so easily. He clarified, "What, on my balls?"

"I mean, I should have guessed . . . you're pretty hairy overall . . ."

Laughter shook his shoulders. "Yeah, I guess I am, I hope you don't mind . . ."

I leaned to press my nose to his chest hair. "Don't get me wrong, I really like it."

He added, "Because I *ain't* shaving. Not my body, anyway. I know guys who do, my friend Joey, for instance, but not me."

I kissed his neck, tasting the salty tang of his warm skin; the air in our tent was hot and humid, the two of us slick with sweat. My lips near his collarbones, I whispered a confession. "I asked Rae if I should shave off my pubic hair before tonight, if guys expect it."

Wy tipped my chin upward so I could meet his amused gaze. "I don't expect it. And I wouldn't change a thing about you, not for the world."

I whispered, "I can still feel you in me. You were *so* deep inside."

He ran a hand downward along my belly, letting his fingertips come to rest between my legs. "I love being inside you. I love how you marvel at things. You see the world with so much joy."

I held his gaze. "How soon can we . . ."

He grew hard just that fast and I pressed immediately closer; he bit the side of my neck, then licked the same spot as he murmured, "We can make love all night long, my sweet baby, but we should take it slow . . ."

"Then we'll go slow. Please, Wy, *please* . . ."

He rolled me to my back, deepening his touch; against my lips, he murmured, "Like that?"

"Just like that . . ."

There was no hesitancy on my part, only need. Wy kept his movements slow and careful once he reentered my body, letting me learn the rhythm, only increasing the pace if I did first. We kissed without end, the intense, wordless sounds of lovemaking caught between our lips; at times, he buried his face in the curve of my neck, his breath coming in pants like that of a sprinter. I stroked his hair, licked sweat from his overheated skin, overcome by both the physical joining and the emotional. Nothing in life had prepared me for this level of feeling. There came a point at which I was aware of nothing but him. *Us.* Joined so closely I couldn't tell where Wy's body ended and mine began. This time when I cried out it was borne of pure, sweet satisfaction. Wy shuddered hard, collapsing on top of me, and I cradled him, holding fast—and from this moment on, I intended never to let go.

# CHAPTER THIRTEEN

I WOKE MUCH LATER TO PITCHY BLACKNESS,
heart slamming against my breastbone.

*What...*

I blinked rapidly, unable to see a thing, disoriented as to time and place before returning abruptly to reality.

*We're at Itasca, it's all right.*

*Everything is all right.*

But my heart refused to calm.

I curled immediately closer to Wy's sleeping warmth; his left arm remained latched over my waist, one sleeping bag beneath us, the second serving as a blanket atop our nude, snuggled bodies. The temperature had plummeted with nighttime and the tip of my nose stung in the chill. A hushed expectancy hovered like a third presence in our tent, manifesting as a strange sense of dread that throbbed at the back of my neck; as much as I wanted to pretend otherwise, I knew something was wrong.

*What is it, what's happened?!*

And then I heard it, just faintly but coming closer—the unmistakable sound of an approaching vehicle. The low growl of an engine, tires grinding slowly over the narrow forest path, headed for our campsite. My heart thrust straight through my ribcage; so acute was my sudden terror that I felt paralyzed, my limbs heavy and useless.

*Oh God, oh God...*

I tried to speak but my tongue had fused to the roof of my mouth.

Wy stirred a second later, murmuring my name with a sleepy sigh. I knew the exact moment he became aware of what was happening because his bearing snapped alert. He whispered, "Is that ..."

"Yes," I moaned, and the twin beams of headlights strafed our tent now, no hiding anything. "Oh no, *oh God* ..."

No sooner had the vehicle braked to a full stop than I heard a door slam and boots hit the ground. I sat up a second ahead of Wy, scrambling through the jumbled sleeping bags for my clothes, certain my dad was about to storm up to the tent and tear open the entrance.

*Oh no, oh shit . . . please no . . .*

I fumbled with my bra straps, my fingers wooden and clumsy, unable to perform simple tasks. The headlights cut into our tent like bright saw blades, amplifying my panic.

Wy tugged on his jeans, taking a moment to cup my shoulders and whisper, "It's all right. I'll deal with this."

He had hardly finished speaking when someone ordered, "Wyatt, get your ass *out here.*"

I paused in the frantic attempt to locate my underwear, feeling a small arrow of relief penetrate my distress as I recognized Uncle Marshall's voice instead of my dad's.

Wy closed his eyes and ran a hand over his face, making no move to exit the tent. "Marsh, let me explain . . ."

Uncle Marshall spoke from right outside the nylon wall and I pictured the angry glint in his eyes. "Explain?! Are you out of your ever-lovin' mind?!"

Before I could think, let alone question the sense of speaking up, I cried, "This is none of your business!"

I sensed Uncle Marshall's surprise as it swelled to existence in the air around him. He didn't immediately respond, and Wy drew me close in a hug, murmuring, "Stay here for a sec, all right?"

He unzipped just enough of the entrance to emerge outside. I refused to remain in the tent like a coward and hurried to dress, energized now, with both anger and a sense of severely misplaced self-righteousness, listening to Marshall chewing Wy's ass.

"Jesus *Christ*, Wy. What in the *goddamn hell* were you thinking? You better thank your lucky stars I'm not Dad. Or Mathias! You realize I have to tell them, don't you?"

The zipper sounded louder than a chainsaw as I parted its tiny plastic teeth. Uncle Marshall, hands latched on his hips and leaning slightly forward, halted his tirade and watched me climb awkwardly out of the tent to join them. He was all but gritting his teeth. The headlights spotlighted the three of us in an uncomfortable tableau of sudden silence, as though we stood facing off on a theater stage. Wy reached for me and I latched both arms around his torso, determined to remain at his side.

With slightly less antagonism in his tone, Marshall invited, "You care to explain yourselves?"

Damned if I was going to let Wy field the blame for something in which we'd been equally involved. Unspoken words hung in heavy ropes around us, a contrast to the cacophony of birdsong echoing through the woods; dawn could not have been more than an hour away. Before Marshall could say anything else, I found my voice, forcing a calm and respectful tone.

"We chose to be here together. I'm not a little kid, no matter what anyone thinks. This really isn't anyone's business but mine and Wy's."

Marshall's hawklike gaze moved between Wy and me, with consternation and perhaps a hint of growing compassion. He didn't resume his haranguing, and I was heartened. I wanted to ask how he had known where to find us, but held my tongue.

Wy squared his shoulders. "Look, I'm prepared to face the consequences of this. I'm no kid either. I love Millie, as I've told you, and I am not taking advantage of her."

Marshall said quietly, "That's the problem, Wy, you *aren't* a kid. You're a grown man who should know better."

"Are you saying I am a kid?" I cried, indignant and insulted. "That I don't 'know better'?"

Marshall's brows lowered, forming dangerous slants. "In everyone's eyes, yes, you are a kid. I know you don't want to hear it, but it's the truth."

"Don't talk to Millie like that," Wy ordered, struggling now to restrain his growing anger. "She's almost eighteen."

"She's a high school senior!" Marshall bellowed, like I wasn't standing right in front of him. "What's next, Wy? Are you going to take her to the prom next spring?"

Hot tears stung my nose and eyes, much to my fury.

Wy said tightly, "Shut your goddamn trap, Marsh. I don't answer to you."

"Maybe not," Marshall conceded. "But you are sure as hell going to answer to Mathias and Camille. *Today.*"

"And I will," Wy said, with admirable fortitude.

Marshall slowly shook his head, angry but resigned.

My throat ached with a growing lump; I whispered, "How did you find us?"

Hearing the choke in my voice, Wy drew me closer.

Marshall said tersely, "Rae. She said Camille tried to call you last night and Rae was worried you were going to get caught. She called Ruthie about an hour ago and told her where you were." He paused for a weighty beat. "I haven't said anything to anyone else. But I'm obligated to, you two realize."

"Ruthie is six years younger than you," Wy said then. "She wasn't much older than Millie when you two were first together. What if you'd met when she was seventeen? You knew she was the woman for you from the first night you saw her picture. I remember like it was yesterday."

With quiet dignity, Marshall said, "I met Ruthann when she was fifteen, at

Mathias and Camille's wedding, as I'm sure you also recall. But I knew she wasn't ready to be with me, not then. I waited until the time was right."

"And what if Ruthie had come to you and told you she loved you, way back then?" Wy challenged, gaining steam. I fought the urge to poke him in the ribs, trusting he wouldn't reveal the way I had begged him to take my virginity.

Marshall's somber gaze pierced both of us. "That's not a fair question. I don't know how to answer it."

"Because you love Ruthie and you would *never* have turned her away. I remember how much you were hurting when she came out to Montana to be with Tish, after the fire. You were dying because she was dating someone else. But that didn't stop you." Wy's expression grew ever more earnest, my sweet, passionate Wyatt.

In that moment, I truly believed everything would be all right.

Uncle Marshall closed his eyes and passed a hand over his face, exactly as Wy had done before exiting the tent; their mannerisms were so similar it was disconcerting. At last he admitted, "You're right. Nothing would have stopped me. Ruthie is my angel, my everything. I could never deny her a thing and you know it." He pinned us with a flat, challenging stare. "You're telling me you love each other this way?"

I spoke without hesitation. "I've loved Wy since I was a little girl."

At the same time Wy said, "Yes. And we'll face what we have to face."

He couldn't have known then.

Marshall was silent for a protracted beat. At last he said, "I'm glad to hear this. But it doesn't change certain facts. Millie, you're still in high school. Somehow I can't see your parents agreeing to let you move in with Wy and start a family just yet." He let that sink in for a heartbeat. "What about college? What about—"

"Stop," Wy commanded, though not as harshly as the word implied. "Can you give us a second, here?"

"Please tell me you used protection," Marshall said, framing it as a statement rather than a question.

"*Jesus*, Marsh!" Wy all but growled. "You can leave now, we'll be behind you in a few, okay? You have my word."

Marshall looked heavenward as if seeking patience. "Fine, I'll head out. But I want you back in Landon in the next hour, do you hear? At Mathias and Camille's doorstep, explaining this."

I recognized that if I wanted to be treated like an adult, I needed to behave like one; but all conviction aside, my heart sank downward toward my ankles at the notion of facing my parents regarding last night.

"We'll be there," I whispered.

Wy nodded acceptance of this condition, and Uncle Marshall turned on his heel without another word. The engine fired to life with a coughing roar, like a reproach. Once he'd backed out and driven away, dust rising in the wake of his tires, I turned and looked up at Wy. Our eyes held as we absorbed what had happened in the last fifteen minutes.

If Wy was as rattled as I was, he hid it well, speaking with resolve. "Everything will be all right, you'll see. We'll face this together. This isn't how I planned to talk to your parents, but I'm prepared to. If Mathias wants to kick my ass, I'll let him."

This possibility seemed so likely the tension in my body cranked up another few notches.

Wy continued, with conviction, "We'll make them understand, I swear to you. I would take a thousand beatings and then some to be with you, don't forget that."

I battled a secondary surge of concern. "I don't want to go yet."

I wanted to linger in this clearing, in our little orange tent, where we'd found such incredible joy last night. Hidden in the cocoon of our love and our lovemaking, where no one could offer judgment or opinion, or enforce rules. Where no one could keep us apart.

"I don't want to go either, but we have to, baby, we can't stay here."

"One more time," I begged. "Before we go back."

Once inside the tent we wasted no time stripping each other's clothing. Greedy with need, we came together with a lack of restraint that was only a thin veil disguising growing fear. Fear of what our families would have to say about all of this; fear of the unknown, the uncontrollable. For that last priceless moment, there was only us.

. . .

The sun was dusting the treetops and creating lacy golden patterns along the road as we headed east an hour later, toward Landon. Wy drove, our joined hands resting on his thigh, the radio playing quietly in the background. A heavy cloak of silence had descended over us as our own thoughts crowded out the need for conversation; anxiety was already beating a steady refrain against my breastbone as I considered what the next hour would bring. But then I recalled what Wy had said before we left our tent to face the rest of this day, just a little while ago.

"It's going to be all right," he'd murmured, poised just above me with his forearms braced on either side of my head. He was still inside me at that moment, our bodies pressed flush and hearts thrusting against each other, but I pulled him even closer, battling desperation, trying to let his words to calm my fears. I couldn't explain why a strange sense of dread was fluttering at the edge of my consciousness, demanding attention. The idea of facing my parents was not pleasant, but I would field their subsequent anger; it wasn't as though they could lock me away forever, or forbid me to see Wy ever again.

*So what is it, what's wrong?*

All my instincts suggested that something was—but I shoved the feeling away, sure I was just overreacting.

"I know," I'd finally whispered, hiding my face against the warmth of his neck, inhaling his scent like someone coming up for the last time. "I just don't want this second to end."

Wy lifted my chin so our gazes could hold strong. His lips curved in a sweet smile, his hair falling over his forehead, his chin and jaws peppered with dark stubble. He was so unimaginably sexy, so very dear to me. A shiver clutched at my spine as he leaned to press a soft kiss to my lips, simultaneously grasping my hips and lifting me gently higher, holding himself as deeply in my body as possible. I shivered hard again, overcome by emotion, threading my legs around his lean torso and squeezing.

"I won't leave your side," he promised.

And I believed him.

We were maybe five miles from the exit to the interstate when my cell phone began buzzing with an incoming call. Startled, I fumbled with it, surprised to see my aunt's name on the screen.

"It's Ruthie," I told Wy, angling the phone in his direction.

"She's just worried," he predicted. "I'm sure Marsh made it back by now and told her about everything. Maybe she talked to Camille and wants to warn us."

"Oh *God*," I moaned, but I couldn't refuse the call, swiping the screen to answer. "Aunt Ruthie?"

The weird thing was, I knew she was there and had heard my voice—but she didn't say anything. The dread in my belly grew dense.

"Aunt Ruthie?" I repeated, with more insistence. "Are you there?"

I heard her clear her throat before asking softly, "Can I talk to Wy for a sec?"

I spoke in a rush. "We're on the way home right now. We're going to—"

She interrupted me, her gentle voice full of obvious concern as she said, "Sweetie, I have to talk to him. Right now, okay?"

"Why?" I demanded; I knew, with total certainty, that I didn't want Wy to hear whatever Aunt Ruthie had to say next.

"Just pass him the phone, sweetie, please." She sounded on edge with worry and I could do little but obey, silently holding it toward Wy.

He crinkled his eyebrows, asking without words what was going on; I shook my head, indicating that I had no idea.

He brought the phone to his ear. "Ruthie, what is it?"

"Where's your phone? Have you listened to your messages since last night?" I heard my aunt question.

"No, it's somewhere in our gear," Wy said. "I haven't seen it since yesterday. Why?"

Aunt Ruthie responded, but this time I couldn't hear her voice over the radio.

"What do you mean?" Wy asked, and I swore I felt the sudden tension rise like a thunderhead within him.

Aunt Ruthie spoke a final time.

Wy went as still as a carving, frozen in place by her words. And then the phone slipped from its position on his shoulder, gliding down his chest before thunking to the floor near the pedals. He appeared so stricken my first thought was that someone had died.

"What is it?" High and startled, my voice sounded like a little girl's.

I watched as Wy gripped the lower half of his face, eyes fixed straight ahead.

"What's going on?" I cried, frightened by the intensity of his expression.

Without answering, he pulled to the pebble-strewn dirt on the side of the road, threw the car in park, and shouldered open the driver's side door. I scrambled after him, ignoring the abandoned phone, dogging his footsteps as he strode across both empty lanes and walked right down into the ditch. About five feet from the spot where the forest began in earnest, in the spiky shadows cast by a hundred towering pine trees, he dropped to a crouch and lowered his head, gripping it between both hands.

Terrified and helpless, I watched as he remained hunched in this position for a good fifteen seconds. The highway was devoid of traffic in the early-morning hour; other than the car's idling engine, there was no sound but birdsong and the sigh of a breeze riffling the wildflowers and rangy grass stalks in the ditch.

"Wy . . ." I begged at last.

He looked up at me, in clear agony.

"What is it? Tell me!" I wanted nothing more than to kneel and wrap my arms around him, but instead I stood immobile, cold hands laced in a death grip near my waist.

It sounded like he was choking. "Hannah is . . ."

"Is what?" I demanded, thoughts rioting—*Oh my God, is she in Landon? Is she here to stake her claim on Wy? Does she know where we were last night? It's none of her damn business!*

"She's pregnant," he whispered.

# CHAPTER FOURTEEN

THE WORLD FELL AWAY. IT JUST FELL AWAY BE-
neath my feet and I floundered in a buzzing gray void, unable to make sense
of the words, let alone consider what they meant in the long term. I retained
no memory of turning and striding through the knee-high grass, leaving him
crouched there in the shady ditch. It wasn't until I was a good ten yards distant
that I returned to reality, with a vengeance.

Wy was on my heels. "Please wait. *Please* . . ."

Blood pounding in my temples and obscuring all but two pinpoints in my
vision, I ignored the plea and started running. I realized I could never hope to
outdistance him but escape was the only viable option just now. I considered
nothing of what Wy might be feeling in the wake of this unexpected news; it was
selfish, I knew somewhere deep down, but pain was ripping through my body,
lacerating organs on its way. Logic, sense, compassion—all burned to ash in the
heat of my shock.

"Millie, *stop* . . ." He clutched my elbow.

I whirled to face him, eyes stinging; he appeared shell-shocked, and fury kept
my tears at bay. Broiling hatred for Hannah exploded through my center, as violent as molten rock. I didn't know her, I couldn't have picked her out of a lineup,
and yet my hatred was potent, coursing like venom in my blood. She had won
after all; her claim on Wy had successfully negated mine.

"Let go!" I ordered.

"Hang on a minute, please just talk to me." He refused to release his hold on
my arm.

I kicked his shin with all my strength. I was wearing flip-flop sandals, so it
couldn't have hurt much, but I accompanied the kick by shoving his chest with
both hands.

He quickstepped backward, stunned by my rage, but I was in survival mode.
I resumed my course east at a jog, fleeing toward what exactly, I didn't know.
Landon was a good twenty miles away along a stretch of two-lane highway. Even
was I capable of maintaining a steady run I would be lucky to make it there before
evening, but I was not about to get back in the car. I couldn't bear to be near Wy,
not when everything that had happened between us last night—only minutes ago

something sacred and exquisite—now ached like third-degree burns covering my entire body.

He thundered, "You think this news was easy for me to hear?!"

I didn't look back, but Wy clearly returned to the idling car, because a minute or so later I heard him driving up behind me. He slowed to a crawl, window rolled down. I refused to acknowledge him, stalking forward without a word. My legs were covered in needle-fine scratches, courtesy of the rampant ditch weeds, and the rising sun beat hotly on my head, but I kept my chin up.

"Please talk to me. You think I expected this? This is the last thing I expected."

I kept walking, unwilling to respond.

"Please just talk to me, I feel like I'm about to die."

I faltered for a second, closing my eyes, hearing the rasp in his throat.

"I love you, Mill, do you hear me? I love you and I won't ever stop."

My hands flew upward, cupping my neck, an involuntary gesture of abject dismay. I didn't open my eyes, feeling the weight of his gaze as I said woodenly, "That doesn't matter now. It's all gone, don't you see?"

"I don't see it that way. Will you get back in the car and talk to me? Please, just talk to me . . ."

Control dangling by an unraveling thread, I turned toward him at last; the sight of his ravaged eyes made further wreckage of my heart. I cried, "There *is* no other way, not anymore! You made someone pregnant! *You* made that choice. And now *she's going to have your baby!*"

"That may be true, but—"

"But nothing!"

"Please come here, please don't walk away."

"Throw me my phone," I ordered. I bit the insides of my cheeks with a savage sort of determination, not about to cry in front of him. Not now.

"I'm not leaving you here on the side of the road!"

"I'll call someone to come and get me." I braved his gaze a final time. "You are all I ever wanted, Wy. But that's gone now. It's all gone."

"It's not gone! We can work this out, I know we can."

"Give me my phone and go."

"I'm not leaving you here."

"Give me my *fucking phone!*"

"Not until you talk to me!"

I bent down and yanked a thick clump of weeds from the ground; the root ball was round and heavy with fresh dirt, small pebbles clinging to the soil. Without another word I flung the bundle, roots first, toward Wy's open window. He ducked, lifting a forearm, but I had another handful of weeds all set, chucking it at him with all my strength.

"Dammit, Millie!"

"Go away!" I screamed, hurtling a third missile. This one struck the door and exploded in a shower of black earth.

Wy refused to leave me alone on the highway, but I walked onward, ignoring the curious stares of those in the intermittent vehicles that came upon us. He drove on the opposite shoulder, keeping pace with me as I marched on through the ditch, my gaze fixed on a point down the road. Time passed. I shut out everything but the necessity of putting one foot in front of the other. When a familiar green vehicle appeared in the westbound lane my heart skittered—but seconds later Rae pulled to a stop on my side of the road, alone in Evan's truck, windows rolled down. Though I couldn't see her expression, I felt the intensity of her concern like oncoming rain. Beyond her, on the opposite side of the road, I saw that Wy had also parked and was opening his door.

I raced up the ditch to Rae and darted inside the truck, ordering, "Go!"

"But, Millie . . ." she implored, watching as Wy hurried across the road.

"Go!" I covered my face, blocking out the sight of him.

"Rae, let me talk to her." Wy had reached the truck and I imagined him leaning in the open driver's side window. "Please, Millie, *please talk to me.*"

I kept both hands over my face.

Rae said, "Wy, just take my car back to Landon, you can park it by the inn and Evan will get it, okay?"

I heard a million questions in her voice as she issued these instructions.

"Don't go," he ordered harshly.

I was about to crack to jagged pieces.

"Rae," I pleaded, and she let her foot off the brake.

"I'm sorry," she said, speaking to Wy or to me, I didn't know in that moment.

"Wait!" he shouted after us. "*Millie!*"

For the first dozen miles, I couldn't stop sobbing long enough to explain anything. I didn't know what Wy had told her—for he'd obviously been the one to call her, using my cell phone—but Rae only cupped my knee, saying nothing, letting me weep.

At last she said in a rush, "I'm so sorry. This is all my fault. I told Ruthie where you guys were because I got scared that your mom knew the truth. What the hell happened back there? I'm freaking out!"

"It's not your fault," I rasped, lifting my face. I crossed my arms and squeezed my ribcage, feeling as though my organs had liquefied and might leak away without pressure.

"Tell me what's wrong," Rae demanded.

"What did he tell you?" I whispered, unable to speak his name.

"Wy said you two had a fight and that you were walking home and wouldn't get back in the car. What in the world did you fight about?"

"We ... we ... " I drew a shuddering breath. "We ... made love."

"And then what?!" Rae recognized that I was omitting critical information.

"Uncle Marshall sh ... showed up this morning ... but that wasn't ... that's not why ... " I clenched my jaws, unable to control my shaking voice. "But then ..."

"Then what?!" Rae thumped the steering wheel with both hands.

"Ruthie called just a little bit ago. And she t ... she *told him* ... " I gulped, barely able to speak. "She told him ... that his old girlfriend, H ... Hannah, is p ... pregnant." My voice wobbled over the horrible truth like bike tires over ruts in a gravel road.

"Oh, holy shit! Oh, my God! You're kidding!"

"*Rae*," I wept. "Oh God, it was so beautiful last night, it was more beautiful than anything I could have imagined. I love him so much ... *how can I let him go* ..."

Rae reached for my left hand, squeezing hard, unequivocally loyal.

"Tell me what you want me to do."

"Drive," I whispered. "Just please drive."

...

I stood on the shoulder of the two-lane, watching as the truck disappeared around a curve in the road. I felt as hollow as a dead tree, blasted by the shock of everything that had happened since Ruthie's phone call roughly thirty minutes ago.

*Hannah is pregnant.*

The words played on repeat in my head, revolving like a broken turntable, slamming me with guilt and dismay and pain.

*My fault*, I thought, again and again. *All of this is my fault.*

The car continued idling and I returned to it, moving slowly, the shield provided by stun and disbelief beginning now to shred away. I curled my hands around the bottom of the open window, feeling the sun's trapped heat penetrate my palms. I studied my knuckles like I'd never seen them before, rushed by images of last night. Of Millie in my arms, the incredible gift of what we'd shared together. She had no way of knowing how amazing last night had truly been; she had never had sex before. But I had, and I knew. I understood. Standing alone in the midmorning sun, the full impact of what I was losing struck viciously.

I understood Millie in a hundred new ways after the past few days, considered myself the luckiest man alive to be on the receiving end of her love. Admitting that we loved each other was just the beginning. Only an hour ago, the possibilities of a future together seemed limitless. I'd been brimming with a level of happiness never before known to me—and now it was gone. Just like that, fucking gone. Alone in the fallout of Hannah's news I fought reality, already knowing that Millie was right. We could never be together after today, not when I'd made another woman pregnant. There was no other choice but to return to Montana and face my purgatory.

*Oh God, please . . .*

*Please don't take Millie away. Don't let me lose her.*

*You selfish, stupid moron, Wy. She's already lost to you. You don't deserve her.*

*And Hannah deserves better than you too, don't pretend otherwise. Hannah deserves someone who loves her, and you don't.*

*You fucked Hannah last spring, you made that choice, and now she's pregnant.*

Crude, insensitive thoughts; we'd fucked and now Hannah was pregnant. There were no excuses for my behavior. Denial filled my chest cavity, thick and painful, as I raced backward through time, trying to count the weeks since I'd last been with her.

*Over two months ago, at least, and you hadn't been with her since New Year's Eve, before that.*

*You were drunk. Probably no condom.*

*Jesus Christ, Wy.*

*But wasn't she on the pill? She swore to me she was using birth control.*

Scalding water seemed to strike my face, bringing with it a stinging awareness.

*What if she lied? What if she was trying to get pregnant?*

*Ruthie and Marshall were saying something about that just a few months ago, remember? That Hannah would do anything to keep you in her life.*

*No—Hannah wouldn't do such a heinous thing . . .*

*Would she?*

I pushed away from the car and stormed to the trunk, digging with single-minded purpose until I found my phone. It was at the very end of its battery life. I had two missed calls from my dad, two from Marshall, and five from Hannah—and as many voicemails. I couldn't bear to listen to any of them and called her, forcing control, forcing myself to get level. No matter how destroyed I felt, I would assume for now that Hannah was also in shock. I was a presumptuous asshole for thinking that she had tried to get pregnant without telling me.

"Where have you been?" she cried upon answering. "Where in the *hell* have you been? I've called your dad, and Marshall and Ruthann, oh my God, Wy!"

"Ruthie told me." No point pretending I didn't know the truth. I softened my tone, with effort. "You're sure about this? You're sure it's . . . ours?"

"Yes, I'm sure! Who else do you think I've been with?!"

The sun was an anvil on the back of my neck. I closed my eyes, leaning forward against the hot metal of the car, free hand clenching into a helpless fist. I didn't know what to say. I wanted to weep. I wanted to shout my agony to the sky, to blame anyone but myself for this. The things I should have said became dust on my tongue.

"I want you to come home. *Now*. I need to see you in person. My parents are flipping out, Wy, they said we have to get married. My dad has been on the phone with Clark twice already today." Hannah sounded about two steps from full-blown hysteria.

My knees simply gave out and I sank to a crouch beside a rear tire, bracing myself against its wheel well.

"Are you there?" she cried. "I said I need you to come home!"

"I heard you," I whispered.

. . .

By the time Rae and I returned to Landon, after eleven that night, Wy was already long gone.

Beside myself with grief and pain, cried-out to the point of physical depletion, I hugged Rae one last time as we sat together in Evan's truck in the parking lot at Shore Leave. I thanked God for Rae's presence; she had carried me through the past fourteen hours, had kept me from sinking completely under. She knew every detail and her listening had been a gift of unimaginable generosity. I found room to be grateful for several other facts—for one, my parents had no idea where I'd actually spent last night. The exploding bomb of Hannah Jasper's news had taken precedence over everything else. Rae had spoken to Aunt Ruthie not long after picking me up outside Itasca, and the two of them concocted a story for the benefit of my parents—that I was so upset after learning the news that Rae and I had decided to ditch Landon for the day.

*Millie, I just heard about Wy and Hannah. Please call me when you get this, honey*, Mom had texted shortly thereafter, sending this message to Rae's phone because mine remained in Rae's car with Wy—not that Mom knew this fact; Rae told her that I'd forgotten my phone at the Johnsons' house. The lies I'd spun in the past twenty-four hours were thick enough to smother in.

My stomach had knotted at the mere sight of Hannah's name in the text message; it was all I could do not to hurl the phone out the window. I sagged against the passenger seat, overcome by despair, my mind stuck in a holding pattern, circling repetitively over the memory of Wy begging me to talk to him. Standing alone on the highway, watching as I exited his life.

*Oh God, oh God, oh God . . .*

After three incoming calls that I begged Rae not to answer, Wy had texted her phone, using mine, which had remained temporarily in his possession. And so I knew where to find it that night once Rae and I returned to Landon, and which was why I requested she drop me off at Shore Leave.

"I'll be up," Rae promised. "Head over once you're done here, okay?"

I promised I would. Shutting out all thoughts attempting to force entry, I hurried to the small wooden shed; the water-warped wooden door opened with a creaky groan, releasing the scent of the lake. I stepped inside, heart quaking, making my way to the plywood shelves lining the back wall. There, on the bottom shelf, tucked behind a stack of ancient foam life belts, I found my phone. Beneath it was a small white envelope.

I fought the urge to crumple the letter without reading it, but of course I didn't; with care, I extracted the folded piece of paper, stationery from Angler's Inn. The handwritten page represented what was likely the last correspondence I would ever have with Wyatt Rawley and I could have no more left it unread than I could have cut off my right hand. I brought it to my nose and inhaled, as if the scent of him was somehow captured on the paper. My eyes, tear-ravaged and grainy, grew wet again. I used the flashlight in my phone, sitting on the floor with my spine braced against the wall and spreading his words across my lap. He'd used a blue pen and his handwriting slanted to the right; he made sharp points on the capital M's rather than rounded.

*Millie,* he'd written. *Nothing has ever hurt worse than leaving this place without seeing you. Marshall is driving Dad and me to the bus station in Rose Lake. You're still somewhere with Rae. I feel like my heart has been ripped out of my body. There are no words to describe how empty I feel. What can I say to explain? What can I say to make you understand? I don't have anyone to blame but me. Accepting this hurts like hell. Accepting that I might never see you again is a thousand times worse. I can't bear it. I love you, Millie, I love you so much I know I won't recover from it, ever. I don't want to recover. I want to lie down and close my eyes and relive every second of our time together. Your voice, your eyes, your face, the way you feel and smell and taste. Nothing in this world compares to you, and it never will, not for me. I'm a goner for you. You have my heart, for always. Please forgive me, sweetheart, because I can't forgive myself.*

He signed it simply, *Wy.*

I clicked out the flashlight, pressure building in my chest with such force I feared I was having a heart attack. I shoved aside an inflatable raft and huddled on the cold floorboards, clutching Wy's letter to my heart, folding my knees inward toward my breasts. He hadn't used Hannah's name, hadn't mentioned the baby. I couldn't know what he intended to do once he returned home to Jalesville; I realized I would eventually know.

*I don't want to recover. I want to lie down and close my eyes and relive every second of our time together.*

Information would eventually find its way to me, whether I wished it or not; early next year, for example, Hannah would give birth to a son or daughter and Wy would be that child's father. I'd done the math, counting forward nine months from May, despising myself for doing so. No matter what Wy claimed, the experience of witnessing a child's birth was one of awe and profound importance, and he would share that experience with another woman at some point next January. He would, forever after, be bound to Hannah in this way, negating the bond he and I had forged last night.

*You have my heart, for always. Please forgive me, sweetheart, because I can't forgive myself.*

I felt as if I'd fallen from a great height, impacting in this moment, the breath knocked from my lungs with a force shocking in its intensity. I hurt so terribly that I curled into a tight, self-preserving ball, wrapping into my arms and squeezing, squeezing, until I was sure my heart wouldn't slip from between my ribs and drain away through the cracks in the floor.

PART TWO

# CHAPTER FIFTEEN

LATER, I WOULD REMEMBER EXACTLY NOTHING about the journey from Landon back to Jalesville, including the duration of a layover at a Greyhound station in Fargo. Marshall drove Dad and me to the bus station in Rose Lake about an hour after Millie disappeared with Rae. Dad was insistent that he would join me on the trip home and that there was no reason for everyone else to cut short their visit to Minnesota on account of my actions.

*My actions.*

I sat in the middle row of my older brother's vehicle, head in my hands, unable to bear the sight of my own eyes in the rearview mirror. Sharp tension permeated the surrounding air as we drove to the small town a few miles down the interstate from Landon; there was no bus station in Millie's hometown. Belted into the passenger seat, Dad rode in quiet contemplation, collecting his thoughts. I knew my father better than almost anyone and I recognized that this sort of calm preceded a monumental verbal ass-kicking. Time and again I felt the concerned weight of Marshall's gaze hitting me like a fist as he glanced back from the driver's seat, but I refused to lift my head.

I hadn't seen anyone else before we left Landon, not even Ruthie. I parked Rae's car in the lot at the Angler's Inn, as she'd requested, before trudging upstairs to the room I'd been sharing with Dad. Things happened quickly after that, leaving me with the sickly sensation of riding an out-of-control carousel. Marsh was already there; Dad had packed our things. I heard the muffled sounds of their conversation as I climbed the wooden stairs, which ceased the moment I turned the doorknob. No matter. I knew I was the topic of their hushed exchange.

They stood facing each other near the window, Marsh bracketing his forehead with one hand as if restraining an oncoming headache, Dad clutching his ancient, battered Stetson to his chest like a shield—his attempt to deflect the unbelievable news that his youngest son had made someone pregnant out of wedlock.

"Son," Dad said, communicating roughly a dozen different emotions with that one word.

I stood framed in the open doorway, feeling like such shit I could have sunk through the floor.

"There's something I have to do." I kept my gaze averted, feeling the small, warm rectangle of Millie's phone in my back pocket. "I have to leave a note for Millie."

Her name scraped my throat.

"We need to go, Wy," Marsh said quietly.

I heard the notes of regret and sympathy blended together in my brother's voice, and braved his unflinching gaze; I knew I looked like shit, my eyes red and swollen, despair having dug a deep trench across my face. Dad's eyebrows drew together in confusion, wondering what Millie had to do with any of this.

"I have to leave her a note."

"Out of the question." Exasperation burned away all traces of Marshall's compassion.

"I'm leaving Millie a note."

Marshall saw something in my eyes because he left off attempting to prevent it and muttered, "Fine, but you're not going back to Shore Leave. I'll make sure she gets it."

"Why do you need to leave Millie Jo a note?" Dad wondered aloud.

Marshall and I exchanged a silent conversation in the space of a few seconds. I saw in my brother's eyes the inevitability of the situation.

"Wyatt Zane," Dad ordered, a clear demand for an explanation.

Tears burned my eyes and clogged my throat. I sank to the edge of the nearby bed.

"Wy and Millie had sex last night, Dad," Marshall said succinctly. There was no challenge in his voice, only resignation, but I flew to my feet, enraged that he'd spoken for me.

"Shut your goddamn mouth!" I shouted, jabbing an index finger roughly against his chest. "It's none of your business!"

Dad gripped the lower half of his face, an age-old gesture of bewilderment.

"It *is* his business, little bro." Marshall retained his cool. "You planned to keep this from Dad? Are you kidding me?"

Dad recovered a fraction of his self-possession, reaching to curl a hand around my right shoulder. "Wy, you're telling me you and Millie Jo . . . that you two . . ."

I closed my eyes, so undone by grief I wanted in that moment to die.

"Yes," I whispered.

Marshall spoke with typical decisiveness. "This isn't the time. You can tell Dad the whole story on the way home. If you want to leave a note for Millie, write it now."

And so I sat on the bed I'd used for the past few nights, feeling as gutted as a dead fish, to compose the letter. I thought of all the letters I'd intended to write Millie in the upcoming year, letters that would tell her about my day and ask about hers; how I couldn't wait for the months to fly past so we could be together again. All the love letters I would have written now condensed into this one, the first and last I would ever send her. My hand shook as I wrote each subsequent line, envisioning her face as she read it. I was as helpless to ease her pain as someone locked in a prison cell. Without a word, I folded the paper into an envelope and passed it, along with Millie's phone, to Marsh.

"I'll make sure she gets it," he promised, and I saw in his eyes the depths of his unspoken sorrow. Marsh understood more than perhaps anyone. He'd once lost Ruthie and only by the grace of God had she been returned to him; I already knew I would not be so fortunate.

Many hours and hundreds of miles later, Dad and I climbed down from the bus in the small station on the outskirts of our hometown, the only passengers disembarking in Jalesville. The evening sky glowed with the setting sun, the air warm, tinged by the summertime scents of pine resin and dust, but the view before my eyes had gone gray somewhere back in Minnesota. I followed my dad like an ambulatory ghost.

"Clark! Wy! Over here!"

We turned to spy Aunt Julie, my dad's little sister, waving from her truck, parked across the street. I saw a newspaper spread open over the steering wheel as she sat waiting for us.

"We'll be right there!" Dad called. "Let me grab the bags."

"I got it, Dad," I offered quietly, touching his elbow.

Dad appeared slightly startled that I'd spoken.

"Thanks, son. I'll go chat with Julie," he agreed.

My heart went into a sort of seizure as I considered what the next hour would bring. I had not spoken to Hannah since midmorning, standing on the shoulder of the highway outside Itasca, despite her numerous attempts to reach me in the meantime, but there was no avoiding it now that we were back in town. It struck me that I was still wearing the same boxers and jeans from last night—I hadn't showered since making love with Millie one last time this morning. Immediately I brought my right hand to my nose and inhaled, as though there was any chance in hell that the scent of her might linger on my skin or clothes. Attempting to remain numb, and therefore somewhat protected, grew increasingly impossible. Images and sounds struck like hail, pelting me with memories of last night.

*Millie.*

*Where are you right now, sweetheart, what are you thinking?*

*I am so sorry, I am sorrier than I could ever say.*

Had she found my letter yet? I knew I could depend on Marsh; that he'd left it, along with Millie's phone, on the bottom shelf in the boat shed as I'd requested. The trunk of Rae's car had contained all of our camping gear, including the sweatshirt I'd used to help clean the blood from Millie's thighs. The thought of her naked vulnerability in that moment, and her ultimate trust in me, tore mercilessly at my heart.

*I remember thinking that everything would be all right because you were there,* she had said. *I was so happy to share that with you, Wy, and now we've shared this too.*

My vision narrowed to tunnels.

*Forgive me, Millie, oh God, forgive me.*

*I would be there to hold you if I could, I swear on my life.*

My phone was tucked in my back pocket, a constant reminder of the illusion that she remained within reach. I had given up hope of receiving a new message from her; all of the texts we'd exchanged since Sunday would represent our last contact. Even so, I scrolled obsessively to my messages, seeking the sight of her name.

My heart stuttered over one that Ruthie had sent six hours ago—*Marshall put your letter in the shed, I just wanted you to know. We're on the way home. We should have left with you this morning so you didn't have to take the bus.*

I almost dropped the phone in my haste to respond—*How is she?*

My question could not have been more stupid; I already knew the answer.

Ruthie did not immediately respond and so I tucked my phone away and collected our bags from the compartment under the bus, watching as it left the parking lot, heading back east. Jalesville was apparently the end of the line tonight, in more ways than one.

As I approached the truck, Aunt Julie demanded, "Wyatt, what kind of a fix have you gotten into?"

My dad's little sister had never been one to mince words. Disregarding the question for the moment, I loaded our bags in the truck bed, running a hand over my face. I felt ready to collapse.

"Jules, give him a little time," Dad admonished, leaning forward so I could climb into the backseat.

"Since when are you and Hannah Jasper still a thing?" Aunt Julie pulled away from the curb, ignoring Dad's concern.

"We aren't," I said shortly, staring outside at the terrain flashing past, land so familiar I could have drawn the exact contours of the mountains to the west from memory.

Aunt Julie sent me a pointed look in the rearview mirror. "Well, you must have been *something* not all that long ago. That girl better pull her act together, that's all I can say. She's been drinking like a goddamn lumberjack in the past month. I'm going to assume she didn't realize her condition, is that right?"

"Hannah just found out," Dad supplied. "Wy's still struggling with all this."

I rested my forehead on the window glass.

"Have you two had supper? You want to come over? Tuck and Netta are bringing dessert later."

"Maybe tomorrow. Thank you, all the same," Dad answered for us.

I sensed Aunt Julie's reluctance to let the matter drop. It wasn't that she was attempting to upset me; she was simply forthright, a purely Rawley trait, in the fashion of her daughters, my dad, and three of my four older brothers. Only Quinn was possessed of a calmer, quieter soul. I wished I could request that Aunt Julie drop me at my brother's apartment; Quinn would make time to listen, without judgment.

"The girls are dying to hear all about everything from your perspective," Aunt Julie said before she left us on the front porch. The fixture above the door threw a cone of yellow light and I watched a moth flapping frantically as it circled the bare bulb, unable to resist the temptation.

I nodded inanely, not even sure exactly what my aunt had just said.

"Come here, give me a hug," she ordered, enclosing me in her embrace.

"You'll be a good daddy, mark my words," she murmured in my ear. "Sweet little Wy, I can't believe you're this old." Drawing back, she clutched my elbows with her usual intensity. "Don't let this stop you from finishing up your degree, you hear me?"

Once alone inside the house I faltered, staring around the familiar space as though I'd never seen it before; the living room rotated on a teetering axis and I reeled, sinking to the closest armchair. And just like that, I lost it like nobody's business. I was solely responsible for the destruction of my own happiness. For the destruction of Millie's happiness, for the plans we had made; a future that could have been ours. It had been within reach only forty-eight hours ago. The thought of what she was feeling at this very second, hundreds of miles away from me in Minnesota, sent me hunching tighter around my aching heart. From this point onward, every passing day, week, month, and eventually year would take me further from our night together. The memory of it was all I had left to hold.

"Wy. Son. It's all right." Dad sounded out of breath, as if he had jogged to reach my side. He attempted to put a hand on my shoulder, but I shrugged it away, not wanting to be touched.

"It's not . . . all right . . ." I wrapped my head in both arms, curling forward over my knees, weeping so hard my skull seemed in danger of exploding. I wished it would.

My father knelt beside the armchair, giving me space but refusing to leave me alone in my grief.

I sobbed, "*Dad . . .*"

I was a little boy again, begging him to make things better, to tell me this was all a terrible mistake, that my life had not been upended, plans razed to ash—the way Dad must have felt the day my mom died. Somewhere in the dark, boarded-over recesses of my memory was a scene, an autumn afternoon, from which I always shied like a spooked horse. Dad was in that memory. And Marshall. But I couldn't let it fully enter my conscious mind. I wasn't brave enough.

Dad rested a hand on my spine, letting his touch speak for him.

I choked, "*I hurt . . . so bad . . .*"

He didn't try to contradict my words, just rubbed my back with small, circular motions.

Time passed. I had no idea how much. Dad waited for the sobs to recede. At last, in his kind way, he invited, "Tell me what happened. With Millie Jo, I mean. Please tell me. You didn't say a word the entire way home."

My chest heaved. Glass seemed to crack in the spaces between my ribs, jagged edges stabbing my heart.

"I love her." I lifted my face and met my father's somber eyes. "I love Millie and now . . . oh God . . . *now it's over . . .*"

Dad studied me as if for additional clues. "And you made love with her?"

"Yes," I whispered, clutching the back of my head with both hands, elbows crushing my temples. I was afraid I might liquefy if I didn't apply pressure with all my strength.

"Might she be pregnant now?" Dad spoke gently; he didn't need to say *this is a fine kettle of fish, son*, the way he usually did when one of us fucked up. I heard it all the same in his tone.

A piercing, momentary hope blazed through my blood. If Millie was pregnant I would not have to marry Hannah. I could be a father to both children but I could marry Millie instead. Maybe everything wasn't destroyed after all—

"Wyatt." Dad's patience was thinning. "Did you use protection?"

"We did," I rasped, realizing any hope of Millie being pregnant with my baby was futile. We'd used a condom each time. We'd been so careful.

"If Mathias and Camille want to talk to you regarding this matter, you will face that conversation. I love you, Wy, you know I do. You're my youngest, the joy of your mother's last years." Dad paused, briefly closing his eyes as if drawing upon a reserve of strength before pinning me with an unrelenting stare. "But I am ashamed of your behavior on many levels here, son. Let's set aside the matter of Hannah for a moment. What in God's name were you thinking, taking advantage of Millie Jo that way? She's a young girl, a sweet and innocent girl. And you've no doubt hurt her deeply with these actions. There's no excuse for any of this."

I held Dad's gaze, needing him to know how serious I was as I implored, "I didn't take advantage, even though I know it seems that way. I love Millie, Dad. She loves me."

Dad's mustache drooped as he said, "I see," his tone infused with sympathy and sadness.

A need to confess filled my throat; maybe some small part of me still believed my dad possessed the ability to change what had happened, that he could force things to work out.

"I've loved Millie since I was a kid. I just never dared to say anything or let it show, at least not until she was old enough. We thought that after she graduated next spring she could move out here to go to college and we could be together. We made love because we wanted to, I wasn't taking advantage, I swear on my life. The timing wasn't the best, I get that, but I love Millie. We love *each other*, Dad."

"Oh, Wy." Dad's voice was full of hurt and my name seemed like the unanswerable question itself—*why? Why?*

*Oh God, please tell me why.*

"And now . . ." Pressure built all over again in my chest. "And now everything is over. Millie is out of reach . . . and hurting. And it's my fault . . ."

"Where does Hannah fit into all of this?" Dad pressed, treading with care. "How sure are you that this baby is yours?"

I wanted to keep silent, ashamed of what could only be interpreted as callous disregard for Hannah's feelings. But I refused to shy from accountability, as much as I wished I could, and said quietly, "It's my baby. Hannah wouldn't lie. The last time we had sex was in May, two months or so ago. I didn't use a condom. I was pretty drunk." My voice was rough with grit. "I was celebrating the end of the semester."

"I don't understand." Dad was shaking his head.

Anger, and the weight of the unendurable, began flattening my control. "What's there to understand? I was drunk, Hannah was there, we had sex. No, I don't love her. I *used* her, Dad, so I could get off. Love was no part of it."

"You will not speak with such crudity about any woman, not in this house, not outside of it! I taught you and your brothers better than that, and you damn well know it!" Dad never yelled but I'd crossed a line.

"It's the truth, Dad, and the truth fucking hurts."

"Watch your mouth!" Dad thundered, and I wished he would hit me, a solid jab straight to the jaw; not that he would dream of laying hands on any of us. I knew my brothers would have no issues aiming a punch at my head, had they overheard my language toward our father.

He stood to his full height, fists planted on his hips. "Women and children are to be cherished and loved, without hesitation, without fail. It's a man's duty. You chose to make love to Hannah, a girl you once cared for, and that choice led to a child. A child who will be *your* son or daughter, your flesh and blood! And no matter what, your children, your kin, come first. You will provide a home for this child and Hannah. There's no other option. I know you for a good man, son, and I know you understand this truth."

Defeated, drained of everything, I sat with forearms braced on thighs, hands dangling like dead birds. I knew he was right; I knew all other choices had been forfeited. The phrase *son or daughter* sent panic screaming through my mind. It made everything all too real.

I spoke the most pressing of many fears. "Hannah said her parents want us to get married."

Dad's angry righteousness deflated a little as he said, "They spoke of it with me, as well." He removed his glasses and passed a hand over his face, pressing hard against his eye sockets as though restraining emotion; worse yet, he appeared resigned. He knew the decision was already made.

"I don't want to marry her, Dad." I gripped my knees, imploring him, certain he would understand. "I can be a good father without marrying Hannah. I'll pay for a house for her and the baby, I'll pay child support for the next twenty years. She can have whatever she wants from me."

Dad crouched to put our faces on a level. He covered my shaking hands with his and applied gentle pressure. "You cannot imagine the toll a new baby takes on a person. You cannot condemn Hannah to raising your child without you. You will marry her and provide for your family. *Your family*, Wy, do you hear me? A child deserves a home with two parents."

My heart thrust like a piston, cold and distant, operating remotely, disconnected from my body.

"Your brothers—" Dad began, and I didn't know what he intended to say but I interrupted all the same, pushed beyond reason.

"My brothers have wives they love!" I yelled through clenched teeth. "I don't goddamn love Hannah! She's forcing me away from the woman I do love! Do you hear me?!"

"Hannah is the mother of your child." Dad struggled to maintain control.

"So you don't give a shit about how I feel? About what I want? Because I don't want this, I don't want to marry her! Why won't you listen to me?" Wild-eyed, I stood, gripping the back of my neck with both hands. "Why doesn't it matter what I want?"

"Because you're going to be a father. What you want doesn't take first place anymore."

The only option my panicking mind recognized was to flee and so I fled, escaping to my truck and slamming it into drive, flying due east on I-94 through the dark, intending to drive without stopping until I reached Landon. Millie was at the other end of this highway, north and east of my current position. I felt her so strongly, her pain stretching across the miles to clash with mine. But gray hopelessness assaulted me all over again, and at last I pulled to the shoulder on the empty four-lane, parallel to the metal road sign inviting me to return soon to Rosebud County. Minnesota was mere hours away, but I knew I could drive no farther. It was useless to even consider it.

I'd reached the end of this particular road.

No matter how desperately I wished otherwise, I could not go to Millie. From this point on, our paths angled in two separate directions. I gripped the wheel until my knuckles stood out like ridges, wanting to rip it from the steering column, feeling more out of control than ever before in my life. The cab of the truck closed in around my body, hot and dense and smothering; a ringing filled my ears, like that following the firing of a shotgun round.

"No," I begged. "Don't let this happen. Don't keep us apart."

But it had already happened; the loss had already occurred, only a few hundred miles east of where I currently sat in an idling, rusted-out truck.

*You can never see her again, you realize this.*

Unable to bear the surrender, I opened the door and stepped outside, facing east on the deserted stretch of interstate. I felt no more substantial than a speck of dust in a fading sunbeam, mattering to no one and nothing.

*You have to live without her.*

*There's no other choice.*

I turned and slammed my fists into the paneling of my truck, one after the other, like it was a punching bag dangling from a garage ceiling. I didn't stop until pain shrieked along my nerves, radiating up my forearms. Shoulders heaving, breath ragged, I looked down at my bleeding knuckles, studying them as though they belonged to a vicious stranger. If I'd broken a bone it was no less than I deserved. I climbed inside the truck and cranked it in a tight U-turn, heading west, back toward Jalesville. Roughly twenty miles later, hardly aware of my surroundings, I pulled into the gravel lot of a roadside bar.

# CHAPTER SIXTEEN

MY BROTHERS FOUND ME MUCH LATER THAT night. I remembered the hour before they appeared at the bar only in blurry patches; having spied my truck out front, Marshall and Sean pulled into the lot and hauled my sorry self back to Jalesville. Marsh and Ruthie had returned from Minnesota only to find out that Dad was beside himself with worry, having no idea where I'd disappeared to and no way to contact me; my phone remained at home. At some point after my arrival at the bar, someone had dumped my ass outside, where I slumped against the wooden boards of the outer wall, feeling the vibrations from the jukebox thrumming against my spine. At last, through bleary, alcohol-glazed eyes I'd spied Marsh and Sean walking in my direction, backlit by flashing neon.

When they crouched down to speak to me, I crawled away in order to vomit without splashing their boots.

There wasn't much talking on the drive back to Jalesville. I hunched forward in the passenger seat of Sean's truck while Marshall followed us, driving mine. Lucky for me I hadn't lost the keys down the john or something equally stupid, given my current near-total annihilation. Despite the fact that Sean usually ran his mouth, offering his opinion whether you wanted it or not, he kept mostly quiet, reaching once to squeeze my left shoulder.

"Marsh told me about Hannah, bud," he said. "It's a shock, I get it."

And a little later, "I get it, Wy, I really do."

As kind and well-meaning as his words were, I knew he couldn't truly understand.

"I want Mom," I heard myself mutter as Sean pulled up at Dad's house, the kitchen lights making bright squares in the darkness. Tears clogged up my damn throat yet again. I clutched Sean's elbow and whispered, "Please get Ruthie . . ."

Sean parked and hopped out, leaving the driver's side door gaping as he jogged toward my truck. I heard him ask Marsh, "Can you see if Ruthie's still up? Wy's asking for her."

Marshall helped me from the truck and toward Dad's house; I could barely walk under my own power. Speaking in the tone of a father, he encouraged, "Let's get you inside, okay? I'll see if Ruthie's still awake."

My brother and Ruthie's house was located just across the yard, but it seemed like an eternity slipped past before I heard her footsteps in the hallway leading to the small bathroom off the kitchen, where Marsh had deposited me. The space was dim, lit only by the fixture in the hallway, and I sat on the floor near the toilet with a towel pressed to the welt on my forehead. I had a clear memory of punching my truck but no idea how I'd sustained the injury to my face; even with my thoughts all whiskey-scrambled, I didn't remember getting in a fight. Blood had dried in a flaking line down the side of my nose. I was ashamed of my behavior for too many reasons to count, but momentary relief rolled over me at Ruthie's presence.

"I'm here," she whispered, kneeling at my side to assess the damage. "I'm right here, honey."

I knew, with no words, that Ruthie understood why I had asked for her. She was the mother I would never again have. I loved her so much, and she had taken care of me in a hundred thousand ways since I was a kid and she'd first married my brother. I tried to respond but heaved instead, bowing forward over the toilet just in time. She made no comment as I hurled up what looked and smelled like a bottle's worth of whiskey, feeling utterly worthless, my insides scrubbed raw.

"I'm . . . sorry . . . Ruthie . . ."

"No, no, it's all right. Don't be sorry." She helped me sit back against the wall, speaking with the same tone she used for her kids as she added, "Let's get you cleaned up, what do you say?"

I grasped her wrist. I had to know.

"Is she all right? What happened after we left?" My voice was a stranger's, hoarse and desperate.

Ruthie hesitated before saying quietly, "She's in bad shape, honey, I can't tell you otherwise."

I covered my face with both hands, pressing brutally hard, but still the image of Millie sobbing, Millie torn apart with pain, filled my skull.

I rasped, "Did she get my letter?"

"I don't know, but I will ask her if you want."

A choking sensation gripped my throat, my teeth clenching up as I sobbed, "I hurt so much, Ruthie, I can't hurt this much and live. *My fucking heart is broken.*" I couldn't stop, punishing myself with every word. "And I know I broke Millie's heart, it's all my fault. We could have . . . *been together* . . ."

"Wy," she whispered, but I barreled on, sobs fracturing every few words.

"Dad says . . . I have to . . . marry Hannah. I don't want to, I can't . . ."

Ruthie couldn't let me continue like this, breaking in more firmly this time, gathering my hands in hers. "You will be such a good father, Wy, don't forget that.

And you'll have your career, think of that. You'll be a vet and you'll have a new son or daughter to teach how to ride horses." She paused, as if considering. "A son, I'll bet you."

But I would not be sidetracked, visions screaming to life in my head—a future that would unfold no matter how much I rebelled against it. A lifetime in which I would be kept from the woman I loved.

"Millie will meet someone else . . . *she'll love someone else* . . . and I'll want to kill him. I already want to fucking kill him and it hasn't even happened yet. And there's nothing I can do. I fucked it up. *I fucked it all up . . . oh, Jesus Christ . . .*"

Ruthie finally said, "Wyatt, *enough*. Now isn't the time for this. You're drunk, for one thing, and injured. I'm going to turn on the light so I can see your forehead. What happened tonight?"

"I don't know." I wasn't trying to be belligerent; I truly didn't know.

Movement crossed the doorway and Marshall was suddenly there, crouching down beside Ruthie. My brother looked grim as he regarded the pitiful mess I'd made of myself tonight.

"Do you think your hands are broken?" he asked.

"I don't know," I muttered for the second time.

"Maybe we should have headed to the hospital, had someone take a look." Marshall rubbed a thumb over his chin. "I think it's a good idea."

"No," I whispered.

"Listen to me, Wy. Do you want to risk permanent damage?"

Before I could respond another bout of retching seized hold and I crawled toward the toilet.

"Maybe Milt would just come over here," I heard Ruthie say to Marsh, naming the local family practitioner.

"That's a good idea," Marshall said quietly. "I'll go talk to Dad and we'll call him."

Ruthie stood to rinse a hand towel at the sink as Marshall disappeared toward the living room. Weak with pain and despair, I released my hold on the toilet and slumped flat on the chilly floor tiles. Guilt swamped me as Ruthie knelt back down and collected my head on her lap, applying the warm towel to my face with care, sponging away the dried blood. I was thankful for her in so many ways, but I couldn't tell her—I could only cry in miserable silence, tears seeping from my closed eyes.

Ruthie smoothed hair from my forehead as she whispered, "It's all right, sweetheart, it's going to be all right."

I tried to respond but a sick, ragged breath came out instead of words.

"It's all right," she kept repeating as I sobbed like a child, ashamed to lose control this way but beyond caring at this point.

"It's not all right . . . I hurt her so much, she's hurting so much, I know it . . . and I can't be there to hold her . . . *oh God, I need to see Millie . . . I need her . . .*"

Marshall returned and knelt on the floor beside Ruthie, curling his hand over my shoulder and squeezing; their worry for me was like a fourth presence in the dim, cramped bathroom, but they said not a word, instead keeping their kind touch on me until the storm had passed.

# CHAPTER SEVENTEEN

I WOKE FROM A DREAM OF BEING CHASED BY hornets, eyelids parting like two halves of a split log, heart hammering. The insects in the dream had been violent in their pursuit, swirling around my head, increasing in number as I tried to flee. I blinked, hazy and disoriented, and realized the buzzing sound still echoing across the sun-drenched room was my phone, abandoned on the floor beside my bed. I rolled to my right and grabbed for it, ignoring the sharp pain stabbing through my hands and behind both eyes.

*Maybe it's Millie . . .*

A long time would pass before this sort of unreasonable hope fully withered.

Hannah's name filled the screen like an accusation, and I wished the hornets from my dream would just get on with it and finish the damn job.

"Were you still sleeping?" she demanded, hearing the telltale husk in my voice as I answered. "It's past noon! How long have you been home? Why didn't you come over last night?"

"Where are you?" I asked, interrupting her exasperated tirade.

"Home, where else would I be?"

Justifiable or not, anger snaked through my blood. "Getting loaded at The Spoke every night, according to Julie. What the hell is that all about? How long have you suspected you were pregnant?!"

I'd expected, maybe even craved, a fight. But the line went quiet in the wake of my words.

"Hannah?" I questioned, after several seconds of tense silence.

"I just found out, I promise you, Wy," she whispered, and her sudden shift into vulnerability deflated my anger. "I know you said we were over back in May. I haven't forgotten that."

"I'm sorry," I said immediately, discomfort twisting through my gut. "I shouldn't have yelled at you."

"Thanks for coming home so soon." She skirted my apology. "I know you guys just left for your trip to Minnesota. I really needed to see you."

I closed my eyes, clenching my jaw; I felt like an imposter in my own life.

*You were the one having unprotected sex with Hannah. So stop feeling so fucking sorry for yourself.*

I recognized the need to be stronger than this. No matter how much I wished to deny everything that had occurred since Tuesday morning, I could not. Hannah's child was also mine, and that child deserved a father, loving and honest, like my own; a father married to the mother. I knew these truths.

I whispered, "I need to get ready. I'll be over in an hour, all right?"

. . .

Hannah's parents were gracious, all things considered; it struck me that they seemed almost happy. They had known me since I was fifteen and first dating their daughter, but I still arrived at their house prepared to face a scene: crying and accusations, the whole bit. Apparently, however, the Jaspers had acclimated to the news of a forthcoming grandchild and were nothing but welcoming as I entered. Hungover as hell and bruised up, I'd showered but had otherwise made zero effort.

*Jesus Christ, Wy, you should be ashamed of yourself.*

But I could not muster up an ounce of reason to care about my appearance.

The first thing Hannah said was, "What happened to your face?"

"I wiped out while waterskiing." I had concocted the tale to explain my injuries. Nodding to her parents, overwhelmed with nauseous tension, I added, "Bill, Irene, hello."

"You got hurt that badly waterskiing?" Hannah's mother asked. "Goodness, I didn't realize it was such a dangerous activity!"

The ridiculous lie ate up a solid five minutes, during which Hannah poured iced tea while her parents and I settled on the wicker chairs in their sunroom. The view opened out onto the foothills east of town, the Jaspers' property tucked on the outskirts of Jalesville. I exchanged polite words with her parents, gripping the arms of the chair with sweating palms; meanwhile, my consciousness hovered somewhere near the ceiling, observing the scene as though attached by nothing more than a thin, invisible cord.

*Focus, Wy.*

*I can't . . .*

From this surreal distance I watched Hannah pour tea, amber liquid gurgling over melting ice, and arrange the tall glasses and a bowl of lemon wedges on a tray. She was wearing a long yellow sundress patterned with blue flowers and appeared her usual self, tall and whipcord-slim, no traces of pregnancy anywhere on her body.

I tried to imagine her stomach belling outward with a child.

I could not begin to imagine the child itself; I was so deeply in shock over its existence that even attempting to visualize its physical reality sent paroxysms through my mind.

*I don't love its mother. I will never love Hannah the way I should.*

*What if I can't love the child? What if I can't overcome this pain?*

A need to beg forgiveness rose in my chest, but I couldn't form the right words, detached from everything occurring in the sunroom, roughly ten feet below my suspended awareness.

Hannah's parents were discussing living arrangements for the three of us—Hannah, the baby, and me.

"My brother's old house, over on Front Street, you know the place, Wyatt. He'll rent it to you for nothing as soon as you're married," her dad was saying. "It'll be a good starter home, mark my words."

"A January baby," her mother enthused. "Maybe she'll come by Christmas, Hannah, wouldn't that be lovely?"

"January eleventh," Hannah said, and I watched her eyes dart my way as she set the tray on a side table. She handed her mother a tea glass. "That's the due date, so Christmas would be too early."

Despite the sunny day unfolding outside, the air in the Jaspers' sunroom seemed grayish and cobwebbed. I could no longer feel the top of my head or my lower legs.

"It's a two-bedroom," Bill continued, still detailing the house. "We'll help you get the rooms painted and the nursery ready."

I retreated further from the conversation below, drifting upward through the wood-beamed ceiling. For a time, I hung suspended above their roof, fixating on each individual shingle, noting the curled edges of a row along the bottom slope. Eventually I rose higher, slow and syrupy, aiming for the massive inverted bowl of the sky, where it appeared peaceful. A place I could escape.

*Wyatt . . .*

I snapped to attention like a lightning rod, struck by the concentrated intensity of her voice. The force of her need bridged the hundreds of miles between us.

*Millie, I hear you . . .*

*Wy, come back, please come back to me. I didn't even get to say good-bye.*

She was weeping; the devastating sound echoed through my mind, a torture I could do nothing to ease—for either one of us.

*All I want in this world is to come back to you, Millie Jo.*

But my words did not reach her.

*Come back, I need you . . . I hurt so much . . .*

*Come back to me, Wy . . .*

. . .

My eyes opened to the sight of Hannah and her mother bending forward over me. I lay supine on the braided rug in the sunroom, sick and unsettled—Millie had been calling for me. I'd heard her, I was certain. I fought the urge to shove both women aside and flee.

"You passed out." Hannah appeared somewhat shocked. She turned to Irene, whose lips were pressed tightly together, forming a thin, irritated line, and quietly requested, "Mom, can you and Dad give us a minute alone?"

Too dizzy to muster the ability to sit, I remained motionless as Bill and Irene left the house. I listened to their footsteps retreat along the sidewalk, momentarily alone while Hannah ran the kitchen faucet, wetting a cloth for my forehead. She returned and knelt beside me on the rug; when she reached for my face, I caught her wrist, halting its forward motion.

"Tell me the truth," I ordered. "Were you on the pill last May?"

She blinked rapidly; whatever she'd been anticipating, it was not that.

"Yes," she said.

"You swear it?"

She jerked her wrist from my loose grip, tucking wisps of hair behind her ears, as pale as skim milk.

"I swear it," she insisted, holding my gaze.

I turned my head to the side, unable to continue looking at her. I didn't know whether to believe her or not.

"Don't you trust me?" she cried, thumping a fist on my shoulder. "Jesus, Wy, this is as much a shock to me as it is to you! I was considering college this fall, you know. Now that's shot."

"College where?" I demanded.

"Billings."

"What program?"

She cupped her forehead with one hand, aggravated by my questions. I knew the college statement was bullshit. Hannah had never expressed interest in attending. After we graduated high school she had continued working at the bank with her mother; she still lived with her parents. It was the reason she was always in town, hanging out at The Spoke when she knew I was home from Pullman. And like a fool, I'd walked down that road one too many times.

"I don't know what program," she admitted, chewing on her thumbnail, gazing out the windows at the sunny afternoon. "It was just a thought."

I rolled to an elbow and then sat up, vision swimming. My guts were in knots and my perception still seemed off—as though the quality of the outside light was filtered through a gray lens. But I'd regained a measure of strength, intention rising in my heart.

Ignoring my dad's words from last night, I said, "I don't want to get married."

Hannah's lips dropped open. "But what about . . ."

"I'm sorry, I really am. I can't change things as they stand right now. I won't leave you in the lurch, I promise you, Hannah. I'll pay for a house for you, if you want, so you don't have to live here anymore. I'll pay child support, I'll share custody. I will do whatever you ask. I just don't want to get married." There was profound relief in simply speaking the truth.

Her eyes narrowed.

"Did you hear me?" I demanded, on edge with rising impatience to get back to my truck and call Millie.

Hannah suddenly reached and brushed aside my hair, leaning in close to scrutinize my neck.

"Is that a *hickey?*" Shock rode high in the question.

The air between us changed, all at once filled with sharp thorns. I twitched away from her touch and gripped the left side of my neck; I hadn't realized.

"Who gave you that?" she cried.

"It's none of your business." I felt my pulse flapping like a bird beneath the protective curve of my palm.

"Who is she?" The pitch of her voice soared through the roof as she rocketed to her feet, hands in fists. "Are you *seeing* someone?"

I struggled to maintain calm. Despite everything, I had no desire to hurt Hannah's feelings. "I told you it was over between you and me last spring."

"Who is she?" Hannah refused to let up. "Is she from town? Did someone beat you up?" She stabbed a finger in the direction of the welt on my forehead. Blood had pooled around my eye in the wake of the injury and I knew I looked like a degenerate. She insisted, "You didn't get that beat up waterskiing. What did you do, screw someone's wife?"

I stood, with some difficulty; my sense of balance had been destroyed at some point last night and the aftereffects had not yet worn off.

"Where are you going?!"

"Home," I said shortly. "I've said everything I have to say. I'll take care of my child, I swear on my life, but we're not getting married. We're not living in your uncle's rental house."

As fast as the flip of some unseen switch, Hannah began crying—horrible, gulping sobs, tears pouring down her cheeks.

"*Wyatt,*" she sobbed, sinking to one of the wicker chairs. "Don't go, please. I don't know what to do, I'm so scared . . ."

My gut went cold.

"Please don't leave," she wept, reaching toward me. "Please just talk to me.

I'm sorry I yelled at you."

*Please just talk to me . . .*

It was exactly what I'd begged of Millie, not two days ago.

I knelt beside Hannah's chair.

"I'm sorry," I whispered; my innards felt paper-dry, ready to scatter at the slightest breeze.

Hannah gripped my right hand and placed it on her lower belly. She heaved a shuddery sigh before saying, "I know this is a shock. But your child is growing in here, Wy, *our* child. No matter what you think, I didn't expect this either. I'm so scared, I can't do this alone. I want him to have two parents who live together." She searched my face, her own soaked by tears as she whispered, "I don't care if you've been with other girls. I love you. I want you to be my husband."

I could barely swallow past the guilty misery in my throat. Hannah's eyes were wide and pale, like water in a translucent blue glass. She'd always been self-conscious of her light eyelashes and brows against her fair skin. Her hair remained long, as she'd always worn it, reddish-blond, its texture more slippery than satin. The hand clutching mine felt wiry and warm. Beneath my palm, her stomach seemed concave; she was a woman constructed of long planes and few curves. I tried again to picture her figure rounding with pregnancy and found I could not.

I cleared my throat. "I live in Pullman during the school year. It's too far to drive back here every weekday."

Grasping desperately at empty air, like someone falling from a cliff.

Her expression became cautiously hopeful. "I don't mind that. You'll come home on the weekends. I have my job here, and my parents, so I'll keep busy all week. And we can talk at night."

How had this come to pass? It was Millie I was supposed to be talking to every night, Millie's voice breaching the distance, the promise of seeing her at some future date making each day bearable.

I withdrew my hand from Hannah's grasp. "I just need a day to think things through, okay?"

"Okay," she agreed after a tense beat of silence. "I understand that."

"Will your folks be upset if I leave before they get back?" I gestured lamely in the direction Bill and Irene had disappeared.

Hannah shook her head. "No. I mean, they were upset at first, but they like you. They always have."

I had little notion of the protocol for a pregnant woman; I'd clearly not paid enough attention the many times my three sisters-in-law were expecting new babies. "Are you feeling all right, taking vitamins and everything? You're not drinking anymore, are you?"

Angry red streaked her cheekbones. "I haven't since the second I suspected." She paused, tucking loose hair behind her ears, fiddling with its length in a gesture I recognized as hesitant; she was buying a second, probably every bit as uncomfortable as me. More quietly, she added, "I have an appointment in Miles City this Friday, if you want to come with. You could meet the doctor."

I heard myself mumble, "Sure, of course."

Determination replaced all else in her expression and she sat straighter in the wicker chair, indicating my neck. "Who have you been with, Wy?"

The lines of my face hardened, beyond my control; in that moment I felt turned to stone, inside and out.

Hannah waited, her forehead crisscrossed by irritated lines.

I thought, *That's the one question I don't have to answer for you.*

"Is it someone from around here?" she pressed. "That's all I want to know."

But I said only, "I'll call you tomorrow, I promise."

. . .

Back home ten minutes later, I found an abandoned yard, Dad's truck nowhere in sight. I'd concocted a plan as I drove and was glad to find myself unexpectedly alone; cell phone in hand, I glanced toward Marshall and Ruthie's house, but no one appeared to be home there either. My brother's work truck and their 4-by-4 were both absent from the open garage. Before I could question the wisdom, I scrolled to Millie's name and pressed the icon to call her. The sound of the first ring dissolved everything I intended to say once she answered; the mere anticipation of hearing her voice annihilated my composure. Heart thundering, sweat forming along my spine, I waited through two more rings before someone picked up.

"Hello?"

I knew at once it was Camille.

"Hello?" she repeated. "Who is this?"

With every ounce of respect I could muster, I said, "It's Wy. I'd like to talk to Millie, if I might."

A terrible silence pressed back against my left ear.

"Please," I whispered.

"How *dare* you," Camille hissed. "You can't possibly think I'd let you talk to her, after everything you've done."

"Please," I implored. "I am so sorry, you could never know how sorry I am. The last thing I wanted was to leave like that—"

"You left because your girlfriend is pregnant! My daughter is *in love* with you, Wyatt, and you led her to believe *you cared for her*. She's devastated. I've never seen her like this. I will never forgive you for hurting her this way." Seething with anger, Camille's words rained like arrows.

I sank to a crouch, knowing I deserved every puncture.

She had paused to inhale and I hurried to say, "I love Millie with all my heart, nothing I said to her was untrue. Please let me talk to her, Camille, I'm begging you. You don't understand, I'm not going to marry Hannah—"

"I thought you were a better man than this," she interrupted, low and deadly, a new barrage of arrows released. "You made someone pregnant and you have a responsibility to her, whether you want it or not. You think *I* don't understand? I was in Hannah's shoes once upon a time, when I was pregnant with Millie! Her father abandoned us and it was one of the toughest things I've ever been through. I would have sunk under without my family. And you're suggesting you'd shirk the mother of your child and then come crawling back to my daughter? *Not happening*, do you understand me? Never contact her again!"

And with that, she disconnected.

...

Night eventually fell.

Supine and motionless, I stared up at the stars, the sky darker than ink with no visible moon to lend its light. I studied the summertime constellations I'd known from childhood, recalling July evenings lying alongside Dad and my brothers in our sleeping bags, the campfire banked for the night, listening as Dad wove tale after tale, or explained how star patterns had earned their names. How I'd loved camping out, secure between the warmth of Dad and my oldest brother, Garth, wrists stacked beneath the back of my head, belly full of beef jerky and roasted marshmallows. Never questioning whether I was loved or cherished.

For the first time since earlier today, when I'd knelt beside Hannah's chair, I allowed thoughts of the baby to dominate. The knowledge of it pressed like a fresh bruise at the back of my mind, ever-present, but purposely thinking of this child, picturing it as an actual tiny person, living and breathing and growing into a young man or woman, hurt like an open wound.

"Forgive me," I whispered for the countless time since stretching out on the ground; there was no one to hear but I spoke aloud all the same. Asking forgiveness alleviated a fraction of the ache in my heart. "Forgive me, please, forgive me."

I kept hearing Camille's voice telling me that Millie was devastated.

*Millie, I will never forgive myself for hurting you.*

*I can bear my own pain, but not yours.*

*I will never stop loving you.*

*I wish to God that you were carrying my baby, not Hannah.*

*Oh Jesus, I am going to be someone's father.*

*Someone's father.*

*I'm not ready, I'm not prepared . . .*

"Forgive me," I repeated, reeling with disorientation and a profound sense of disconnect, as though I was severed from all I knew as real, and existed now outside my own body. Somewhere nearby I'd tethered Shadow to an iron stake, giving him a long lead so he could graze. The dry heat of the day had disappeared along with the sunset, but I felt beyond the cold, lying parallel to the remnants of the foundation of my ancestors' nineteenth-century home, a structure disassembled in the intervening decades in order to build a new house, the one in which my brothers and I had eventually been raised. I rested my left hand on the crumbling stone, absorbing its familiarity.

*This is where my ancestors lived out their lives.*

*My child will be their newest descendent, the newest Rawley on this land.*

I rubbed my palm over the cool roughness, feeling small bits of rock tumble to the earth in its wake. I tried to imagine a little kid who looked like me, or Hannah, or a combination of the two of us; a child who deserved its parents together under one roof, a child who deserved no less than to be loved and cherished and born to a stable home. What would I teach this child, what would I tell her when she asked me how I'd proposed to her mother? How could I teach my son to marry for love, and no other reason, as had been instilled in me from my earliest memories?

*You have to pretend. For your child's sake, you have to pretend.*

"Forgive me," I whispered again, slinging a forearm over my eyes, blocking out the sight of the distant stars. "Please, forgive me."

# CHAPTER EIGHTEEN

HANNAH AND I WERE MARRIED ON A FRIDAY AF-
ternoon a few weeks later.

The ceremony was short. I remembered that much. It was attended by our extended families and a handful of friends, held in Hannah's church. A calm sun shone from sunrise to sunset, the landscape burnished with approaching autumn. My third-year classes would start in Pullman next week. I wore a rental tux, along with Quinn, who I'd asked to stand up as my best man. Hannah had just begun to show. I couldn't bring myself to admit, later, that I would not recall the expression on her face, the words of our vows, what color her bouquet was or even if she wore a veil. I saw only the smooth bulge between her hipbones, the growing baby whose existence had brought about this day. I felt once-removed from reality, a sensation that rendered my face and limbs wooden and jerky, like those of a puppet.

August twentieth, my wedding day.

Marsh, Ruthie, and Dad remained the only members of my family who understood the real reason behind my numbness as I stood before the altar with yellow sun spilling at my feet, stupidly fantasizing that the woman who appeared at the back of the church on her father's arm was Millie. Garth, Sean, and Quinn realized I was marrying Hannah because I'd gotten her pregnant, but they knew nothing about what had taken place in Minnesota. Ruthie assured me that she would never tell anyone, even her sisters—especially Camille, who already despised me, and I understood why. I deserved to be despised; shit, I despised myself. I hadn't even told the guys I lived with during the school year about my wedding. I figured that next week, once we were all back in Pullman, was soon enough.

After the service, Hannah's parents hosted a reception at an upscale restaurant in Miles City. Had this been a day of true celebration, the reception would have been held at The Spoke, and Marshall and Case, along with Garth, would have played music late into the night. I would have kept Millie in my arms on the dance floor for the entire night, everyone else be damned. I would have told her over and over how much I loved her, how grateful I was that she was mine—that I would never take a single day of our lives together for granted. I would kiss her soft lips, her taste as sweet and familiar as anything I'd ever known, and she would tuck closer like she always did, her beautiful hazel eyes shining with the promise of our wedding night and every night thereafter; shining with love for me, and no other.

*I'm so happy, Wy*, she would say as we swayed to the music.

*Millie Jo Rawley*, I would marvel in return. *My sweet love, my wife.*

Hannah was talkative at our head table, chatting with her cousin, who'd been the maid of honor, and her friends who wandered over with cocktails in hand, all of them admiring the decorations Hannah and her mother had chosen. Their words rippled over me like currents in a stream. No one seemed to pay much attention to the fact that I'd been throwing back booze like a fucking sailor on leave—no one, that is, except my brother. Quinn, seated to my left, had already advised that I lay off unless I wanted to get carted out of my own wedding reception in a wheelbarrow.

"Wy, come on." Quinn was a person of few words but I heard the mild reprimand in his tone, all the same, as I snagged yet another champagne flute from a circulating server.

"I got it," I muttered, gulping the sickly-sweet liquid, in no mood to be lectured even as I heard the slur in my words.

My brother sent a pointed glance toward Hannah, roughly ten feet and several thousand miles away. He lowered his voice. "She won't be happy if you can't walk out of here on your own, bud."

I knew he was only concerned; of all of us, Quinn's personality was the most even-keel. He was seven years older than me and had been the youngest until I came along, but his calm nature and ability to listen sometimes made him seem even older than Garth.

"I can . . . walk," I muttered, reaching to push back from the table to prove it and almost tipping my chair over; Quinn stopped me from making a complete fool of myself, steadying the chair with a quick, discreet motion. I looked his way, my head sloshy and probably about eighty-proof. I marveled, "It jus' hit me. *I* was a whoopsie-baby. 'Member when you guys used to call me that? And now *I'm having* a whoopsie-baby . . . whatta you know about *that* . . ."

Quinn would have yanked me up by the scruff if it wouldn't have caused an unforgiveable scene; as it was, his expression was proof enough of his shock. He hauled me upright by an elbow and proceeded to lead me through the restaurant, all the way to the main entrance. Once outside, he didn't stop walking until we were safely hidden from view in a small, grassy alley on the west side of the building. A bench was situated there, in an oblong patch of shade, and Quinn plunked me down on it.

"You are being one hell of an asshole right now, little bro," he said.

I knew he was right but I just sat there and shook my head, slowly, like a wind-up toy losing steam.

Quinn crouched down; he was the tallest of us at six foot three. He rested his forearms on his thighs and regarded me with unmistakable sympathy, speaking quietly this time, all sense of judgment washed away.

"I remember the day Dad and Mom brought you home from the hospital. The snow had finally let up, it was an outright blizzard the night you were born, I remember it perfectly. You came early and Dad was trying to hide how worried he was when he brought us to Aunt Julie's, but we all knew. None of us slept that night, just waiting for Dad to call."

Quinn paused for a moment, gripping my shoulder and continuing the story instead of commenting on the tears leaking down my face.

"Dad finally called around five in the morning, almost breakfast time. He was so happy, everything was all right, and we had a new baby brother. Aunt Julie made us stacks of blueberry pancakes. We were cheering and laughing, and saying you were supposed to be a girl. When they got to come home the next day, you know what Mom said?"

I buried my face behind both hands, shoulders heaving.

Quinn finished the story, which I knew well from its many retellings.

"Mom said that you were our gift, our little angel. She doted on you, Wy, even if you don't remember it like we do. You were her baby. You may have been a surprise but you sure as hell were no accident. There *are* no accidents, bro. Sometimes it just takes a while to figure out why we have to go through tough times to understand that."

I couldn't lift my face, locked in a stranglehold of emotion.

Quinn remained hunkered near my knees; he suddenly said, "Guess you saw us head out."

Marsh and Ruthie were there; I felt Ruthie's arm slid over my hunched shoulders.

Marshall said, "Let's get you out of here. I'll gather up the guys and we'll pretend we're taking you out for a round of barhopping, okay?"

"Where are you taking him?" Ruthie wondered aloud. "He's in no shape . . ."

"We'll get him to their house over on Front Street," Marshall said, naming the rental property I would live in with Hannah and our child, presumably for the rest of my life. "I'll take the blame for letting him get so drunk that he passed out, maybe take a little heat off him." He paused, lowering his voice as if this would somehow magically prevent me from hearing. "I suppose there's no way Hannah's not going to be angry, huh?"

"Well, it's not exactly any woman's first choice of a wedding night," Ruthie murmured.

The three of them helped me to Quinn's truck; I was so drunk my head lolled forward, my chin bumping my chest. I knew I would be vomiting violently within the next quarter hour.

Ruthie maneuvered my legs out of the way so she could shut the passenger door. She added, to Marshall, "I'll handle damage control around here. Tish and Netta will help me."

Marsh said, "I'll see you at home, love, don't worry about us."

But I knew she would worry no matter how sincere his words of comfort. Ruthie knew as well as I did that this day marked, for me, the beginning of a steep uphill climb.

# CHAPTER NINETEEN

MY EYELIDS PARTED WITH DIFFICULTY, AS though glued shut at some point in the night hours. The view directly before my nose was dim and reddish; I lay sprawled on my belly, head and left arm dangling over the edge of a mattress, with no idea of the time or where in the hell I was. My mouth tasted like week-old shit. I tried to roll over but the throbbing in my skull inhibited movement. I exhaled, ribs aching, struggling to recall the previous evening—and one fact took sudden precedence.

*You're married.*

The words penetrated the haze like a discharged gun.

*Yesterday was your wedding.*

*Hannah is your wife.*

*Your wife.*

"Wy?" came her whispered voice, as though the thought had conjured her. I felt the mattress shift as she rolled my direction. "How are you feeling?"

I tried to answer but there wasn't enough moisture in my mouth to form words. Pins and needles radiated through my dangling, upraised left arm. I made a loose fist to dispel the numbness, feeling the weight of the gold band around my third finger.

Hannah put her palms on my back, leaning to plant a kiss on my shoulder. I realized, with a start, that I was naked other than my underwear. I had no memory of anything that occurred after Quinn and Marsh helped me inside this house at some point yesterday evening. I felt reprehensible, in more ways than one.

"Good morning," she whispered gleefully, in sharp contrast. "It's our first day married."

I licked my dry lips.

"Your brothers brought you home," she explained, though I still hadn't managed to speak. "They apologized for getting you so loaded. I know it's not your fault." She ran a hand along my spine, cupping my ass and gently squeezing. "Do you need some water?"

I croaked, "Yes, please."

Hannah disappeared, leaving me alone on the bed; I realized, belatedly, that this dim space was the bedroom in her uncle's rental house, a place I'd visited twice since July, both times with Hannah's parents in tow. The bed was queen-sized, shoved beneath the only window in the room, over which dark red curtains hung, blocking out the midday sun; I hated the subsequent burgundy shade tinting the air. I clenched my teeth as I sat up, jamming both hands through my hair, wildly scouring my memory for a clue as to last night's events. I had no memory of undressing, or sex of any kind, unable to imagine that I'd come close to getting hard in such a drunken state.

*You should be ashamed of yourself.*

I had married my child's mother because it was the right thing to do and I understood that I must learn to love her; Hannah deserved no less and I meant to try.

*God help me, I can't do this . . .*

*You have to, there is no longer another choice.*

Hannah and I hadn't exchanged any true physical contact since I returned from Minnesota other than kissing yesterday, at the wedding service. Earlier in the month, I'd accompanied her to an appointment with her obstetrician, during which Hannah underwent her first ultrasound; we returned to Jalesville with a roll of sepia-tinted images. I had examined those pictures until my eyes all but crossed, turning the images sideways and upside down, studying the placenta and the umbilical cord, silently identifying the baby's developing spine and femurs, organs and brain stem, marveling that these grainy images were of my child. My son or daughter. It was too soon to determine gender.

"Here you go."

The mattress sank as Hannah returned from the kitchen, handing me a glass of water. Other than our clothes and a few personal items, most everything in our possession had been borrowed or gifted to us, right down to dinner plates and towels. I had never before noticed Hannah's predilection for red things; our sheets and pillowcases were a deep scarlet, and I found the effect of so much red unsettling.

"Thanks," I whispered, accepting the water, gulping it down. I realized the need to apologize; no doubt Hannah had been angry, let alone embarrassed, last night. There was no way to sugarcoat the fact that I'd ditched her at our wedding. I tried to clear the rasp from my voice before speaking. "I'm sorry I left early. I didn't mean to leave you there alone. What time did you get here?"

"Around ten. You were already in bed, snoring. It's all right, I know your brothers are a bad influence, I don't blame *you*."

It took a second for her words to penetrate.

"A bad influence?" I repeated, somewhat confused by this statement; maybe I'd misunderstood. "Why would you say that? You know they're not."

Watching me closely, Hannah hurried to say, "I mean, they probably just thought it was funny to get you loaded, it's probably what they did to each other on their wedding days."

My brothers would never have dreamed of drinking to excess on their respective wedding days—but then again, their circumstances had been worlds different than mine. Even though I'd inadvertently skipped out on half of my own reception, I didn't feel as though I'd missed a thing. Sitting at a fancy restaurant in Miles City, listening to piped-in classical music while guests murmured at remote tables was not my idea of a celebration. Hannah and her mother had planned every aspect of the wedding while I strayed to the periphery, swept along in a current outside my control. I realized my attitude must change, that I had to take charge. I could not be a passive observer in my own life.

*But it's not the life you want, it's so fucking unfair—*

I shut out those thoughts and turned more fully in Hannah's direction; she was wearing a short robe that gaped open, revealing her otherwise bare body beneath. It wasn't as though I'd never seen her naked before, but it created a strained intimacy between us, a forced acknowledgment of our new status as a married couple. My stomach pitched as the water landed there and I prayed she wasn't expecting sex just now. I knew, without a doubt, that I would be unable. Desire seemed dead inside my body.

But no such luck.

Hannah plucked the water glass from my hand and set it aside, linking her arms around my neck as she murmured, "We didn't get a chance last night, but you can make it up to me this morning."

I turned my face to avoid her mouth, mumbling, "My breath is really bad, let me brush my teeth . . ."

"Hurry back!" she commanded.

I ignored this request and hid out in the shower, scalding my skin, bending forward at the waist, resting my forehead on the slick, dreamsicle-orange tiles, attempting to convince myself that I belonged here in this house, with Hannah. She was hardly a stranger; I'd known her most of my life and we had dated in high school, for fuck's sake, but I felt so horribly alone and it scared the shit out of me. I'd never experienced such disorientation. Water poured over my skull and flowed down my body, and I closed my eyes, relenting to need, imagining that Millie stood just outside the shower stall. I pictured her pressing both palms to the damp glass and I lifted my hands, aligning them with hers; only a flimsy piece of cheap, rippled glass separated us.

*You married her*, Millie whispered, without accusation. I heard only the razor edge of her pain. *I can't believe you married her.*

*I had no choice. This isn't what I want. I would give anything if you were here with me, Millie Jo. Anything at all.*

*There is always a choice. And you chose someone else.*

*She's pregnant. She's carrying my child. What else could I do?*

But Millie did not answer, fading softly away. My fingers curled against the steam condensing on the glass, becoming fists. A stranger's hands, the left with its unfamiliar gold ring.

*Please don't go—*

Behind the screen of my closed eyes I saw Millie's face exactly as it had looked when I entered her body for the first time, her beautiful eyes locked on mine, full of need and trust and love. So very much love—far more than I deserved, as life had promptly proven. Again I felt her surrounding me, felt the hot silk of her skin, tasted her mouth and belly and the slippery sweetness between her legs. The pale orange of the shower stall became the deep orange of the little tent we'd shared. I gave over to remembrance; gripping firmly with a soapy hand, I came in less than a minute. Gasping and shuddering, I bent my head in the shower spray, wanting to die even as I knew how much I had to live.

. . .

Days passed into weeks and the sick, murky haze refused to recede from my perception. I battled the constant urge to retreat into sleep, only to be plagued by nightly insomnia. I'd drift into fitful stretches of unconsciousness, then startle awake with two hours to go before dawn, heart slamming, drenched in cold sweat. My third-year classes began in earnest and I lived during the week in the off-campus rental property that I'd found during my first year living in Pullman; as a Montana resident, my first year in the DVM program had taken place at the university in Bozeman, before I transferred to Washington State for my second year. My roommates were two fellow veterinary students, Kyle and Joey Quick, twin brothers from Yakima.

"What the hell, you're *married* now?" Kyle had asked the first night we were back in our shared apartment, settled around our battered kitchen table with its mismatched chairs and the charred circle where Joey had once missed the ashtray and ground out his cigarette on the tabletop.

"When did this happen? Why weren't we invited?" Joey followed up before I could offer even the most pathetic excuse for not letting them know.

I muttered, "I'm sorry, you guys."

Kyle flicked a finger against the ring on mine. "Where's your wife, why aren't you living with her? Is she a student?"

We had all rolled into town earlier that afternoon, finding the tiny, furnished apartment stale and dusty and otherwise untouched, exactly as we'd left it in May. The last time I'd been in the company of Kyle and Joey the mood had been merry, second-year finals complete and a group of us drunk and exhilarated, crowding into a local tattoo shop with beers in hand. If someone had told me what would transpire between that night and this one, I would never have believed it. I still couldn't; I'd left Hannah behind in Jalesville with a feeling of undeniable relief. Driving west toward Pullman felt like a jailbreak. Even the looming threat of fall semester of third year—rumored to be the most difficult in the program—was nothing compared to the reality of waking up alongside a woman I did not love.

I looked between the Quick brothers, drinking beer and eating pizza as they sat waiting expectantly for an explanation. They were identical twins whose personalities were so different I had never once confused the two of them since our initial introduction. They were competitive and driven but very protective of each other; Joey was gay and had yet to reveal this fact to their parents. Both had become trusted friends in the past year and I was glad to see them. I felt far more at home in our rundown, tobacco-scented apartment than I did in the rental house on Front Street. I pictured Hannah there, over eleven hours away and alone this week; she told me she would call her parents if she needed anything.

*First things first*, I thought.

"You guys remember me talking about Hannah Jasper, my old girlfriend?"

They nodded in unison.

"I got her pregnant." I released a slow sigh, hunching my shoulders as though expecting one of them to aim a punch at my head.

They shared a brief, intense glance in the way of siblings, exchanging an entire conversation in about two seconds before looking back at me, tempering their surprise, I could tell.

"That's big news," Kyle said at last. "I take it this was unexpected?"

Joey set aside his beer; perceptive as always, and blunt, he recognized, "They made you get married, didn't they? You're in total shock, I can see it in your eyes."

Instead of answering, I drank deeply of my beer, draining the bottle.

"When's the baby due?" Joey asked.

"January eleventh," I rasped; the alcohol had momentarily stripped my vocal cords. "Hannah works in Jalesville and her family is there, so it doesn't make sense for her to live here all week, where she doesn't know anyone."

"You two broke up after high school, right? What gives? You've been hooking up since?" Kyle used his beer bottle to nudge my shoulder. "Without wrapping up your johnson, apparently."

"It happened last May, the night I got home from school."

They waited silently for further explanation and I recognized the generosity of their listening. I debated telling them about Millie, but was too afraid I'd fall apart.

I admitted, "I'm scared shitless. I didn't want to get married. It was the last thing I was ready for, but I was raised to be accountable, to do the right thing. And you're right, my dad and her parents were pretty insistent." I gripped my forehead, squeezing hard for an endless moment. "A kid deserves both his parents in the same house."

"I don't disagree, but this is a huge issue, Wy. This is your *life*. Does Hannah know you didn't want to get married?" Joey pressed.

"She knows." I felt lower than ever as I admitted this fact, staring at the tabletop like a kid in the middle of a lecture, unable to meet their sympathetic gazes.

Kyle scooted his chair backward about five feet and opened the fridge, collecting each of us another round.

"And?" Joey prompted, not about to let me avoid explaining.

"And she didn't care in the end. She loves me, even if I don't deserve it. She's trying really hard, planning everything for the baby, and I know I should be excited. But it doesn't seem real yet."

"It will once the kid shows up," Kyle predicted. "Will you still live here during spring semester?"

I finally looked up at them. "That's the plan, at least for now. I'm going to talk to my advisor tomorrow morning, see if I can possibly be assigned residencies closer to home."

"I respect what you're saying about kids needing both parents under one roof, I think that's honorable of you." Joey shifted position, settling his feet on the adjacent empty chair. "But what do you mean about not 'deserving it'? Why wouldn't you deserve Hannah's love?"

"Because I don't love *her*. What kind of piece of shit doesn't love the mother of his child?"

When I closed my eyes, I didn't see my pregnant wife. All I saw was Millie. I saw her in the bright sunshine, riding her horse alongside Shadow and me through the foothills; I saw us holding each other close in Flickertail Lake as rain coursed over our heads; I felt her safe in my arms and pressing ever closer, as though she couldn't get enough of my touch, the orange canvas walls of a little tent surrounding us in our finite heaven. I found it impossible to accept that the amount of time I'd been allowed with her was only a handful of days, barely a flicker of an eyelash in the whole of my life.

"Hold up." Kyle lifted one hand like a traffic cop, rising from the table. "Shit, I didn't think I'd have to break out the hard stuff quite yet, but this conversation requires more than beer."

"You're *not* a piece of shit, Wy, don't get melodramatic on us," Joey said, as Kyle reappeared from their room clutching a bottle of bourbon; he tossed a crumpled pack of smokes Joey's way.

If only they knew what a piece of shit I really was; the only way I'd been able to force a hard-on in the past week, my first week of married life, was to leave the bedside lamp off and picture Millie instead of Hannah. I felt so wretched afterward that I'd been unable to meet my own gaze in the mirror. Not only was it unjust to Hannah on many levels, but the act served to slice through the sacred memories of everything I'd shared with Millie. My heart felt like wreckage.

"Here, bro." Kyle slid a bourbon on the rocks my way.

Joey fixed his earnest gaze on my avoidant one, exhaling smoke through both nostrils as he said, "Plenty of people get married for the sake of their kids. I'm not saying it's the most ideal reason out there, but it's the most honorable one. If you're trying to be a good father, you did the right thing. I mean, there's really no greater thing you can be, in my modest opinion."

"And think how many more couples *stay* together for the sake of their kids. I don't have an exact percentage but I'll bet you it's more than half, our folks included." Kyle rejoined us, settling the bottle in the middle of the table. He sipped his drink with an appreciative sigh before lofting it high. "Here's to third year, boys."

"And fatherhood," Joey chimed in, as we clinked glasses.

I drained the booze in a clean gulp.

"Just keep us in the loop, Wy. We're your best friends," Joey said, overstating the last two words with a touch of humor. He squeezed my shoulder before throwing back his shot.

"Thanks for being here, you guys." I meant it, even in my present terrible state of mind.

"Hey, we got your back, you know we do." Kyle poured round two as if we didn't have alarms set for dawn, and their combined support and the welcome oblivion of the alcohol pulled me through to morning.

# CHAPTER TWENTY

I MEANT TO TRY. I TRULY DID.

But as the months passed, I found my bitterness increasing like a cancer, sapping my will to continue moving forward.

Lying awake through the endless dark of those winter nights, I would think, *You are an ungrateful asshole, acting like your life is so bad. Think of all the good things you're neglecting to consider.*

Not the least of which was a healthy son, growing a little more each day; we had discovered this news at an appointment in October. The closest moments I shared with Hannah were a direct result of the baby. Sitting on our couch with both my hands cupped on the firm, basketball-roundness of her belly inspired the only true tenderness I felt toward her. She was delighted by the way he kicked and moved; he was always most active just before bed. She pored over name books, painted the nursery a soft denim-blue, and installed a crib and dressing set along with the help of her parents. Because I was only home on the weekends, the house had become Hannah's unchallenged domain. She chose paint colors and window fixtures and furnishings, and I said nothing except versions of "That looks great."

Despite the escalating wail inside my head, the one that begged me daily to contact Millie, I did not. Doing so would solve nothing, I realized, but so much remained unsaid between us. And there were so many new things I wanted to tell her, like the fact that Tuck had secured the proper zoning and ground was scheduled to be broken for the rehabilitation center. Had fate taken a different path, I knew Millie would rejoice with me over this news, the sort of thing we would have discussed every night. I wanted to share with her even the most mundane facts, like how my classes were progressing or what I thought about something I'd come across in required reading. Craziest of all, I longed every day to tell her about my son, whose due date was rapidly approaching.

In turn, I wanted to hear about her days and nights and every last moment in between. I missed her face and her laugh and her voice; I missed *her* so terribly it was a constant ache. Time had healed nothing—time only served to highlight exactly what a toll living without her demanded. Searching online revealed nothing, as I suspected; Millie had said she thought social media was a waste of time.

But I tried anyway. Late at night, in my bed in Pullman with a laptop open over my thighs, I tried. I found Rae with no problem and scrolled obsessively through her dozens of pictures in an attempt to spot Millie, so far with no luck. I stopped myself a hundred times from sending Rae a message, begging for any news. But I couldn't; I knew it was dishonorable even to consider. I couldn't risk hurting Millie more than I already had.

Though it almost killed me to admit, I knew it was best to sever all connection.

. . .

Winter break between semesters stretched like a featureless desert. Without the ability to escape to Pullman, I had no convenient excuse for prolonged absence from the house on Front Street, and the strain between Hannah and me increased with each passing day. I had grown all too acclimated to our weekend relationship and felt useless without the distraction of nightly reading and studying. I missed the easy camaraderie of Kyle's and Joey's company in the evenings. At the very least, they were interested in hearing what I talked about.

*Nothing is going to change unless you try harder,* I told myself a dozen times a day. *You have to make an effort. Hannah is your wife and she loves you. She is carrying your son and they both need you. It doesn't matter that she isn't excited about the rehabilitation center, or that she doesn't want to come with you to family dinners.*

To some extent I understood that Hannah's anticipation over the rehabilitation center, which Tuck and Netta had recently named Bitterroot Ranch, was bound to be less focused than mine. She did not intend to work there, nor was she particularly interested in listening to me talk about my classes or fieldwork, which I had come to realize in the months since our marriage. But the family dinners were another matter entirely. My dad and Aunt Julie had taken turns hosting Sunday dinner for the entire extended family since before I was born. Hannah had accompanied me plenty of times back in high school, and she knew how much it meant to me to attend. But I had come to suspect something I'd never before noticed about her—she didn't like my family. It was innocuous at first, a comment here or there expressing displeasure about one of my brothers, or Dad.

"Clark is very controlling of you, isn't he?" she asked one Sunday afternoon in November. "Always expecting you to spend every last minute with him when you're only home for two days a week."

Dad didn't expect that, but Hannah somehow refused to see this; she believed her own opinions without question.

Or, "I can't stand how your brothers and their wives just show up here on Saturday nights without calling first. We wouldn't show up at *their* houses without calling."

"They're my family, they just want to say 'hi' and hang out with us a little," I contradicted that particular night, embarrassed after telling Garth, Becky, Sean, and Jessie it was a "bad time" for them to stop by. I couldn't understand why Hannah resented them so badly. They had left without pressing the issue, but I saw the puzzled look in my brothers' expressions and I could tell that Becky and Jessie, who had both grown up in Jalesville and known me since birth, wanted to ask what was wrong.

"*I'm* your family," Hannah had countered immediately, covering her belly with both hands. "The baby and I are your family. You should worry about what we think, not *them.*"

I couldn't understand why she always phrased it that way, constantly pitting herself against Dad and my brothers, and never without an undertone of challenge.

Guilt motivated so very many of my actions I could hardly remember a time when I was without the weight of its presence. Guilt prevented me from talking about my classes at home, or attending Sunday dinners with my family, and prompted me to ask my brothers to give me a quick heads-up before stopping by on the weekend. I tried to be sensitive to Hannah's point of view; she was an only child and unaccustomed to the chaos that typically characterized my family's get-togethers. And then one day we crossed a line and had our first real fight. Not just a petty disagreement about something trivial; this one was a true manifestation of repressed anger.

Ruthie called me a week before Christmas to make sure Hannah and I planned to come to dinner at their house on Christmas Eve.

"For sure we do," I said, grateful to hear my sister-in-law's voice. I missed her and Marshall, not only because I loved them dearly, but because there was a sick holdout part of my soul that longed to be around Ruthie because she reminded me of Millie. She was Millie's aunt, after all, and her eyes were the same clear, beautiful topaz; her brown hair was long and curly. Even Ruthie's smile was similar, and though it hurt like a double-bladed knife to see the resemblance, I also craved it like a drug. And I knew Ruthie would answer anything I dared to ask about Millie.

"How are you doing?" she wondered aloud, as if sensing my thoughts to some extent. Since the advent of fall semester, I'd had little chance to talk to Ruthie; at least, to her alone.

"All right. I'm just making us dinner," I said, my free hand falling still. I was in the middle of stirring chili on the stove, intending to have dinner ready when Hannah arrived home from work, any minute now. I'd made cornbread and chicken chili, two of her favorites, determined to put forth more effort.

"Good," Ruthie said softly. "You two must be getting excited. Marsh was saying you have the nursery all set to go. I have about a million baby clothes to pass along at Christmas. Trust me, you won't have to buy a thing for the first two years at least."

"Thank you." I heard the back door open. "Hey, Hannah's home. I'll tell her we're happy to come next Friday. Can we bring anything?"

Hannah entered the kitchen behind me as Ruthie said, "No, just yourselves. We can't wait to see you, you've been such a stranger."

"We'll be there," I promised. "Bye. Love you."

"I love you too, honey," Ruthie said before disconnecting.

I said over my shoulder, "Hey there. Welcome home. You hungry?"

Hannah did not reply, and I turned more fully her way, surprised to observe that her face appeared pale and set above her bright red scarf. A pulse of concern caught me unaware and I hurried to her side.

"Are you all right?"

She sidestepped my outstretched hand, demanding, "Who were you just talking to?"

"Ruthie," I said, mystified by Hannah's unmistakably hostile tone. "She invited us to Christmas Eve dinner at their house."

Hannah's lips compressed. "Why would you tell her you love her?"

Stunned that she'd ask such a bizarre thing, I had no idea how to respond.

She mistook my silence and snapped, "Does *Marshall* know you say that sort of thing to his wife?"

I located my voice. "They're my family. Of course Marsh knows I love Ruthie."

"She was pretty quick to say it back. Why would she call you 'honey,' anyway?"

"Are you crazy?" Too shocked to reconsider the question, I could do little but stare blankly at my wife.

Hannah unzipped her coat with terse movements; beneath it, she wore a baggy sweater dress and black tights. Her due date was less than a month away and she moved somewhat awkwardly as she stalked to the fridge and flung it open.

"Please answer me." I kept my voice level with effort.

"Answer what?" Hannah threw back. "Whether or not I'm crazy? Real nice, Wy."

"I want to know why in God's name you'd ask such a crazy question about Ruthann."

Extracting a jar of iced tea, Hannah slammed the door and faced off with me. "Because I can't stand her, that's why! I never could. She's way too involved in our business, especially yours. I think if Marshall knew how interested she was in you, he'd have a thing or two to say."

I could not stomach another word. "Hannah, *Jesus Christ.* Are you hearing yourself? I refuse to let you talk about Ruthie or Marsh like that. They would do just about anything for us and you know it. And for fuck's sake, they have one of the happiest marriages I know."

"As compared to what, compared to *yours?*" she hissed, jutting her chin in my direction; two slashes of angry red color stained her cheeks. "And where do you get off, defending another woman to me?"

"Quit twisting things around! You're making ridiculous accusations and you know it."

"We're not going to their house on Christmas Eve," she announced, abruptly changing tone. "I already told my parents we'd come over there."

"You can go to your parents' house; I'm going to my brother's," I told her, stubbornness overriding sense. "I miss them. I've hardly seen them since school started."

"No, you're not! You're coming with me. It's time we started our own traditions instead of always blindly following your *father's.* It's not fair to me." And without another word she burst into loud, messy tears.

Dumbfounded by her attitude, not to mention the extremity of her fury, I found myself speechless yet again. And then I smelled burning chili and turned back to the stove, clicking off the element. I felt sick and shaky inside, like I'd ridden too long on a ride at the county fair, a ride I was helpless to exit. I had no idea what to do or say next.

"You don't even give a shit that I'm so upset, do you?" she shrieked, intensifying my unease. Since our wedding, I had come to learn that when Hannah didn't get her way in any situation, no matter how trivial, she sobbed and carried on until I relented. Tears poured down her cheeks as she screamed, "I'm standing here crying and you're stirring the fucking soup!"

"Hannah . . ." I began, but she interrupted.

"I live here all week without you and then you ignore me when you are home! Do you ever stop to think about how *I* feel, you selfish asshole?"

"'Selfish'?" I repeated, anger rising hotly in my chest.

Wild-eyed, she yelled, "You don't care about me at all, you never tell *me* you love me unless I say it first, just Ruthann. Well, screw her!"

Guilt diluted the heat of my anger; Hannah had me by the nuts there, no denying.

She railed, "And you just stand there, not saying a word! Do you love me, or don't you?"

My teeth came together on their edges. "Hannah, I . . ."

"You what?!"

"We're married, aren't we?" My voice had gone as hoarse as an old man's.

Crying hard, she fled the kitchen. I heard our bedroom door slam, then lock.

I followed directly after. "Hey, listen to me, I'm sorry. I didn't mean to hurt your feelings."

"Go away!" she raged. "I want to be alone."

"Please just open the door so we can talk."

"Leave me alone, *you asshole!*"

And so I left.

# CHAPTER TWENTY-ONE

I COULD HAVE DRIVEN TO DAD'S, OR AUNT JU-lie's, or any of my brothers' houses, not to mention my cousins'. They would have made time for me on this chilly winter night, I knew without question, would have listened and sympathized, offered kind advice, and fixed me a plate of whatever they were eating for dinner. My family loved me—I was goddamn lucky to have them—and I had shut them out for months now, at my wife's request. I did not believe any of the things Hannah flung my way when she was upset—that my father was controlling, or my brothers overstepping, or that it was inappropriate to tell Ruthie I loved her. Nor did I believe that Hannah and the baby were the only ones I should consider family simply because we were married and Hannah didn't like my dad, my brothers, or their wives.

But I was too ashamed to retreat to any of their homes. Shit, I was terrified. What if I cracked and confessed to all the apprehensions crawling under my skin like insects? Clutching the steering wheel in both hands, the words I wanted to say coursed, panic-stricken, through my head.

*Dad, please don't make me go back there. Can I just stay here tonight?*

*That house on Front Street is not home. I'm scared it will never feel like home.*

*Hannah is like some stranger. I never know what to expect from her.*

*She hates our whole family. Did you guys notice that when we dated in high school? How did I never see this about her before now?*

*She's going to have my baby, but it still doesn't seem real yet.*

Shame had me in a stranglehold. I was a grown man, not a child. I could face what was required of me—

*But what if I can't . . .*

The Spoke appeared on the right as I cruised along Main, driving with no purpose other than avoiding the rental house on Front Street. The Spoke was our family's perpetual gathering spot, and I could hide out there for a few hours, at least. Pushing through the front doors of my aunt's bar served to calm my nerves, despite the rowdy scene of a typical Friday night; important events in our family had been held here since long before I was born and the space was cheerful, lit by warm neon and bare-bulb string lights, familiar in every way. A local father and son were onstage with their fiddles; plenty of people were dancing and clapping along. I spied Lee circulating the crowd and Netta behind the bar. I hoped maybe I'd find Tuck hanging out at the bar counter, as he sometimes did when Netta worked. The thought of talking about Bitterroot Ranch buoyed my spirits.

"Hey there, Wy," my cousin said as I claimed a barstool. "Long time no see."

I tried for a smile. "I've got a bit on my plate, just now."

Netta was no one's fool; the older she got, the more she resembled Aunt Julie, in both personality and looks. She rested her palms on the gleaming wooden bar, searching my face as if for clues. She finally muttered, "I'd say that's an understatement. What'll you have, hon?"

I considered for a second. "A whiskey sour sounds about right."

Netta made no comment but she kept her eyes on me a little too long before gathering up a glass, clearly communicating that she knew something was up.

"Is Tuck around?" I asked as she slid the drink my way.

"He's out at his folks' place just now. You want me to call him, have him swing by?" Netta knew how much I enjoyed talking to Tuck. The plans for Bitterroot would be in full swing as soon as the snow began melting—and I could hardly wait.

I did, but I said, "No, that's all right. He sounds busy."

Netta couldn't resist any longer. "What's Hannah up to tonight?"

"She's resting." I downed the drink in two swallows after replying, no longer meeting her gaze.

Netta absorbed this statement, continuing to study me until I started to feel like a little kid, all but squirming. Lee saved me, elbowing up to the bar alongside my stool, holding her empty drink tray out of the way.

"Hi, Wy," she drawled cheerily, planting a kiss on my cheek; her breath smelled like red wine. "What're you doing here?"

I held up my empty glass.

Lee grinned at her older sister. "Netta, get this boy another round!"

It was busy enough that my cousins couldn't spend too much time interrogating or teasing me, both of which they loved to do, and had since I was a kid. The first two whiskey sours unhinged the tension in my spine and I found my way to one of the few free chairs left in the main room. I plunked down with a group who had graduated with my brother Sean and his wife Jessie, and they welcomed me with drunken magnanimity. The music was upbeat and fast-paced, the mood in the bar boisterous. I could have blamed my choice to get loaded like a cargo train on numerous factors, including my fight with Hannah, but in the end it was my own fault—like so very many things were these days. The next thing I knew, Ruthie was standing beside my chair, her puffy winter coat folded over her arms.

"Hey, Ruthie!" I was so glad to see her. I tried to stand in order to give her a hug, but failed.

Everyone at the crowded table offered drunkenly enthusiastic greetings. Kelly Anne Collins, sitting to my right, reached and squeezed my thigh as Ruthie was momentarily snagged in conversation, then kept her hand settled on my leg. Kelly Anne was Sean's age, somewhere around eight years older than me, recently divorced. Probably I should have switched seats, or even left the bar, after she started dropping hints about an hour ago, whispering things in my ear about us maybe getting out of here. I shifted so her hand was displaced, but she scooted her chair immediately closer; her breath was harsh with booze, practically flammable.

Ruthie turned her attention back to me and I stared up at her in silence, absorbing the expression on her lovely face, which communicated her concern. In that moment, with the bar lights glowing and the candle lantern on the table flickering, Ruthie looked younger than her age and more like Millie than ever. Her curly hair fell all over her shoulders and her green eyes shone with hints of gold; her mouth was somber. Without warning, tears stabbed at the backs of my eyeballs. I wondered how she'd known where to find me, and why Marshall wasn't standing here instead of his wife, ready to drag me home by an ear.

Ruthie leaned closer, politely ignoring Kelly Anne. "You ready to go, Wy?"

"You wanna sit?" I invited. Never mind that there weren't any empty chairs.

"Not just now. Let's get you home, how about that?"

"No, thanks," I muttered.

Ruthie tried another tactic. "Why don't you come back to our house, have a cup of coffee with Marshall and me?"

"How'd you find me?" I squinted up at her as if this might minimize the undulations across my vision.

"Netta called me," she explained quietly, her eyes flickering to Kelly Anne, whose hand was back on my jeans, stroking up and down, uncomfortably close to my crotch.

It wasn't that I'd encouraged Kelly Anne's attention, but explaining this was beyond my capability just now.

Ruthie's patience began to wear; she shifted her coat to the opposite arm, overenunciating her words. "She was going to call Hannah, but *thank goodness* she didn't."

Kelly Anne, listening with rapt attention, snorted at this statement. She leaned over my lap to address Ruthie, releasing a gust of disbelieving air as she said, "*Please*. Everyone knows that girl's been trying to get Wy to knock her up since high school."

A sharp blade of consternation jammed between my ribs.

Ruthie ordered, "Wyatt, get up. You're coming with me."

This time, I obeyed.

Kelly Anne called after us, "Call me sometime, Wy!"

Ruthie muttered, "*Jesus*," keeping her arm tucked around mine as we headed for the main entrance; I was just sober enough to navigate the crowd without bumping into anyone or falling down.

Once outside, she did not mince words, her breath appearing in misty clouds in the cold night air. "What were you thinking? What good could possibly come of you acting like that? People talk in small towns, Wy, in case you'd forgotten. What would your wife have to say about Kelly Anne Collins draping herself all over you?"

I held up both hands, able to focus on only one thing. "What'd she mean about 'everyone knows' . . . ?"

Ruthie fell silent too quickly.

I leaned toward her, weaving on my feet. "Is that what you guys think?"

I saw the way she was searching for the tactful thing to say.

"It is, isn't it?" Heat seized my chest, followed immediately by a bone-deep chill. "God, you all think that, don't you? Hannah got pregnant on purpose."

Ruthie reached for my arm but I jerked away, spurred on by mounting anger and redoubled frustration.

"Why didn't someone—" But my voice trailed away as I realized the gaping fault in my logic.

Ruthie knew well that she'd said it plenty of times. I just hadn't listened.

"Come on, let's get you home," she whispered.

"To Dad's," I insisted, unwilling to face my wife in this state of mind. I'd already said too many things I regretted in Hannah's presence.

We were roughly a mile from the bar when I choked, "*Pull over . . .*"

Ruthie heard the urgency, the tires grinding over the snow-topped gravel on the shoulder as she braked. Not a moment too soon; I fell to my knees in the icy ditch and vomited until I was dry-heaving, ashamed and sickened and wanting to just die.

Ruthie was there, standing near me as I curled around my midsection, and I was stricken all over again at the sight of tears on her face, shiny in the crisp starlight as she said, "I'm so sorry, this sucks so much. I know you're hurting, we know you're unhappy . . ."

"I'm losing my goddamn mind, Ruthie. I miss her so much, I can't handle it anymore. It's like living every day without my heart. I can't stop thinking about her, I don't even want to try. And as much as it fucking hurts, it couldn't hurt worse than *never thinking about her again . . .*"

"I'm so sorry," she repeated. "Oh, Wy, I'm so sorry."

I clutched her hands, clad in woolen mittens while mine were bare and stone-cold. "Have you talked to her, do you know how she's doing?"

"I don't. I've only just started talking to Camille again and she hasn't mentioned anything about Millie. I'm almost scared to ask, but I will if you want me to."

"I keep pretending that it's Millie who's carrying my baby, Millie I get to come home to at the end of the week. I can almost convince myself *every time* that she'll be there when I open the door. I would give anything, you have no idea. Things would be so beautiful if she was there, oh God, life would be so *right*. None of what's happening now is right, it's not what's meant to be."

Ruthie squeezed my hands. "But it's what *is* happening, Wy, you can't pretend otherwise. Hannah is going to be really angry if someone tells her about how Kelly Anne was hitting on you."

"I didn't do anything with her, how could you think—"

"I know that, I really do. But you weren't stopping it either. And Hannah won't know it unless you explain."

Fire blazed in my chest. "Hannah hates our family, Ruthie. She hates all of you, thinks Dad controls me, doesn't want you guys coming over. She won't go to our family dinners. You know what she said earlier tonight? She said that she can't believe I tell you I love you, and then she asked what *Marsh* would think if he knew. Can you believe that shit?"

I saw Ruthie's surprise; I saw her strive to make sense of it. At last she said, "A lot of this probably has to do with her being pregnant. It's such an emotional upheaval, not to mention a physical one, and your hormones get so thrown off. Trust me, I've been there five times."

"You think?" I whispered.

"I'd say that's part of it. She came to plenty of family dinners with you in high school and I don't remember her ever acting like she hated any of us. I'm sure if she was in the right frame of mind, she would realize her accusations are way off base. Right now, she's just too upset." Ruthie tugged at my hands. "Come on, it's cold out here. A little coffee will do you a world of good."

Emotionally and physically depleted, I kept silent as Ruthie drove on to Dad's house, knowing there was nothing left to say, nothing to ease the pain.

Nothing short of Millie Jo Gordon.

# CHAPTER TWENTY-TWO

LANDON, MINNESOTA

A BLIZZARD WATCH WAS POSTED FOR THE GREAT-er Landon area, but as usual, this did not deter anyone's evening plans. I sat at the bar with Rae, both of us clapping along with the music of a foot-stomping bluegrass band. The annual winter music fest, typically held at Eddie's Bar, had been moved to Shore Leave at the last minute, due to a dead generator at Eddie's. With the heat produced by the riled-up, beer-drinking crowd, though, a furnace seemed completely superfluous. Our entire family was in attendance: Mom, Grandma Joelle, Aunt Jilly, and Barry, the daytime bartender, were busy serving drinks, and the atmosphere was typical mid-January, cabin-fever crazy.

"I didn't know Zig was such a good singer!" Rae said, putting her mouth directly beside my ear so I would hear over the music, referring to Eddie's grandson, currently onstage.

"Yeah, usually he just plays the drums." I reached past Rae's right shoulder for my hot chocolate, taking a careful sip before replacing it well beyond anyone's stray elbow. Unlike my cousin, I had not added a generous glug of rum to my drink.

"He's *so* sexy," Rae gushed, staring with rapt attention, squeezing my knee. "When did he graduate, again? He can't be that much older than us . . ."

It was the third Saturday of January; we'd only just composted the two Christmas trees that had adorned Shore Leave during the holiday season, and the café appeared a little forlorn in their absence. Tonight, however, the mood was one of happy abandon, the café packed to the gills with locals and out-of-towners alike, people clad in jeans and sweaters and snow boots, keg cups in hand. The music fest drew bands and singers from across the state, a perfect excuse to celebrate and fend off the winter blues. Tables had been shoved aside to create a makeshift dance floor; I spied a couple dancing close despite the fast pace of the current song, smiling at each other as if the rest of the crowded bar didn't exist.

I looked away, focusing my concentration in other directions with all my effort, wondering if I should offer to help take orders. Mom had said not to worry about it, to just enjoy myself, but suddenly I could no longer abide sitting motionless. I poked Rae's side, leaning in close.

"I'm going to see if they need help with drinks," I told her.

"Don't leave me!" Rae cried good-naturedly, gripping my elbow. "At least wait until Evan gets here."

"There he is," I said gratefully, spying her boyfriend entering from the dining room. I waved him over. "Here, take my seat."

Evan asked, "You guys want to get out of here? I'm having some people over later."

Rae tugged on my wrist. "Come on, it'll be fun. You could use a night out."

I mumbled, "Maybe later."

I met up with my mom behind the diner counter, where she was brewing coffee.

"You need help?" I asked, already tying my server apron into place.

Mom looked over her shoulder and I tried to pretend I didn't notice the way she was gauging my mood. She'd tread so carefully during all our interactions since last summer that some days I felt like a patient in a psychiatric ward. I supposed it figured; early on, I'd hardly been able to muster the strength required to leave my bed, let alone get dressed and step outside. The unbearable, splintered spike of pain had eventually tempered itself to the dull ache of an unhealed bruise—as long as I didn't touch it, I was all right.

"Thanks, honey," Mom said, resting a hand on my shoulder. "That would be great. I still haven't gotten to that new bunch at eleven."

I collected my notepad and a handful of pens, stifling the urge to duck away from her sympathetic touch. Table eleven was a high-top out in the bar, surrounded by a group of twenty-something guys and girls. They were talkative and exhilarated, ordering three pitchers of Guinness and a round of tequila shots.

"Those don't really go together," I said to the guy who ordered for the table.

He appeared amused, tilting his stool back on two legs as he argued, "They're from the same continent."

"Not really." I tucked my pen behind my ear. "Think about it."

He jabbed one of his companions. "Hey, where's tequila from?"

"Mexico," the other guy said.

"Darlin'!" heralded Eddie from a nearby table crowded with locals. "Grab us another couple pitchers, won't you?"

"On it!" I called as I hurried to the bar, grateful for the busy distraction. I found stillness the hardest to bear, stretches of silent contemplation in which I was left unguarded and could not rally the strength to fight off memories.

I ducked behind the bar, joining Barry and my dad.

"I've been pressed into service," Dad explained, hands flying as he loaded cocktail glasses with ice while Barry spun the blender.

"Who orders piña coladas in the middle of winter?" Barry grumbled, pouring frothy liquid into tall flutes.

"Those *have* to be for Aunt Tina and Aunt Elaine," I said, giggling at Barry's consternation. They were two of my dad's older sisters. "They just got here about ten minutes ago."

"Who else?" Barry groaned. "Like we have pineapple slices to go on the rim! Where do they think we are, Honolulu?"

"They just might," Dad said, with amusement. "No telling how long they've already been drinking this evening. What can I get you, hon?"

"I got it," I said. "You guys are busy."

I lined up four pitchers beneath the taps and then thought better of it and said over my shoulder, "I need seven tequila shots and a bowl of limes, Dad, if you have a second."

I delivered the drinks, receiving ample gratitude from both tables.

"Will you join us, love?" asked the guy I'd teased about tequila, affecting an Irish accent.

"No, thanks," I replied. "I don't drink."

"Ah, a smart *and* bonny lass. It don't get no better than that!"

"That's a *terrible* brogue," I told him.

"Russell Morgan, at your service." He maintained the accent, to my amusement. "Might I have the pleasure of your name? Do join us, love."

"Millie Jo," I said, shaking his proffered hand. "And the answer's still no."

It wasn't until much later, the music fest having reached its rowdy, impressive grand finale, Shore Leave empty of all customers, that I found the business card, tucked neatly under the receipt of their extensive drink tab. I ran a fingertip over the embossed words—*Lake View Stables, Champlin, MN.* Beneath an address and several phone numbers it read, *Dan and Dee Morgan, proprietors.*

*That's strange,* I thought. *Why would he leave this?*

It wasn't as though there was a chance in hell I was going to call any of the numbers—or require the services of a stable many hundreds of miles south. I would have chalked it up to an accident if Russell Morgan hadn't taken the time to place the card beneath their payment receipt, which included a hefty twenty-five-dollar tip; and upon the receipt he'd included a handwritten thank-you complete with a smiley face. Without thinking twice, I tucked the card in my apron and began collecting empty glasses.

. . .

We all congregated at the lake house once the café was restored to order; the adults gathered around the long dining room table to play cards while the little kids overtook the living room to watch movies. It was far too cold and snowy to venture outside for a walk, even though I craved one, and Rae was still somewhere with Evan, so I loaded a plate from the leftovers arranged along the kitchen counter—glazed ham, au gratin potato hotdish, bowtie noodle salad, creamed corn, crescent rolls, and caramel-apple pie. Then I holed away upstairs, situated on one of the twin beds in the attic bedroom, bracing my back against the wall, a surface painted the color of faded roses.

I ate slowly, staring into space; it was good to feel hungry again. I had lost so much weight last summer that Mom, in a moment of desperation, had threatened to hospitalize me. I'd had no intention of courting drama or acting out—it was just that my stomach had been reduced to a hard, painful knot, unwilling to receive food, leaving me unable to eat more than a few bites at a time for several months. The sounds of my family's chatter and easy laughter drifted from downstairs, becoming a muted background cadence as my thoughts coasted like feathers in a gentle breeze, aimless, bound for destinations unknown. At last I finished eating, set aside my plate, and tapped my phone to open a page I'd saved months ago.

I swallowed hard, inhaling through my nostrils as I studied the picture, captured probably without his knowledge by a campus photographer. The banner across the top of the page advertised the university and the veterinary medicine program, but I saw only Wy, crouching in the foreground of the shot among dozens of students, forearms braced on his thighs, wearing boots, jeans, and a white lab coat, his face in slight profile, mouth somber as he listened to the instructor, a woman kneeling near the head of a coal-black horse; a class in the middle of a lesson. I used my thumb and forefinger to enlarge the image, wishing for the countless time that his eyes were visible instead of directed away from the camera.

*Oh God, Wy, I miss you so much . . .*

I traced the outline of his nose, his jaw, his shoulders and legs, ending with his hands, fingers loosely interlocked, the pads of his thumbs resting together. There was no way to know exactly when the photo had been taken, except that it was after his wedding; a gold band was visible on the third finger of his left hand. Despite my initial and obsessive online searching, I hadn't found additional pictures; like me, Wy was not a fan of social media. Besides, since the horrible evening I stumbled inadvertently across pretty, smiling, redheaded "Hannah Jasper Rawley"—the equivalent of huge iron pokers rammed simultaneously through my lungs and heart—I had taken care to limit my searches.

Despite all attempts to shield myself from such knowledge, I knew their wedding date, August twentieth.

I knew their child's due date, January eleventh, already four days past.

I knew they were expecting a son.

I knew because Rae knew, thanks to her mom, who talked periodically with Aunt Ruthie. I had stopped myself a thousand times from texting either of my aunts in Montana, recognizing that contacting Wy, even indirectly, was a stupid, useless idea; I'd unwillingly relinquished all hold on him and the promise of a future together. I remained grateful that my parents had never discovered the full extent of last summer's events. Even so, they had both spent plenty of late nights holding me close as I sobbed uncontrollably while my poor siblings tried to make sense of my endless despair. I couldn't begin to imagine the extent of the damage had they known about our night together at Itasca.

My phone vibrated with an incoming call, startling me so much it fell to my lap. I scooped it up and said gratefully, "Hey there. Are you headed home?"

No response.

"Rae? Are you there?"

"Hannah's in labor." Her tone was somber, her voice soft. "Ruthie called me a little while ago and I wanted to be the one to tell you."

My heart issued a pitiful thud, sending an immediate chill through my blood. Rae said quickly, "Come over. We're at Evan's, there's a few people from our class here. Come have a drink, Millie Jo-Jo, please. Don't be alone."

"I don't drink," I reminded her; my voice was drier than yesterday's ashes.

"You need one tonight," she insisted.

I disconnected without another word and set aside my phone. Turning sideways, I sank to the rumpled pink blankets and curled my knees toward my chest, hugging hard, wishing for the ability to just say *fuck it* and go get wasted with my friends at Evan's house, to temporarily numb this pain; no matter that it would just wait patiently to ambush me as soon as the effects of the alcohol wore off. But I was terrified to lose control, terrified that if I was drunk I would relent to the desperate need to call or text Wy. I fantasized almost constantly about doing so, and had since the day we parted ways on the side of the highway. Instead of subsiding, the desire to contact him had only escalated with the passage of time.

He appeared to me frequently in a vivid dream sequence, always riding Shadow hard across a stretch of the foothills, his eyes fixed on something in the distance. Wy was a strong rider, at ease in the saddle as he had been since childhood, and in the early parts of the dream, setting eyes on him was a gift. But without fail, as I watched from a small but impassable distance, Shadow's front legs folded as he crumpled mid-gallop, pitching Wy over his head like a bullet fired from a gun. Night after night I was forced to witness Wy strike the rocky ground, and I was unable to run to his motionless form. And every time I woke in a cold sweat of fear, limbs thrashing, alone in my bed; the nightmare's power to shatter me never decreased. In those smothering moments, the inability to contact him was more devastating than ever.

*Are you all right, Wy? What's happening to you that I keep dreaming that you're hurt, broken beyond repair?*

When I finally told Rae about the nightmare, she pondered only a few seconds before concluding, "It makes sense, if you think about it. What you're seeing is an interpretation of his heart getting broken."

*And mine.*

It had taken as many months to muster up the strength to leave his letter at home in a drawer instead of carrying it tucked close to my body. I had long ago memorized every word, had composed a hundred imaginary responses.

*What would you say if Wy actually answered his phone?*

*There's nothing either of you could say that would change a thing, and you know it.*

*I just want to hear his voice . . .*

My phone buzzed twice more; Rae, both times, and I refused to answer. But roughly a minute after her last attempt to reach me, I heard someone climbing the creaky attic stairs.

*Fuck,* I thought. *Rae called Mom and she's coming to talk.*

The last thing on the face of the earth I wanted was to sit through another hushed, well-meaning conversation with my mother. I sat quickly straight, smoothing tangled hair from my eyes, somewhat surprised to spy Aunt Jilly appear in the open door. Petite and pretty, wearing a soft indigo sweater that exactly matched her stunning eyes, my aunt peered into the room. Her long golden hair was arranged in a complicated braid adorned with tiny jeweled barrettes, courtesy of Lorie.

"Hi, babe," Aunt Jilly said softly. "You up for a little company?"

My throat was too tight for speech, but she understood, crossing the room with quiet steps and perching on the edge of the mattress; wordlessly, she patted her right thigh, and as though I was about five years old, I rested my head on her lap, covering my face with both hands. I cried in bitter, agonized silence, wracked by shudders I could not control. Aunt Jilly bent forward over me, stroking my hair with gentle hands. She offered no advice or commentary, letting her touch speak for her.

She spoke only once, murmuring, "Let it all out. It's the only way."

If only I had the words to explain why I couldn't do such a thing, that letting it all out would leave me as empty as a shell washed ashore; I refused to release my memories of Wy—because I would rather bear the pain forever than lose all I had left of him.

# CHAPTER TWENTY-THREE

CLASSES HAD RESUMED IN PULLMAN, BUT WITH the imminent arrival of our child, I was sticking close to home, determined to be at Hannah's side the moment she went into labor. The eleventh, a Tuesday, passed without event. Other than constant pain across her lower back and difficulty going to the bathroom, issues that had plagued her since November, nothing seemed out of the ordinary. I walked on eggshells, determined since December to reinvent my attitude, to make things work between us. I shut out, with determination, many small, barbed realizations—we hardly touched, we never laughed. Hannah hated my family and I was not overly fond of hers. We had almost zero common interests. Our conversations centered primarily upon our son, whose name we hadn't yet chosen. We wanted to set eyes on him first.

Most difficult to shut out was the fact that everyone thought Hannah had tried to get pregnant, had maybe even lied about being on birth control. I could not force the thought of Kelly Anne's comment, not to mention Ruthie's subsequent reaction, from my head. At times accusations burned so hot on the tip of my tongue it took all I had not to fling them Hannah's way—but what could I say? When all was said and done, she had hardly become pregnant on her own. And I'd been warned. I had, in a manner of speaking, dug my own grave in this situation. I focused on what our life would be like once the baby arrived; our son would bind us together. Our son would make us a true family.

Or so I hoped.

It was after ten on a frozen Saturday night, and I sat alone in the living room, doing my best to catch up on assigned reading, a plate of leftovers balanced on my lap. Wind howled around the house, throwing pellet-like snowflakes, and I hoped the noise wasn't keeping Hannah from sleep. She'd retreated to bed two hours ago, but had ventured to the bathroom at least five times since. I was exhausted, eyes grainy, and when I found myself rereading a paragraph for the third time, I marked my place and set aside the textbook and my unfinished dinner. I knuckled my eye sockets and was about to stretch out on the couch to sleep when I heard my name. I hurried to the bedroom to find Hannah sitting up, her head bent forward and both palms resting on her enormous belly.

I went to her at once, curving an arm around her shoulders. "I'm here, it's all right."

"I think my water just broke." Her voice shook.

My heart began pumping like a piston. "Then it's time, let's get you to the hospital."

"I'm scared," she admitted, clinging to my hands. "The baby doesn't feel right."

Fear spread like ice water through my veins. "What do you mean he doesn't feel right?"

"I don't know, something just doesn't feel right," she insisted. "I feel like my insides are about to pop out." I felt the trembling in her upper body and squeezed her closer at once.

"Well, that's sort of true," I said, immediately regretting the stupid comment. I backpedaled quickly. "Everything's all right, it's all right."

"Oh my God, *shut up*. You're not helping. But that's no surprise."

I ignored the jab, knowing she was scared. I offered, "I'll call your parents. Do you need help getting dressed?"

"I'll call them. Grab our bag and get the truck started. I don't need help getting dressed."

Thirty minutes later, I dropped her at the emergency exit of the hospital in nearby Miles City, where she was immediately whisked away in a wheelchair. I found a spot in the adjacent parking garage and then hustled to the front desk of the obstetrics wing, jittery and short of breath when I should have been a rock, calm and stable.

"Just down the hall," a nurse instructed, with a smile. "First door on the left, Dad."

*Dad.*

The realization struck harder than ever before, right between the eyes.

*You are about to become someone's dad.*

I squared my shoulders and entered the small room to find Hannah situated in a narrow bed while a nurse attached her belly to a fetal monitor. A saline drip was already inserted in the top of her left hand and she appeared pale and frightened, undeniably vulnerable. I felt a pulse of intense concern, realizing afresh just how much she and our son needed me. Accountability cut deep, scoring my flesh; how undeserving I was of Hannah's love, how selfish I'd been these past months, letting pain override my responsibility. But apologies were not what she needed just now.

I reached for her free hand, tucking it securely between both of mine.

"We'll get a full examination going once the doctor arrives," the nurse said briskly. "You two hang tight."

"Like we have anywhere else to go," I murmured as the nurse left the room, trying for some levity. I snagged a chair and drew it to the bedside. "How are you feeling? Do you need anything?"

"They took a sample of the fluid to make sure it was really the water breaking," Hannah said, settling a palm on the fullest part of her stomach, a perfectly round dome beneath the pale blue hospital gown. She held my gaze, as if sensing the depth of what remained unsaid between us. Speaking with reverence, she whispered, "I can't believe we're finally going to meet him."

I positioned my hand gently over hers, emotion building in my chest. "I know, I can't wait."

"He hasn't been moving much," she worried. "Not since yesterday."

"That's normal, it means he's in position and ready to be born." As though a small, glowing lantern cast a sudden light, a picture of Twyla lying on her side in the horse barn filled my head. I felt Millie's fingertips on my shoulder as palpably as if she stood beside me in this moment, and my next breath lodged in my lungs.

*No*, I thought, determined to focus on the here and now. *Please, I can't bear it tonight. I have to move forward no matter how much it hurts.*

"You look beautiful," I told Hannah, my throat tight. "Things are going to be different from now on, I promise."

She closed her eyes without replying and a contraction rippled over her abdomen. It lasted a good fifteen seconds before tapering off, and she released a tense breath. Sweat had formed on her temples.

"We're here!" cried a voice behind us, her parents inundating the room and clustering around the bed.

"Mom," she said gratefully, reaching to accept a hug from Irene. "I'm *so* glad you're here."

Irene gathered Hannah's hair in both hands. "Let's get your hair in a ponytail and out of the way. Where are your things, for heaven's sake?"

"I forgot the bag in the truck," I admitted. "I'll be right back."

I knew it was important to Hannah that her parents were present for the birth, and had refrained from voicing my opinion to the contrary. I strode back outside, blasted at once by the chilly bite of the wind and increasing snow. I'd neglected to grab my coat in the rush to get to Miles City and ducked my head. The wind was so harsh I didn't at first hear my phone ringing. I hurried to the parking garage to answer, seeing Marshall's name on the screen.

"Hey, little bro," he said as I answered. "I hear you're at the hospital!"

"I meant to call you guys. I called Dad on the way." Shivers overtook my ribs and I wrapped an arm around my torso. "I'll keep you posted tonight."

"You need any moral support? We can head over there in minutes," Marshall offered. "The guys are already here, we've been playing cards."

The warmth of gratitude filled my heart; I'd neglected my brothers and their families this past winter, per my wife's request, and it was in moments such as these that I realized all over again just how much I missed them. They were my family, they loved me, and I loved them. They wanted to share this momentous occasion with me, the night my son entered the world.

"Thanks, Marsh. I appreciate that."

"You two would rather be alone for now," he understood quietly. I knew Ruthie told him everything and that he was well aware of the things I'd said on the side of the road back in December, after she picked me up at The Spoke. I had apologized to Ruthie more than once, ashamed of losing control like that, admitting to things no one should have to know.

"Hannah's folks are here," I explained. "We're not exactly alone."

"Well, let us know as soon as your son shows up. I remember the night you were born, as clear as a bell. There was a blizzard that night too. I love you, Wy, keep us posted, okay?"

"Yeah, I've heard that story a time or two. I love you too, Marsh, thanks for being there." My voice was gruff with restrained emotion.

"Call if you need anything."

"I will."

But there was very little news during the next twelve hours, as Hannah's labor crept inch by torturous inch without progress. Her amniotic sack had indeed broken, but hours passed between increases in her cervical dilation, during which she grew increasingly exhausted and agitated; I was more grateful for her mother's presence with each passing minute. Unable to sleep, I wandered the hallways, detouring to the cafeteria for coffee as an icy white dawn began painting the eastern sky. Over ten inches of fresh snow blanketed the frozen ground, and my son was in no hurry to venture to the outside world.

"Please, let him be all right," I whispered, staring outside at the raging weather. I'd found a window at the end of an empty hallway and rested a fisted hand to my lips, whispering the prayer. "I know I haven't been a good husband, but I want to do better. I want to be the man they need, my wife and son. I want to be a good father, to teach my boy how to be a good person. Please, let him be all right. He's coming so slowly and I'm scared. I'm so scared."

I rested my forehead to the cold glass, closing my eyes, unreasonably frightened that I deserved punishment, that somehow my continued devotion to another woman was responsible.

I pressed harder against my mouth. "I still love Millie, I can't deny that. I'll never stop loving her, it would be a lie to pretend otherwise." I gritted my teeth, momentarily unable to continue. At last I whispered, "I'm learning to accept that we can't be together in this life. I'm willing to accept it. Please just let my son be all right, I'll do anything. Don't let my mistakes hurt my son."

There was no immediate response, no lightning flash of awareness, but I found a measure of comfort in simply speaking the words aloud.

"Wy, you over here?"

I turned in a rush, spilling coffee down the front of my shirt. Bill stood at the opposite end of the hallway, calling for me. I jogged toward him.

"Hannah just wondered where you were, everything's all right. Irene was in labor for more than thirty hours with Hannah, so I suppose it figures that her own labor would take time. How you holding up?"

"I'm all right," I assured him.

Back in the room, Irene was stationed alongside her daughter, holding out a plastic cup of ice chips for Hannah to suck on, one at a time. Guilt spread along my limbs; I should have been the one performing this task, but Irene had usurped my position at the bedside and Hannah seemed not to mind. I realized that she found more comfort in her mother's presence than mine, but I had no one but myself to blame.

I tried for a cheerful tone, observing Hannah's red, angry-looking expression. "How's everything in here?"

"Does it look any different?" Hannah snapped.

"Give the man a break," Bill said, with an air of gentle teasing. "He's just as tired as you, Han."

"Oh, really?" Hannah fired the words at her father like pellets from an air rifle.

The doctor bustled in at that moment, providing a welcome distraction, but her examination revealed little progress.

"We'll get you on a Pit-drip," the doctor said. "See if we can get things moving along."

But morning inched to late afternoon before Hannah was given the order to begin pushing. All of us were beyond depleted by that point, Hannah tearful or screaming by turns. I had given up trying to offer any words of comfort, holding her hand as she cried and swore and begged for the ordeal to end. We'd been relocated to the delivery wing and the doctor was situated on a rolling stool near Hannah's bent legs, which I prayed meant things were picking up. Irene and I were at her head, on either side; Bill had opted to stay in the waiting room and I didn't blame him.

"Come on, another!" ordered the nurse stationed at the doctor's side.

"I can't," Hannah sobbed. "*It hurts . . .*"

I was so tired that everything around me seemed a step outside reality, as if on a slight delay; it took a second to realize something was wrong. The fetal monitor registering the baby's heartbeat had changed—his heartrate was swiftly dropping.

Hot, sick fear swallowed me whole.

Hard-edged orders flew from the doctor's mouth, and nurses scrambled to do her bidding in a slow-motion reel. And then the doctor's face, swathed in a surgical mask, loomed near.

"Mrs. Rawley, your son is in fetal distress. We're going to perform a C-section. We're taking you to the surgical wing right now."

The following minutes became a blurry rush of sound and color, a span of time I would never be able to fully recall; my defense mechanism against abject panic. It was only in the aftermath that I was able to piece together what had actually occurred, a bullet-list of cold, hard facts. Irreversible, just like a rising sun or a fading life.

Our son was in respiratory distress as he emerged from the womb, barely breathing.

Hannah's uterus had prolapsed, she was in danger of hemorrhaging, and an emergency uterine hysterectomy was performed on the spot.

She would never bear another child.

I did not learn the last two facts until later because I rushed alongside the team hustling my son to the neonatal intensive care unit, unable to bear letting him out of my sight. Tiny and blue-tinted and wrinkled, with tightly-closed eyes and a head of thick black hair. My son, in distress; my son, who needed me more than anyone ever had. Nauseous with fear, bile in my throat, I refused to be removed from the room, watching from an unbearable distance of several yards as nurses worked over his fragile body, attaching him to oxygen and an intravenous catheter. By the time they deposited him in an incubator that was shaped, grotesquely, like a small glass coffin, I felt as if a truck had slammed me repeatedly against a brick wall.

I sat as close as I could, unable to remove my eyes from my child; if I took my eyes from him, he might die. I had been given gloves and was allowed to touch his tiny feet, determined to show him that I was here, that he was not alone among machinery. A nasal cannula, a small tube with tiny prongs, had been placed in his nose to assist with oxygen circulation, and an IV fed nutrients and fluids through the stump of his umbilical cord. He wore nothing but a pint-sized diaper, tiny thick socks, and a blue cap tugged down over his ears. His eyes were closed, the lids forming tight seams, but his mouth was slightly open, moving with little suckling motions. Love clouted my senses and inundated my heart. It was love on a disproportionate scale, binding and absolute.

I curled the gentlest of touches around his impossibly small feet, whispering, "Hi, little one. I'm here, I won't leave your side. We're going to get through this, do you hear me? Soon you're going to come home with me and your mom. We love you so much, sweetheart."

I kept talking, tears flowing down my face, holding fast to my son.

# CHAPTER TWENTY-FOUR

"CHEERS, MEN, RAISE 'EM UP!"

Rousing applause sounded in the wake of Kyle's toast, cheering and whistling and shouts of congratulations. The pride of accomplishment, of fulfilling a lifelong desire to become a veterinarian, rose in my chest, eradicating the petty irritation of Hannah's absence from this moment.

"I came to your graduation. Besides, you guys are just going to get drunk. I don't know why I have to be there," she'd said last night, barely pausing on her way toward the washing machine, a laundry basket braced against her hip.

Though I resented the jab, I let it go, saying only, "Dad and Aunt Julie arranged the entire thing. Kyle and Joey are driving over from Washington."

*It's a big deal. It means something to me,* I wanted to say, but the words wouldn't clear my mouth. I felt, however unreasonably, my wife should comprehend this without me spelling it out.

The Spoke glowed with warm welcome this Saturday evening, the first week of a mellow June. My brothers, their wives, and everybody's kids were in attendance, in addition to Aunt Julie and my cousins and their husbands; Dad was holding my son, eighteen-month-old Zane Alexander, who had attended at my insistence. Kyle and Joey arrived yesterday afternoon and were staying at Dad's house. On Monday, Netta and Tuck would officially open the doors of Bitterroot Ranch, their rehabilitation center. Having passed my boards and certifications and earned my licensure to practice veterinary medicine in the state of Montana, I would soon be in their employ. It seemed centuries had passed since I'd experienced such bursting anticipation and excitement.

"We really made it," Kyle said as we drained the round of whiskey. "There were plenty of days I didn't think we would."

"You and me both," I agreed, clapping him on the back.

Joey gazed around the bar. "I think I'm going to like this area."

Though he'd once planned to reside in Seattle and open a private practice, Joey had been enticed by Tuck's offer of a job at Bitterroot Ranch. Because I would specialize in large-animal, agricultural veterinary work and Joey's focus was small animals and exotics, Tuck had offered us both the chance to rent office space at the center; I'd been the one to suggest the idea to Tuck, who enthusiastically agreed.

"Come here, Dr. Rawley, give me a hug," said Ruthie, reaching with both arms.

I set aside my drink and squeezed her close, rocking side to side.

"I am so damn proud of you, Wy," she said in my ear. "This is such a big deal."

"Thanks," I whispered emotionally, briefly closing my eyes, pretending for no longer than a half-second that the warm, sweet body I held close and the abundant curly hair brushing my cheek belonged to Millie. I swallowed hard and drew away.

"And you two, come here," Ruthie insisted, catching Kyle and Joey for hugs. "Welcome to Jalesville. You'll love it here."

"Thank you, ma'am," Kyle said, flushing a little, smiling at her with a subtly flirtatious air. "I don't technically plan to live here, but thanks all the same."

"But *I* do," Joey said. "Any recommendations would be much appreciated. Where do people shop for local produce? What's the farmer's market scene around here?"

I grinned, threading my way through the congratulatory crowd to Dad's side, craving Zane in my arms.

"Look at my boy, the doc," Dad said, mustache twitching, tears in his eyes. "Your mother would be so proud, Wyatt. I know she's looking down on you."

"Thanks, Dad," I whispered, cupping his upper arm before collecting Zane and kissing his forehead.

My smiley son bounced on my forearm, excited by the noisy activity and chatter. Despite his harrowing entrance into the world, Zane had sustained no long-lasting negative effects. I didn't believe I was biased in my opinion that he was the sweetest, most adorable child to ever exist. He'd grown like a champion— a year and a half after his birth, he was chubby and energetic, with cheeks like pink apples. His eyes were brown and lively, his smile almost constant. His hair was dark, forming soft curls all over his perfect head.

"Hi, buddy," I murmured. "How's my boy?"

"Come and grab a plate," Dad encouraged. "We have all your favorites."

Before I could set foot in the direction of the food tables, I was surrounded by a noisy, giggling group of girls: my nieces, intent on claiming Zane. He was their own personal teddy bear, upon whom they lavished attention and affection. And he loved every last minute, accustomed to kisses and squeals and hugs.

"I want him, let me hold him first, Uncle Wy," pleaded Harleigh. "I haven't seen my Zany all week!"

"I haven't either, you can't hog him!" ordered Tansy.

"I get him next, you promised!" said Celia.

"Careful, now," I ordered, surrendering Zane to Harleigh's outstretched arms.

"How's my sweet widdle Zany?" she cooed, bouncing him before planting kisses all over his irresistible cheeks, leaving behind faint lip-gloss smudges.

"Thank goodness I never worried too much about germs," I muttered to Dad as the girls whisked off in the direction of another table. I spied Sean and Jessie already seated there, along with Lee and Pam and Aunt Julie, so didn't worry over following them.

Zane spent plenty of time in the company of his cousins. Since his birth, I had been much less tolerant of Hannah's dislike of my brothers and their families. The sad truth was that Zane would never have any siblings, and it was my opinion that he needed the company of other little kids as often as possible. I couldn't imagine a childhood without my brothers. When Hannah railed about how often Zane and I hung out with them and their families, I turned a deaf ear. I'd grown adept at doing so since the rainy March night, over a year ago now, when Hannah had screamed that she blamed me, unequivocally, for her hysterectomy, claiming that if I'd stayed at her side instead of rushing away with Zane, I could have stopped the surgical team from making the decision.

My promise to be a better husband had fallen miles short of the mark.

I put every ounce of effort into fatherhood instead.

I loaded a plate with pork ribs, spicy shrimp gumbo, coleslaw, steak fries, jalapeño poppers, bacon-stuffed mushrooms, and a heaping slice of chocolate lava cake before joining the Quick brothers, who were seated at a rowdy, crowded table that included Marsh, Ruthie, Quinn, Garth, Becky, Netta, and Tuck.

"There's the man of the hour!" heralded Garth, raising his beer mug in a salute. "The first doc in our family!"

Marshall squeezed my shoulder. "Damn, kid, we're proud of you. In case you hadn't guessed."

Quinn added, "I suppose this means we have to leave off picking on you for the rest of our natural lives."

"Little Wy," said Becky, with a fond smile. She narrowed one eye, perusing my face. "Look at you, you handsome thing. I wasn't sure I would, but I really like the goatee."

"It gives you a very distinguished air," Ruthie agreed.

"Like a real doctor?" I teased, stroking my trim beard in the exaggerated fashion of an academic.

"God, dude, don't do that, you look like Dr. Ribald," Kyle said, with a shudder. "I didn't think I'd live through my rotation at that man's clinic."

"What are your plans this evening, guys?" asked Tuck, leaning forward on his elbows.

I had known Tuck for many years, long before he and Netta started dating; his family, the Quillborrows, were longtime residents of the area. Tuck was one of very few men I could envision keeping up with Netta's endless energy; the combined intensity of their focus had been the driving force behind the creation of Bitterroot Ranch. I tried hard to shelve my jealousy over their happy, loving marriage, the way they shared so many interests and goals. I couldn't begin to imagine working alongside Hannah on a daily basis.

Looking between Joey and me, Tuck elaborated, "I have a surprise for you-all out at Bitterroot. I wanted you to see it before the ribbon-cutting on Monday."

Joey set aside his beer. "A surprise, for us?"

Tuck nodded, patting Netta's thigh with a smile of deep contentment.

"We've been so excited we can hardly sleep," Netta added.

"Sure, we can head out there tonight," I said, mouth full; I hadn't felt so hungry in months. "I actually wanted to drive past anyway, to see it before it opens for real."

"Same here," Joey agreed. "I just need time this evening to haul a few things to my new place. Not that I'm in a hurry to leave your dad's house. Talk about feeling at home." He looked toward Quinn. "Thanks again for the tour."

Quinn, always a man of few words, simply nodded acknowledgement.

"Clark has to be the nicest man alive," Joey continued. "You guys are lucky."

"Yeah, he could teach our father a thing or two," Kyle added. Recognizing Netta as the clear authority at our table, he leaned toward her and asked in the hushed tone of a conspirator, "Any chance your sister Lee might want to dance with me once the music starts up?"

Netta grinned. "I think she just might."

. . .

A molten sun was melting toward the distant mountain peaks by the time we all drove out to Bitterroot, a sprawling, hundred-acre property tucked at the base of a ridge on the west side of the highway, surrounded by wide-open foothill country. I had hitched a ride with Ruthie and Marsh, and sitting in the middle of the backseat in my brother's old, rusted-out truck, leaning forward to peer out the windshield as we followed Tuck's 4-by-4, reminded me so much of the first time the three of us had ridden somewhere together that I had to laugh.

"What's so funny?" Ruthie turned to look over her left shoulder. She added softly, "It's so good to see you happy, Wy."

"I was just thinking about the day the three of us drove from Bozeman to Jalesville, way back when Case was in the hospital. Remember that?"

"Like it was yesterday," Marsh said, shooting a wicked grin in his wife's direction, reaching across the short distance separating them to squeeze her thigh. "That was the first time I had Ruthie all to myself and I was not about to let that opportunity slide. I thanked my lucky stars, let me tell you."

"You two made me stay home so you could ride back to Bozeman alone," I said, recalling that long-gone afternoon.

"No, you had a headache, Wy, it was pure chance that we got to ride back together." Ruthie flicked a finger against Marshall's knee as she added, "And *you* were the perfect gentleman," unable then to stave off a contradictory giggle.

Both Marshall and I had a good laugh over that statement.

"Oh, wow," Ruthie suddenly murmured, leaning forward. "Oh, *look*. It's gorgeous."

Bitterroot Ranch appeared in the distance, angelically lit by the evening sun like something not quite of this world. I let the beauty and promise of the place resettle around my heart—here was my future. A degree, a job, an opportunity to provide, and then some, for my son. This was what I'd worked my ass off for all these years. I was more quietly proud of my accomplishments in that moment than I'd yet been.

"It's quite a sight, isn't it?" I murmured.

Tuck pulled to the shoulder of the road just before reaching the front gate. He climbed down from his massive vehicle and waved at us to do the same. Marsh parked and left the engine idling while Kyle and Joey, in their car behind us, followed suit; Quinn had ridden along with them.

"Wy, Joe, come over here," Tuck ordered solemnly, beckoning us forward. "I wanted you two to see this before anyone else."

He led us the remaining dozen or so steps to the front gate, with its magnificent arch of interlocking elk horns, and brandished a hand at the new wooden sign adorning the entrance. Hand-painted, constructed of reclaimed barn wood like most of the buildings on the property, it read *Bitterroot Ranch, Tucker and Netta Quillborrow, proprietors.* Beneath that, in similarly formal, elegant script, was written *Wyatt Rawley, DVM* and *Joseph Quick, DVM*.

It was the first time I'd seen my name and title on anything other than my licensure documents. Tears brimmed immediately on my lower lids; from the corner of my vision I noticed Joey pressing his thumbs to either eye, similarly affected. I cleared my throat to speak.

"Tuck, this is beautiful. I'm so honored."

"It looks fantastic. We need a picture, right here," Joey insisted.

Netta and Ruthie snapped photos, using everyone's phones, and then all of us ambled around the property in the warm glow of the sinking sun, marveling anew at the outbuildings, the main offices, the equipment and sheer space. Forty-six horses were currently stabled in two barns, not counting the massive steel-pole shed housing a training arena. Tuck was a licensed psychologist specializing in equine therapy, and Netta would run the business office, a natural fit for her as the daughter of a first-class entrepreneur like Aunt Julie. Joey and I would practice medicine both on- and off-site. There were a dozen or so other employees, from tiny, fiery Mae Hanson, who had worked as a secretary in the main office at the high school until retiring to "take it easy," to five teenagers paid to muck stalls and haul hay.

"Shadow and Scout are already here," I told Marsh and Ruthie, leading them through one of the barns. I'd brought my horses from Dad's house only a few days earlier.

"How many are rescue animals?" Marsh asked, pausing to offer his hand, palm up, to a nearby mare. She nosed it and immediately began licking, attempting to lap up every trace of salt on his skin.

"That's Patsy, she licks everything. She's worse than a toddler," I explained, patting the mare's warm, solid neck. She began energetically nibbling at my shirt, expecting her customary treat. "About half are rescues rather than boarders, just now. The south barn—we call it Recovery Barn—is where they're stabled."

"You do such good work here," Ruthie said, stopping to scratch the big square jaws of a nearby gelding, Brand, who stuck his inquisitive face out of his stall at the sounds of people.

Marsh said, "Last Sunday at dinner, Tuck and Netta were telling us about the animals you've already rescued. Their website is pretty great; it showcases every new rescue. The kids love it."

"Netta's fantastic about posting everything. It is pretty great, isn't it? But it makes you wish you could save all of them, like back when I was a kid and wanted to rescue every stray dog." I thought of that summer night in Landon, sitting with Millie at the ballfield, talking about Bitterroot and what happened to racehorses. I thought about how I would feel if I turned around and saw her walking across the corral toward us, sunlight in her hair and her eyes fixed on me. How she would share the joy in this moment with me; she would understand the importance of Bitterroot's grand opening.

"Or cat," my brother was saying.

"Right," I muttered. "You do your part where you can, and try to make peace with the rest of it." I reached Shadow's stall and he came immediately to the gate, nuzzling my chest. I murmured, "There's my boy," and kissed him between his wide-spaced eyes, scratching his neck with a hand on either side of his head. Scout was one stall over, turned so that only his broad golden flank was visible.

"Can you finally get a couple of dogs now?" Ruthie asked. "They could live out here, right?"

"Hell, yes," I said adamantly. "That's the plan. I want Zane to know what it's like to raise and care for animals, since he can't have a dog at home."

I tried not to grit my teeth over the futility of the argument. Hannah claimed to be allergic but I knew the truth was that she didn't want pets in the house. She'd never once come horseback riding with me, even though I'd assured her many times that it was safe and I'd teach her everything she needed to know. But it was no use. She responded by arguing that I never tried the things she liked, a statement which always left me wondering exactly what those "things" were; other than shopping and paging through home design magazines, there was very little else Hannah seemed to enjoy, including my company. Whenever we went anywhere or spent extended time together, we always included Zane. Focusing on him was a welcome relief, for both of us.

I stepped over to Scout's stall, my mind straying again, imagining Millie at my side, dressed for riding. I closed my eyes, letting the fantasy play out, torturing myself as I pictured us racing Scout and Shadow out into the foothills, where tall spires and round boulders provided plenty of secret, sheltered spaces. I'd have a blanket tied on my saddle, but we wouldn't spare a second to spread it out—I'd have Millie in my arms and her legs around my hips before she even set foot on the ground, and she would laugh, teasing me about how I had no patience before I'd kiss her, tasting her from the inside out as I unbuttoned her jeans, and she would have mine unzipped and around my ankles—and then I'd be deep inside her, hearing the sounds I had cherished so goddamn much, the way her breath came in gasps and small, sweet moans—

Ruthie had said something, but her voice was as remote as someone speaking from the top of a mountain.

I gripped my forehead; damn my evil fucking imagination. I missed every last thing about Millie, not just the physical connection we had shared, but sometimes missing *that* overpowered all else, inspiring a deluge of guilt. It wasn't that I didn't recognize why; Hannah barely touched me. And it wasn't as though I longed for sex with just anyone—I wanted Millie. I wanted her every damn second, even knowing the futility of it. There were times, usually late at night, stationed on the couch in the living room and sleepless yet again, when I needed so badly to be touched that I didn't think I could bear the lack of it, both passion and affection; on the rare occasions that Hannah and I had sex, it was always over quickly, with little of either.

My brother was saying to Ruthie, "Honey, let's go take a look at the henhouse. I want to get an idea of the layout before I start building anything."

The evening had cooled, the air dusky; stars had winked on across the chilly canvas of sky, as far as the eye could see. Netta and Tuck showed Marshall the extensive henhouse, explaining the intricacies, while I lingered in the background with Ruthie, who seemed introspective. Seizing this brief moment alone with her, I dared to ask the one question I knew I shouldn't.

"How's Millie?"

I felt the flicker of Ruthie's quick gaze but kept mine directed at the western horizon, where a vivid stripe of pink afterglow backlit the mountains. Just the fact that I'd asked outright took Ruthie by surprise, I could tell; I didn't usually. I searched out information where I could, without being obvious. Dad often mentioned little things, seemingly offhanded, but I recognized that he knew damn well I longed to know about Millie's life. She had started at the University of Minnesota in Minneapolis last fall, for example, as a freshman in the psychology program.

"She enjoyed her first year at college. She liked her classes," Ruthie answered at last. She folded her arms in an almost defensive manner, no longer looking my way, and though there wasn't so much as a hint of an undertone to her words, I knew immediately. A sixth sense; a crawling sensation beneath my skin.

"What is it?" I demanded.

Ruthie kept her gaze trained on the horizon and her reluctance was plain.

My dread tripled.

"She's seeing someone," she admitted quietly.

A cinch strap seemed to tighten around my chest.

"It wasn't that I wanted to keep this from you, Wy, I just didn't want to tell you like this, especially not today." Ruthie spoke now in a rush.

"It's all right," I managed to say. I had known this would happen, I'd prepared myself, but reality struck with the impact of a rockslide all the same.

Ruthie knew I was lying; I was far from all right.

"Who is he?" I knew it was none of my business, but I could not have kept quiet in that moment had my life depended on it.

"His name is Russ Morgan." She did not divulge additional details.

*Russ.*

"Who is he?" I repeated, attempting to convey the real questions blazing at the back of my throat—*who the fuck is this guy, how did they meet, how fucking dare he thinks he can weasel into Millie Jo's life?*

*Please, God, no . . .*

"His family owns a stable outside Minneapolis. Millie started working there a few months ago. I guess this place specializes in a horse training technique she wanted to learn. I can't think of the name, it sounds something like 'parallel' . . ."

"A stable?" I repeated roughly. "The bastard is teaching her Parelli?"

I wanted him dead. I wanted to be the one who snapped his neck, an acute, savage sort of insanity swamping my blood. I knew Parelli, I knew it damn well. It was a hands-on approach to horse training, the teachings intended to utilize a horse's instincts and mimic the way a dame would pass knowledge to a foal. Tuck was a certified instructor. I pictured this guy, this Russ Morgan, standing alongside Millie in a corral as they worked with a horse, stepping closer to guide the movements of her arm with his own . . .

And that was just the tip of the iceberg of terrible visions crowding my head.

I covered my mouth with one hand, squeezing hard, digging my fingertips into my cheeks.

"I shouldn't have said anything." Ruthie was agonized. "I'm so sorry."

"Don't be sorry," I muttered, but I was already striding away, headed back to the horse barn, where I saddled Shadow and took off alone into the foothills, sending him into a rippling canter, then a full-out gallop, already knowing it was a wasted effort. Time had long since taught me there was no way to outrun the pictures in my head; no way to get beyond this level of pain.

# CHAPTER TWENTY-FIVE

## MINNEAPOLIS, MINNESOTA

I STOOD JUST INSIDE THE DOOR TO MY SHOE-box-sized dormitory, a space I had shared since September with two other freshmen girls, one from southern Minnesota and one from Nebraska. Because I'd still been on the schedule at Lake View Stables until last night, I was the last to leave our dorm this balmy June afternoon, my car packed with boxes and reusable grocery sacks and a stack of books I hadn't wanted to return at the exchange. Taped to the concrete wall opposite the door was a small picture of the three of us, taken last fall at the first real party we attended together, standing with our arms draped around each other and our necks adorned with Hawaiian-style leis; I'd been in the middle and my smile appeared genuine, at least from a distance.

I cast my gaze around the room one last time before shouldering my purse strap and heading down the long hallway. I was unaccustomed to the empty silence, my footfalls echoing along a corridor typically jammed with a crush of bodies, girls walking, running, shouting, singing, laughing . . . occasionally puking. I hurried down the stairs to the wide front doors, toward the bright golden sunlight spilling across the floor, lifting my face to its brilliance as I stepped outside. The campus was already a few weeks beyond the end-of-semester bliss, but I still stole a hit off the aftereffects lingering in the air—the promise of a sweet expanse of summertime haze and relaxation to counteract the tension of studying for finals, revising essays, and cleaning out nine months' worth of dorm room junk.

My phone beeped with a text and I fished it from the back pocket of my jean shorts, swiping the screen to see a message from Rae.

*Hurry home! We're having a huge party this weekend to celebrate!*

A smile pulled at my mouth. I pictured Flickertail gleaming like a polished agate and the bustle at both Shore Leave and White Oaks, Dad's parents' lodge, as tourist season kicked into high gear. I imagined the spring wildflowers growing tall along Fisherman's Street and the food being prepared in my honor. I missed my family tremendously, even Henry; I'd driven home for spring break, but that was over two months ago. I crossed the blacktop parking lot with sun beating on my head, a small rush of anticipation swelling in my heart.

*On the way!* I wrote back, adding a few smiley faces and hearts.

There was just one place I needed to stop before heading home. I took the exit for 94-W, following what had become a familiar route since last December, when I'd first driven the twenty-mile stretch of interstate to Russ's hometown. Lake View Stables was situated on the outskirts of Champlin and functioned primarily as a boarding facility, with room for up to two dozen animals; the stalls were typically occupied by horses, but the stable was currently housing a mule and two small, adorable burros. The mule, a shy, gentle creature named Wallace, was my favorite of the bunch. Lessons were offered in various horse-training techniques; Russ, his parents, and his two older brothers were all certified by EAGALA, a national equine therapy organization. Russ's mother, Dee Morgan, specialized in Parelli, the technique in which I was most interested.

It had been last December at an off-campus party I attended with my roommates that Russ's path again crossed mine. Almost a year had passed since our brief initial meeting at Shore Leave, when he'd attended the music fest and ordered Guinness and tequila shots, and I didn't at first connect the dots when someone behind me said, "I thought you didn't drink."

Startled, I turned to see a guy dressed in jeans and a black wool sweater, clutching a keg cup and studying me as if he knew every last secret I possessed. He had merry blue eyes and dark blond hair and jaws peppered with stubble. When I didn't immediately respond, he adopted the Irish brogue and added, "Now, don't be tellin' me ye don't remember me."

I blinked, peering up at him from the battered couch where I'd been hiding out with a keg cup full of cola, *sans* alcohol, waiting for my roommates to get tired of the noise and chaos; I was their sober cab, as usual. I thought hard for a second before saying, "Russell Morgan."

His answering grin was wide and joyful and there was something in it—something that caught me off guard with the suddenness of a lightning bolt—that reminded me of Wy. Their coloring was different and Russ wasn't nearly as tall, but his face was lean and his smile echoed Wy's, forcing me to inhale a small, sharp breath as he stepped closer.

"Might I join you?" he inquired, gesturing at the otherwise empty couch shoved along one wall in the small enclosed porch, a narrow space lit only by a purple lava lamp undulating through its paces. The main activity of the party was happening in the adjacent living room and kitchen; the porch faced the quiet darkness of a residential street, snow banked hip-high along either curb, and provided a welcome escape for someone like me—uninterested in throwing back shots of Bacardi or playing Quarters.

I shifted position, bringing both feet to the floor and thereby making room on the sagging cushions as I said, "Only if you drop the accent."

"It's a deal," he agreed easily, taking a seat on the opposite end, a polite gesture that proved he didn't want to crowd me. The couch was small enough as it was; he was still less than two feet away. He gestured at my cup. "You broke your own rule?"

I angled it his direction. "It's just soda. No booze."

"You won't believe me, but I had a weird feeling that we'd see each other again someday," he continued. "Did you find the business card I left that day? That's my family's stable."

"I did. I think it's probably still in my apron pocket. Thanks for the great tip, by the way."

"No problem. And look, I was totally right. We meet again!" He grinned afresh, lifting his drink to toast with mine. I obliged, lightly bumping our keg cups, as he asked, "Are you a student at the U?"

"First year, psych major," I explained, already answering what would surely be his follow-up question. "How about you?"

"I'm finishing up my undergrad in business administration," he explained. "I'll graduate in May. This is my roommate's little brother's party, so we thought we'd stop by."

Something occurred to me. "Were you twenty-one when I was serving you drinks that day? You must be younger than I thought."

He laughed. "Yeah, I was. I'll be twenty-three next June. What about you?"

"I was seventeen that day we met," I said, giggling a little at his resultant expression. "I'll be nineteen in two months, on Valentine's Day."

He released a low, disbelieving whistle. "I know women don't like to hear they look older than they are, but you really do. No *way* would I have believed you were only seventeen."

"Should I take that as a compliment?" I demanded, half-teasing.

"For sure you should." He nudged my bent knee with his cup. "You are one fine-looking woman. Is your hair naturally curly?"

I was completely silent for a heartbeat, wondering if he had somehow adopted the erroneous idea that I was an easy mark because I'd separated myself from the other partygoers.

He saw or sensed my apprehension and said quickly, "I'm not trying to make you uncomfortable, I swear. I don't usually throw around compliments to girls I just met."

"Thanks," I said at last.

"Are you seeing anyone?" was his next question.

"Right to the point, aren't you?" I stared at him, mildly stunned. No guy I'd met yet this year had been so forthright. Then again, I typically avoided parties or, if dragged along, found a place to hide out; some people were natural-born flirts—Rae, for instance, and both of my roommates—but I was definitely not one of them.

"If you want to get coffee sometime, let me know." Russ was not to be deterred. "We can talk about the origins of alcohol."

"Or horses," I blurted.

His expression grew instantly more animated. "Horses? You like horses?"

"I do. I plan to specialize in equine therapy."

Images of Bitterroot Ranch filled my mind at the words—the magnificent rehabilitation center where Wy intended to work, which I'd viewed online so often I could have described every last inch, watching as, day by day, the buildings took shape. The website included before-and-after pictures detailing each step of the journey, and featured a variety of new horses in a section called "Rescues." Every single time I clicked on the "Team" link my heart all but exploded—but so far the only employees with linked bios were Tucker and Netta Quillborrow. I recognized Netta as Wy's cousin, a woman I had met in summers past. I checked back every other day, sometimes more often, looking for Wy's picture and link.

*Once he's licensed*, I figured. *Next June.*

Russ was saying, "You should come out to the stable. I'd be happy to show you around anytime. It's just over twenty miles from Minneapolis, in Champlin, where I grew up. My folks own the place, and my brothers and I all work there."

"Maybe," I hedged, although the idea was appealing; I hadn't been around horses since the last summer I spent in Jalesville.

"You can bring your roommates along, it doesn't have to be us alone," Russ assured me. "I mean, I know you don't know me very well yet, so I understand that it seems weird for me to ask you to come to my family's business twenty miles away."

"Actually, it sounds fun," I said honestly.

I found myself relaxing in his easygoing company; we sat chatting for nearly two hours that December evening, and not once was there an awkward, silent gap. Russ was a talker, blunt and quick to voice his opinion, but he was also funny, making me laugh more than once during that first conversation. We parted after exchanging phone numbers; he promised to call, and by the following weekend, I'd driven out to Lake View and ended up meeting his mom, Dee, and one of his older brothers. The scent of horses called Wy so strongly to mind that the first visit to Lake View was about three-quarters pure agony—but I had made myself a promise to move forward, no matter how difficult, one small step at a time.

Since December, I'd spent plenty of time in Russ's company and was a frequent visitor to the stables. Dee had offered me a job in March, which I happily accepted. I had come to like Russ's mother tremendously, a cheerful woman with observant blue eyes and strong, sinewy hands. She handled horses as though born to it, a certified Parelli instructor who took me under her wing. Dee, along with her husband and sons, spent most of her time at the stable, working with the horses. And while Russ was a good teacher in his own right, Dee's instruction was invaluable.

*You're a natural, Millie,* Dee had told me on more than one occasion, and that kind observation was on my mind as I drove up to Lake View under the hot glow of June sunshine, snagging a shady spot near the small grove of maple trees that grew along one edge of the parking lot.

I smiled, spying Russ's beat-up white truck, glad he was here. I wanted to tell him good-bye before we parted ways for the summer. He had graduated with his business degree in May, a ceremony that I attended along with his parents and brothers. He had discussed grad school options with me, confessing that he was ready to take a small break from coursework, which I completely understood. Besides, he loved his job at his family's business. The stable was a large, echoing, steel-pole building, shaped like a long, narrow letter *L*, with an enormous attached paddock. The animals were housed in stalls along the south wall; the main arena occupied most of the space within the structure, a massive, dirt-floored training area surrounded by wooden benches. I had spent plenty of happy hours there, with both Dee and Russ.

Dee stood in the center of the arena, working with a mother and daughter from Champlin, helping them learn the basic techniques with their new horse, a beautiful, rust-red yearling mare named Iris.

"Don't let her back you up," I heard Dee firmly instruct the daughter. "Use the Carrot Stick."

She was referring to one of the Parelli games, all of which were played with the horses to help them learn directions. The Carrot Stick was clutched in the daughter's small hand, a slender, four-foot long stick, painted orange, with an attached five-foot long rope. The games were meant to help build confidence in both horse and rider, create a sense of mutual trust, and develop a partnership through verbal and nonverbal communication.

Dee ordered, "Now, gently swing the string over Iris's back, get her attention," and I smiled at the familiar words. They were playing Friendly Game, part of the first level of instruction; the Carrot Stick was supposed to feel like the swishing of a mother horse's tail.

I waved to Dee and headed straight for the stalls, skirting the hay shed, already calling to Wallace, the mule.

"Hi, boy," I murmured as he poked his long nose over the top of his stall, neighing happily as I cupped his jaws and kissed him between the eyes. Wallace was slightly smaller in stature than the horses, with quirky, rabbit-like ears and huge square teeth he often exposed in his version of a smile. His coat was a dull grayish-brown, soft but bristly, like the knap on an old-fashioned sofa. His nose was pure white and two white blotches encircled his dark eyes. I was totally in love with him; I'd long since recognized the occupational hazard involved in working with animals. I wanted to bring every last one home with me.

"Millie, hey!" Russ called, sticking his head around the office door; the office was a small enclosed room at the front of the stable.

"Hey!" I called back, fishing a sugar cube from my pocket to offer to Wallace, who gobbled it up and then kept licking my palm.

Russ joined me at the stalls, patting Wallace's neck. "I'm glad you stopped out. I was hoping to catch you before you headed home. I'll miss you this summer."

I stared up at him, this man that, for all practical purposes, I considered my boyfriend. Our relationship was tame—especially by college standards—and Russ had never pushed me beyond my comfort zone; we had kissed on many occasions, several times while half-naked, but had not yet advanced further. We talked about past relationships, admittedly without much detail on my end. I'd lied, telling Russ that I'd had sex a few times with my "high school boyfriend," whose name Russ never even asked for. By contrast, I knew far more about his former girlfriends.

*You're so innocent*, he'd said during one of those conversations, and I hadn't interpreted the statement as insulting. He added, *But I find it sexy, if you want the truth. We can take it slow, I respect that.*

"I'll miss you this summer too," I said.

"Maybe you can drive down here a time or two." He spoke lightly, refraining from suggesting that he drive up to Landon instead. Even though he'd been there before—the weekend of the music festival, during my senior year of high school—I wasn't yet ready for him to visit my hometown and meet my entire family. He must have sensed my reluctance, because he had not pressured me about it.

I smiled. "How else would I get to see Wallace?"

Russ grinned widely in response and I hated myself for seeing that trace of Wy in his expression; it was so unfair, on so many levels.

"Right," he murmured. "Wallace is going to miss you so much that he can hardly think about the next two months without you."

My heart melted, ice cream left in the sun. "Aw, he never told me that . . ."

"He's not that great at expressing himself." Russ gathered me in his arms.

I giggled at his words, hooking both arms around his neck. "Tell him that two months goes by really fast."

"Says you," Russ muttered.

I hugged him, tucking my chin over his shoulder, squeezing my eyes shut. I liked Russ so much. I longed for the moment when I'd feel that deep-seated pull, that firecracker awareness of being in love.

"Call me once you get home," Russ said. "I want to know you got there safely."

"I will," I promised.

Five minutes later I was headed north, the interstate rumbling away beneath the tires, bright sunlight pouring in through the driver's side window. By the time I reached Highway 64, I was singing along with the radio, delighted by the prospect of spending the summer at home; working lunch and dinner shifts with Rae, swimming in the lake, taking out the pontoon for evening cruises with the entire family. My grandparents, Bull and Diana Carter, were planning a huge dinner in my honor at White Oaks this weekend.

I arrived in Landon at just after five in the evening and drove out to Shore Leave first, knowing everyone would be there at this time of day on a Thursday.

"Millie's here!" I heard Rae yell from inside.

Rae, Mom, Aunt Jilly, and Grandma Joelle all ran outside to greet me as I parked. They caught me in a five-way hug, everyone talking and laughing at once, and tears filled my eyes as I returned the enthusiastic embrace; I could always count on the homecoming at Shore Leave. The café was bustling with tourist-season business, but they ignored the customers in their excitement. Grandpa Blythe jogged down the porch steps and lifted me right off the ground, spinning me in a circle.

"Little Millie, we're so glad you're home," he said.

"We've missed you so much around here, honey," Grandma Joelle said, smoothing a hand over my hair once Grandpa set me down. "It's just not the same."

Mom kissed my forehead, scrutinizing my face. "You look good, sweetie. How's Russ?"

Despite the fact that they'd never officially met, my mother seemingly adored Russ; I'd told her about him, and all about my job at Lake View, and suspected her adoration stemmed primarily from the fact that I'd shown even minimal interest in someone.

"He's great," I said, then quickly changed the subject. "Man, am I glad to be home! You guys need help this evening?"

"You just got home, babe, you don't have to go to work already," Aunt Jilly said.

"No, let her!" Rae insisted, holding my gaze; she always knew.

"Let me grab my apron," I said gratefully.

. . .

It wasn't until after eight that I found a moment alone. I scurried down the incline to the dock, wanting to catch both the sunset and my breath. It had been a busy dinner shift and I ditched out on rolling silverware, claiming exhaustion. My intent was to call Russ and fill him in on the drive and my evening—he'd sent a text already and I replied with a brief response, not wanting him to worry—but once I collapsed on the glider and swiped my phone's screen to life, I found myself tapping my favorites tab and pulling up the homepage for Bitterroot Ranch, craving a sight of the place where I frequently, foolishly fantasized about someday working. One banner in particular caught my immediate attention. There, front and center for the first time, were the words *Wyatt Rawley, DVM.*

The sinking sun poured hot orange light over my shoulders. I clutched my phone with trembling hands, as strung out with tension as if I intended to commit a crime, almost too afraid to touch the link. I inhaled a shaky breath, blood hopping as I read and reread his name. At last, unable to bear the suspense another second, I opened it.

"*Oh, God . . .*" I whispered.

I pressed hard against my lips, devouring the image, a candid shot rather than a standard head-and-shoulders photograph like his fellow employees, taken as though by someone much shorter than him—one of the kids, probably—and catching him in mid-laugh, the back of one hand lifted to his forehead as though he meant to adjust his same old gray cowboy hat. He'd grown a goatee and a closely-trimmed beard, lending him an aura of maturity for which I was totally unprepared; a perfect frame for his beautiful mouth. I couldn't swallow past the sudden daggers in my throat, rushed by an onslaught of memories—those lips all over my body; those lips speaking words of love and promise. I had so desperately believed I would share my life with this man. His familiar eyes shone with good humor; he appeared content.

"*Wy,*" I breathed, aching and overcome.

His bio read, *A Montana native, Dr. Rawley's goal since the age of three was to become a veterinarian. After earning an undergraduate degree in General Agriculture from the University of Montana in Bozeman, he attended the School of Veterinary Medicine at Washington State University in Pullman, graduating with honors and specializing in equine studies. He lives in Jalesville with his wife, his young son Zane, and his horses Shadow and Scout, and spends his free time caring for animals of every kind and teaching his son to ride.*

Names jumped out at me—*Dr. Rawley; his young son Zane; Shadow and Scout.*

He was teaching his son to ride; he cared for animals of every kind. My heart leaked from a hundred new stab wounds. It was Scout's name in the bio that set me over the edge, that propelled the burst of insanity which inspired me to open a new text and type in Wy's cell phone number—assuming he hadn't changed it in the past two years. My fingers were trembling almost too hard to compose a brief message. Because he wouldn't recognize my number, which had indeed changed, I added, in parentheses: *This is Millie.* And then, before I could reconsider and despite all the very valid reasons I knew I should not, I hit "send." My heart, already thrusting, almost broke through my breastbone. I bent forward over my phone, agonized and exhilarated, unable to believe what I'd dared to do—after two years of total silence, of zero contact with him, I'd texted Wy.

# CHAPTER TWENTY-SIX

I WAS DRIVING FROM BITTERROOT, HEADED FOR downtown Jalesville, when my phone beeped with a new message. I figured it was Hannah, wondering when I'd be home, so I put off checking; it wasn't until much later, after I returned a borrowed air compressor to Nelson's Hardware, where I'd worked after school as a teenager, chatted for a spell with my old boss, and admired a new kitten belonging to his youngest daughter, that I even remembered I'd received a message. Back in my truck in the gloaming light, I used my teeth to remove one of my work gloves, swiping my screen with undeniable reluctance. But I realized at once that Hannah had not sent the message: there was no identifying name, only a phone number. The 218 area code caught my instant attention—northern Minnesota.

My heart lobbed a hot rush of blood through my body as I opened the message.

*I've been learning Parelli and I really love it. (This is Millie.)*

Sent at 7:17 my time, which was an hour behind her time zone, and nearly two hours ago now.

I almost dropped the phone in my haste to respond. Instead of returning the text, I pushed the icon to call her, heart thundering as I held the phone to my ear with one hand and gripped the steering wheel with the other, listening to the distant ringing. She must have thought I didn't care enough to write back immediately. The line rang five times before the call was disconnected without going to voicemail. I was about to call again, determined to explain that I'd only just now read her message, when a new text from her number popped up on the screen.

*Is this Wy?*

I could hardly draw a full breath. I wrote back at once—*It's me*—and then waited on tenterhooks, each moment a new, piercing agony of expectation.

Seconds ticked past before her next message appeared—*I don't think I can handle talking, if it's all the same to you. Can we just text?*

There were a hundred things I wanted to say and yet I sensed on a deep, instinctive level that I needed to let Millie speak first. She had initiated this conversation; I had to trust that she would tell me why she'd chosen tonight, a warm June evening almost two years later, to make contact. A stripe of pale blue decorated the western horizon while bright stars spangled the eastern, and I sat staring mutely at her words. At this unexpected contact I felt lighter than a sunbeam, joy expanding through my entire body—but then, Millie had always had this effect on me, without fail.

I wrote, *Of course.*

Almost immediately, she wrote back—*What are you doing right now?*

*I've been running errands since I left work. What are you doing?*

*Sitting on the dock. I've seen Bitterroot Ranch online, it's so incredibly beautiful. You must love working there.*

I closed my eyes, bringing the phone, and her words, to my lips.

*Oh God, Millie, my sweet Millie. You are what's incredibly beautiful. I'm still in love with you—you know that, don't you? You have to know I've never stopped loving you for one day, not for one minute, and I can't tell you because it would be so fucking dishonorable—*

I didn't send those words, only thought them.

I responded, *It is a beautiful place. I've only been working there a few weeks but it already feels like home.*

*Congratulations on your degree. I'm so completely proud of you. I hope you're proud of yourself.*

*Thank you. I am. Ruthie told me your first year at the U went well. And you're learning Parelli, you said.*

I would not, if it killed me, mention Russ Morgan.

*I am. I've been working at a stable this past winter. I think of you every time I work with horses. I'm sure you must know all about Parelli.*

Gratification flooded my senses, logical or not; she thought of *me.* I wrote back, *Tuck is an instructor. I'd like to earn my certification when I have time. It's a great method. Are you certified yet?*

*Not quite yet but I get to practice every time I go to work.*

*You were always a natural with horses.*

*My favorite horse at the stable is actually a mule! His name is Wallace and he's the sweetest creature I've ever known. I want to bring him home with me. He seems to listen to every word I say.*

*I'm sure he does. Mules are actually easier to train than your average horse, not the stubborn animals most people think they are. They just have good memories and are wary of anything they remember as a negative experience.*

I settled into a more comfortable position in the driver's seat, cradling the phone as though it was Millie's hand, reminded of the night in Landon when we'd texted until almost dawn, the night before we made love for the first time. My phone beeped with a new message.

*I've read that. I already miss Wallace. I might go visit him before this fall.*

*Are you home in Landon for the whole summer?*

*I am.*

Such surface conversation, when I was dying to hear her voice.

*Take it slow,* I warned myself, *just like the first time around.*

Another text appeared—*How's your son? I've wanted to text you more than a hundred times and tell you congratulations for him.*

*Zane is wonderful. I love that kid like crazy.*

*Ruthie has shown me pictures of him. He's adorable. I know you're an amazing father.*

*He's one of the few things that makes my life worth living every day.*

I would not dare edge any closer to intimating that I was unhappy with Hannah, that our marriage was a joke; anyone reading between the lines could already glean such things from the text I'd just sent.

*I'm happy for you, Wy. I've learned so much this past year at college, so many things I wish I could talk to you about. I know that's probably stupid.*

A brutal fist gripped my heart.

Immediately I wrote, *It's not stupid. I want to talk to you too.*

*So much was left unsaid between us, you know? Everything just ended so fast.*

I damned it all and called her number for the second time; again, she didn't answer, disconnecting the call before it went to voicemail and texting almost immediately after.

*I'm sorry. I just can't.*

Terrified that she'd cease communicating altogether, I wrote, *I understand. I promise I do.*

No response.

I kept writing, spurred on by a flood of emotion I usually kept at strictest bay—*There hasn't been a day in the past two years that I haven't wanted to call you. That day I left Minnesota was the worst of my life. I am so sorry for leaving like that. It was the last thing I wanted.*

*It was what you had to do,* she finally responded, and my heart resumed beating. *I understood that, even back then, but it hurt so fucking much. There was a long time I didn't think I'd make it past the pain.*

Tears burned my eyes and pulsed at the bridge of my nose. I was a breath away from texting that the years separating us had changed nothing, that I still loved her with an undying devotion. But it would be wrong on a scale I couldn't stomach. Dishonorable to my wife, to Zane, to Millie herself.

*Forgive me,* I wrote. *Please, forgive me. I can't forgive myself for it.*

*I forgave you a long time ago, I promise. I'm all right, I really am.*

*Will you let me call you?*

*Maybe sometime. Not tonight, I'm sorry.*

*Don't ever be sorry, you never had anything to be sorry about.*

Nearly a minute passed while I waited in silent misery—and then a new text appeared.

*I have to go. It was good to talk.*

I wrote, *Text me anytime.*

No response.

I sent a final plea—*I mean it, day or night.*

But my phone remained dark, as quiet as a hundred well-kept secrets.

. . .

I lay awake for hours after that conversation, reading Wy's last two texts until my vision all but blurred. *Day or night,* he'd written. Did he mean it? Did such words suggest he perhaps felt sorry for me after all this time? Had I come across as pitiful and desperate, admitting how much I hurt in his absence? Tears had ambushed me earlier, sitting on the dock clutching my phone as if it was a physical connection to Wy. I hadn't cried so hard in a long time, sobs that seemed to rip my body in half; it scared me that I could lose control so quickly, as though the defenses I'd constructed in the meantime meant nothing.

*No,* I decided at last. I knew Wy well enough to realize he would never see me in such a light. He was only concerned about me; he admitted to wanting to call me and had tried, several times just this evening. I told myself repeatedly there was no point hoping or pretending he still felt something for me—at least, something beyond the need for forgiveness. As much as I had longed to answer those calls, I simply wasn't ready. I would have fallen apart in front of him, so to speak, far worse than falling apart alone; all intent to remain neutral would have been destroyed. I might have admitted things I should not if I'd heard his voice, things I would regret tomorrow.

*Wy, oh God, I miss you so much.*

*How long does it take to stop wanting you? To fall out of love?*

*I never imagined a future in which we weren't together.*

*But you've moved on, I realize that, and I have to do the same.*

. . .

Too restless to lie awake in bed, I sat for hours in the living room, gazing outside at the dim, indistinct shapes of the neighborhood, cloaked in new-moon darkness. Though I knew I should have already deleted our conversation, I hadn't yet found the strength. I saved Millie's number under the name "Scout," as she'd once hidden mine, and attempted to set aside all guilt, rationalizing that there was nothing inappropriate about Millie and I occasionally exchanging a few messages; for one thing, I owed her a thousand times more than that. I had scarcely let the phone out of my hands since her final text, repeatedly rereading her words while my conscience kept up a steady barrage of commentary.

*You know you can't do this, Wy.*

*You can't contact her again.*

*It's wrong, no matter what you try to tell yourself.*

There were facts about my life I could not deny—I was unhappily married; I was lonely. I closed my eyes, covering my face with one hand as a familiar argument raged inside my skull. In the past six months, I'd begun seriously considering what divorcing Hannah would entail, what it would alter in my life. I could not shake the insidious feeling that divorcing her was akin to abandonment; my salary supported us almost completely. Despite everything, including our frequent arguments over issues often petty and inconsequential, she was a good mother to Zane. I didn't doubt her love for our son. Far worse than any issues concerning finances, I knew that divorcing Hannah would mean fighting her for custody of Zane, a fight that I did not, for one second, fool myself over.

It would be a battle to the death, I was well aware, and the odds were not exactly stacked in favor of my survival.

*You're a father before you are anything else.*

*I can be a father to my son without being married to his mother.*

*But what would you do if you couldn't see Zane every day, if he lived in a separate house? How could you survive only seeing him every other weekend?*

It was the realization that stuck it to my gut, every time; the thought of living apart from my son was unbearable, as unbearable in its own way as the thought of never seeing Millie again.

*Just let me have this—let me sometimes talk to Millie.*

*You don't get to have it both ways, you realize this. Delete that number, do it right now.*

*I can't . . .*

*You can. You've learned to live without her. Delete her number.*

A small sound caught my attention from the direction of Zane's room, and I set aside my phone, heading down the dark hallway before he woke Hannah. The nightlight lit his blue-painted bedroom with a soft, peachy glow, and I entered to see my boy standing in his crib, clinging to the top bar. At the sight of me, his face split with a grin and he reached with one arm, bouncing up and down on his chubby legs. He wore a diaper and a white T-shirt that exposed his round belly, and I scooped him into my arms, inhaling against the downy softness of his hair, the scent of pure innocence, of pure love. Since his birth, I felt as if I'd grown an entirely new heart, one separate from all that had come before. A heart devoted to Zane.

"Hi, buddy," I murmured, rocking side to side. "You need a hug, huh? Me too."

He needed a clean diaper, in addition, after which I resettled in the rocker near the front windows, cuddling him against my chest. My hand was exactly the length of his back. Sitting there, one palm resting upon him as his breath evened out with sleep, I felt the familiar surge of protectiveness, the knowledge that I would do anything required to prevent Zane from being hurt. Anything at all—even remaining married to a woman I did not love. Anything less was cowardly and unthinkable. How would I live with myself if I left his mother and relinquished a single minute of precious time with my boy? How could I consider living in a house separate from my child?

Once Zane was asleep and returned to his crib, I picked up my phone and slipped quietly outside through the front screen door, taking a seat on the top of three pitted cement steps leading to the front walk, hoping that, by some miracle, I would find a new message from Millie. It was 4:48 in the morning, 5:48 in Minnesota, and there was no reason to think she was awake there in Landon, many hundreds of miles from where I sat in the grayish tinge of dawning light, holding my phone, staring at its message screen and rereading her words. One message in particular stood out—*It was what you had to do. I understood that, even back then, but it hurt so fucking much. There was a long time I didn't think I'd make it past the pain.*

I thought, *It still fucking hurts. And I still haven't.*

The air had lightened in minimal increments, enough that the streetlamp on the corner blinked out; at the exact moment its light disappeared, a sudden, prickling awareness crawled over my skin, a sensation strong enough that I sat straighter at once. Without questioning why, I opened a new message to Millie and wrote, *Are you all right?*

No response. I waited with a hard-pounding heart, certain my imagination was not just playing tricks as minutes ticked past.

I called her then, seized by a strange fear.

Just as last night, she disconnected the call before I could leave any sort of message and my phone vibrated almost immediately after with a text.

*Please don't ever call me again. I made a mistake texting you last night. It won't happen again.*

I stubbornly, stupidly, ignored this, determined to speak to her.

When she didn't answer for the second time, I wrote, *Please talk to me. You wouldn't talk to me that day.*

I swore I felt the crackling bolt of her anger as palpably as an intensifying lightning storm. Within seconds my phone blazed with a new message.

*You married someone else. No matter what you felt for me, you fucking married someone else! Do you know what that did to me???!!!*

Raw emotion stormed through my chest, propelling forth words I'd kept buried too long.

*If you think I was any less destroyed, you are wrong. I died that day, I fucking died and you drove away with Rae without a word, without even saying good-bye!*

*Because I knew I was losing you and I couldn't bear it! I still can't bear it. I should never have contacted you and I never will again, you have my word.*

Hands shaking, sweat forming on my chest, I called her number yet again.

And this time, she answered.

...

My pillow was damp beneath my face when I woke and I rolled slowly to one side, working hard to inhale past the sharp pain in my chest. The dream in which I'd so recently been immersed continued to play out in my mind—refusing to become wispy and gray, or fade to nonexistence. Tears rolled over my temples in the pearly light of predawn; the lump in my throat swelled. It had not been my old, recurring nightmare, but in its own way this dream was even more painful. I'd been running with Wy across a field of blooming daisies, summer sunshine warm on our heads, hands linked. We were married; it had been our wedding day, and in my free hand I held up the train of a long, silky dress, allowing my feet leeway to fly. Flowers in my hair, both of us laughing, overflowing with love and happiness.

I rose from my bed without a sound, tugging shorts beneath my pajama top and zipping into a sweatshirt. With bare, silent feet, I slipped down the stairs and then outside, immediately surrounded by humid air and abundant birdsong. Phone in hand, I made my way through the woods to the lake, stepping with care, avoiding sticks and pebbles. I headed for the edge of the shore, the spot just where it met the quietly lapping water. The top curve of the sun appeared on the eastern horizon as I neared the lake, a glowing sliver of scarlet light. I meant to throw my phone out into the water, but to my surprise, it suddenly buzzed with an incoming message.

*Are you all right?*

That Wy had written such a question just now was strange enough to invoke a sense of the surreal; indicative of a connection between us that nothing seemed capable of severing, not time or distance or circumstance. I stared at his message, wondering if I was hallucinating. I'd hardly slept, and when I finally fell into an exhausted stupor, I'd been hammered by the dream of our wedding day. I sank to a crouch on the shore, feeling as though I was still webbed in a dreamworld, and my phone began ringing—he was calling.

*Answer*, my heart begged. *Please answer.*

I declined the call and texted, *Please don't ever call me again. I made a mistake texting you last night. It won't happen again.*

But he called back immediately, ignoring the plea.

No more than seconds later, he wrote, *Please talk to me. You wouldn't talk to me that day.*

His words brought memories surging—terrible memories of that morning on the side of the highway outside Itasca, of helpless despair. No one, before or since, had hurt me as profoundly. Maybe it was pure survival, but sudden fury throbbed through my blood, momentarily overpowering the pain. My index finger flew over the tiny digital keyboard on my phone's screen.

*You married someone else. No matter what you felt for me, you fucking married someone else! Do you know what that did to me???!!!*

Almost instantly, he responded—*If you think I was any less destroyed, you are wrong. I died that day, I fucking died and you drove away with Rae without a word, without even saying good-bye!*

Pain clogged my throat.

*Because I knew I was losing you and I couldn't bear it! I still can't bear it. I should never have contacted you and I never will again, you have my word.*

The phone buzzed to life in my hand.

Anger lent me strength—or stupidity, depending on the viewpoint. But no sooner had I answered when I found I couldn't speak. I held the phone to my ear, sensing him there on the other end, many hundreds of miles west of me in Montana—my Wyatt, the man my entire being, inside and out, could not stop loving.

Tears seeped from my eyes like acid as he said intently, "Millie? Are you there?"

I knew he could hear me breathing but I couldn't respond, unwilling to let him know how undone I was at the sound of his voice. His deep, familiar voice, rough with concern and strain. I cupped a hand over my mouth and pressed hard, squeezing my cheeks, feeling the edges of my teeth.

He spoke with the same low-voiced intensity I remembered all too well. "Please don't hang up. I just want to talk to you. The last sight I had of you was watching that truck disappear down the road." He paused before asking, "Did you find my letter that day? I never knew."

I had to respond; it took all my effort to maintain a steady voice. "I found it that night after Rae dropped me off. You were already gone."

I heard him exhale. "It's so good to hear you, it's been so long. Leaving was the last thing I wanted. You have to know I would have stayed if I could."

"I know," I acknowledged, eyes closed, but it did no good—tears streamed past the barriers of my eyelids all the same. "I still have the letter. I meant to throw it away about a thousand times, but I never could go through with it."

He spoke in a rush. "Not a day has passed that I haven't wanted to write you another letter, or call you. After Zane was born, you were the first person I wanted to call. I know it makes no sense, you probably would have hung up before I could speak a word, but I just wanted to tell you about him. Oh God, Millie, there are so many things I want to tell you . . ."

It was too much, the pain returning in razor-edged waves. I couldn't listen to these words, not when Wy belonged to someone else, a pretty, redheaded woman named Hannah who had been the recipient of his tender, passionate touch for the past two years; his wife, the woman who had taken his name and given him a child that made his life worth living every day. The woman he held close every night and made love with, the woman who shared his life and his dreams. She was probably pregnant with their second baby already.

"I met someone, he's a horse trainer," I blurted. The lifting sun burned my eyes, creating a reddish haze in the gauzy layer of mist over the lake. The lie bulged like a bullfrog in my throat and before I could think twice, I said, "We're really happy."

A thick wall of silence before Wy said, "Then I'm happy for you." Another pause, before he asked, "Is that Russ?"

"How do you . . ." I was stunned.

"Ruthie told me. His family owns the stable where you work, she said."

"Lake View," I whispered.

"He's teaching you Parelli?" Wy sounded hoarse, there was no denying.

"Yes." I gnawed the insides of my cheeks to keep from admitting things I had no right to admit—the entire reason I had avoided answering his calls in the first place. I rallied every ounce of strength in my possession and said, "I have to go, Wy."

"Not yet." Somewhere between an order and a plea.

I whispered, "Good-bye," disconnected the call, and then reeled sideways, slammed by a wave of dizzy nausea. I scrabbled through the beach rocks until I found a large, jagged-edged one. I grasped it, hampered by tears, and hammered it against my phone, sweating, breathing hard, until I had splintered the digital screen into a pinwheel of cracks. And then I stood and chucked it with all my strength, watching as it hit the glass-smooth water with hardly a splash, disappearing forever beneath the surface.

# PART THREE

# CHAPTER TWENTY-SEVEN

OF ALL THE FARMS AND RANCHES WHERE I TREAT-
ed livestock in my vast territory of Montana counties, Jarred Watkins' was the
only I disliked.

At first, I worked primarily in and around Jalesville and therefore knew most
of the surrounding families; in the year since graduation, my practice had expanded exponentially and I traveled hundreds of miles during any given week,
visiting outlying operations, performing herd checks, vaccinating or examining
or treating, as required, and confirming insemination for mares and cows, often
thinking as I did so of the conversation I'd once had with Millie on the subject.
I'd purchased an ultrasound machine for the procedure, one that strapped across
the tops of my shoulders, with a small sonogram screen that fit neatly along my
left forearm.

I spent the early part of each week, usually Mondays and Tuesdays, on site at
the rehabilitation center. They quickly became my favorite days of the week, spent
caring for the stock at Bitterroot, which by now included over five dozen head of
horse, two dozen Dexter cattle, a breeding pair of Berkshire swine, five dogs who
roamed with all the freedom of wild wolves, Netta's chickens, and uncountable
barn cats. I ate lunch with Netta, Tuck, Joey, and, more often than not, Quinn,
who met us if he could swing it, the five of us clustered around one of the picnic
tables in view of the foothills if the weather was fair—which, that spring, it was
almost every day.

The camaraderie of that first year at Bitterroot helped me in countless ways.
I could never quite find the words to vocalize this, but they must have known at
some level how much I depended on their friendship and support, how much
they carried me through. Though I never spoke openly about it around anyone
but my brothers or Joey, my miserable marriage was not exactly a secret. The brief
conversation I'd been allowed with Millie last summer had only made everything
worse, serving to highlight the glaring contrast between my current life and what
it could have been.

Because Hannah worked every weekday, we took turns bringing Zane to
either Dad's or Irene's; whichever of us finished work first picked him up, usually
Hannah. I did my best to show up in time for dinner, but some days, depending

on the distance between Jalesville and a call, it just wasn't possible. And before heading home, I always stopped at Bitterroot's empty office, closed for the evening, to shed my work clothes and boots—perpetually filthy with a combination of mud, saliva, and dung, and which Hannah refused to allow in our washing machine—and to take a final walk around the property, bidding the animals goodnight, ending with Shadow and Scout. I'd considered purchasing a pair of mules ever since Millie had mentioned Wallace.

Stupid, irrational thoughts; imagining her joy over the animals, fantasizing about a day in the distant future in which she would be here caring for them along with me.

Tuck and Netta lived less than a quarter-mile up the road from Bitterroot, and sometimes one or both of them would still be around in the early evening, turning out a last light or locking up the main office. I always made sure the dogs were kenneled for the night. My favorite of the bunch, a collie mix named Otter, usually accompanied me on calls, riding in the passenger seat of my vet truck with his tongue lolling, shaggy head sticking out the window. I'd always harbored a special fondness for animals with black and white coats, reminiscent of my first horse. I longed to bring Otter to the house on Front Street—Zane adored all of the dogs at Bitterroot—but Hannah was insistent on the no-pet rule. Not even a single goldfish lived within our walls. All of Zane's exposure to animals occurred at Bitterroot or at one of my brothers' houses, where dogs and cats and various other critters ran rampant.

*Am I so narrow-sighted that I can't see beyond the way I was raised?* I often wondered, the long drives I made almost daily through the wide-open foothill country inspiring endless introspection. *Is it wrong to think a home should include animals, and laughter, and messes? It doesn't have to be perfectly clean and quiet at all times; we don't live in a library, for Christ's sake.*

The rest of the week, and an occasional Saturday or Sunday, I drove to calls near and far in my work truck, a two-ton diesel I'd recently purchased. I met dozens of new families, made contacts, and collaborated with vets from neighboring counties, people whose lifestyles were comfortingly familiar—farmers and ranchers, men and women who wore coveralls and work gloves and heavy boots, who drove tractors and hauled trailers and made conversation about grain prices, livestock auctions, and weather patterns. Men and women whose children had learned to drive farm equipment around age ten, who knew the value of a dollar, and to whom manual labor was part of a typical day. People who were not squeamish about tasks that needing accomplishing, who would have laundered dirty work clothes in their home washer without blinking an eye.

I made countless comparisons as dozens of miles disappeared beneath my truck tires, weighing my options. And though I'd been in a low, shitty mood when I met Jarred Watkins on a Wednesday afternoon in mid-May, having driven out to his ranch after a sleepless night, it was not why I disliked him. Jarred was a somewhat surly man, about a decade older than me, and it wasn't so much his abrupt attitude either; I came across the occasional gruff customer and usually didn't think twice about it. Something about the man just plain troubled me, on a gut level. He'd been quick to inform me that his wife had called for a vet, not him. The disdainful tone with which he spoke the word "wife" reminded me of the way a cop on a crime drama would say "perp."

I'd been called out to his ranch to examine a foundering pony. The poor creature could hardly walk, and I collected a blood sample and administered an anti-inflammatory drug to relieve her pain, disturbed by the conditions in the Watkins' unclean barn. Jarred stuck to my side like a tick as I worked over the pony, and so I cast my gaze as surreptitiously as possible at his additional livestock, which included two donkeys, two mules, and a gelding quarter horse, all six of which, counting the pony, appeared underfed. The pony's hooves badly needed trimming, which I pointed out to Jarred, who mumbled an unintelligible reply. A dog, a skinny pit bull mix, slunk about the edges of the barn, watching our exchange with wary eyes, and I felt an acidic lump swell in my chest. All my instincts suggested that Jarred Watkins mistreated, maybe even beat, his animals.

"We have an on-site farrier at Bitterroot," I pressed, attempting to swallow away my misgivings. Nothing raised my ire faster than the suspicion of animal abuse. "He can stop out here this week."

"Nah, I'll take care of it," Jarred insisted.

"Take care of it soon," I said, holding his gaze. He didn't respond, but he retreated a few steps away, perhaps intuiting my growing anger. "She's in serious pain. If you don't care for her hooves, her condition will only get worse. Same goes for the rest of your stock."

I turned my attention back to the pony whose small, elongated head lay in my lap as I knelt in her stall. I rubbed her nose, wishing I could lift her into the bed of my truck and haul her back to Bitterroot. I gently lowered her head to the hay scattered on her stall floor, collected my equipment pack, and stood, brushing my hands on my jeans as I issued directives to Jarred.

"You need to strictly control her diet and keep her on complete stall rest. I'll stop back in a week to check on her and I'll call you with her blood work. In the meantime, get those hooves trimmed. She can recover from this."

He studied me in unpleasant silence before nodding curtly.

Outside, a lead-colored cloud bank had massed, the air dense with an approaching thunderstorm, and the atmosphere in the barnyard seemed tainted with ill will. The pit bull trailed us, his head and whip-like tail hanging low. The window curtains in the adjacent house were drawn, but I saw them suddenly part about two inches, conveying a fluttery sense of anxiety, as though whoever stood behind them wished to watch without being seen; Jarred's wife, probably, the woman who'd called for a vet when he clearly would not have. Everything seemed too quiet, the sort of eerie silence that held the land in a tense grip just before a violent storm broke. Otter, waiting for me in the truck, issued a sharp bark, as though urging me to get a move on.

I shifted my pack to my left hand, extending my right. "I'll be back next week."

Jarred briefly shook. "No need."

"I'll see you then." I was not to be deterred.

"I mean it, doc, there's no need." His eyes appeared hard and flat, like a sheared-off stone. "I already owe you for this visit, I'm not paying twice."

"No charge for a follow-up." I climbed inside my truck and started it, ruffling Otter's fur in an attempt to calm down.

Jarred stood watching as I drove away; as glad as I was to leave the cheerless place, I was reluctant to drive away knowing the animals in his possession were not properly cared for. Rain began spattering the windshield as I turned left on the gravel road leading back to the highway, and only by chance did I happen to glance in the rearview mirror in time to witness Jarred boot the old pit bull hard in the ribs, sending the animal jolting to his side. I hit the brakes and then angled my truck in a tight U-turn, observing the bastard's surprised face with a certain amount of grim satisfaction as I reentered his barnyard.

"You forget something, doc?" he inquired sharply as I stepped down from my truck and approached through the increasing downpour. The poor old dog hunched near the porch steps, favoring a front leg.

"I saw you kick that dog." Hostility pumped through my blood. "I don't stand for animal abuse."

Jarred snorted. "I didn't abuse that mutt."

"I saw you."

His jaw jutted. "Kicking a disobedient dog isn't animal abuse."

"Touch that dog again and you'll be sorry." I may have been out of line but I didn't care in that moment.

"Get off my property or *you'll* be fucking sorry!" he railed.

I strode around him without another word and collected the pit bull in my arms. The soggy creature probably weighed fifty pounds, but he didn't struggle against my hold. Rain rolled down my shoulders and gathered in my hat brim, and I was unprepared for Jarred's swinging fist. He caught me in the mouth and

I staggered, but retained my hold on the dog. I deflected his next blow by turning and hunching a shoulder, just as my brothers had taught me long ago; pure
adrenaline kept physical pain at bay. I deposited the wet dog in the truck bed and
faced off with Jarred, who was cursing, steaming-mad, howling for his wife to
call the sheriff. When he advanced on me, I shoved him in the chest with both
hands, setting him hard on his ass. Otter lunged against the passenger door, barking frantically.

"I'm pressing charges, you sonuvabitch!" Jarred bellowed as I drove away.

"Go ahead," I muttered, gripping the steering wheel so furiously my knuckles
stood out like ridges. It was a little late to worry about legalities now. I pictured
the way the pit bull had struck the ground before limping away from Jarred and
vented to Otter in a hopped-up rush of vitriol, "Fucking piece of shit *animal-
abusing motherfucker*, I should have taken all his livestock, should have broken his
fucking nose. Goddamn piece of shit."

Once out of sight of the Watkins' property, I pulled to the shoulder of the
road and lifted the pit bull from the truck bed, depositing him in the backseat
where he would be protected from the rain. The poor thing wagged his wet tail,
licking my hand as I rubbed his graying muzzle, which bore evidence of scabbed-
over abrasions, likely from being struck. His intelligent eyes were golden-brown
and drooped at the outer corners, sorrowful in the way of abused creatures the
world over, and though I'd technically just stolen him from his owner, I felt completely justified in the action.

"I'm so sorry that bastard hurt you, boy. You can live with us from now on,
how's that?"

I drove the forty miles back to Bitterroot in a cocoon of self-righteousness,
not realizing until after I parked outside the main office that the lower half of my
face ached and my limbs felt rubbery. I let Otter out of the truck and then carried
the pit bull inside the work space I shared with Joey, a building adjacent to the
main office where Netta worked. Joey looked up from his laptop at my sudden
entrance, eyebrows raised.

"A stray?" he guessed, already hurrying from behind the desk.

"You could say that," I muttered, transferring him to Joey's arms. The dog issued a low moan, legs scrambling.

"Hey there, dog, it's all right," Joey soothed, switching up his hold to contain
the movement, hustling to the examination room. "You're all right now. Some-
body hurt your nose, huh?"

"I should have beaten the shit out of the guy," I said, grabbing an antiseptic
wipe from the container on the counter, scrubbing at my knuckles.

"What the hell does that mean?" Joey demanded from down the hall.

"It fucking means I fucking hate animal abusers." I joined Joey, where he'd situated the dog on the exam table and was busy angling a light.

"Don't we all?" Joey looked up, peering more closely at me. "Your lip is bleeding. Where have you been?"

"The Watkins' ranch, west of here, out by Torch Gap Road. I took this dog from his owner. Without permission, I mean." I leaned against the doorframe, resisting the urge to look over my shoulder for the first sign of a police cruiser rolling into the lot with top lights spinning.

Joey whistled a low, falling note, a nonverbal *uh-oh*.

"I don't stand for animal abuse," I said stubbornly, pressing the antiseptic wipe to my split lower lip; it stung like hell on the wound there.

An admiring half-smile appeared on Joey's face. "If someone comes to haul you to the clink they'll have to get through me first." He gestured at the dog. "I'll x-ray him, but I'd say this poor mutt has at least two fractured ribs. You did the right thing, Wy, you're a good person."

"Thanks, buddy."

"All the same, you better call Travis," Joey advised, naming the local sheriff, whose father, the former sheriff, was a longtime friend of my dad's. "Fess up before this gets out of hand."

I figured he was right and called Travis Woodrow from our office landline, explaining the situation. He told me to hang tight and called back a few hours later to say that nothing had been reported; for whatever reason and despite his threats, Jarred Watkins had not issued a complaint to any local authorities.

"Thanks, Trav," I said, running a hand over the back of my neck. My unease had grown with each passing hour as I imagined possible long-reaching ramifications of my actions, everything from losing my license to practice medicine to Bitterroot being fined or shut down.

"It doesn't mean he *won't*," Travis continued. "But if he hasn't yet, I'd say chances are good that he doesn't plan on it. Maybe he's smart enough to know you'd be more credible than him. You said you suspected additional abuse or neglect?"

"Yes," I confirmed. "He probably beats his wife and kids too, he seems just the type. I should have taken all the livestock from that place."

"Funny that you'd say that, since he has multiple priors."

"For what?"

"Nothing to laugh at. Misdemeanor assault. A couple of drunk-and-disorderlies that stuck, one aggravated assault that didn't." Trav sounded like he was reading from a printout. He issued a low whistle before saying, "Way to go, Wy, you made the shit list of a first-class asshole."

"Figures," I muttered.

"I'll make a call, try to get someone out there to check things out." Travis paused before saying, "I hear that tone in your voice. Don't make Clark have to bail your ass out of jail for trespassing. Or worse, you'd get gut-shot with a twelve-gauge and this Watkins guy would let you bleed out in his corral. I peg him as the sort who prefers to take matters into his own hands."

I briefly envisioned the picture Travis had just described, which likely wasn't far from the truth. It wasn't that I intended to go looking for trouble. I just hated knowing there was nothing I could do to prevent helpless animals from suffering. The pit bull was sedated, sheltered in one of our kennels for the night. Joey had treated the animal's injuries and was now loading his backpack to head home. He'd overheard my conversation with Travis, and after I hung up, he invited, "You want to grab a beer? It's on me."

"Thanks, but I better get going. I've been late too many times already this week." I leaned on my elbows over my desk, grinding my eye sockets with both fists. I sensed Joey's compassion; though I'd never yet told him about Millie, he knew Zane was the only reason I wanted to return to the house on Front Street on any given night.

"What will Hannah have to say about all this?" Joey inquired quietly.

"God only knows," I mumbled.

"You *stole* someone's dog?" was exactly what she had to say, fifteen minutes later. "Are you out of your mind?"

"I would have taken the entire barn of animals, if I could have," I said, unapologetic. I stood near the stove, loading a plate with warmed-up leftovers from dinner, which I'd missed once again. Zane was already in bed, curled up with his teddy and his blankie. I'd bent over his crib to kiss his downy cheek before joining Hannah in the kitchen.

Near my right elbow, she stood gaping at me. She was wearing an old T-shirt of mine over pajama shorts, her hair hanging loose to her shoulders. Her limbs were long and pale in contrast to her sunburned face, her feet bare. She heaved a frustrated sigh, unwilling to let the matter drop. How I wished we could just talk, have a normal conversation without a subtle—and sometimes not so subtle—undercurrent of irritation at each other.

"Did you even stop to think how that might affect us?" she wanted to know. "What if you'd been arrested? You care more about animals than your own family!"

"That is not true." I turned to look at her, studying the pale blue eyes I'd regarded at close range for the past three years; my wife's eyes, the woman with whom I'd promised to share my life and who had given birth to my son.

I heard Millie say, *We're really happy.*

*No doubt Russ Morgan's happy,* I thought bitterly. *He has you.*

Hannah cried, "It *is* true! You let yourself get punched in the face over a stupid dog, a dog you stole from someone's property! How could you do such a thing?!"

I skirted her, grabbing a beer from the fridge before taking a seat at the table; I wanted a whiskey but held off, unwilling to listen to yet another accusation that I was an alcoholic. Even though I figured it wouldn't do much good, I attempted to explain. "I saw that dog get kicked. I can't stand seeing animals hurt. The poor thing had two fractured ribs and evidence of past abuse. My face is the least of my worries."

Hannah sank to a seat across from me. "But it's not your problem. I don't get why you care so much."

I knew she didn't, and so did not bother replying.

Not that it mattered; she continued nagging with no prompting. "You have to face reality. You can't save every animal, even if you want to."

"Right. But I can save the ones I see getting mistreated right in front of my eyes."

Hannah tucked hair behind both ears. "Well, you're lucky nothing came of it. At least, not yet. I just wish you'd think twice before doing something like this. Think about me and Zane. What would we do if you lost your job? *Jesus,* Wy."

"Don't act like I don't think about the two of you."

"What am I supposed to think when you do a stupid thing like this?"

"It wasn't a stupid thing."

"It was!" Her eyes narrowed. "I can't trust your judgment. You're at work most of the week and half the time when you're actually home, you're drunk."

I set down my fork. "That is not true."

"You drink every night!" She jabbed a finger at the beer can near my elbow.

"I have a few drinks, nothing out of line." I thought of the whiskey bottle hidden in the back of the cupboard near the dishwasher, the one I sipped from late at night, alone on the couch or the front porch steps.

She continued glaring, probably well aware of all these things.

"Can I just eat in peace?" I asked, suddenly unbearably weary.

Hannah flounced from the table and stormed to our bedroom; moments later, loud sobs sounded. She hadn't even bothered to shut the door. I set aside my plate and ventured after her, worried that her crying would wake and scare Zane. I had long ago learned that Hannah's tears were for the most part staged. She acted hysterical whenever she didn't get her way; oddly, her parents seemed the most susceptible to it, without seeming to realize that it was an unhealthy way to seek attention. When I tried broaching the subject with Irene, she snapped at me, claiming that if I only tried harder to make Hannah happy, she wouldn't have reason to cry so often.

Hannah was lying on her stomach, and mine ached at the necessity of having to deal with this sort of situation yet again.

*Just leave her alone*, I thought, but felt guilty relenting to the instinct. Besides, I didn't want Zane waking up and hearing his mother in inconsolable tears.

"Don't cry." I sat near her on the mattress and rested a hand on her waist, but she twitched my touch away, as she usually did.

"Go away!" she sobbed.

"Fine," I muttered through my teeth. I started to rise but she suddenly shifted and grabbed for me, clutching hold of my wrist.

Her red-rimmed eyes brimmed with fresh tears as she demanded, "Where are you going?"

"Nowhere. To the goddamn kitchen."

Her constant mood swings were more exhausting than a day spent loading hay bales on a flatbed trailer. And then she caught me off guard as surely as Jarred Watkins' first punch had. Digging her nails into my skin, she hissed, "Who is she?"

A cold arrow shot through my center.

"What do you mean?" I whispered.

"The woman you're seeing, that's what I mean!" Hannah cried.

It took all I had to keep a level expression, even as my thoughts raced and spun.

*Did she somehow see my texts to Millie from last summer?*

Even though it had been nearly a year I had not yet deleted them, despite all the very good reasons I should have.

"I'm not seeing anyone," I said quietly, but I tugged my wrist free at the same moment, which somehow served to contradict the statement.

Hannah rolled to her knees on the mattress and her pale eyes gleamed with a weird sense of triumph. "I know you're lying. You work late all the time, you never return my texts. God knows we hardly have sex. Who is she, some vet in the next county? Some bitch who sticks her arm up a cow's ass all day too?"

It was times like these that a surge of pure revulsion swelled in my chest, as noxious as a cloud of poison.

"You'd demean my entire career that way? The career that keeps a roof over your son's head and food on our goddamn table?" I demanded, unwilling to address the potshot about our lack of a sex life. We were both to blame for that.

"You're not denying it!" she hollered.

"There's nothing to deny, that's why. Keep your voice down! Do you want Zane to hear you?"

"Don't order me around! Not when you're probably screwing some vet in another town!"

"*Jesus Christ,*" I muttered in disgust, turning to leave, closing the door behind me.

Hannah flung something after me, a hard object which struck the door and no doubt left a divot in the cheap wood. I went straight to Zane's room, relieved to find him asleep, snuggled on his tummy, his lips moving like he was nursing. I shut his door and dragged the rocking chair closer to his crib, listening for sounds indicating that Hannah was about to burst into the room. I did not intend to let her wake Zane or scare him with her yelling. She resumed sobbing but didn't follow after me, and I thanked God for small favors. My erratic heartbeat slowed as I studied my sleeping son. Time slipped past and eventually I dozed off, waking at some later point with a startled twitch.

I sat straight, sensing that hours had passed. The house was silent, deep with night. Outside Zane's airplane-patterned curtains the sky appeared dense, and as I watched, a cluster of heavy clouds were suddenly backlit with lightning. Seconds later, thunder grumbled like someone delivering bad news. I hunched my shoulders and rolled my neck to ease the kinks. Zane was snuffling baby-sized snores. I rested a hand to his back before leaving him in peace, intending to sleep on the couch, as per routine. My phone sat abandoned on the coffee table and I picked it up before stretching out on the cushions, scrolling to the contact labeled "Scout."

The small digital clock on my screen read 3:19. There was no reason to believe Millie was awake this early spring morning.

*But, what if . . .*

*Don't even think about it, Wy.*

*If she's expecting a text from anyone, it's Russ Morgan. Not you.*

*You have to stop this. She told you she's happy with him and that she didn't want to talk to you anymore.*

*You need to respect that.*

*It doesn't matter how much you want to talk to her.*

And though it nearly killed me, especially when I already felt so goddamn wrecked, I deleted every message we'd exchanged last summer.

# CHAPTER TWENTY-EIGHT

THAT FRIDAY, SEAN AND QUINN, WHO WERE both employed by the county and often rode to work together, stopped out at Bitterroot at the end of their shift to see if Joey and I wanted to join them for a drink. Dad was already watching Zane since Hannah was over in Miles City shopping with her mother, and I took a moment, as I did several times every day, to acknowledge how goddamn fortunate my brothers and I were to have our father in our lives. Dad was pushing seventy these days and yet still insisted on caring for our kids whenever necessary, which was to say on about a daily basis. I knew Dad truly enjoyed their company, but his presence was a gift of immeasurable magnitude, one I would never take for granted.

"Sure, that sounds great," I told Quinn, who stood holding open the front entrance while Sean waited in the work truck. I called over my shoulder, "Joe, you want to join us?"

"Give me just a sec!" Joey responded from the exam room; I thought he sounded somewhat on edge.

"Is this the famous mutt?" Quinn asked, coming inside, letting the door thump shut behind him. "The one you stole on Wednesday? Should have named him Otis Lee the Second."

I nodded wryly, thinking of the long-ago afternoon when I'd saved the cat; I only wished it was in my power to save every abused animal from harm. I rubbed a thumb over the top of the pit bull's grizzled head, which lay on my right thigh as he sat on his haunches alongside my desk chair. Because we hadn't known the dog's name, we'd taken to calling him Lucky, or Lucky Dog, using the same intonation as the old commercial jingle. Since his rescue from Jarred Watkins' ranch two days ago, Lucky stuck to my side as soon as I set foot on the ground at Bitterroot; I hated leaving him behind in the evenings.

"Hey there, fella," Quinn murmured, bending down to scratch Lucky's head. He nudged my shoulder in a gesture of affection as he added, "You did the right thing, little bro. I would have done the same. I can take him if you don't have room here. Or Sean said he and Jess can too. Their kids would love this guy."

"I just might take you up on that. This poor guy needs a little love." I squelched the sudden rush of resentment; Hannah and I had barely spoken since the accusations of cheating she'd flung my way two nights ago.

"We'll be right out," I assured Quinn, reaching for my hat. "I'm glad you guys stopped in; I could use a drink tonight."

The four of us entered The Spoke ten minutes later and I let the customary noisy space work a temporary spell over my shitty mood. I inhaled the aroma of tobacco, fryer grease, leather, and alcohol, mixed with various perfumes and colognes and the scent of warm, perspiring skin. The bar was decorated in honor of the rapidly approaching summer season, with canning jars full of early wildflowers, and the atmosphere inside was typical warm-weather rowdy. Lee came from behind the bar to give us quick hugs, standing on tiptoe; she wasn't as tall as Pam and Netta.

After hugging Joey, Lee complained, "You make me miss Kyle! You look just like him and I haven't seen him in two weeks."

Joey grinned. "He misses you too."

"Get him to move here!" my cousin nagged; she and Kyle had hooked up after our graduation party last year and my brothers and I, in addition to Joey, loved teasing them about their subsequent long-distance romance, not to mention age difference. All kidding aside, I wished Kyle would decide to relocate to Montana. Joey and I talked often about it. But Kyle loved his job in Washington, and so, for now, he and Lee contented themselves with visits once or twice a month.

Joey added, "And *please* tell him you think we look just alike; I'd love to hear what he has to say about that."

Sean elbowed Lee with a longtime combination of teasing and good humor. "Kyle's still putting up with your shit, huh? Dude must really like older women."

Lee delivered a sharp jab to Sean's midsection. Fussily adjusting her long ponytail, she snapped, "Older woman, my ass!"

We all loved picking on Lee; Quinn joined in next, saying, "It's not like Kyle is young enough to be your teenage-pregnancy baby or anything. He's only, what, like ten years younger . . . "

We were all laughing by then, including Lee, even though she pretended to be angry.

"Go sit the hell down, leave me alone!" she ordered.

Lee sent over two pitchers of lager and a round of whiskey sours. The band was a group of locals and we enjoyed a few minutes doing nothing but unwinding, draining the first round as we listened to the music. My brothers were dressed similarly to me, in well-worn jeans, scruffy T-shirts, and work boots; neither had shaved in a good three days. By contrast, Joey, after having shed his lab coat back at Bitterroot, had changed into clean dress pants and a crisp collared shirt, the outfit that hung in his locker for unexpected occasions which he felt required nice clothing; Joey would never consider appearing in public without a fresh shave. I noticed for the second time that he seemed restless—and all of these things inspired me to nudge him with my elbow as my brothers were drawn into conversation with a group at a nearby table.

"Spill," I ordered my old friend in an undertone.

Joey sent me a withering look, eyes narrowed.

I hid a smile, leaning back in my chair, subtly scanning the unruly crowd. "You don't fool me. Who do you have your eye on?"

"No one," he insisted, sitting straighter, but I knew him well enough to recognize the signs.

"Don't get prissy on me," I said, messing with him a little; the truth was I hoped he would find someone in the area. Despite having gone on an occasional date in the past year, all with guys he'd met online, I knew Joey was lonely, and Jalesville didn't exactly have a significant gay population. Selfishly, I just wanted him to stick around; not only was he my best friend, but I also worried he would grow tired of the small-town vibe, something to which he was not accustomed.

"Fuck off," he responded irritably, twitching his shoulders, avoiding my gaze as he sipped carefully from the skinny cocktail straw in his whiskey sour; he would kill me if I kept teasing him right now.

*Don't be such an asshole, Wy,* he would say.

"Come on," I pestered. "Who?"

My brothers turned back to our table at that moment and it was only by chance that I happened to be looking at Quinn; for no more than two seconds his gaze held Joey's, and that was all it took for realization to dawn. My mind skipped blankly for a moment, absorbing what I'd just witnessed.

*Hang on a sec . . .*

*What the . . .*

*Quinn is gay?*

*Since when?*

*How did I miss this? I am that dense?*

Quiet, thoughtful Quinn, who hadn't really dated anyone since high school, or expressed genuine interest in any woman, local or otherwise. Awareness flowed over me in waves, and I felt like an inconsiderate, not to mention unobservant, jerk. All the conversations I'd had with him, all the kind advice he'd given me over the years, flashed through my mind in the fashion of someone drowning. And meanwhile, I'd been so wrapped up in my own problems that I'd never recognized a basic truth about my own brother.

*Think about it, genius. He and Joey have been hanging out together since that first night Quinn gave him a tour of Jalesville.*

The idea of my brother and my best friend as a couple, while wholly unexpected, grew quickly in appeal. I kicked Joey's ankle beneath the table, letting him know I intended to grill him the minute we were alone. He angled me his most prissy glare and a sudden surge of contentment infused my soul, unbelievably welcome. But I should have known not to trust it—not five minutes into my good mood, I spied Travis Woodrow enter the bar and scan the crowd; he was obviously looking for me, because he strode our way before I lifted a hand to wave him over. He was in uniform and his expression was grim.

*Shit.*

*There's trouble.*

Noticing what had to be the sudden, sickly green tinge to my face, my brothers and Joey stopped talking and turned their gazes in the direction of mine.

"Trav looks pissed," Sean observed.

I squared my shoulders, trying hard to inhale a deep breath, certain Travis was about to clap me in cuffs.

He reached our table before anyone could reply and said without preamble, "There's a problem."

Sean and Quinn both spoke at once.

"If you're here to take Wy away there's been a mistake . . . "

"This is complete bullshit . . . "

Travis heaved an exasperated sigh. "I'm not here to take anyone away, guys." He pinned me with an earnest gaze as he explained, "I just got word from a deputy over in Jarred Watkins' county. He stopped out there this afternoon, just a few hours ago, and talked with Watkins. Watkins got all riled up when the deputy said he needed to provide better care for his livestock. Watkins told him that a vet from Jalesville stole his dog on Wednesday. He named you, Wy."

I tried hard to appear braver than I felt. "I would do it again, you can put that on record if you want."

"I think you did the right thing," Travis continued. "But you may very well be in a situation here." He paused, clearly reluctant, before adding, "Watkins had recently shot a foundering pony. It was still lying in its stall."

My blood boiled. "That *piece of shit*. I would have taken that pony with me, there was nothing wrong with her that time wouldn't fix."

Travis leaned forward. "Listen, I explained the situation to the deputy, Clemens is his name. I told him you saw Watkins kick the dog and that you acted with compassion when you took it away. But Clemens is on the way here to question you about it, I wanted to give you a heads-up. Watkins told him that you used violence, shoved him down when he tried to take back his animal."

Adrenaline pierced the self-righteous haze clouding my brain. Thank God

Hannah was out of town and not there at the house to answer the door to a deputy; wouldn't that supply her with ample ammunition to lob my way?

"When's he getting here?"

Travis glanced at his watch. "Probably within the hour. You should head home."

"Thanks, Trav. I appreciate you warning me like this."

My brothers and Joey were a concrete wall of defense, surrounding and bolstering me; I was so grateful for them. They all accompanied me to the house on Front Street and followed me inside, where I clicked on lights and paced the living room rug until a county sheriff's beige, official-looking SUV rolled into the driveway. Pulse racing, I met him at the door, trying to assess the man even before he began speaking, searching for a hint as to his reasonability. He was somewhere in the vicinity of my dad's age, with eyes like a basset hound's beneath the wide, curved brim of his no-nonsense O'Farrell hat.

"Wyatt Rawley?" he inquired, and at my curt nod, he stopped just out of reach on the front walkway and indicated his badge. "Deputy Mason Clemens. I'm here regarding a matter that took place this past Wednesday on the property of Jarred Watkins. What can you tell me about that afternoon?"

"Would you like to come inside?" I asked after a moment's pause. My insides were hopping, but I forced a calm tone, not wanting to appear unduly guilty.

"No, thank you, son," the deputy said. "I've driven a piece to get here and would like to get home, if you want the truth. But I need a few answers first. What can you tell me about Jarred Watkins' claim that you stole a male pit bull from his barnyard on Wednesday afternoon?"

"I took the dog." No point denying what Clemens already knew; slightly heartened by his use of the word "son," I added, "I saw Watkins kick him in the ribs. I would do the same again, I'm not pretending otherwise. I'm a veterinarian and I don't stand for animal abuse. My colleague confirmed the dog's broken ribs later that same day."

Joey was at my side. "Officer, I can attest to that. The animal's nose was marked by healing lacerations, suggesting repeated strikes with a weapon, possibly a stick or some sort of whip. I treated Lucky myself."

"Lucky?" the deputy repeated.

"That's what we've been calling him. I kept the dog; no one else was involved," I explained, poised to defend Tuck and Netta.

Deputy Clemens adjusted his hat brim as he admitted, "I observed livestock in poor condition at Watkins' place. I don't stand for animal abuse myself, gentlemen, but that doesn't necessarily give you license to forcibly remove someone's property. What can you tell me about putting hands on Jarred Watkins, Dr. Rawley?"

"I shoved him aside when he tried to take the dog back. And then I drove away."

"He give you that split lip?" Clemens gestured at my face.

"The bastard hit Wy's face, twice," Joey put in before I could answer, though I hadn't asked him to reveal that particular detail.

"Who struck first?"

"Watkins. He decked me but I wasn't about to leave the dog there. Travis Woodrow told me that Watkins shot the pony I treated on Wednesday. I can tell you with certainty there was no need to put that animal down. None whatsoever."

Clemens nodded slowly, studying me with a silence I found unnerving.

At last I could stand it no longer and asked outright, "Am I under arrest here?"

My brothers were crowded in the doorway by now, the three of us, plus Joey, facing the deputy as he stood alone in the yellow glow of the porch light. I hoped we didn't appear overtly threatening; I knew my brothers would stand up for me to their last breaths, as I would for them. Behind me, I heard Sean crack his knuckles.

Clemens said succinctly, "No. Thank you for your time, Dr. Rawley. If Jarred Watkins moves ahead with pressing charges, we will meet again. He was pretty burned up when we spoke this afternoon, and I'm glad to have heard your side of things."

I wasn't sure what to offer as a farewell; *you're welcome* and *good-bye* both seemed stupid. I nodded and the deputy had just turned to head back to his SUV when I saw Hannah's car appear at the end of our street.

My heart plummeted toward my boots.

She parked at the curb across the street, unable to enter the driveway until Clemens backed out. I saw her gaping mouth, her wide eyes, as she sat gawking while he drove away. Zane was sitting in the backseat, also staring, but he wouldn't know anything was wrong if Hannah didn't make a scene.

*Right. No chance in hell of that.*

Hannah zoomed into the driveway and stalked up the front walk without unbuckling Zane from his car seat. Red-faced, all but sputtering, she started in immediately.

"I *told* you, Wy! That *stupid* dog!"

"*Jesus,*" muttered Sean, just too low for Hannah to hear. He rested a hand briefly on my shoulder and muttered, "We'll get going."

I turned to my brothers and Joey. "Thanks for being here, you guys."

They each wore an expression of compassion.

"Anytime," Quinn said.

"You know it," Joey added.

"Join us later if you can, we're heading back to The Spoke," Sean said, and this time Hannah heard his comment.

"He will *not*," she spat as though she was a warden.

After they left, I stepped around Hannah and headed for her car, where poor Zane was still waiting in his car seat. I leaned in and unbuckled him, scooping him into my arms and murmuring, "Hey, buddy."

Hannah was right on my heels. "Tell me what's going on!"

"The deputy was here to get my side of the story," I explained, carrying Zane toward the front door. "I'm not under arrest."

"But that guy must be pressing charges if a sheriff was here!"

"Not quite yet. I told him that Watkins was abusing the dog. Watkins actually put down his pony, the one I treated a few days ago, can you believe that?" As I spoke, Zane burrowed against my chest, popping a thumb in his mouth, and I immediately lowered my voice. "There was no reason for that, nothing but pure cruelty."

"This is all because of a dog!" Hannah cried. "A stupid *dog*, Wy. You'd risk your family's well-being because of an animal?"

I was not about to get sucked back into this particular argument. I said, "Let me get Zane to bed and then we can talk."

"Of course, ignore me like you always do. What do I expect?" Hannah stormed away, slamming our bedroom door.

I read Zane two stories, rocking him in the chair by his crib. After the second book, he implored, "One more, Daddy!"

"One more," I agreed, resting my chin gently on his head, thinking of my father and the countless patient ways he'd taken care of me during my growing years. What would I have done without my dad's love, if he hadn't been there for me every day of my childhood?

Zane scrambled down to the carpet and ran to his books, digging industriously until he found the one he wanted. His chubby-cheeked smile stretched from ear to ear as he climbed back on my lap and resettled against my chest, and I felt a deep, gouging ache in response to his innocent joy, the fearful knowledge that no matter how hard I tried I couldn't completely protect my child from the pain of life. I wanted more than anything to be a good father, but I couldn't force aside my longing for the woman I loved.

*Millie, oh God, if only it was you out there in the kitchen.*

*I'd pay any price to see your face tonight . . .*

I heard Hannah slamming things around as I read Zane's third bedtime story and slowed my reading pace, lingering over the words. Fuck if I wanted to interact with her right now. But Zane was growing drowsy, eyelids sinking as I finished the last page. I changed his diaper and tucked him in his crib, leaning down to whisper, "I love you, son. Good night."

"Night, Daddy," he whispered, before requesting, "I want to see horsey."

I smiled, obligingly rolling back my T-shirt sleeve so Zane could see my horse tattoo. He giggled, poking my arm, and said, "Good-night, horsey!"

I kissed his forehead and clicked out his bedside lamp. "Horsey says it's time for sleeping."

Hannah was heating something in the microwave; though I hadn't eaten dinner, I wasn't remotely hungry, my stomach in knots from the evening's events. How I longed to enter the kitchen and talk to my wife without a confrontation. I wanted to hold her, to feel warmth and love and caring. Loneliness gaped like a bottomless hole through my center. I stood near the closed door of our son's room and leaned my forehead against it, desperately seeking reassurance.

*How the hell has my life come to this?*

I thought back to the Hannah I'd known as a teenager, laughing about things with me, coming to family dinners, joking around without a hint as to the disturbing personality that lay hidden inside her. Had she been this volatile back in those days and I'd just never noticed? Or had that side been dormant—the strange, manipulative part of her that used tears and threats and endless drama to get her way?

I eased shut Zane's bedroom door and entered the kitchen. Hannah looked my way, hard-faced, but I was determined to try.

"Zane's sleeping."

She nodded curtly in response.

"Did you have fun shopping with your mom?" I asked, making the sort of conversation one would with a distant relative. I felt useless, exhausted and hollowed out. I couldn't exactly recall the last time we'd had sex. No wonder Hannah thought I was cheating.

She sighed, her chair scraping along the floor as she sat down.

I sat across from her and looked square in her pale eyes, trying to make her understand. "I saved that poor dog because it was the right thing to do. I can't stand to see someone hurting an animal. I'd like to think anyone would have done the same thing."

Hannah's brow wrinkled. "Are you saying that I wouldn't?"

"Would you?" I honestly didn't know.

"I wouldn't risk myself over an animal," she said without hesitation. "And neither should you. If this man presses charges, what if you lose your vet license? What the hell will we do then?"

"I don't think it will come to that," I said, though I wasn't completely sure. Guilt and regret tangled like thorn-covered vines inside my chest. I reached and collected Hannah's right hand. "I'm not having an affair."

She dug her nails into my palm. "Then prove it. Make love to me right here, on the table."

"Right now?" I asked, like a goddamn fool. It was the worst possible thing I could have said.

Hannah yanked her hand free. "You don't want to, do you? Like always."

"I do," I insisted. "Come over here, let me kiss you instead of pulling away."

Her eyes remained locked on mine but she didn't move. I forced myself to continue holding her gaze, afraid to appear guilty.

*You have never cheated on your wife. At least, nowhere but in your mind.*

She whispered, "Who is she?"

"Will you let it rest?"

Without warning, Hannah shoved back from the table and stood—and before I had a hint as to her intention or a hope of ducking the blow, she cracked me across the face with the back of a fisted hand, the one holding her fork.

My chair toppled as I stood in a rush, clutching my cheek, but I was in far less pain than I was simple stun. "You just hit me!"

She flung the fork against the wall above the sink, her tear-filled eyes bright with fervent emotion that seemed just this side of insanity. I stared in mute horror as the utensil clattered off the counter and struck the floor.

"You're lying!" she seethed. "It's the same bitch who gave you that hickey back when I was pregnant, isn't it?"

Hoarse with shock, I repeated, "You just *hit me*."

"I'm not apologizing for it!"

I turned from the table and Hannah lunged around it, grabbing my elbow.

"Where are you going?!" she cried.

"To Zane's room." I yanked free of her grip. "We're spending the night at my dad's."

"What?" she screeched. "You will not take my son from this house!"

"He's just as much my son and yes, *I will*." Keeping anger at bay was a monumental effort; I was so furious I felt almost ill with it.

Hannah stepped in front of me, jabbing an index finger against my chest. "I'll call the police! I'll tell them you're taking my son away without my consent!"

Forcing a bravado I did not feel, I challenged, "Go ahead and call the cops."

Hannah flicked hair out of her eyes. "I will if you take Zane out of this house. Just try me, Wy. The sheriff was already here once tonight. I'll tell them I'm scared of you."

I stepped around her without further comment and continued down the hall to Zane's room, grateful to find him snoring; he had not heard the events of the past ten minutes. I shut his door and reclaimed my seat in the rocking chair, only then realizing that my heart was chugging and my kneecaps trembling. I tried for a deep breath, fixing my gaze on the small glow of the nightlight as I tried to process what had just happened.

*Go home*, my instincts screamed. Home still meant my dad's place, the home where I'd been raised, not this fucking rental house on Front Street. But the longer I considered the possibility of retreating to my father's, the shittier I felt.

*If you go home, you'll have to tell them what happened. You'll have to admit that you made your wife so upset that she hit you.*

*Hannah wouldn't really lie to the cops, would she? She's not scared of me.*

I felt sick and pathetic; worse than that, I felt helpless. When it came down to it, I realized that I was ashamed—too ashamed to confess to my dad, let alone my brothers, that Hannah had actually struck my face. It made me seem weak and ridiculous. I rested my forearms on the edge of Zane's crib and lowered my head; when morning began staining the sky a pale gray, I was still in the same position and hadn't slept for a minute.

# CHAPTER TWENTY-NINE

RUSS AND I HAD BEEN SEEING EACH OTHER AL-
most constantly since I returned to Minneapolis for my sophomore year at the
university and resumed working part-time at Lake View Stables, and for the first
time since the advent of our relationship, he started pressing for more. He had
already demonstrated more patience than most guys were capable of; I hadn't
ventured south to Champlin during the summer months, limiting our contact to
phone calls and text messages. And Russ had not complained or pressured for a
visit. Lying awake in my dorm room that autumn, I sifted through contradictory
thoughts, turning them over in my mind the way I would have a pile of beach
rocks, cupping the weight of each in my palm, rubbing a thumb over smooth
planes or jagged edges, noting small imperfections.

*Russ is a good person.*

*He's smart.*

*He loves animals.*

*He obviously likes you.*

*I like him too. But I can't pretend that I love him.*

*He isn't Wy, but no one will ever by Wy.*

*Maybe your feelings for Russ will grow into love over time.*

*Just because it didn't happen right away doesn't mean it won't.*

*Especially if you don't even try.*

And so I tried; somehow it did not occur to me to question why I was both-
ering, or to wonder why I felt I needed a boyfriend in the first place. Jealousy?
Loneliness? Desperation to prove that I was capable of moving past the memories of our time together, as Wy obviously had?

"You really like this guy Russ, the horse trainer?" my dad had asked over the
summer, before I left for Minneapolis.

We'd been sitting together on the dock near Dad's childhood home, where
Grandpa and Grandma Carter still lived, just around Flickertail from White
Oaks Lodge. Dad was flicking bits of day-old bread to the sunfish and bluegills
in the shallows; he'd stayed behind with me when the rest of the family left for

an evening pontoon cruise, an activity common to most lake residents in the heat of late summer. Dad was so much easier to talk with than Mom, though I would never have admitted this to her; Dad's personality was just more relaxed, his conversation style appreciably less intense. I didn't resent knowing that Dad had lingered behind because he wanted to talk with me, the way I would have resented Mom doing the same thing.

I watched the palm-sized fish dart to the surface to gulp bread crumbs, splashing and displacing each other, their shiny bodies glinting with brilliant colors, silver and sapphire-blue and rich yellow. The tint of the lake was deep green at this point in the summer but remained clear; it was like peering through the translucent prisms of an enormous emerald. These little fish were accustomed to us; they were fed almost every evening, either by my siblings or Grandpa and the cousins. Dozens pooled near our feet, which dangled in the lukewarm water. They scattered if I swished my legs.

I finally muttered, "I do like Russ."

Dad silently handed me a piece of stale bread so I could join him in feeding the fish, and it seemed like an invitation to elaborate.

I continued, "I've learned so much about horses at Russ's family's stable, like I was telling you guys at supper. Parelli is so intuitive. But you have to be really patient, and willing to take it one day at a time. You know what's funny? I've really come to see how much individual personality horses have, just like people. Some are sweet and willing to please, and good listeners, others are rowdy and wild, and some are just plain assholes."

Dad laughed. "That's been my experience with horses too. When we'd—"

I looked his way, wondering at the abrupt way he'd cut off the sentence, before realization struck. I closed my eyes for a second before whispering, "It's all right, Dad, you can talk about them."

He sighed, his barrel chest expanding as he acknowledged quietly, "Aw, hon, I know. I'm sorry. I don't purposely avoid talking about them. I just don't want to say the wrong thing. There's nothing worse than seeing your child hurting."

I chucked the piece of bread without ripping it apart and then leaned forward, bracing my elbows on my thighs, linking my fingers, watching the fish attack the floating toast. I muttered, "I'm all right, I promise."

If Dad knew I was lying, he didn't comment, which I truly appreciated. He only said, "I think you've come a long way this year. College has been good for you."

I remembered that Dad had graduated from the university I currently attended, and attempted to picture him there as a student in the business department. I struggled with the image of my big, outdoorsy dad squeezing behind a classroom desk to attend a lecture.

"Wy was my first love," I suddenly blurted, raspy with emotion; Dad always managed to get to the heart of the matter, even without a word. "And no one around here will even say his name, for fear of hurting me. It's like the Rawleys don't even exist anymore. Mom and Aunt Ruthie barely talk. I miss them all . . . *so much* . . ."

Dad tucked me gently to his side.

"I feel like I'm broken," I whispered, slumping against him. "Like nothing can heal this pain. I know that's dumb . . . I know I should be over it by now . . ."

"It's not dumb," Dad said firmly. "And you're not broken, Millie Jo. You are far from broken. I don't think you have to put a time limit on your feelings."

"But it's been two years."

"Well, maybe it'll take two more. Don't beat yourself up about it in the meantime. Especially if you like Russ. From what you've told us, he seems like a pretty good guy. Speaking of that, your mom and I would like to meet him."

"Maybe this fall," I muttered, unwilling to commit to the idea.

I'd since revised the timeframe, figuring that *next* summer would be soon enough for Russ to meet my family. It was late October by now, close to Halloween, and I had stuck around after work to wait with Russ while Felicity, one of their younger mares, labored; the closest I felt to Russ occurred when we worked together at Lake View. Felicity was the last of their mares to foal for the season and the birth was her first. She had shown signs of early labor around dinnertime; the process had unfolded in the past few hours without complications, but Russ was reluctant to leave before full delivery.

Alone with him and the horse, I found myself increasingly unable to stop my thoughts from straying to the summer evening of Scout's birth. The tint of the stable lights and Russ's gentle encouragement of Felicity only strengthened both the memory and my longing for the man in it.

"I'm going to head over and see Wallace for a minute," I told Russ.

Crouched in the stall, he looked up at me over his shoulder. "I'll yell if the action starts. At this rate, it should be any minute." Referring to the local veterinarian, he added, "I don't think we'll have to call Bert."

I didn't answer; merely thinking the word "veterinarian" never failed to hammer my heart with aching blows. My stupid gaze roved to the front entrance, imagining how I would feel if the door suddenly opened and Wy strode inside the stable from the darkness outside.

"Are you all right?" Russ asked, startling me; he appeared somewhat alarmed and I took care to neutralize my expression.

"I'm fine," I insisted, not meeting his eyes. "I'll be right back."

I walked slowly along the familiar dirt path that rimmed the arena and linked up with the stalls; most of the stock was bedded down for the night, but a few curious noses poked from stall doors at the sound of my passage, seeking a treat or a pat. I stopped beside Charger, a lovely gray gelding who reminded me a little of Shadow, resting my forehead to his warm, firm neck and inhaling the comfort of his horsy smell. I closed my eyes, relenting to need and letting the fantasy play out—that of Wy stepping close behind me, his arms gliding around my waist and bringing me against his body.

Hunger quickly replaced tenderness and my breath grew short as I imagined gripping the top rung as he bent me forward and stripped my jeans down to my knees. I swore I could almost feel him there, clutching my hips in his strong hands and thrusting deeply inside, taking us both beyond all words. Safely hidden in the semi-darkness and well away from Russ, I reached down to press hard between my legs, quivering and wet, seeking respite from the torture of my memories—at times I craved Wy's easy, familiar sweetness and at others, like now, I craved the passionate heat that had flowed so strongly between us, craved it down to my bones. Nothing I did with Russ came close to what I'd felt with Wy.

The horse, maybe sensing the energy rolling from my body, stomped his back hooves and neighed, echoing my restlessness.

*Stop this shit, Millie.*

*You're pathetic, and what's more, you're deluding yourself.*

*What you had with Wy is over and you have to accept it.*

I stepped away from Charger and continued to Wallace's stall; he brayed happily to see me, nosing my ribs with such enthusiasm I was lifted to my toes. I kissed his velvet-plush nose, murmuring, "Hey, buddy. How are you tonight?"

I scratched up and down along the sides of his slender neck, loving the way his eyes drifted closed and his big, goofy front teeth showed as he enjoyed the attention.

"I'm going to miss you, Wally. Dee told me your owners are moving out to Oregon." Tears wet my eyes but I continued talking to the mule, as I did so often when alone. "You remember the man I told you about, the vet? He lives in Montana, so you'll probably drive past his hometown on your trip out west. It's called Jalesville. It's tucked right in the foothills and the air smells so good there, wilder than around here. And when it rains, this huge, crackling storm rolls down from the mountains and looks like it's going to destroy the whole town, but then it just races past and before you know it, it's already in the next county."

I had never lived in Jalesville but I was distinctly homesick for it nonetheless.

*What are you doing tonight, Wy? Are you out on a call somewhere? Or are you done with work, at home having dinner with your family?*

*It was so good to talk to you that night back in June—but it hurt like a fuck-*
*ing burn later. Like a branding scar on my heart, in the shape of your initials, WZR,*
*scorched straight into the surface . . .*

"I might have lived and worked these past years in Jalesville, with Wy, if
things had worked out differently," I whispered to Wallace, my throat aching. But
I refused to cry; I would not cry over Wy, not anymore.

Wallace nickered as though he understood.

"Hey, it's time, hurry!" Russ called from the front of the stable.

I tucked loose hair behind my ears and drew a slow breath before jogging
back to them, arriving just in time to spy the foal emerge from her dame in the
birthing sack, umbilical cord trailing over her slim, delicate back. Within minutes
she was already attempting to stand; her hide was the same gleaming russet as
Felicity's. I knelt near Russ on the soiled hay, resting a hand between his shoulder
blades; his skin was taut and warm beneath his faded old T-shirt.

I said, "You did good work."

He grinned at my compliment, extending his touch toward the foal. "I didn't
do a thing, it was all Felicity. Hi there, tiny little horse, look at you. You're adorable."

"She's pretty precious, isn't she?"

"Felicity did great," Russ enthused.

"She was a champ," I agreed. "Your mom will want to hear the whole story."

"I'm glad you stayed out here tonight, Mill, that we got to see this together."
Russ patted the filly's slender neck, using his knuckles like a gentle curry brush.
He'd never called me "Mill" before. "What should we name her?"

I bit the insides of my cheeks, watching as Felicity licked and nuzzled her
newborn.

"It's not up to me to choose," I said at last, standing to brush hay bits from
my jeans.

Russ continued watching me. He appeared solemn, like someone about to
deliver bad news, as he muttered, "I don't get it."

"Don't get what?" I asked, even though I knew damn well what he meant.

"What are you holding back?"

While I knew he'd sensed it, he had never yet asked outright, leaving me
faltering.

"Nothing," I mumbled, fidgeting with the hem of my flannel shirt.

Russ's jaws squared; he was clearly done sidestepping. He remained hunkered in a crouch as he said bluntly, "I want us to make love. It's time, don't you
think? We've been together since last winter."

"I told you I don't want to rush things." After the better part of a year, it was a pretty weak excuse, I realized.

Russ's expression grew subtly more irritated, his eyebrows drawing inward. "I don't think wanting to have sex tonight exactly qualifies as rushing things, do you?"

"What about last summer?" I heard myself ask; I hadn't even thought to question him before now, but we hadn't seen each other even once during those months. "Were you with anyone else?"

He appeared legitimately surprised. "What the hell is that supposed to mean?"

"Apparently you're the one who can't wait to have sex; it's a fair question." It wasn't, but at that moment I didn't care.

He rose to his full height, upset now, face suffused with redness. "That's a shitty assumption. You know I wasn't. Why, were *you?*"

I shook my head, submerging all thoughts to the contrary as silence grew edgy between us.

"I love you," he suddenly blurted.

"Russ . . ." I faltered to silence again, at a complete loss.

"You don't have to say anything," he went on, speaking fast. "I just want you to know how I feel. I love you and I want to make love with you. I have ever since the night we sat on that couch and talked. Shit, I have since the day you served me tequila in your family's bar."

Confusion welled in my heart.

*Maybe this is what you need.*

*Maybe if you have sex it will change things . . .*

*How will you know if you don't even try?*

And so it was that less than an hour later, in the privacy of my roommate-free dorm, Russ was in the process of unbuttoning my shirt. To shut out the wailing cry inside my heart, I reached down and assisted him with the task.

His warm breath fanned my forehead. "You're sure about this? I wasn't trying to pressure you into anything by telling you I love you."

I whispered, "I know."

"I want you so much. I've been dying." He clutched my breasts as he spoke, hurrying to unfasten my bra as he added, "I have condoms in my wallet."

"Grab one," I insisted before I lost my nerve, rolling to an elbow on my narrow bed as he sprang up to do just that. Wearing nothing but unzipped jeans, Russ knelt and dug around in his coat pocket.

He said over his shoulder, attempting to tease me, "They're ribbed for your pleasure, it says right here on the box."

Grinning, he bounded across the carpet with the condom packet in hand.

He looked more like Wy in that moment than he ever had and I begged silently, *Don't let me notice that about Russ tonight. I can't bear it.*

I scooted over so he could stretch out beside me on the bed. He cupped my face, leaning to kiss me as he immediately slid his other hand inside my panties, and it took all I had to fend off the crashing deluge of memories. Behind my tightly-closed eyelids, I saw warm lantern light striking the orange walls of a little tent—

*Stop. Please, oh God please, just stop.*

But as I much as I begged otherwise, memories flooded without my consent. Russ and I proceeded to have sex.

And I pretended to take pleasure in it, feigning more enthusiasm than I felt; later, once he fell asleep and left me to my own thoughts, I was ashamed of my behavior. I owed Russ an apology for many reasons, not the least of which was using him in an attempt to put my memories of Wy behind me, once and for all. What kind of fool thought such a thing was possible? What was the matter with me? It wasn't as if sex with Russ was bad; it was the comparison that was unbearable—the difference between experiencing these private, beautiful things with someone I loved versus someone I just liked. At some level, I'd never really imagined letting another man so close to me, of sharing such intimacy with anyone other than Wy.

Once I was certain Russ was asleep, I climbed carefully from the twin bed, wrapped into my robe, and then made my way to the communal bathroom at the end of the otherwise empty hall, bending over the sink and splashing my face, craving a scalding shower and pints of body wash—again, for no good reason; it was hardly Russ's fault he failed to live up to an unfair ideal. I squeezed my eyes shut, picturing the way his face had gone slack as he came just a little while ago, with a grunting moan and a final deep thrust, before collapsing over me. And then I replaced this picture with the remembrance of another moment. The stunning joy of the night at Itasca versus the chilly remorse of this one was intolerable.

I stood for long moments studying my reflection in the glow of the bathroom nightlight, having failed to click the overhead fixture on. My hair was tangled, my eyes hollow with despair.

*It was the first time with someone else.*
*You knew this wouldn't be easy.*
*It will be easier the next time . . .*

I tried to pretend the words were true.

# CHAPTER THIRTY

## JALESVILLE, MONTANA

I DROVE OUT TO BITTERROOT AFTER MY SLEEP-less night in Zane's room, unwilling to deal with Hannah by morning's light. A quick examination of my reflection in the bathroom mirror revealed the faint stripe of a bruise on my cheek, but I could easily explain that away, if anyone noticed; I worked with large animals on a daily basis and often sustained minor injuries. I entered the bedroom just long enough to grab a clean shirt, informing the silent shape beneath the blankets that I was headed out on a call; no response other than Hannah shifting her legs to a different position. No apology, certainly nothing resembling love. My teeth on edge, I worked hard not to slam the door to the garage as I left, all the shit I'd felt last night amplified by the effects of no sleep. I rolled my head in a slow circle in an attempt to ease the aching kinks in my neck.

Bitterroot was calm by dawn's soft light; it was just past sunrise as I parked, spying Joey's car in its customary spot; he liked to get an early start on the day too. Gladness overrode some of my distress as I entered our familiar vet office—I would have someone to talk to, at least. Lucky jumped up from his spot on the rug and hustled to my side, and I dropped to one knee to rub my knuckles over his ears, planting a kiss on the smooth, shiny fur at the top of his head.

"Hi, buddy," I muttered as he nuzzled my chest with his wet nose.

"That you, Wy?" Joey called from down the hall.

"Yeah."

"Did you bring coffee?"

"No."

"Get some brewing, will you? But not that diner-issue sludge you like. I have some Lifeboost Organic in the top drawer."

"On it." I was a man of few words today.

Joey appeared in the main office a minute later, and I suddenly remembered what I'd intended to ask him last night. The ugliness with Hannah had temporarily overridden everything else in my mind—but then again, hadn't that been the theme of my life for the past three years?

*Jesus Christ, Wy.*

Joey caught sight of my expression and demanded, "What?"

"How did I not see this?"

He knew exactly what I meant, studying me in silent contemplation for a few seconds, at last sinking to a seat on one of the chairs lining the wall.

"He's not exactly obvious about it," he finally said.

"How long have you known? Shit, *I* didn't even realize and it was right there under my nose all this time. I can't believe I'm this dense; he's my brother, for Christ's sake."

"I've known since the first time I met him, when Kyle and I were here for graduation," Joey admitted, linking his fingers over his stomach. "That he was gay, I mean, not that I *adore* him. I don't think he knows how I feel, even though I act so ridiculous around him, all tongue-tied and shit. It's like junior high all over again."

"You've honestly known since you met him? And you never *said* anything?"

Joey pursed his lips. "It's not my business to say anything. I knew he'd tell your family when he was ready. I think Marshall and Ruthann know."

"Does Quinn know *you* know that he's gay?" I was still wrapping my head around this discovery.

"Of *course* he knows. Jesus, Wy. I get the sense he likes me, I really do, and I have great instincts for that sort of thing, but he's so damn shy . . ."

"He always has been," I confirmed.

"Who was the last person he dated?"

"Honestly? His high school girlfriend, Ellie."

"I want to rip her hair out by the roots. Does she live around here?"

"Yeah, but she's married and has three kids. I don't think you have much to worry about there, big guy." Half of a grin pulled at my mouth at the nickname; Quinn towered over Joey.

"Don't tease me, Wy, I mean it. I haven't liked someone this much in a long time. Honestly, I haven't liked someone this much ever. Why do you think I've been treading so lightly in this situation? I've lived here an entire year now and I haven't even attempted to make a move."

I paused a moment, touched by his sincerity. "That's great, Joe, I mean it."

He continued glaring at me.

"I wonder why he's never told us. He must think we wouldn't understand?" I spoke as though thinking aloud, somewhat offended that Quinn had never confided in me; but then again, Marshall was the only one of my brothers who knew about Millie.

"It's not an easy thing to tell your family, trust me. Even a close family like yours. Besides, he's subtle," Joey acknowledged. "And *so* sexy, I'm sorry, but it's true. I'm crazy about him. I feel like I'm *going* crazy."

I laughed, lightly punching his arm. "Don't worry about offending me; you're my best friend. Why would I care that you're hot for my brother?"

Joey muttered, "I don't know why I tell you a goddamn thing." He blinked, gaze at once sharpening, honing in on the bruise on my face. He leaned forward as he asked, "What happened there? Don't tell me you had a run-in with Watkins last night."

All my amusement drained as swiftly as whiskey from a tipped bottle. I wanted badly to tell him the truth—hadn't he just trusted me? But this was different.

But if I knew him, Joey knew me just as well. He guessed, "That bitch hit you, didn't she?"

I looked away, embarrassed to answer; I didn't even bother to call him out on the slur.

"Has she hit you before?" he demanded.

I shook my head, gaze fixed on the floor near my boots.

Joey was silent, absorbing this; I sensed he thought I was withholding information. At last he said quietly, "That's abuse, buddy, there's no spinning that shit. What happened last night?"

I felt a tightness in my throat—all the words I longed to let loose collecting there, begging for release. I made a hook of my right hand and dragged it through my hair, stalling, angry and frustrated. I was grateful for Joey's compassion; he might not have been family, but I knew he cared. And somehow it was easier to tell him the truth than it would have been Marshall, or Dad. Even Ruthie.

"Yeah, Hannah hit me," I finally admitted. "She accused me of cheating and then lying to her about it. We were sitting at the table and she smacked me before I had a clue that she meant to. She's convinced I'm messing around."

"Are you?" Joey studied my eyes, digging for secrets. "Kyle and I have known something was wrong ever since you got married. I mean, beyond the fact that you didn't want to get married in the first place. But I've never taken you for a cheater. You're not the type."

The tightness in my throat grew small spikes. I tried to swallow past them, totally unable.

"Wy, come on. What is it?"

Studying my hands, I admitted, "There's someone else, yeah."

"I *knew* it. Who? Is it a man?"

I looked up at the last question, startled, before recognizing his intent of making me laugh.

"Yeah, you *wish*," I muttered, and Joey laughed too.

"For real, who is she? Is she from around here?"

"No," I whispered. "She's from Minnesota."

"Wait, what? When did you meet someone there?"

I crumbled like a broken dam, starting with the way Millie and I had been part of each other's lives since we were little, omitting nothing. Joey listened with total absorption, the two of us sitting on chairs in the waiting room of our vet office as organic coffee perked and bright morning sun stretched across the tile floor. We had no scheduled appointments today; both of us had intended to catch up on paperwork, remaining open for any walk-ins; the usual routine for a Saturday. Bitterroot would be busy within the hour, people arriving for riding lessons or Parelli lessons, or to take out the horses they paid to stable here, but we remained alone as I spoke more openly than I had in years, all but hoarse by the time I finished.

"Thank you for listening," I finally said, emotionally depleted but grateful for the excuse to talk about Millie without restraint.

Joey continued to study me; after a moment he muttered, "Shit, Wy."

"You're telling me." I knuckled my tired eyes.

At last Joey sat straight and stretched his spine; he said somberly, "This explains so much about you." He tapped an index finger against my chest. "You need to tell Millie you still love her. I feel strongly about this."

"What about . . . him? *Russ*. Millie said she was happy with him." I could hardly speak the bastard's name, let alone the words.

"Fuck him! If what you just told me is true, this guy has no chance against you."

Hope surged in my chest despite all better judgment, despite my current reality.

Joey was gaining steam. "Call her and tell her the truth."

"You don't think I would in a second, if I could? You know why I can't."

"You can be a good dad to Zane without staying married to Hannah. You know this is true."

My chest ached all over again. "But he's my son. I wouldn't see him every day if I left Hannah; I'd have to wait for the weekends, or worse, every *other* weekend. She would make it ugly as hell, you know she would."

"Then you tell the court that she physically abuses you. I'm serious. No one should have to live like that. I mean, let's examine the irony present here." He brandished a hand toward Lucky, who sat patiently nearby. "You rescue a dog from an abusive situation, risking bodily harm and possible legal charges. You need to rescue *yourself*, dude, before it's too late."

I muttered, "I don't think Hannah is going to kill me, if that's what you mean."

Joey disregarded my sarcasm. "What do you think Millie is doing today? Right now, at this moment?"

"How would—"

He interrupted, "She's at work, I'll bet, at that stable you mentioned. And my car has a full tank."

I felt my eyebrows crinkle, confused.

"I'm up for a drive," he went on, and I finally stumbled to the conclusion.

"Joe . . ."

He ignored me, standing and bouncing on the balls of his feet as he ordered, "Shut up and come on." He turned to Lucky, changing tone as he invited enthusiastically, "You wanna get some fresh air, boy? Huh? You wanna go on a road trip with us?"

The pit bull's tail whipped side to side in a frenzy of joy; my heart did the same damn thing.

Joey was already out the door, Lucky on his heels, and less than five minutes later we were driving east beneath unabated springtime sunshine, the sky a cloudless blue as far as the eye could see, as amped up as two teenagers embarking on a forbidden journey in a stolen car. Joey sat behind the wheel, flicking cigarette ash out the open window while I rode shotgun with my right boot braced on the dash, in mild shock at this turn of events. But I could not deny the welcome anticipation pumping through my blood; I felt like a prisoner escaping his cell, inhaling freedom in huge gulps. The radio blasted a local station and sunlight shone in bright arcs on the windshield. Lucky, in the backseat, sat on his haunches, head sticking out an open window.

We reached the interstate exit, and Joey accelerated, sending a grin my way.

"Turn around. I can't do this." I prayed he wouldn't heed this request.

"Shut the hell up," he said cheerfully.

"I can't tell Millie I'm in town. I can't risk it." But the mere thought of setting eyes on her, even from a distance, intensified my exhilaration to a fever pitch.

"Wy, man, you love this woman, you just spent an hour telling me how much. That *means* something. You think everyone finds that kind of mutual love in this life?" he demanded. "Because they don't!"

"I just want to see her. Just for a second." I tried to pretend this would suffice.

"For a second? Like, to store up for the rest of your life without her? You know that's not enough." Joey thumped the steering wheel, abruptly changing the topic as he ordered, "Find us a better radio station."

By late afternoon we were driving through the western suburbs of Minneapolis. My heart was going triple time, and had been since North Dakota.

"Where to?" Joey inquired, peering at road signs.

"Champlin," I ordered. "Lake View Stables."

I figured there was a good chance Millie would be at work there on a Saturday, rather than at school, and besides, I had no idea where she lived on the university campus—which appeared enormous on the map I pulled up on my phone.

"We'll just drive past." I tried to sound like I was capable of just driving past the place where Millie worked. "I want to see it, that's all."

"Whatever you say."

We had spent the hours of our drive intermittently listening to music and talking, stopping twice for food and to walk Lucky. Joey had smoked his way through half a pack and sat now with the tail end of a cigarette clamped between his teeth. The car's GPS led us to the stable in Champlin with no delays, not a single wrong turn. Before I knew what was happening, a collection of outbuildings appeared on the left side of a two-lane highway; a wooden sign proclaimed *Lake View Stables, Dan and Dee Morgan, proprietors.* While the place wasn't grand in scale in the way of Bitterroot, it was still impressive, and boasted a view of a large expanse of blue water, reminding me immediately of Flickertail.

Joey slowed and turned left into the parking lot while I experienced what felt like a moderate heart attack.

"We can't ..."

"Calm down. We're not doing anything wrong."

I frantically scanned the cars and trucks in the lot. The stable appeared busy, but that worked in our favor; we weren't conspicuous, at least. A group emerged from a barn door into a nearby paddock, a woman leading a mare by a halter rope, and my heart about came through my ribcage—but it was not Millie.

Joey killed the engine and stubbed out his smoke in the ashtray. "You ready?"

"We're not ... we can't ..." I sounded like a little kid.

"We drove *all this way.*" He matched my tone.

"I can't just walk in there." But I wanted to so fucking badly.

"How about this? I'll go in and ask around a little, see if she's here. I'll fill you in and you can decide what you want to do next."

"But ..."

"Trust me."

"Are you sure ..."

"Let me help you, Wy, come on." Joey flipped down the visor and smoothed his hair, taking a moment to pop a breath mint and sanitize his hands with a small bottle of lime-scented cleanser he kept in his car.

And without another word he strode across the parking lot and entered Lake View Stables.

The idea that Millie could be standing just behind those doors, only steps away from me, was unbearable. I could hardly sit still, my gaze locked on the front entrance. Lucky, sensing my distress, rested his jowly face on my left shoulder, snuffling in my ear. A miniature eternity slipped past before Joey emerged and returned to the car, while I tried to discern from his expression what had taken place inside.

"Is she here?" I demanded.

"Not yet, but she's due in at five," he said, leaning down to talk to me through the open window.

Our dashboard clock was an hour behind the local time, which meant Millie would arrive at the stable in twenty minutes, give or take.

"Who did you talk to? Is *he* in there?"

Joey rested his forearms on the car. "I don't know, I didn't ask about him. I spoke with his mom, I think. Nice lady. Knows her shit."

"Who did you say you were?"

"An old friend of Millie's."

"Oh Jesus—did you say you were a vet from Montana?!"

Joey rolled his eyes. "Give me a small break, please. Why don't you get out and we'll take Lucky for a quick walk."

"Not here!"

"Where, then? We should stick close if you want to catch her in the parking lot."

I nodded agreement, too tense to continue discussing the matter; sweat had begun to form on my chest. Fifteen minutes dragged by as Joey walked Lucky up and down the block while I stayed in the car and scrutinized every vehicle entering the lot. I didn't know what Millie drove these days, unable to keep from picturing the car we'd borrowed from Rae that night in Landon, when we drove out to Itasca. As the final few minutes before five ticked past, my nervous anticipation grew to towering heights; I had no idea what I would say to Millie when she appeared, couldn't even begin to imagine how she might respond to my unexpected presence in Minnesota. Would she even *want* to see me? I realized there was a decent chance she would simply tell me to leave, that she never wanted to see me again.

Joey returned to the car with a minute to spare.

"Any sign?" he asked, opening the driver's side door to let Lucky clamber inside. He caught a look at me and said, "Wy, man, take a deep breath."

A beat-up white truck rumbled into the lot before I could either breathe or respond, and just like that, there she was, in the same physical space as me for the first time since the side of a highway in northern Minnesota almost three years ago now.

*Millie.*

*Oh, Jesus . . .*

The sight of her was a sharp blow between my eyes, my response swift and total. Maybe twenty running paces away, her beautiful curly hair falling all over her shoulders and down her back, one arm bent and resting on the edge of the open passenger window. Joey saw the abrupt change in my expression and turned to look.

"Is that . . . " he asked softly, trailing to silence as he noticed what I already had—Millie wasn't alone in the truck.

A guy wearing a cowboy hat was driving.

He could be none other than Russ Morgan.

Adrenaline slammed through my body, hotter than blood, tensing my muscles, priming me to bolt over there and fight for her. At the same time I couldn't move, could hardly feel my legs. Russ parked the truck, he and Millie now unknowingly facing our direction, and then he leaned across the small distance separating them and tugged her closer, saying something to make her smile. She put her hands on his shoulders and they kissed, his hat almost falling off in the process.

Joey muttered, "*Shit.*"

They exited the truck, and Russ—tall, skinny, blond, *please let me beat him to death*—hurried around the hood to catch up with Millie, who wore jeans and riding boots and a faded green T-shirt. She reached up as she walked, catching her long hair in both hands, winding a band around it to hold it in a ponytail; Russ snaked an arm around her waist, pulling her close to his side as they disappeared through the front entrance. No more than three minutes had passed, but it was more than enough to annihilate me for good.

"Joe . . ."

He understood without another word. I didn't speak again until we'd driven roughly two hours west, and then made only a simple request.

"Stop there."

"I don't think that's a good idea . . ."

"Stop there."

Joey sighed, slowing to enter the gravel lot of an off-sale liquor store.

# CHAPTER THIRTY-ONE

## CHAMPLIN, MINNESOTA

"MILLIE, HON, YOU JUST MISSED AN OLD FRIEND of yours!" was the first thing Dee said as I entered the office to say hello. Russ had gone on ahead to the arena, where he was due to teach a riding lesson. Dee sat with her boots resting on her desktop, riffling through papers stacked on her lap.

I leaned a shoulder against the doorframe. "A friend of mine?"

"That's what he said. He's probably still out there somewhere." She gestured behind me, toward the stable. "It couldn't have been more than fifteen minutes ago."

My heart gave an unexpectedly intense thump as I absorbed this news. "What was his name?"

Luckily, Dee did not catch the tension in my voice. Without looking up from the papers on her lap, she said cheerily, "If he told me, I don't remember, I'm sorry. He seemed sweet. Very polite. I told him to stick around since you'd be in soon."

My kneecaps had begun to tremble; it took all I had to maintain a casual tone as I asked, "What did he look like?"

Dee tapped her index finger on her lips. "About my height, slim, kind of built like a gymnast . . . really pretty blue eyes."

My heart resumed a more normal rhythm; her description was in no way connected to Wy, no matter what my oddly strong first instinct had been.

"That doesn't sound like anyone I know," I told Dee. "Weird."

But as I entered the stable a minute later, I found myself unable to shake the strange little prickle along my spine. The busy space seemed supercharged, the way the air back home felt just before a thunderstorm broke over the lake. With a growing sense of urgency, I hurried through the crowd, my gaze roving over faces and forms—as inexplicable as it might seem, I couldn't escape the overwhelming feeling that Wy had been *here*, at Lake View.

*What's wrong with you?*

*As though Wy would show up here to find you, are you crazy?*

*There's no way.*

*Obviously the person asking about you was not him, unless Dee was really off-base in her description.*

While I recognized plenty of people in the main arena, including current students or those who boarded their animals at the stable, I spied no one fitting Dee's description and no one I knew outside of this place.

*An old friend of mine, Dee said. But who?*

*Why would a friend of mine ask about me and then just disappear?*

I strode past the stalls, ignoring the horses for the first time ever, shoving through the side doors that faced the parking lot. The May evening was warm and windless, but as I scanned the familiar blacktopped lot I shivered violently, the hair on my nape standing perfectly straight, as though stroked by an unseen hand. Walking fast, I made a circuit of the parked vehicles, searching for one with Montana plates.

*None.*

*What did you expect?*

*You're losing your mind.*

But I swore I could feel him—I was not just imagining it.

I fumbled for the phone tucked in my back pocket, realizing too late that I had no way of reaching Wy; his contact information had been lost in the lake along with the phone I'd chucked last summer. My options were limited—I could text Aunt Ruthie and ask for Wy's number, or even Auntie Tish, but could not think of a feasible excuse for needing to contact him. There wasn't one and I knew it.

"*Wy,*" I whispered painfully, turning in a slow half-circle, the movement kicking up a dry scattering of maple seedpods; my gaze skittered down the empty highway. I braced both hands on top of my head, roughing up my hair. "Were you actually here? What in the hell?"

I retreated to the fence surrounding the paddock, leaning against it as I called Rae.

"Was he here?" I asked my cousin the second she answered. I heard the bustle of a busy Saturday evening at the café in the background behind Rae and pictured her standing near the diner counter, balancing the phone on her shoulder as she tied on her server apron in preparation for the evening shift. Beyond that, I heard the way she was considering my question, the soft sound of her breath meeting my ear; I felt her stretching out with her senses, searching for me through the distance separating us.

"I haven't had a notion, if that's what you mean," she said at last, her somber tone matching mine. "What's going on?"

I filled her in on the past twenty minutes.

"But that description doesn't match Wy, not by a long shot. 'Pretty blue eyes'?

Does that sound like any guy you know?"

"No one I can think of. I mean, Russ has blue eyes, but obviously it wasn't him. I'm so confused."

Rae spoke gently. "You've thought this before, remember?"

I recalled the conversation exactly; last October, after the first time Russ and I had sex, I'd spent the entire next day pelted by the sense that Wy was looking for me, certain he would magically appear in Minneapolis to confess that he was still in love with me.

And that hadn't happened.

Rae was saying, "It made sense you'd think Wy was in Minnesota that first time, once you'd moved on in a significant way. Your subconscious was experiencing shock." She paused. "Russ didn't propose today or anything, did he?"

"No!" Despite the warm air, I shuddered.

Rae suggested, "Maybe you have a stalker!"

"Fuck off," I grumbled.

My bitchiness never deterred Rae. She only said, "Hurry and get your ass home! When are you leaving school?"

"My last final is next Monday afternoon. And then I'm heading straight for Landon on Tuesday morning."

"Thank God! Don't bring *him*."

"I wasn't planning to," I assured her. Russ had accompanied me home last December, over winter break. While my parents had enjoyed his company, Rae had been unimpressed; she said I didn't act like myself around him, that I was too quiet. I begged her one last time, "Are you sure Wy wasn't here? I swear to God, Rae, I'm not imagining it this time . . ."

"Millie *Jo*."

Defeated, I muttered, "You're right. I have to go," and disconnected before Rae could say another word.

. . .

The whiskey, as they say, wasn't working anymore.

"This was a shit idea," Joey said for the third time.

The view out the windshield was flat, unforgiving black; we were driving through the emptiness of western North Dakota but might as well have been flying along on a road carved into the surface of the moon. Clouds had massed, blotting out the stars; the headlights cut two stark swaths through the otherwise impenetrable darkness. The radio volume was low, but as a commercial ended and the song "Wicked Game" suddenly came over the airwaves, I slammed the side of a fist against the controls to shut it off, almost spilling what remained of the bottle balanced on my right knee.

"*Fuck*," I muttered. "I'm sorry, Joe . . ."

"Don't be sorry," he said immediately. "*I'm* the one who's sorry. It was a shit idea. I don't know what I was thinking."

"I didn't stop you." I tried again to inhale past the nails pounded into my lungs and heart at the sight of Millie in another man's arms. "Maybe it's better to know the truth."

But it wasn't better. It was only a thousand times worse, knowing.

*What did you expect? Millie told you herself she was happy with Russ.*

*What you did today amounts to stalking and you know it.*

*Let her go, Wy, you unbelievable asshole.*

Joey was saying, "Look, this makes sense if you think about it. No matter what Millie feels for you, you're married to someone else. You've *been* married for almost three years. Does Millie have any way to know you're unhappy in your marriage? Or that you're still in love with her?"

"No," I muttered, alcohol and exhaustion and sadness crushing inward on my heart. "I don't deserve her, Joe. I hurt her so fucking bad, it's no wonder she moved on. Oh, God . . ."

It was past midnight, and I had four missed calls from Hannah, none of which I'd returned; I didn't have the strength to listen to her voicemails. Not just now. A text, sent an hour ago, summed them up anyway—*Where have you been today? If you're not home in five minutes, don't bother.*

And I wouldn't have bothered—but for my son.

. . .

I had told Rae that I intended to leave for Landon right away on Tuesday morning, but I had lied without realizing. My car was packed, textbooks returned, dorm room emptied of all but memories; sophomore year complete. Russ was teaching a class at Lake View, where I had worked my last shift over the past weekend. I was supposed to stop out to tell him good-bye before I drove home for the summer. I enjoyed working at Lake View and would miss the animals stabled there—though none had taken Wallace's place in my heart—but felt only relief at the idea of three months away from Russ, who, once the dam had broken, wanted sex constantly.

In the long, icy winter months following our first time, I sought refuge in my classes, striving for perfect scores on all assessments, in addition to working weekends at Lake View, and was busier than I'd ever been. But I enjoyed the focus and the challenge; at the most basic level, I simply needed the rapid pace to occupy my mind and my heart. My relationship with Russ had evolved more quickly than my instinct preferred, leaving me torn between what I felt and what I *wanted* to feel; as ridiculous as it sounded, it was the only way I could describe my feelings for Russ. I *wanted* to feel more for him than I did. I exerted real effort to convince myself that I would fall in love with him eventually; that liking someone was just the first step in the process.

So far, no luck, and an unmistakable sense of escape washed over me, more welcome than the springtime sun glowing across my windshield as I angled west on I-94. I meant to stop at Lake View, I really did—but I didn't decelerate as I approached the exit to Champlin. Heart thudding, I sped up instead, gripping the wheel with sweating palms—only to find my little car flying west as the sun inched upward in a hot blue sky; a cloudless sky the true blue of fulfilled promises. I was halfway across North Dakota before reality began to set in, pulling no punches.

*What the hell are you doing?!*

*Are you crazy? Turn this car around.*

But I didn't listen.

Late that afternoon, I took the familiar exit into Jalesville; a sharp decline toward the little settlement tucked in the Montana foothills, the bump over the railroad tracks, and then the town itself, Main Street suddenly rolling beneath my tires. My heart was contracting and releasing so forcefully I couldn't breathe—I felt criminal, sweat pooling in my armpits, palms slick as I drove past The Spoke; I could not have felt more conspicuous had my car been equipped with loudspeakers announcing my presence in Wy's hometown. My dashboard clock read 5:27, which meant it was 4:27 local time on this Tuesday evening, and now that I was in Jalesville, a place where every sight was tied to some memory of him, my longing grew disproportionate, swelling past all reason.

*He could be anywhere. Oh God, anywhere around here . . .*

I continued past The Spoke's cheerful neon lights, checking out sights I hadn't beheld since age fifteen, vacillating between wild exhilaration and sweaty near-insanity. There was Nelson's Hardware, where Wy had worked in high school, and Auntie Tish's law office—I scrunched down low in my seat as I drove past, spying people inside—and the grocery store where I'd tagged along to shop for food in summers past. At the westernmost edge of town I parked in front of the ancient building housing a barber shop, remembering how Wy had once explained that this part of Jalesville was the oldest, the original structures dating back to the nineteenth century; hitching rails, complete with iron hardware, still ran the length of the boardwalk for two blocks. Plenty of people in the surrounding area rode horses to town for business. It was not uncommon to park a vehicle alongside two or three of them, tethered to the rails.

I studied the mountain peaks in the distance as my car idled.

*I love this town so much.*

*This is where I would have lived these past years, if things had worked out differently.*

And sorrow grew potent, pooling inside me with a piercing sense of loss; my current life seemed a terrible deviation from the path I should have been walking right now, alongside Wy. Our separation was so very wrong, I felt it to my bones—and yet, how could it be wrong when Wy's beloved son was a part of it, the very *result* of it? Surely Zane's presence was meant to be, despite the wrench he had unwittingly thrown in my life three years ago. The thought of Wy's little boy restored my senses as swiftly as a hard slap across the face.

*What are you doing, Millie? What are you thinking?*

*I just want to see Wy's face one more time.*

*Please just give me this one day.*

*One day to get me through the rest of my life . . .*

I shoved down all doubts and drove onward, clearing the city limits. The promise of summer tinged the air as I entered the gorgeous foothill country beyond town, open range dotted with sagebrush, its scent rising like turpentine in the static air. I soon spied the county road that led out to the Rawleys' homestead, but there was no way I'd dare arrive there unannounced; not even Rae knew I was in Montana, and I intended to keep it that way. I pulled to the shoulder roughly fifty feet before the turn, resting my forehead momentarily on my knuckles. When I looked up at the sound of a vehicle approaching from the opposite direction, the afternoon sun stabbed my eyes, creating a bright copper blur. I blinked rapidly, craning my neck to stare after the truck, which had slowed to take the turn. My heart stuttered before I realized I didn't recognize the driver.

*What if that had been Clark and he'd seen you?*

*What would you say to explain?*

*Showing up like this is totally insane and you know it.*

*How, exactly, did you envision this playing out?*

But I had no good answers; nothing seemed capable of parting the fog of madness that had inspired this journey in the first place. The only information I possessed with any certainty was Wy's place of business, Bitterroot Ranch, the address of which was stored on my phone.

*I'll just drive past. I want to see it in real life, that's all.*

Within minutes I followed the directions, kneecaps jittering as I approached the rehabilitation center north of town, which must have sprawled over a good hundred acres—massive outbuildings of both log beam and steel-pole construction dotted the landscape in a rough horseshoe pattern, all tucked neatly at the base of a soaring, pine-dotted ridge. A tall wooden gate, complete with an arching entrance constructed of interlocking elk horns, graced the lane to their main office; a beautiful, hand-painted sign announced *Bitterroot Ranch, Tucker and Netta Quillborrow, proprietors.*

And beneath that, two additional names—*Wyatt Rawley, DVM,* and *Joseph Quick, DVM.*

My heart went into immediate overdrive, propelling a burst of emotion; seeing Wy's name and title displayed so prominently sent a visceral thrill of pride through my blood, and the next thing I knew I'd driven beneath the majestic arch, crawling at five miles an hour along a gravel lane edged with impressive, intermittent boulders, absorbing the bustling activity of a thriving business. I was pushing my luck, but I no longer cared. After years of seeing nothing more than pictures of this gorgeous place, I was actually here, witnessing its full glory.

*It's even more beautiful than I imagined.*

Horses everywhere, their hides gleaming in the ever-present river of molten sunshine, dozens spread out between three huge corrals, two built with pole fences painted the cheerful green of pine boughs, the third of split-rail construction, evocative of an earlier century. People dressed for manual labor, most in wide-brimmed hats, moved about between buildings; there was a woman on a four-wheeler, hauling a flatbed trailer loaded with hay; a pair of teenage girls wearing lanyards, one holding a megaphone, drove by on a dandelion-yellow golf cart. My heart stopped as I caught sight of a tall, lean man in the center of the split-rail corral, setting a horse attached to a long lead line through its paces, but a rapid closer examination revealed that it was not Wy.

*But he could be here, anywhere here.*

*You're crazy, Millie, batshit crazy.*

*Turn the car around and go!*

Instead I parked in the paved lot adjacent to the main office, a small building built to resemble a settler's log cabin. A wooden shingle above the door read *Tucker Quillborrow, LP, MS, LLC,* the very degrees I intended to earn. I cast my gaze around, peering out the windshield, side windows rolled down; the pleasant scents of hay and horses filled my nose. I was inconspicuous as long as I remained in my car; there were at least a dozen vehicles parked in the hot melt of evening sun, nothing out of the ordinary about one more. An addition to the main office bore a shingle of its own, and there, in black letters, were the vet clinic's hours of operation; Wy's place of business, only steps away. The vet office was currently closed.

After hours of speeding westward without stopping, I now sat paralyzed. Chances were Wy wasn't here, not if his office was closed, but no doubt someone inside the main office knew his current location.

*And then what?*

I had no good answer for this question either. Before I lost all my nerve, absolutely palpitating with anxious energy, I exited the car and approached the main office, entering to the tingle of a bell tied above the door, so overwhelmed by emotion it took seconds for the dancing gray spots to clear from my vision.

"Hi, hon!" called a woman standing behind a hip-high front desk, glancing around the young couple stationed in front of her. "Have a seat, I'll be with you shortly! New client paperwork is just over there," and she indicated an antique wooden hutch to my right.

A man around my dad's age, three kids in tow, nodded hello as I walked past him and sank to a wing chair beside the front windows; in the next second, I realized the woman behind the front desk was none other than Wy's cousin Netta. Tall and slim and pretty, with a wide, animated smile and sun-streaked brown hair, the family resemblance was unmistakable.

*You need to leave before she recognizes you!*

*It's all right, she doesn't really know me. Besides, she hasn't seen me since I was fifteen.*

I studied Netta surreptitiously as she chatted with the couple at the desk, fiddling with the ragged fringe on the hem of my jean shorts. I felt torn in half with panicky indecision, at war with myself.

*Just go ask her if Wy will be here today.*

*I can't! I shouldn't even be here!*

*Then just leave! Get out of here before anyone else sees you.*

*You* want *to get caught, don't you?*

*You want Wy to know you were here, that you came looking for him.*

*I just want to see his face—it's been so long—*

*Then stand up and go introduce yourself to Netta.*

I was just about to do that very thing when all my options were promptly stripped away. A large blue pickup coated by a fine layer of dust pulled up in front of the windows, no more than a dozen feet from where I sat. Time froze, along with every muscle in my body, as Wy climbed from it; by contrast, my thoughts whirled in a frenzy of frantic observation, noting every detail.

*Oh God oh God, Wy . . .*

Clad in his battered gray cowboy hat and a red T-shirt, well-worn work gloves and faded jeans, he was so immediate, so achingly familiar and handsome, that I wanted to sink through the floor and simply die. There was no denying he remained my ideal in every way, the love of my life, the man who rendered all others lacking. He was tanner than saddle leather, his arms lean and strong, his shoulders wide; he exuded calm and competence, as always. The only difference was the facial hair he'd grown since I'd last seen him, which lent him a new depth of maturity—Wyatt Rawley, only steps away from me for the first time in three unendurable years. Motionless, utterly transfixed by the sight of him, I could do nothing but watch as he leaned into the backseat of his truck, emerging moments later holding an adorable little boy.

My heart ceased functioning all over again.

Wy planted a kiss on his son's forehead before setting the boy on the ground, and Zane immediately ran ahead, pushing through the front door before I could catch my breath.

"There's Dr. Rawley now," I heard Netta saying, her voice as remote as if she was broadcasting a crackly transmission from a distant planet. "He can answer your questions about your horses."

I almost knocked over my chair as I stood—the only option my panicking mind recognized was to flee, and so I fled. Exiting through the front door meant crossing directly in Wy's path. A restroom sign loomed across my vision and I raced for it, nearly colliding with Zane. The women's room door had barely closed behind me when I heard the bell tingle again out in the main office and knew Wy had entered the space. I stood with both hands covering my mouth, listening as hard as I could.

Netta was saying, "Zany! Hi, honey, I haven't seen you all week!"

"Hey, Netta," Wy said, and my blood pulsed at the sound of his deep voice. "Thanks for watching Zane for me. I won't be gone long."

Netta responded, "No problem, hon. These folks have a few questions for you, if you have a minute before you go."

I imagined him nodding. "Sure. Let's head over to my office."

Other voices momentarily obscured his and the next thing I knew, the outer door opened and he was gone. Just like that. No less than I deserved.

*You need to leave, immediately.*

And this time, I knew there was no other choice, insanity washed away for good by the reality of seeing Wy with his son. No matter how much I longed otherwise, Wy was not mine. He was married to another woman and they had a child. And I belonged exactly no place in that picture.

*What in God's name were you thinking, showing up here?*

*You saw his face one last time, you have that now.*

The ancient wound throbbed, reclaiming its stranglehold on my heart.

I waited for another few minutes before slipping from the restroom, until I was certain Wy was no longer in the outer office. Zane filled my sight as I fluttered past the desk where Netta stood talking to yet another client; Wy's beloved son unexpectedly looked my way and offered an endearing smile. Zane Rawley was a pint-sized version of his father, a brown-eyed darling of a boy; he would turn three next January, I knew well. It was all I could do to keep walking forward when I wanted to crumple in pain, staring at this boy who, had life taken a very different turn, might have been mine and Wy's.

*Go*, my mind screamed. *You don't belong here, Millie. You know this.*

My car seemed to exist at the other end of a long tunnel, the world closing in around me as it always did when it hit me all over again just how much I'd lost. I scanned the parking lot; thankfully, Wy was not in sight, and I scurried past his truck—dark blue, with his name and title stenciled on the doors in yellow letters—keeping my head down. Less than thirty seconds later, I turned left onto the main road, en route to the interstate, trembling with cold, aching grief. And as much as I longed to, I did not look back.

# CHAPTER THIRTY-TWO

I TOLD NO ONE ABOUT DRIVING TO JALESVILLE and seeing Wy, not even Rae.

I arrived in Landon close to dawn the next morning, after driving straight through from Montana, gritty-eyed and road-weary, feeling as gutted as a dead fish. And the summer proceeded to pass in a blurry whirlwind of working lunch and dinner rushes at Shore Leave and staying out late with Rae. My cousin had broken up with Evan over the winter and was currently seeing Zig Sorenson, which she kept strictly confidential; at thirty-one, Zig was eleven years older than us and Rae knew her dad would kill him on sight if he caught wind of their relationship. Zig was a decent guy, but not above a little subterfuge to avoid Uncle Justin's legendary temper, and he gamely played along when Rae insisted that they stay under the radar.

What struck me most that summer was the increasing numbness I experienced, a feeling like ice at a slow creep through my veins. Hanging out with Rae and Zig those humid summer evenings, usually in the company of Zig's friend from work, Jeremy Hanley—who, at twenty-six, was Wy's exact age—seemed like fun in the moment, but left me emptier than ever by morning's light. The more desperately I tried to fill the gaping hole in my chest, the deeper it grew, a hollowness that terrified me. As the days passed, one bleeding into the next, I realized I needed to end things with Russ, once and for all. I knew I would never love him the way he wanted, and no amount of time would change that fact.

Rae, Zig, and Jere became my constant companions that summer, the four of us hanging out in Zig's double-wide in the small trailer court south of Landon most nights, a twenty-by-forty space ironically perfect for clandestine gatherings and subsequent debauchery. The surface of the coffee table was perpetually cluttered with booze bottles, packs of smokes, a plastic ashtray, Zig's yellow lighter and Jere's red one, half-eaten pizzas, and our respective shot glasses; the air was always tinged by residual smoke, classic rock in the background, the volume turned low on an old stereo. I felt increasingly disconnected from reality as the hours of those nights waned toward morning, thanks in no small part to the alcohol that flowed hotly through my otherwise icy insides; I still hated the taste of booze but craved the temporary oblivion it supplied.

"You're such a librarian, Mills." Zig teased me with variations of this statement almost every night.

Rae, stationed on his lap, neatly downed her vodka before saying, "Leave her alone. Millie is smarter than you and Jere put together."

Zig and Jere laughed hard at this, nodding enthusiastic agreement; Jere poured me a shot, my fifth or so of the evening, with a wink. I accepted it and swallowed the fiery liquid in a quick gulp. Nothing I did within the walls of Zig's trailer was against my will—I chose to drink and get loaded and play stupid drinking games; I chose to straddle Jere while he sat on the sagging couch and let him kiss me and glide his hands under my shirt and inside my panties; I chose to give him half-drunken hand jobs. I chose not to listen too hard while Rae and Zig had repeated energetic sex in his bedroom, separated from Jere and me in the living room by nothing more than a flimsy plywood door.

Though Jere asked me all the time to consider it, I drew the line at sex with him, even after I broke things off with Russ, not long after my disastrous trip to Jalesville. I was already plagued by guilt and ashamed of my behavior on more than one front—Russ loved me, and no matter what I did, I couldn't make myself love him back. Jere was fun and good-looking and I liked him just fine, but I knew even the first night we made out that we had zero chance of a future together, and that we were in actuality just using each other to alleviate our respective loneliness. I had dreaded Russ's reaction to the necessity of ending our relationship, but was totally unprepared for the speed at which his disbelief morphed to anger. In all my nervous imaginings of breaking up with him, I had not once considered that he would respond with such fury.

"How long have you been planning this?" he had yelled into the phone that particular morning, and even though he was many dozens of miles distant, my spine twitched in alarm at his furious tone. "You can't tell me you decided *just today* to break up with me!"

"I'm so sorry—"

Russ interrupted at once. "What started this? Is there someone else? I *knew* it. Is that why you go home alone every summer? To be with someone else?"

"*No,*" I insisted. "Can you please stop yelling—"

"'Stop yelling?' Are you serious right now?! Out of nowhere you tell me this shit and you expect me to stop yelling?! I can't believe this. You're like some stranger I don't even know!"

Tears filled my eyes and throat, water slamming through a gorge. I stammered, "Russ, I'm so sorry . . ."

"I've *waited* for you!" he raged. "It's not like I couldn't have dated other people in all this time. *Jesus Christ*, Millie. I was going to propose to you once you graduated! What do you think about that, huh?! What have you been doing with me these past two years, *just fucking around?*!"

That was the first night I let Jere pull me on his lap after Rae and Zig disappeared into his bedroom.

My cousin was uncharacteristically unaware that summer, but I recognized the signs; I knew them all too well. She was in love. Starry-eyed, she gushed about Zig without letup. She didn't care that he was eleven years older and lived in a trailer and bartended at his grandpa's place for extra cash. She didn't care that her dad would kill Zig if he knew they were having sex as often and vigorously as bunnies. She only cared about how he made her feel. I loved Rae, and was hardly one to judge; I worried that she was setting herself up for an obvious and major heartbreak—but then again, who was I to talk? She was unfailingly supportive of me, especially regarding my decision to cut ties with Russ.

"I think being a librarian would be a great job," I mumbled in response to Zig's teasing, tossing back yet another shot, with a shudder.

"You'd be one of those sexy librarians who takes off her glasses and then makes you come in the storage closet with her." Jere appeared dreamy-eyed, as if envisioning this exact scene, and I giggled, watching as he drew on his small metal pipe. He smoked a lot of weed and wasn't exactly the smartest guy on earth, but he was funny; he made me laugh. And even though his mouth tasted extremely herbal, he wasn't a bad kisser.

"Makes you do *what*, Jere?" Rae teased.

"Come in the storage closet . . . " He suddenly got the joke, exhaling both laughter and smoke.

Zig slid a hand across Rae's thigh, squeezing her as they smiled into each other's eyes.

They retreated to his bedroom a minute later, and Jere invited politely, "You wanna get high, Mills?"

"No, thanks."

"You wanna take off your glasses?" he asked next, sliding closer to me on the battered couch cushions.

"I'm not wearing glasses," I murmured, moving into his embrace.

He grinned, still all dreamy-eyed. "My kind of librarian."

. . .

I returned to Minneapolis for my junior year in late August, exhausted and sunburned and unemployed—I hated the thought of never again setting foot at

Lake View, but continuing to work at the stable was out of the question, now that Russ and I were over. I'd left Landon with promises to call Rae every night, the two of us holding each other close before I climbed into my car in the parking lot at Shore Leave. I'd said my good-byes to Dad and Mom and my siblings at home, but stopped over at the café for a last round of hugs from Grandma Joelle and Aunt Jilly; Rae had walked me out.

"Don't work too hard this semester." Rae rocked us slowly side to side, her chin hooked over my shoulder. I inhaled the scent of her soft golden hair, which I'd always thought smelled like sunshine. She whispered, "I'll miss you so much. It was so good to have you all to myself this summer."

"You liar," I responded. "*Zig* had you all to himself this summer."

She drew back, cupping my elbows. "I'm sorry, I know I've been obsessed with him."

"You love him. You think I don't understand?"

Our gazes held steady for a few beats of silence.

At last Rae said softly, "You'll meet someone else. The *right* someone else."

I fought the horrible sensation of everything inside me toppling inward, like a demolished building; I couldn't bear to ask her if she'd seen it in a notion. My lips trembled as I whispered, "But what if—"

"*No.*" She spoke adamantly, shaking me a little, still holding my elbows. "You have to let Wy go. For your own good, Mills."

That night, alone in my tiny, non-air-conditioned dorm room, I curled beneath my top sheet, gripping my shoulders in either hand, muffling my frantic weeping in a pillow. Every aching sob I had not allowed over the past summer gushed forth in a choking rush of pain, emotion so violent I was terrified by it, numbness annihilated beneath the flood. I had stood within steps of Wy back in May, had laid eyes upon him, and in the end, I'd been too cowardly to do anything but flee—and even still, I could not heed Rae's words and fully concede the loss of him. To make matters all the more unbearable, today's date was August twentieth, Wy and Hannah's third wedding anniversary, and I was tortured by images of what they were surely doing to celebrate.

*Oh God, does she feel the same way I did when you touch her?*

*Does she even know how lucky she is, to be loved by you?*

*Do you think of me at all, Wy, ever at all?*

I figured he did, at least sometimes—I would never doubt that Wy had once loved me.

*But you don't anymore, do you?*

*And I can't bear it . . .*

# CHAPTER THIRTY-THREE

WINTER CAME EARLY AFTER A BOUT OF WARM weather in the last week of September, one blizzard atop the next as a dreary October drained into a bleak November. I made a concentrated effort after the disastrous trip to Minnesota back in May to stop purchasing hard liquor; no more hiding bottles in the cupboard. When I met Joey and my brothers at The Spoke, I limited myself to a couple of beers, nothing stronger. I continued to seek refuge in my work, finding comfort in the care of animals as I had my whole life and in the developing relationship between my brother and my best friend. Quinn had, at last, shared the truth with us—during a Sunday dinner at Aunt Julie's—and apparently, I had been the only adult in the family who hadn't suspected for some time. I felt more like a self-centered jerk than ever.

"It's about time you came out of the woods," Sean had said that afternoon. "Jesus, bro, you know we love you. You can tell us anything."

"Out of the *woods?*" Becky was already giggling. "Sean, you're a moron."

Jessie added, "Honey, come on, we've talked about this."

Quinn said kindly, "It's the thought that counts."

Lee leaned across the table. "For the love of God, *ask Joey out.* You two would be perfect for each other. Kyle and I both think so."

Joey joined Quinn for Thanksgiving at Dad's; my brothers and their families were all in attendance, and the festive mood worked to temporarily lift my spirits, despite a confrontation with Hannah earlier in the day.

"I'm bringing Zane with me." I was unwavering. "It's bad enough that you won't come with. It's Thanksgiving, for Christ's sake."

She hissed, "Your family hates me! They run me down in front of Zane!"

"You know that shit is *not true.*"

"It is!"

"You live in some sick fantasy world," I accused, flinging aside the armful of laundry I'd toted to the bedroom. Almost immediately, I thought, *As though you should talk, Wy.*

Quinn had chopped down a blue spruce from the back acreage of our homestead, as per family tradition. He and Joey worked together to steady it in the stand and string the lights; later, after turkey dinner, the kids decorated its branches. I snagged a seat on one of the leather sofas, smiling to watch Zane hang the candy canes his cousins handed him, one at a time, working with somber concentration. The whole house was blanketed in the warmth of holiday spirit; the air smelled like pumpkin pie, and the radio played Christmas songs, and I found myself imagining what it would be like if my mother had not died all those years ago. My mother, who had lingered at the back of my mind all day. I'd dreamed about her the previous night, as I sometimes did, but couldn't remember exact details, only that she'd been trying to tell me something.

*What was it, Mom?* I thought, squinting as though this might stimulate my rusty memory of the dream. *What did you want me to know?*

I imagined her scolding me for my negative attitude.

*You have a lot to be thankful for, including a beautiful, healthy little boy.*

*Don't take that for granted, son.*

*You need to focus on the here and now.*

*Hanging on to Millie Jo is destroying you.*

*No one's life is exactly how they wish it was, Wyatt.*

But as the holiday season and eventually the spring progressed, I found myself straying to the outskirts of things at family gatherings, staring into space, avoiding conversations. Though I always feigned a cheerful attitude around Zane, it became harder around anyone else. Other than Joey, no one knew about the insidious ways in which my relationship with Hannah had deteriorated. Though she hadn't again lashed out physically, our interactions remained strained. She refused to apologize for either hitting me or threatening to lie to the police, preferring to avoid both issues—and me—altogether. My despondency grew stronger every day, which terrified me. When I found myself at the liquor store after work on a rainy Wednesday in mid-May it was hard to imagine sinking much lower.

*Don't do this. What will it solve?*

I hesitated, teetering on a thin edge between reason and total despair.

*Fuck it,* I thought at last, grim with resignation.

That was the first time I thought I saw Jarred Watkins in Jalesville. Driving along Front Street minutes later, the slim brown paper bag containing my booze shoved beneath the bench seat, I passed a truck in the oncoming lane that seemed somehow familiar. I didn't get a clear angle on the driver as our vehicles crossed paths, but felt a surge of unease, as though I'd missed something important, some necessary detail. I slowed to a crawl, looking over my left shoulder, but the taillights of the other truck were fast disappearing in the opposite direction, obscured by the light but steady rain, and I chalked up the strange feeling to my low mood.

*You haven't heard a word from Watkins since last fall,* I reminded myself as I pulled into the garage, windshield wipers slapping.

Travis Woodrow kept me apprised of the situation involving Jarred Watkins; he had not pressed charges against me, for which I was thankful, and had instead himself been the recipient of animal neglect charges, thanks to the untiring efforts of Deputy Clemens. I'd learned that Jarred had been forced to surrender his remaining livestock to the county at the end of February, and I'd been on alert for a few weeks after that, concerned about a possible confrontation. But nothing occurred and eventually I dropped my guard.

*That wasn't Watkins in the truck just now. You're imagining things because you feel guilty about buying whiskey.*

I parked beside Hannah's car, making sure the booze remained hidden in my truck until I could retrieve it later. The house smelled like pasta and cheese, and I heard Zane laughing as I entered through the kitchen; a small measure of comfort replaced the dull ache across my gut.

"Hi, guys," I called toward the living room, stepping out of my boots.

"Daddy!" Zane ran with arms widespread, and I scooped him up for a hug.

"Hi, buddy." I kissed his forehead and he patted my cheeks as I asked, "What are you and Mommy doing?"

Hannah appeared in the archway between the two rooms, arms tightly folded, and answered for him. "Watching a show. Supper's been ready for over an hour."

Because he remained in my arms, I felt the way Zane's small shoulders slumped at the tone of his mother's voice. He looked expectantly at me, brows lifted, as though to gauge my potential reaction; he was obviously troubled, and I hated myself more in that moment than ever before in my life. My boy was only a toddler and already expected and feared confrontations between his parents. I was fooling myself to think he always slept through our fights or Hannah's frequent, wild sobbing.

*Fuck,* I thought again; I felt like someone had shot acid into my veins.

"It smells great in here." I forced a smile, heartened by Zane's subsequent grin.

Hannah retreated to the living room without another word, and so I carried Zane with me to the kitchen, scooping us each a plate of lasagna, settling him in his booster seat at the table while the television droned in the background. I talked brightly with my son, doing my best to atone for my lateness, my guilt; for the booze in my truck and the pit of depression in my center. Much later, once I'd tucked Zane to bed and Hannah was asleep, I settled on the front porch with the whiskey, comforted at last by the warm haze induced by the alcohol propelling through my blood. I sat drinking until I felt exhausted enough to steal a few hours' worth of sleep, but as I stood to head back inside, I happened to notice a vehicle a few blocks down the street pull quietly from the curb and drive away.

A truck.

I squinted after it, on sudden alert.

*What the hell?*

I was too far away to discern a license plate and stood there in the darkness, all but weaving on my feet, trying to convince myself I was just imagining trouble.

*It's nothing. Go to bed.*

...

I found Lucky when I arrived at work the very next morning. I was the first to arrive and spied him lying on the damp concrete near the front entrance to the vet office, as though sleeping. But I knew within a few steps that he was not asleep, even as my mind tried to deny the obvious truth. I jogged the last few yards, heart thudding, and dropped to a crouch alongside him, already recognizing what I couldn't bear to admit—his unnatural stillness, his stiff legs.

"Lucky, buddy, come on," I said. "*Dammit*, buddy."

I cupped his heavy head, which was limp and cold; his lower jowls drooped and his eyes were not quite shut, but there was no denying that he was gone.

"*Shit*," I muttered, gripping my forehead, pressing hard.

I heard Joey's car approaching along the gravel driveway and stood; spying me standing there motionless outside our office, staring mutely at him, he recognized that something was off and hustled across the parking lot.

"What's wrong?"

I gestured at Lucky, my throat raw.

Joey knelt and ran a palm along the dog's side, then looked up at me with clear surprise. He demanded, "What in the hell? Wasn't he in the barn last night, with the rest of the dogs? How did he get out here?"

Suspicion rippled over my nerves; I couldn't believe it had only just occurred to me. I said through a clenched jaw, "Jarred Watkins was here last night. He killed this dog."

Joey stood in a rush, as though concerned I was about to charge to my truck, roar out of the lot, and make tracks to Watkins' ranch. Holding up a hand, he said, "Hang on a sec, Wy, we can't go jumping to conclusions like that."

I shook my head, grinding my teeth; I resumed my crouch beside Lucky, this time minutely examining him, searching for any sign of inflicted harm. All I knew for sure was that he'd been in his kennel last night, with the rest of the dogs, and now he was outside in the dawn light, dead. I rolled his body over, taking care; his fur was short, aiding my ability to spy a wound, but I found no evidence of damage. At last I curled my fingers around Lucky's soft ear and said quietly, "I will figure this out, buddy, I promise you."

Joey had disappeared inside our office, returning to let me know that nothing within had been touched. He added, "But we should check the kennels, come on."

The dogs slept in the north barn, where the cattle were also housed. Other than padlocking the large outer doors, we didn't typically lock up the arena or the stables on a nightly basis, only the tack rooms and main offices; there was no cash kept on-site, and the only other logical reason to break into a vet office would be to steal the controlled medical substances. It would be no difficult task for someone to creep inside one of the barns under cover of darkness; we didn't even have security cameras. Our remaining dogs were in their kennels, barking and excited to see us; how I wished they could speak up and tell us what had occurred last night. I strode to Lucky's kennel to find the door unlatched, gaping open a few inches, the only sign of something amiss in the entire space.

"Mother*fucker*." My hands were in fists. A wave of heated sickness rolled over me as I imagined Jarred Watkins standing right here at some point last night, probably aiming a small flashlight to find the right dog. Had Lucky known it was him and resisted? What kind of sick fuck would kill a dog just to prove some point? It could be none other than Watkins; only he would have taken the time to arrange Lucky right where we would be sure to find him in the morning, sending a clear message. It *had* been his truck last night, skulking around Front Street.

"He fed him rat poison or the equivalent, I'd bet my license," Joey said, his voice reaching me from a long, hazy distance even though he stood at my side. "It's available at any drugstore. I can do a necropsy to confirm it."

"I'm going out there," I rasped, turning blindly from Lucky's kennel.

"No. *Hell* no." Though I hadn't specified, Joey recognized my intent and grabbed my arm.

"Let go."

"I won't."

"Let *go*."

"What are you gonna do, punch me out? *Jesus*, Wy." Joey released my elbow. "We'll call Travis, first thing."

Fury swarmed across my vision, egging me on—I envisioned smashing my fists repeatedly against Jarred Watkins' smug face, one after the other until he was pulp—but I knew Joey was ultimately right. There was nothing to be solved by losing control. Nothing I did now would bring Lucky back.

"Let these guys out," I muttered, gesturing at the rest of the dogs. "I'll go call Trav."

I was scheduled to visit three separate ranches and couldn't cancel; instead, I used the long drive times to contemplate my next move. Travis stopped out at Bitterroot and took my statement, during which I told him I was sure I'd seen Watkins in town last night; Travis called back later, while I was driving east, to let me know that Deputy Clemens had been informed and meant to pay Jarred Watkins a visit later today.

"It doesn't mean anything is going to happen," Travis warned me. "As much as I hate to admit it. Everything in this situation is circumstantial. Worse yet, this kind of thing happens with animals, they get into the wrong thing, accidentally ingest something harmful."

"Are you telling me you think this was a goddamn *accident?*"

"You know me better than that." Travis sounded irritated. "Shit. You know I don't. I'm just trying to prepare you." He paused. "In the meantime, don't go doing anything stupid, you hear me?"

"I hear," I muttered, but it was more difficult with each passing hour not to consider doing something stupid, especially after Trav called a final time to let me know that Mrs. Watkins had confirmed her husband's presence at home last night, thereby providing him with a neat alibi.

When I arrived back at Bitterroot later that afternoon, I found my brother in the vet office, sitting on my desk, using his pocketknife to dig out a splinter in his palm. The moment I appeared, Quinn set aside the knife and rose, engulfing me in a brief, tight hug.

"I'm sorry," he murmured. "Joe told me about Lucky."

"Thanks."

Quinn held my gaze, obviously concerned. "What are you planning?"

I looked immediately away. "Nothing."

"Bullshit," my brother said.

I spied Joey heading across the parking lot from the main office, carrying a bundle of mail. On impulse, I said, "I'm happy for you guys. I'm glad you found each other."

Quinn cupped the back of my neck for a moment, studying my face as though deciphering an algebra problem, brows drawn inward in a combination of compassion and concern—and I knew right then that Joey had told him about Millie.

But he only said, "Thanks, little bro."

Joey explained that he'd conducted a postmortem on Lucky while I was out on calls; we both knew results of the necropsy would take days, but it was an important step toward any hope of proving that Jarred Watkins was responsible.

"Do you want me to take care of burying him?" Joey asked, resting a hand on my shoulder; he didn't need to clarify why.

"No, I should . . ."

"Let us take care of it," Quinn insisted. "You don't have to face that. You look like hell, Wy. I know you loved that dog. We'll bring him over to Dad's, put him to rest out by the old homestead."

Tears stung my gritty eyes. "Thanks, you guys, I'll stop over later. Let Dad know I'm all right, okay?"

But I was far from all right. I drove aimlessly after leaving Bitterroot, lost in thought, the familiar sights of my hometown appearing ashen before my eyes.

*Stop this, Wy.*

*Stop feeling sorry for yourself.*

*It's no goddamn use . . .*

I had turned twenty-seven this past February—my birthday was two days after Millie's, which fell on Valentine's Day—but I felt closer to a hundred, ashamed of myself on too many levels to count. There was no denying that I spent nearly all my energy wallowing in delusion and self-pity, drinking to dull a pain I knew in my heart could never be fully numbed. I had a wife, a son, and a career; a life in this town. The past needed to remain in the past, no matter how much I rebelled against the notion. It was more important to be a good father, the father my son needed. Zane was only three years old; he needed me in every way, and would continue to need me far beyond his teenage years. He hadn't asked to be conceived, let alone born. God, I loved him so, more than I ever would have thought possible before his birth.

I drove to the edge of town, where I parked facing the mountains and sat with my truck idling, watching as weather blew in from the west. Ever since I was a little kid I'd loved watching thunderheads build, blue-black and menacing beyond the distant peaks. When a spring storm rolled across the foothills, it seemed the sky was about to engulf the town; I recalled many afternoons sitting with Dad and my brothers as we watched the clouds broil, exclaiming in awe as lightning sizzled and thunder shook the ground. Weather moved fast over the long stretches of land near Jalesville; we'd only just start to appreciate the storm before it was gone, sailing away, hitching a ride toward Miles City on the back of the wind.

In the past year, I'd spent time storm-watching with Zane, the two of us safe in my truck, enjoying the wonder on his little face as he peered at what he called the "angry sky." As light rain spattered the windshield, I looked at the empty passenger seat, recalling other times, other summer afternoons; I heard an eight-year-old Millie say, *Wow, I've never seen a storm move so fast!*

*Not even over Flickertail?* I'd been in the backseat with Henry and Brant while Millie sat up front with my dad.

*Not that fast*, she insisted, her eyes bright with excitement. *Aunt Ruthie al-*

*ways says everything is a little wilder out here and I think she's right.*

I slammed the steering wheel with the base of my palms, fury and despair making knots in my gut. Today had pushed me over the edge in more ways than one. I felt sick with helplessness, every bit as unable to fix what was wrong in my life as I was to punish Jarred Watkins for his unbelievable cruelty.

*There you go, feeling sorry for yourself again.*

*Pull it together. You can't just drive around town all night.*

*Maybe Hannah will actually come to put some flowers on Lucky's grave with you and Zane.*

"You really think that guy took the time to kill a dog?" was the first thing she asked after I explained the morning's events. I found her alone in the kitchen, Zane having stayed for supper at Hannah's parents' house.

"I just told you exactly what I think." I leaned against the doorframe, arms folded, while Hannah bustled around; I didn't like the hard edge I heard in my voice.

She contradicted, "Dogs die all the time. Wasn't that dog old?"

"Not that old."

"You're imagining things, Wy. You're paranoid when it comes to animals."

"Thanks a fucking lot."

Hannah paused in her frenetic movement, staring at me with obvious irritation. "I mean that you're making more out of the situation than necessary. Be reasonable. I can't believe you told Travis Woodrow you think someone *murdered* that dog. How embarrassing. Did he actually take you seriously?"

I left without answering, ignoring what she yelled after me, resisting the urge to slam the door to the garage hard enough to shake paint off the walls.

# CHAPTER THIRTY-FOUR

I COLLECTED ZANE FROM HIS GRANDPARENTS
and brought him with me to Dad's.

"I have some bad news, bud," I told him as we drove through a bright, dripping landscape; the earlier rains had passed, leaving the foothills glinting with jewel light in the fading sun. "Lucky died."

"He did?" Zane's voice held surprise and sadness. "How, Daddy? Did a car hit him?"

"No, not like your grandma's cat. Lucky was just old." I had no intention of telling Zane anything beyond. "Uncle Quinn and Joey buried him and I thought maybe we could put flowers on his grave, what do you say?"

"Is he by Grandma Faye?" Zane asked.

"Somewhere close by, probably," I said, closing my eyes for the space of a heartbeat. My mother was buried in the maple grove where the original Rawleys on our land had been laid to rest for generations; the oldest headstone there belonged to Miles Rawley, my grandfather's grandfather, who had died in 1881.

"That's sad," Zane said. "Lucky was a good boy."

"He was, wasn't he? I liked how when he wagged his tail, his whole body shook."

Zane giggled. "I liked his kisses!"

"He liked to lick your face, didn't he?" I parked near Quinn's truck, inundated with relief to be home. Every inch of this house, the barns, and the surrounding acreage were a familiar balm to my nerves.

Dad met me at the door for a hug, before scooping up Zane and kissing his cheek. He invited, "Come on in, boys, you're just in time for dessert."

Marsh and Ruthie's kids were all present, in addition to Sean's two youngest, Harleigh and Mikey. The kids were clustered around the dining room table, scarfing slices of pie; someone had spilled milk. Zane raced for his booster seat, elated to be around his cousins, as usual. Joey and Quinn were out in the kitchen, chatting as they worked together to do the dinner dishes. Joey was wearing an old apron of my mother's tied over his jeans, washing while my brother dried. It was such a scene of domestic contentment that I was a little taken aback—but they seemed so right together, and I truly was nothing but happy for them.

Dad caught my eye and winked, his mustache twitching with subtle amusement as we observed them.

"This is a good look for you," I told Joey, stepping into the kitchen and tugging at the bow tied around his waist.

His hands sunk in soapy dishwater, Joey didn't even fire back a sarcastic comment; his eyes held a depth of calm I'd never before witnessed in him. He said softly, "We took care of Lucky. We were waiting for you to have the ceremony."

Quinn asked in an undertone, "Hannah didn't join you guys, huh?"

I shook my head, feeling my lips compress, unwilling to elaborate; I suddenly wondered how much Joey might have told my brother about this additional aspect of my life. But now wasn't the time to wonder.

"Come grab a seat, Wy," Dad said. "Julie brought over a couple of blackberry pies."

The sun had worked its way under the horizon by the time we all ventured outside to pay our respects to Lucky; Marshall and Ruthie weren't home, or I knew they would have joined us. And while not all of the kids had known Lucky, they were appropriately solemn and subdued as we gathered around the freshly turned earth a quarter-mile from the house. The air was still and soft as a purple twilight advanced, warm with spring, and I didn't feel foolish presiding over a dog's funeral as everyone waited expectantly for me to begin; I felt only the unwavering support of my family and my best friend.

*You have so much to be grateful for, don't take it for granted.*

*I know, I really do . . .*

I cleared my throat. "Lucky was a good dog and I'm really going to miss him. I wish I could have known him a little longer."

Joey followed up. "Lucky was perpetually in a good mood. Even for a dog."

Quinn added, "Nothing brought that little dude down, that's for sure."

Zane piped up, "Me and Daddy taught him to sit and stay."

Dad said, "He was a smart dog."

"When he wagged his tail, he knocked things over but he looked so damn happy," I said.

The littlest kids, including Zane, were sniffling and wiping tears; for the first time, I noticed that all of them were clutching wildflowers. A catch formed in my throat.

Celia said, "I only met Lucky a couple of times but I liked him a lot."

"His face always looked like it was smiling," was Axton's contribution.

"He never jumped up on people," Gus said.

Harleigh added, "He liked to play catch."

Colin whispered, "He runned fast."

Mikey and Luke nodded somberly at their older cousins' words.

"We'll miss you, boy," I concluded, hunkering down and touching the turned earth. As soon as I could, I intended to haul a stone over here and carve his name.

The kids set their flowers atop the grave and took turns patting the ground, following my example; by now I was choked up and pressed my knuckles hard against my nose, not wanting Zane to see me upset. The poor kid saw enough of that as it was, thanks to his mother. As his cousins began drifting back toward the house, Zane came to my side and leaned on me, resting an elbow on my head, and I tucked him closer, protectiveness surging; he was so little my arm wrapped more than double around him. My knees were covered in dirt. Zane smelled like blackberries. I studied his sweet face in the last of the daylight; he would never know how much his presence healed my heart, at least not until some future day when he had his own children.

I murmured, "I love you, bud. I'm glad you're here."

"I love you, Daddy," he whispered, and planted a sticky blackberry kiss on my cheek.

. . .

Two days passed, and the news from Travis was disappointing.

"We got nothing, Wy, I'm sorry. I believe what you suspect and so does Clemens, if you want to know the truth. But we got nothing recent on Watkins. I mean, there's clearly motive. He was forced to surrender his stock and has no love for you, but there's no hard evidence that he was on Bitterroot property the other night."

"You're saying I should just let this go, aren't you?" I stood filling my truck at a roadside station west of Jalesville, on the way to my second call of the day. A storm was on my heels, the wind picking up as the diesel pump clunked, and Otter barked at me to hurry. I was so exhausted I wanted to crawl into the backseat and sleep until tomorrow, and it wasn't even noon.

"Yeah, that's what I'm saying. I'm sorry," Travis repeated. "If it makes you feel any better, I don't think Watkins will make another move. He probably feels avenged, like he got away with something by poisoning that poor dog with no consequences."

"It doesn't make me feel better," I muttered; none of this was Trav's fault and so I added, "Thanks, I hope you know I appreciate everything you've done."

"I'll keep you posted," Travis promised. "And hey, it's Friday. You head on home after work and have yourself a good evening. I don't think you'll see Watkins again."

I caught Joey on his way out when I finally returned to Bitterroot late that afternoon, beneath a driving rain. He stood checking his reflection in the small office bathroom; the door was wide open as he leaned toward the mirror, carefully fixing his hair.

I leaned a shoulder against the doorframe, unable to keep from smiling as I teased, "You look real pretty."

"Don't make me say it," he warned cheerfully.

"I know, I know." I headed for my locker, shaking water from my hat. "I hope you have an umbrella all set, it's a real piss-cutter out there."

"How was your day? Any good news?"

"No, unfortunately. What are you guys doing tonight?"

"Dinner in Billings. Quinn should be here any second, he's on the way."

Quinn hurried inside a few minutes later, ducking his head against the rain. The floor grew wet in a wide arc in the mere seconds the door was open.

"Holy shit," he said, swiping water from his jacket sleeves, one after the other. "It hasn't rained like this in ages. I could hardly see past the windshield."

"Maybe you guys should stick around town," I said, shivering as I hurried to button a flannel over the dry T-shirt I'd just slipped over my head.

From down the hall, Joey called, "Don't worry about us, Wy, I'm driving."

My brother grinned at this statement, before asking me, "You hear back from Trav?"

"Yeah, he basically told me to drop it."

Quinn studied my face. As usual, his silence spoke more than words.

"What?" I grumbled.

"Nothing," he muttered, turning from me as Joey emerged, offering him such an endearing smile that I felt almost embarrassed to witness it.

"You all right, Wy?" Joey took the time to ask.

"You want to join us, little bro?" Quinn added.

I was touched by their concern, but assured him, "I'm heading straight home, you don't need to keep an eye on me. No vigilante shit in mind."

"You swear?" Quinn pestered.

"Go, seriously. Have fun. Don't get too wet."

Joey glared at me. "If that's supposed to be some sort of stupid double entendre . . ."

Alone thirty seconds later, I sank to a seat behind my desk and stared blankly at the opposite wall, trying to pretend I didn't want to call Millie so much it hurt. The obsessive urge to do so had only increased since Lucky's death.

*I just want to talk to her for a little while, I'd be satisfied with even a minute . . .*

A minute. Right. Trying to interject rationale, trying to convince myself that a minute would suffice. I was no better than an addict, scrabbling around for one more hit of what I craved, already knowing deep inside that nothing could satisfy it. The two years since we'd last spoken seemed more like a hundred; this July would mark four years since our night together at Itasca. Millie was close to the end of her junior year of college by now, and I had forced myself to stop asking Ruthie about her, terrified that at some point all too soon, the news would be that she and Russ Morgan were engaged.

*Give me the strength to bear it when it happens,* I thought for the thousandth time. *Please, God, give me the strength.*

Seconds ticked by while I sat motionless, listening to the rain batter the roof and battling my better judgment. When I jolted awake at some later point, my heart was going triple time. Thunder detonated directly overhead. I didn't remember falling asleep over my desk, but hours had passed. The wall clock read 9:32, and Joey and Quinn had left before five. I scanned the desk for my phone, riffling through various junk before realizing it was out in the truck. The storm had not abated as I slept. Rain continued to strike the windowpanes like pellets as I checked on the animals in the exam room before heading out; two cats and a rabbit barely stirred in their kennels as I clicked the light switch. I threw on my jacket before heading into the downpour, tugging the hood over my head—and that was exactly why I didn't see him coming before he struck.

One moment I was striding through the empty parking lot toward my truck and the next, someone rushed me from behind. I heard him only a fraction of a second before the bat made contact—he must have been aiming for my spine or head, but timed the swing wrong and caught my left shoulder as I threw out a defensive elbow, propelled by pure instinct. The storm was deafening, but I heard the crack of bone. There was no time to crumple despite the shock of the pain, and I ducked in a rush and avoided his next blow, his body nothing but a dark blur through the haze of rain and adrenaline. Breathing hard, grunting with the effort, I seized hold of Jarred's forearms and dragged him toward the ground, determined to disable his weapon. I knew it was him, despite the fact that his head was covered by a dark ski mask.

*"You piece of shit . . ."* Raw with rage, I didn't recognize my own voice.

We grappled viciously once we hit the pavement and I was unable to process what was happening in anything but small bursts.

*Get him, get him, get him*—the refrain roared across my brain, momentarily numbing the searing ache in my shoulder.

I managed to pin the bat—aluminum and slippery as hell—but doing so pulled my concentration from his other arm, and Jarred slammed a fist against my jaw, knocking us both sideways. I retained my grip even though he landed with the advantage, positioned slightly above. Rain washed over my face and leaked between my clenched teeth as I struggled to regain the upper hand, clinging to the bat so he couldn't use it to inflict worse damage. My back and boots scraped over wet gravel. I tried to knee his ribs but he was too close. Jarred landed another punch, and I lost momentary focus as stars exploded across my vision.

He leaned in close. "My wife left me, you fucking thief. She thinks I killed that dog."

I tasted blood as I rasped, "You did kill him."

"I oughta kill you, *you sack of shit . . .*"

He jerked free from my weakened grip and rose swiftly to his knees. With a groan, I rolled to the right just in time to avoid his brutal downswing. The bat smacked the wet ground with a hollow, metallic pop and the fraction of a second during which he straightened back up allowed me the chance to twist sideways and boot him in the stomach—this time I made solid contact and knocked him backward. I scrambled to my feet, dizzy and reeling, and kicked his chest with all the strength I could muster. He curled around his midsection and I stomped his arm flat to the ground, at last forcing him to lose hold of the weapon. I bent and grabbed it, and for a burning moment considered smashing his skull like a rotting pumpkin—

*No.*

*Jesus, Wy, no.*

Jarred lay moaning but unmoving. Keeping the bat clenched in one hand, I staggered back to the office. My joints were swiftly turning to melted rubber and I struggled to manage the code on the lock pad. I slammed the outer door shut, locked it, and fumbled to dial 911 on the landline, then went to my knees on the tile floor, all of the pain held at bay during the fight screaming along my nerves in unbearable flashes. I crumpled to all fours, curling my left arm toward my chest like a dog favoring a broken leg, unable to bear my weight on that side. By the time two cruisers wailed into the parking lot, I had lost consciousness.

PART FOUR

# CHAPTER THIRTY-FIVE

## MINNEAPOLIS, MINNESOTA

COLD WEATHER ARRIVED EARLY THE AUTUMN OF my junior year, blasting in with an ice storm the day before Halloween. I had not found a new job, nor had I confessed to my parents that I was no longer seeing Russ. Instead I flung my concentration into third-year coursework with feverish intensity, determined to keep at the top of my class. I shelved all of the thousand things I still longed to tell Wy on a daily basis and instead talked to Rae every night, as promised. Despite all odds, by December she and Zig were still together and she intended to reveal the truth to Aunt Jilly and Uncle Justin before Christmas. I was considering using the shock of Rae's revelation about Zig to dampen my own news—I hated letting my parents think I was still with Russ, but it was so much easier than fielding what I knew would be Mom's disproportionate concern.

"Aunt Jilly already knows about you guys, I don't have to be precognitive to know *that*," I told my cousin during a late-night phone call in December. I was wrapped in my quilt like a burrito, a textbook open on the bed near my knees. I had spent the past week studying for finals without letup; midnight had come and gone, and my eyes were blurry with lack of sleep. Fluffy new snow edged my tiny window like lace.

I imagined Rae chewing her thumbnail. "I know, Mom totally knows. But she isn't who I'm worried about. Dad'll be ballistic."

"Not necessarily. You're a grown woman, not a kid."

"Not in Dad's eyes. I'll always be his little girl; you know how protective he is." I heard her rearranging pillows. "I forgot to tell you. Clint knows."

"How?"

"I told him. I'm so sick of keeping secrets. We were hanging out at his place on Sunday, and I just wanted his opinion. I think there was some part of me that thought Clint might offer to talk to Dad for me. Or at least, *with* me."

"What did Clinty think about everything?"

"He was pretty calm about it. I mean, Clint *knows* Zig, knows he's a good guy. He thinks our age difference is pretty extreme. But plenty of people are more than ten years apart."

"Is 'Zig' his actual name? I've never asked."

I knew Rae was smiling even though I couldn't see her face. "His full name is Zigfried, isn't that great?"

"You'd never guess his family was Norwegian, would you?"

She giggled before adding, "But I could tell Clint doesn't buy how serious we are." I was silent too long, and Rae demanded, "What?"

"Serious as in, what, you're ready to settle down with Zig and have his babies?"

Now it was her turn for silence. At last she asked softly, "Would it be crazy if I said yes?"

"Not crazy at all," I whispered.

"Thanks, Mills."

I had a few admissions of my own. "I saw Russ the other day."

I sensed her sit straight up, surprise crackling across the line. "What?"

"He's been calling and texting since I got back to school, apologizing for the things he said when we broke up, pretty much begging to get back together."

"Yeah, you told me about that. But you were ignoring that shit!"

"I was. We ran into each other at the coffee shop off campus, the one he knows I go to."

"He totally premeditated that, you know he did. What happened?"

"It wasn't bad. We just talked. I told him I was sorry about everything, and about ending things over the phone." I fiddled with the edge of my quilt. I was omitting the fact that Russ had offered me my old job at Lake View, and that I'd agreed to consider it.

"*No*," Rae insisted. "Don't let him manipulate you. You aren't yourself around him, I've seen it with my own eyes."

A small burst of irritation detonated in my stomach. "I know, you've *told me*. Besides, I don't even know what you mean. I'm 'myself' around Russ."

"You aren't," she disagreed. "He only knows about one-tenth of who you really are."

"You are so frustrating!" I yelled, irritation morphing to anger. "I'm lonely, all right? I'm fucking *lonely*. I miss the horses. I even miss Russ."

*But not for the right reasons.*

Rae misinterpreted. "Mills, if you need sex, we'll get you together with Jere when you're home for Christmas. He's been missing you. He talks about you all the time."

"It's not that. Besides, Jere and I never—"

"I know," she interrupted. "But you could easily change that when you're home on break."

"*Rae*," I groaned.

"I'll take that as a 'maybe,'" she said cheerfully.

. . .

I knew there was no chance in hell of anything happening with Jere Hanley while I was home in Landon for Christmas, but I did find myself considering Russ's offer of returning to work at the stable. I was not blind; I knew without a doubt that Russ hoped for plenty more to resume than just my old job. I weighed options in my mind, often lost in thought while I was home for the duration of winter break. Other than creating an excuse for his absence, I said nothing else about Russ to my parents, and instead strayed to the periphery of things; it wasn't difficult to manage, what with the ensuing drama over Rae introducing Zig as her boyfriend on Christmas Eve. She cagily arranged for the entire family to be present in order to minimize her dad's potential response.

Zig, clad in a festive Christmas sweater, appeared unduly pale, his usual smile nowhere to be found, but I gave him credit for having the guts to show up. I'd known Uncle Justin my entire life and was accustomed to the intimidating scars on his face and his quick temper—even though we kids knew well it was all bark, no bite—but I could clearly see how someone would be wary of him, even tough Zig Sorenson. Uncle Justin reacted well for the first few seconds after Rae admitted that she and Zig had been a couple for months. The entire living room went silent, everyone's gazes darting between Uncle Justin and Zig while the blinking Christmas lights on Grandma Joelle's tree flickered over all of us, bathing the big living room in the candy colors of a carnival midway—and I restrained the sudden urge to giggle.

Rae stood with her hands clasped at her waist, her brown eyes wide with expectation as she awaited her dad's reaction, a piece of silver tinsel caught in her hair. You could have heard an icicle fall outside.

But then Uncle Justin slammed a big, curled fist on the arm of the couch and demanded, "What is this really about, Louisa Rae?"

Before Rae could sputter a reply, Uncle Justin directed his menacing gaze at Zig, stabbing his index finger toward the front door. "If your next words are about becoming a father, Sorenson, you better get a goddamn good head start!"

To his credit, Zig did not flinch. He strode to Uncle Justin and extended a hand as he said with quiet dignity, "Your daughter is not pregnant. And I would like to ask permission to continue dating her. I should have asked before now, and I am here to apologize."

Aunt Jilly was hiding a smile behind her coffee mug; Rae was speechless, her mouth literally hanging open. I saw my dad wink in amusement at my mom, who poked him in the ribs.

Grandma Joelle said, "For heaven's sake, Justin, shake the man's hand."

Zig stayed for dinner that night.

Without coursework and constant studying to occupy my thoughts, and with Rae preoccupied, loneliness dug an ever-increasing trench through my heart as winter dragged on, one snowstorm atop the next. I wanted to resume my job at Lake View, but was afraid it would send the wrong message to Russ. While I had missed some aspects of our relationship, they weren't the key ones; I missed the camaraderie we shared while working with horses and teaching classes, but I had not, for one second, missed his constant need for sex, or his insistence that we move in together. Boundaries would be necessary, were I to return.

Shortly after arriving back at school in bleak mid-January, I called Russ at Lake View.

"I'd like to come back to work," I said immediately; no point making stupid small talk.

I heard him exhale. "That's so great, Millie."

"But that's *it*. It doesn't mean I want to get back together, like I've told you."

He spoke quickly. "Right. I understand."

Working again in Champlin every weekend as classes resumed for spring semester, I was busier than ever before, but I had made up my mind to graduate early. Instead of spending another summer in Landon, drinking and messing around and wasting time, I took overloads both semesters of my junior year and registered for summer term, determined to earn my undergrad degree by next December. I intended to start a graduate program immediately afterward, and far too often I opened and reread the grad studies webpage for the University of Montana in Billings—which was less than two hours from Jalesville, pitting me at war with my better judgment.

*And then what?*

*You'll show up at Bitterroot again, hoping to see Wy?*

*Would you really sink so low?*

*You'd pursue an affair with a married man?*

*Yes, God help me, yes. If that was all I could have of him.*

*No, that's insane. You could never settle for such a despicable thing.*

But I applied to the university in Billings, all the same.

. . .

Once, long ago, Wy had told me that the last time he had sex with Hannah, the night Zane was no doubt conceived, that it "just happened." I'd only pretended to understand what he meant that night, the very night we admitted our feelings for each other in the darkness at Shore Leave, far too inexperienced to comprehend such a statement, let alone the lonely despair that might motivate such a decision. I certainly didn't understand the potential long-reaching ramifications of that choice.

But I understood now.

Shortly before the end of spring semester, on a warm, sunny Friday in the middle of May, I received my letter of acceptance. Pending my December graduation, I would be enrolled as a student in the graduate psychology program in Billings. I held the unfolded letter to my heart for a long time, staring into the middle distance, feeling something shift, deep inside my gut. The letter seemed like a premonition, but of exactly what, I could not have said; I just knew, without words, that something beyond me had changed with the ripping open of the envelope.

I drove to work in complete silence, the letter folded on the passenger seat, radio off.

"Montana?" Russ repeated when I told him the news, not two minutes after arriving. His incredulous tone suggested I'd been accepted to a university on Mars.

"I love Montana. I have family out there, remember?"

Russ had been an undeniable gentleman in the months since my return to Lake View, treating me like a fellow employee rather than a former girlfriend, for which I was abundantly grateful. Because I was no longer burdened by the strain of trying to make a serious relationship with him work, I found I enjoyed just being his friend. Only a few times during the past spring had he hinted that he was interested in more than friendship, subtle advances I immediately shut down.

"Yeah, I guess," he said, studying me intently, one forearm braced on the edge of the wooden beam above his head; I'd interrupted his work of mucking out Charger's stall. He offered, "Can I take you out to dinner to celebrate?"

I hesitated a little too long, and he rushed to say, "Just friends, I swear."

And I agreed.

Much later that evening, with Russ snoring alongside me in the twin bed in my dorm room, I lay with both forearms making an *X* over my eyes, teeth clenched, furious and ashamed of what I'd let happen. What had *just happened*, exactly as Wy had once described. Dinner included a bottle of expensive wine— Russ made a big deal about not having taken me for dinner on my twenty-first birthday, which had come and gone last Valentine's Day—and wine led to a lowering of my better judgment, a surge of lonely misery tangling together with my own pathetic, twisted motives. Russ had no clue that I'd applied to grad school in Montana for the sole purpose of being near the man I had never stopped loving.

*What the hell is wrong with you, Millie?*

I wished that my love for Wyatt Rawley would wither and die once and for all, leaving me in solitude, if not peace. It had become almost a curse, a blazing torch I could not set aside no matter how excruciatingly it burned me, time and time again.

*If I can't be with him, let me stop loving him, please, dear God. I can't bear it anymore.*

*I want you so much, Wy, you couldn't know how much I want you. It's like a hunger that won't go away. I want to make love with you until I find some sort of absolution, until I can't remember how much loving you has destroyed me . . .*

And now here I was, ending the night with Russ in my dorm room, stifling my guilt at his obvious joy as we had sex three times over the course of an hour. He had condoms in his wallet, as always.

*What have you done, Millie, what the hell have you done?*

When my phone vibrated to life a little past one in the morning, I was unsurprised to see that Rae was calling; no doubt she had sensed something and was calling to reprimand me. I had been lying there awake and almost ignored the call, unwilling to attempt an explanation, but the buzzing insistence would only wake Russ, so I eased from beneath the sheets and attempted to find my jeans in the darkness. The screen's firefly glow lit my way as I hurried into the hallway, intending to head to the concrete steps out front of the building.

"I know what you're going to say—"

But Rae immediately cut me off.

"It's Wy," she said succinctly, her voice loaded with concern.

I froze mid-step, my heart seizing like a beetle beneath a sharp point—skewered through at the very suggestion that something might have happened to him.

"What . . ."

"He's in the hospital, he's been hurt. Someone hurt him, I mean. I don't know exact details."

"What . . ." I had been reduced to one-word utterances.

"I wish I knew more, Mills, God, I'm sorry. Mom just talked to Aunt Ruthie a minute ago and then called me. You should call her."

I disconnected without further prompting and dialed my aunt with shaking hands, standing there in the hallway beneath the aggressive buzz of the overhead lights. I hadn't talked to Aunt Ruthie in a very long time. The line rang five times with no answer, at last defaulting to her voicemail.

I blurted, "It's me, it's Millie. Please call me when you get this."

Tears rolled like floodwater down my face as I wrapped my free arm around my torso, squeezing, squeezing; trying desperately to counteract encroaching panic. When Aunt Ruthie's name suddenly filled the screen, I almost dropped the phone in my haste to answer.

"Is he okay?!" I cried.

"Yes," she said at once. "His shoulder is broken, but the doctor told us he'll be all right. I'm here at the hospital with Marshall and Clark."

"Oh my God, what happened? *Tell me* . . ."

Aunt Ruthie heard the hysteria in my voice. "Millie, honey, he's all right, I promise you."

I knew I had to pull it together.

"I'm here," I whispered. "Please tell me what happened."

"It's a long story, but it all boils down to the fact that Wy was attacked outside the vet office by a man who is now in custody—"

"Attacked?!" I sank to a crouch.

"I'll tell you everything I know," she promised.

A pulse of sudden instinct prompted me to whisper, "Is Hannah there with you?"

Aunt Ruthie had said Marshall and Clark—but not her.

A pause; at last my aunt said, "No, not at this second."

There were many layers in her tone which I could not interpret, but I didn't press for clarification. The fact that Wy's wife was not present gave me the courage to make the request.

"Please, let me talk to him."

# CHAPTER THIRTY-SIX

## MILES CITY, MONTANA

IT WAS PAST MIDNIGHT. DROWSY FROM PAIN medication, I was situated in a small hospital room, the space lit by the glow of a rerun of the evening news. I heard Ruthie and Marsh talking in low tones in the hallway. Quinn and Joey had left an hour ago, along with Dad; after confirming that I was not in danger of dying, Hannah said she would come to pick me up tomorrow afternoon, the earliest I could be discharged. I could not begin to imagine explaining my injuries to Zane—my face resembled a Halloween mask, my back was covered in abrasions, my left arm was immobilized in a tight sling. Jarred's initial swing had impacted against my shoulder blade, fracturing the bone, and the sclera of my right eye was redder than blood. I'd been evaluated for both a concussion and chest injuries associated with my broken scapula.

I felt like I'd been hit by a train—but there was a grim comfort in knowing that Jarred Watkins was currently in custody; no doubt of the bastard's intentions or guilt this time around.

Someone knocked on the partially-open door and seconds later Ruthie appeared at the bedside. She smoothed hair from my forehead and then cupped my face.

"How are you feeling?" she murmured.

The last thing I wanted was for her to worry more than she already had tonight. I said, "I'll make it, I promise. You guys don't have to stick around. It's late."

I thought I heard wrong when her next words were, "Millie wants to talk to you."

I tried to sit straighter at once, heart slamming—for a split second, I actually thought Millie was about to walk into the room.

"What . . ."

Ruthie passed me her phone and then politely retreated, drawing the door closed as I brought the phone immediately to the less-injured side of my face.

"Millie?" I croaked.

"It's me, I'm here." And just like that, her voice was there in the room with me, the one voice that swept all loneliness, all despair, from existence. "Are you all right? I told Aunt Ruthie I needed to hear for myself, I've been so scared since I heard you were hurt."

Her words were more healing than anything any doctor could prescribe. Inhibitions momentarily lowered, I admitted gruffly, "Just hearing your voice makes me all right."

Millie sounded out of breath. "Aunt Ruthie told me someone attacked you. Oh, Wy, oh my God, I'm so worried. Rae called me first and she didn't know exactly what had happened. I told Aunt Ruthie I needed to hear your voice so I could know for sure that you were all right. Are you okay to talk? Oh God, you must be in so much pain . . ."

Afraid she might hang up and years would pass before we spoke again, I rushed to say, "I'm okay. I'm glad you called, I'm so goddamn glad."

"Oh, Wy," she whispered again. "I was so scared."

I swore I could almost feel her soft breath against my cheek and wished for a visual of her face in this moment, to better gauge her feelings. The tenderness in her voice was unbearable, leaving me shaken and confused—was I only hearing what I wanted to hear in her tone?

"Tell me everything," she invited.

The measure of relief I felt just hearing those words, knowing I was at liberty to talk to her, was almost unimaginable. As though I could quantify such raw gratitude. I told her everything, starting with how I'd taken Lucky last year, and what had happened since, concluding with the moment Jarred Watkins appeared in the parking lot at Bitterroot wielding a goddamn baseball bat. I didn't mention the fact that I'd been in Minnesota last spring, at the end of her sophomore year, and seen her at Lake View; it would only highlight what a jackass I was capable of being.

"You did the right thing, taking Lucky that day," Millie said once I finished explaining. "No one could possibly think otherwise. You saved him. You gave him a good life before he died, I know you did."

"I'd do it again."

"Of course you would. It's who you are," she said softly.

For the first time in nearly an hour, I didn't know what to say next—I wanted to beg her to stay on the phone with me all night, just so I could hear her breathe when she fell asleep. I'd only been allowed that privilege one night of my life, the one we spent together at Itasca. The dim little hospital room had become a sanctuary. I realized afresh just how much Millie understood me on levels my wife never would.

As though reading my thoughts, she said, "I hate that you're in the hospital because of all this, but I'm so glad to talk to you. It's been so long. I'm sorry for how I acted the last time we talked, telling you I would never contact you again. I was behaving like a child."

"Don't be sorry, not for anything. I miss talking to you more than you could know."

In the background of her call a door suddenly creaked open; an instant later, a male voice inquired, "Is everything all right? What are you *doing* out here?"

Alarm bells clanged in my skull.

"I'll be right in," she said to him, clearly angled away from the phone. "Just give me a second."

Sounding irritated, he demanded, "Who are you talking to?"

"I'll be *right in*," she repeated, with more insistence.

I had no way to know if he left her alone or not, but I assumed he retreated, because her voice came back onto the line, low with regret as she said, "I better go. It's late and you should rest."

"Was that Russ?" The grit in my voice was unmistakable.

As though admitting defeat, she whispered, "Yeah."

"He doesn't like you talking on the phone, or what? Are you outside?" There wasn't much disguising the protective, jealous edge in my tone—I knew I had no right, unable to help it.

"No, just in the hallway of my dorm." She hesitated and I wished more than ever for the ability to see her face, to know what she was feeling in this moment. She finally whispered, "I did something really stupid tonight."

My heart jolted—did she mean our conversation? Or asking to talk to me in the first place?

I was about to ask when she caught me off guard again, saying quietly, "Why isn't Hannah there with you?"

There were many excuses I could have offered for my wife's absence, but Millie spoke before I could answer.

"I asked Aunt Ruthie if she was there, at the hospital. If she'd been there, I wouldn't have asked to talk to you." Millie paused to inhale before saying in a rush, "I wish I was there with you right now, Wy, you have no idea how much I wish it."

All defenses reduced to dust, I admitted, "I would give anything if you were."

Suddenly I could tell she was crying, and trying to hide it, and my heart seized all over again.

"Millie—"

I heard the choke in her throat as she interrupted me to whisper, "I have to go. Take care of yourself. Please, oh God, please take care of yourself. For me." And without another word, she disconnected the call.

*I would do anything for you, Millie Jo.*

*Anything at all.*

*And I mean it and I can't fucking mean it, at the same time.*

I stared at the flicker of the television screen for a long time after the line had gone dead, clutching Ruthie's phone, imagining Millie hundreds of miles away in Minnesota and returning inside to Russ Morgan as I lay here alone in a goddamn hospital bed, my world fading to gray static all over again.

# CHAPTER THIRTY-SEVEN

## MINNEAPOLIS, MINNESOTA

RUSS WAS SITTING UP IN BED, CLEARLY AGGRA-
vated, as I reentered my dorm room. I had detoured to the bathroom, hiding
out in a stall until I could draw a reasonably full breath. But my knees were still
trembling, my heartbeat erratic, as I closed the door behind me. He had clicked
on the bedside lamp, encasing the claustrophobic space in a muted auburn glow.

"Russ, I . . ." My tongue was sandpaper-dry.

"Who were you talking to? How long had you been out there?"

I could barely hear past the realization that spun on repeat through my head.
*Wy is still in love with you.*

The need for survival had almost convinced me otherwise.

Russ slammed both fists against the mattress and my attention jerked back
to him.

"Are you listening to me?" His volume escalated. "Who were you talking to?
You were crying out there, I heard you."

"And now you're yelling at me?" I whispered, suddenly recalling what he'd
said last summer, when I ended our relationship—that I was like a stranger. I
restrained a shudder, experiencing the exact sensation in this surreal moment,
standing here facing a man I had known for the duration of my time as a college
student, whose mother had taught me many things, whose family I cared about;
this man I had allowed inside my body too many times to count, whose face I
had watched grow slack as he came, again and again. Justifiable or not, revulsion
stirred in my gut.

I straightened my spine and said, "Please leave."

His lips dropped open. "What?"

"I am telling you that I want you to leave."

He stared at me, stunned.

Increasingly uncomfortable, I babbled, "I'm sorry I let this happen tonight,
Russ, truly sorry. I shouldn't have; it was a mistake."

My words sank in for several tense seconds before he shoved aside the sheet
and rose, jamming his shirt over his head, scrabbling around for his jeans and

shoes. I watched in miserable silence, torn between wanting to continue apologizing and wishing he would just hurry and get the hell out of my room.

He took a moment to pause and hurl a few final words in my face. "You're right it was a mistake, I don't know what the hell I was thinking. You're a selfish flake. *Fuck you.*"

I held open the door without another word, slamming it behind him and resisting the urge to scream a parting shot after his retreating form, hopped up on a surge of contradictory overwhelming emotions. I stripped the bed in a rush of angry energy, flinging the soiled sheets and pillowcases to the edge of the room, and at last sank to the bare mattress, seeking my phone, cradling it as I opened the recent calls list. Sixty-four minutes I'd been allowed to talk to Wy. It seemed more like five, in retrospect, that hour having flown past on swift, silent wings. I'd taken a chance admitting that I wished I was in Montana with him.

*I would give anything if you were,* he'd said.

I stared out the window at the darkness pressing against the small glass pane, recognizing that I could be in Jalesville by morning if I left immediately. I couldn't bear thinking of Wy in a hospital bed hundreds of miles away with a fractured shoulder, alone and hurting. Restless energy flowed beneath my skin, begging me to jump behind the wheel and drive to Montana as I had a year ago—but this time I wouldn't run away; I would go to him, wrap him in my arms and never let go, like I should have done in the first place.

*And then what?*

*He's married, no matter how much you wish otherwise.*

*But he's unhappy, I know it, I could hear it in his voice . . .*

*Why wasn't Hannah at the hospital with him?*

I held the mute phone to my lips, closing my eyes.

*Oh God, Wy, call me back and admit that you still love me. I will come to you in a heartbeat.*

. . .

But weeks passed and he did not call, did not text; I kept my phone next to my body without letup, waiting, hoping, only to hear no word. There were moments of aching doubt and weakness when I felt I could never forgive him for this silence.

*It's up to you to make the first move, Wy, don't you understand?*

*Maybe you're just fooling yourself, Millie. Maybe you misunderstood.*

But I knew in my heart that I had not, that Wy still loved me as much as I loved him, a love from which neither of us had ever recovered.

*That may be true, but what do you expect from him? You're as selfish as Russ said.*

*Wy is a parent, with responsibilities above and beyond any of yours, and you have no idea how that feels.*

Finals complete and junior year over, I drove north to spend precious time in Landon; summer term was scheduled to begin in mid-June, and Rae was insistent that I return home until then.

"I'll tell Zig I'm dedicating all my time to you," she promised over the phone.

"Uh-*huh*," I muttered in response, but she was as good as her word. When we weren't working at Shore Leave, we spent long, gold-tinted afternoons lounging on the water in inflatable chairs, drinking beer or lemonade and gossiping, our noses and chests sunburned by evening. Zig only showed up once, to say a quick hello. It wasn't as though he didn't get Rae all to himself every night anyway; since Christmas, they had rented a small apartment in downtown Landon.

By Saturday of that first week home, I had not yet assembled the necessary courage to tell Rae about sleeping with Russ or talking to Wy later that same night. I hated keeping secrets from her, but I felt as though I was floating in a strange grayish void—a sort of purgatory, desperately waiting for something that may never happen. As much as I fantasized otherwise, I was realistic enough to understand that there was a good chance Wy would never confess the truth, let alone leave his wife. I could spend the remainder of my life wishing for the impossible. And I wasn't strong enough to withstand Rae's commentary on this; I already knew what she would say, because she'd said it a dozen times before. It was advice that anyone with even an ounce of logic would offer.

*You have to let him go.*

But knowing he still loved me had allowed for a small seedling of hope to take root in my soul, rendering all logic null and void.

As long as there was a chance, a terrible part of me would hold on to that hope.

The sun had melted along the curve of the sky like strawberry ice cream left outside in the heat. The entire sweep of western horizon was decorated by hot-pink stripes in the wake of the setting sun as Rae and I settled on the end of the dock, evening shifts at the café over for another Saturday night. Rae had swiped a smoke from her mom's pack, both of us dipping our bare toes in the lukewarm water lapping the moorings. Uncle Justin's speedboat was tethered nearby, gently undulating with the motion of waves stirred up by passing pontoons; every other family either waved or called hello to us, sometimes giving a couple of honks on their boat horns.

"You're coming tonight, right?" Rae blew a stream of smoke toward the far shore.

"Maybe," I hedged. I'd been practically a recluse since returning to Landon, avoidant of everyone other than my family. My parents finally knew that Russ and I were over for good.

"Everyone wants to see you," my cousin went on. "It'll be fun. Most of our class will be there."

"What about Evan?" I was grasping at straws, trying to change the subject.

"What about him? We're still friends. I just think you should—"

Rae stopped dead in the middle of the sentence for no apparent reason. The half-smoked cigarette fell from her fingertips and landed in the lake with a soft *plip*, extinguishing its tiny flame and sending miniature concentric rings outward. Startled by her sudden silence, I turned her way, and chills erupted like land mines beneath my skin, hairline to toes.

I knew that look.

I grabbed her elbow, inexplicably frightened. "What is it?"

Rae blinked in slow motion, as though in a trance; her face was paper-white. "It's the strangest thing," she whispered.

"What did you see?!" I shook her arm; to the best of my knowledge, Rae had not experienced a notion of this magnitude since the horrible afternoon she witnessed Dani's death.

She turned her dark eyes my way and searched my face, severe with focused intensity.

"Rae!" I pleaded in a desperate croak. "What did you see?"

She whispered, "When was your last period?"

My heart froze solid.

"When?" she insisted.

Saliva stuck to the back of my throat, stripping me of the ability to tell her that it had been at least a month. Possibly a month and a week—my thoughts lurched backward in a frantic attempt to recall the last time I'd bled.

Rae clutched my knee. "I just saw you holding a baby. Your daughter. I saw her eyes. She was *looking back at me*. Oh, my God . . ."

My hands flew to cup my belly. A sick, sour taste spread across my tongue.

"*No*," I breathed, fighting the urge to leap to my feet and run. Flee even the remotest possibility of such a thing. "No, it can't be."

Rae shook my leg, as though to interject reason into the situation. "You haven't had sex recently?"

Desperation swelled in my chest, damp and horrible, like a grove of poisonous mushrooms. Rae was never wrong, just like Aunt Jilly. When they experienced a notion, you could count on its occurrence. I thought again of Dani's cancer, and my fear grew out of control.

*There is no way, oh God, there is no way this could be true.*

*But what if—oh Jesus Christ, what if—*

*I'm pregnant.*

For the first time since the morning it happened, I understood with sterling clarity what Wy had felt upon hearing Hannah's news of impending parenthood. I crossed both forearms over my chest, gripping my shoulders on either side, ambushed by the same helpless despair, the inevitable knowledge that life had picked me clean of any choice but one.

"*Rae . . .*"

"With who? When?" she demanded.

I was fading fast. "With Russ . . . back in May . . ."

She wrapped her arms around my torso, squeezing me against her side as my arms and kneecaps started shaking, pitiful little leaves in a rising wind.

"And you haven't had your period since? Did you use protection? Aren't you on the pill?"

Too many questions. I mumbled thickly, "Not anymore."

"Protection?" she insisted.

"We used condoms," I whispered.

Rae maintained calm. "Let's go get a test. I'll drive us to Bemidji."

But it would only confirm what Rae already knew—what she had seen in her vision.

*Your daughter*, she'd said.

A shiver sliced through my ribs.

"Rae, *oh God . . .*" I moaned, bending forward, already knowing I was a goner. Thoughts flew hard and fast, swooping to take shots at my head like birds on the hunt.

*A baby . . .*

*A baby with Russ . . .*

*How can I possibly tell him?*

*I never want to see him again!*

*What if he thinks this means we have to be together?!*

*What if our parents make us get married?!*

*Oh God oh God, they'll make us get married . . .*

I stood in a rush, then proceeded to sink to a crouch, unable to support my own weight.

Rae hauled me upright and kept her arm around my waist. "Come on, let's get out of here. We'll go buy a test."

I implored, "Tomorrow. Please. Let me pretend it's not true *for one more night . . .*"

A sob annihilated any additional words.

Rae hustled me through the woods, past the silent windows of our family's café, upon which the last vestiges of sunset glinted like an ironic benediction, as yellow as the slim spokes of dandelion petals, as yellow as the coward of a woman who should have had the sense to end, once and for all, a relationship with a man she had never loved. The sickest part was that this all seemed somehow *familiar*, this massive log suddenly blocking my path had been waiting my entire life, anticipating the moment when I stumbled upon it. My pregnancy was practically predestined—from great-great-grandmother forward, and probably even before, the Davis women had given birth young and out of wedlock. Mother to daughter, again and again, an endless cycle. I was simply the next link in that age-old chain.

# CHAPTER THIRTY-EIGHT

## JALESVILLE, MONTANA

HANNAH ARRIVED AT THE HOSPITAL TO PICK ME up late in the afternoon, the same hospital where Zane had been born and where we'd brought him for each subsequent checkup; the hospital where Hannah had undergone her hysterectomy. I sat waiting for her in the small lobby, stationed in a wheelchair—I'd balked, but was informed it was part of the discharge procedure and therefore not optional—wishing I'd asked Dad, or Marsh and Ruthie, or Joey and Quinn, to pick me up instead; anyone other than this woman who strode across the tile floor with no hint of a smile, barely acknowledging we knew each other, let alone lived as a married couple.

Maybe it was the surreal haze induced by pain meds, but I felt as though I sat watching a complete stranger advance toward me. This woman had been my high school girlfriend and had taken my name and given birth to my son—and yet I had no idea who she really was. Maybe I'd never really known, except in the most surface of ways. I blamed myself as much as I blamed Hannah; the misery of our marriage weighted both our shoulders, heavier than iron, heavier than guilt.

I had realized something last night, a truth my instincts had known all along; a truth I had buried in order to survive day to day.

*Millie is still in love with you.*

Hannah stopped two steps away from my knees, her mouth drawn up like she'd just bitten into a lemon wedge. I refused to speak first. The daily activity of a hospital front desk surrounded us; people chatting and talking and waiting for the elevator while quiet cello music floated from overhead speakers.

"You look terrible," Hannah finally said, moving behind me to grasp the handles on the wheelchair. "I'm sorry you got hurt, Wy. I should have come last night, but I didn't want to bring Zane all the way here in the middle of the night."

"What have you heard about Watkins?" I asked. And then, as she pushed me in the direction of the door, I added, "I have to stop at the pharmacy before we go."

"I haven't talked to the police, if that's what you mean," Hannah said as we waited in line for my prescriptions. She rested a hand on my uninjured shoulder, her voice softening as she asked, "Are you in pain? Will you have to take a leave from work?"

I resisted the urge to shrug from her touch. "What do you think?"

She withdrew her hand. "You don't need to snap at me. I was just asking."

"Where's Zane?"

"At my parents' house."

Driving toward Jalesville fifteen minutes later, I stared out the passenger window of Hannah's car, leaning slightly forward so my shoulder wouldn't make contact with the seat. The western horizon gleamed like an opal. As I watched, the lowering sun pierced the thick clouds, sending banners of light spiking toward earth, blinding-bright.

*Millie is still in love with you.*

Hannah parked in the driveway of her parents' house, and Zane, peering out the living room windows, hurried to open the screen door and run outside.

"*Dammit*," Hannah grumbled. "Stay in the car."

I ignored her and opened the passenger door, realizing my mistake as Zane stopped short, bursting into tears at my mangled appearance. Immediately I crouched down to his height and held out my right arm, the one not restrained in a sling.

"It's all right, buddy, I'm all right," I assured him. "I just got a little banged up."

He dove for my chest, hiding his face, and I cupped the back of his head.

"I missed you, Daddy, you were gone all night," he said, voice muffled against my shirt, and I felt the knife in my heart sink to the hilt.

"Zane, get in the car," Hannah ordered caustically. "You'll hurt your dad's arm."

"Let him be." I kept my voice level. "I'm fine."

Irene followed Zane outside and stood nearby, hands on hips. She pronounced, "Wyatt, you look just awful."

I gritted my teeth, wishing I was at liberty to say, *Someone took a baseball bat to me, what the fuck do you expect?*

I drew back from Zane and said quietly, "Why don't you hop in the car, honey, and we'll get going."

He obeyed without a word, but Irene prattled on.

"What happens next? Did they arrest this man? Will you have to go to court? Why would someone attack you outside your vet office, for the love of God?"

"Because Wy stole this man's dog, Mom, like I was telling you," Hannah said.

I rose, and Irene actually retreated a step; I knew I looked like someone emerging from a junkyard brawl, not only beaten black and blue but with sleepless eyes and days' worth of scruff on my jaws. I said, "It's a long story. There's more to it than that."

"You won't be able to work in that condition. Will your insurance cover it?" Irene wouldn't quit. "What will you do if you lose your job?"

I turned to confront Hannah, aggravation rippling over my skin. "Did you tell her that? You know that's not true."

Hannah stood with both hands planted on her hips. "How am I supposed to know?"

She had no idea about so many things, about nearly every aspect of my life.

"Netta is my *family*. Tuck is one of my dearest friends. You actually think my job would be in danger over something like this?" I suddenly realized Zane was watching us with a somber expression. I shut my mouth and returned to the car, making a point of asking him what he'd had for breakfast, what he'd done this morning in my absence—anything to override the heartbreaking concern in his eyes.

. . .

I collapsed into bed after taking two pain pills, and was out cold until the following morning, waking groggy and disoriented. It had been a long time since I'd slept in bed rather than stretched out on the couch. The house was silent and empty; I listened hard but heard no sign of anyone else. My shoulder hurt like hell, hot, sharp pain that radiated all the way to my fingertips, and my head ached with a dull throb. I eased to a sitting position, nude except for an old pair of pajama pants, my body prickling with pins and needles; I'd slept almost without moving. Hannah had left a bottle of water on the nightstand, along with the two prescription bottles. I reached, knocking one to the floor with a clicking rattle, my vision swimming.

It took several minutes to maneuver from bed and down the hall. I felt as frail as an old man, shuffling along with my right hand on the wall. I wasn't hungry, but I heard my phone from the direction of the kitchen. I had three missed calls in the past hour, from Dad, Ruthie, and Joey. A note on the table, scrawled by Hannah, informed me that she and Zane were grocery shopping. I sank to my chair and stared at my phone, furious at myself for thinking I would find a missed call from Millie. A missed call, a text, anything . . .

Any hint that she had tried to contact me since we talked on Friday night.

*She still loves you.*

I exhaled in a rush, turning my phone over and over in my right hand, thoughts racing.

*Millie Jo, I don't deserve your love, not anymore. You deserve to be happy, you deserve so much more than me. You deserve everything life has to offer.*

*We were supposed to be together, I know this, and life robbed us of each other.*

*But I can't imagine my life without Zane. He was meant to be, even if that forced us apart.*

*I wish I could explain so you would understand—*

*It's my punishment to live without you. But it's punishing you just as much, and I don't know how to live with that.*

# CHAPTER THIRTY-NINE

A FEW WEEKS PASSED. I FINISHED MY COURSE OF
pain meds but was still plagued by woozy restlessness. Despite being on medical
leave, I drove out to Bitterroot with Zane almost every day while Hannah was at
work, visiting everyone and hanging around the barn and corral with Shadow and
Scout. I'd found Zane a gentle yearling mare named Sage and purchased her from
a rancher over near Billings. Sage was petite for a horse, rust-red with a white
star on her slender nose, and Zane was over the moon to call her his own. I took
advantage of the lack of far-ranging appointments to work with Zane and Sage,
teaching him the rudiments of tacking. It did my heart good to see the way he
took to horses, and they to him; a natural, just like Dad, just like me.

One afternoon, Zane told Joey that he wanted to be a vet when he grew up.

"You're a good kid, Z-man," Joey said in response.

Zane ran off with Netta to feed the hens a few minutes later, but I stuck
around the vet office with Joey, discussing Jarred Watkins. I'd pressed every
charge I was able against the bastard—aggravated assault in our state commanded a twenty-year prison term at the high end—enough to keep him in county jail
without bail until his sentencing. He had sustained a cracked rib but no additional damage, and I sometimes imagined what would have happened if I'd slammed
the bat into his skull that night instead.

"He could very well have done permanent damage to you. But I'm glad you
didn't brain him, all the same," Joey said, when I confessed this. I pretended I
didn't feel the weight of his continued gaze. He asked, offhandedly, "How are you
holding up?"

I shrugged, immediately regretting the motion; my left arm remained in a
sling, and would for at least another week. "I'm healing."

Joey knew me too well. "What aren't you telling me?"

"Nothing," I insisted.

He tried a new tactic. "Kyle's headed to town for the weekend; he'll be here
by six or so. What do you say we go out for a few rounds?"

"Sure, that sounds good." And it really did; hanging out with my brothers
and Joey and Kyle always lifted my mood.

And so it was that I ended up at The Spoke that evening, along with Joey,

Quinn, Sean, and Kyle; after prying Kyle away from Lee, we found a table near the stage. I had not consumed a drop of alcohol since the week before Jarred Watkins' attack, and didn't at first intend to drink in the fashion of everyone else. But it was a Saturday night, summer was in the air, and Joey, Kyle, and my brothers were in the mood to party. Lee didn't help, leaving the bar to join us for periodic rounds of shots, and I felt my defenses slipping as I justified giving in—Zane was safe at Dad's, along with a bunch of his cousins, and Hannah was out of town at some wine-tasting with a group of women from the bank.

*Please let her decide to stay out all night. I don't want to deal with her until morning.*

Lately Hannah had been pressing for us to move, or maybe build a new house, a bigger one. We could afford it, thanks to my salary, and she was sick of living in her uncle's rental on Front Street.

When she reiterated the issue, I usually said some asshole-sounding thing like, *I don't know right now.*

By the time we left the bar, my vision was amber-tinted and my shoulder no longer ached.

"Hitch a ride with us, little bro," Sean insisted, reaching to snare me in a headlock, knuckling my scalp. "You're loaded, you lightweight."

"Lemme go," I muttered, ducking away. "I'm fine."

"No way." I heard the authority in Quinn's tone. "We're all headed to Dad's anyway."

The stars over the parking lot of The Spoke shone with a hard-edged, glittery brilliance. I realized there was no point fighting them and climbed into the backseat of Quinn's work truck. It wasn't until my head lolled backward against the seat that I realized I was drunker than I thought. I looked listlessly to the right, staring at the landscape flashing past, a horizon so familiar I could have traced its contours with my eyes closed. Quinn slowed to take the final turn to Dad's, and I knuckled my sore eyes with my free hand, figuring I'd brew some coffee at Dad's and sober up. Or, I thought, the idea growing in appeal, maybe Zane and I could just stay the night.

The living room was chaotic, as usual, as we entered. I smiled to see Zane running wildly, dodging furniture, screaming with laughter, pursued by Tansy, Harleigh, and Celia, their hands formed into snapping claws as they chased him. He turned on a dime and raced in my direction, crashing against my knees and encircling them with both arms. He tilted his head to look up at me, smiling, brown eyes shining.

"Wanna stay at Grampa's!" Zane announced. "Play wif the girls!"

I bent and cupped the back of his head. "Hi, buddy. You having fun?"

Zane nodded so hard his hair flopped. He chanted, "Stay, stay, stay!"

"All right," I agreed, taking a seat in the recliner, not wanting Dad to spy my red-rimmed eyes, which clearly gave away my whiskey consumption. Quinn, Joey, and Sean continued on to the kitchen to chat with Dad, while Celia, out of breath, came to perch on the armrest, displacing my right arm.

"Uncle Wy, we're going to Landon next week!" she announced.

"I know, hon," I muttered. "Your mom told me."

"You and Zany should come with. He's never been." She removed my hat and settled it atop her head, where it sank and covered her to the nose. From beneath the wide brim, she went on wheedling. "I know he would love it and I'd help watch him, I promise."

The familiar living room faded away as I pictured Landon and Shore Leave and the lake, the place in full summertime swing, as I had not seen it in four years.

"Why can't you guys come with?" Celia wanted to know. "We haven't all been there since I was little!"

"You're still pretty little, there, kid." My voice sounded like ash.

"Millie's even gonna be there, Mommy said," Celia went on.

Zane leaped on my lap, shrieking, "Hide me, Daddy!"

Harleigh snatched the hat from Celia's head and raced away, calling over her shoulder, "Me and Tansy made pineapple upside down cake, Uncle Wy, come have some!"

Zane tugged at my hand and I could not refuse, allowing him to lead the way to the kitchen.

...

"Is he here?" I heard my wife demand sometime later that night.

I slung a forearm over my eyes, chilled and shaken from the nightmare Hannah had unknowingly interrupted. The only illumination in the room came from the small light fixture above the stove in the adjacent kitchen. I lay flat on my back on the long, battered leather sofa at Dad's house, an afghan drawn to my waist. I knew I should get up and deal with this situation, but couldn't muster the will.

I heard Dad's calm voice near the front door. "He fell asleep on the couch. How about I have him call you tomorrow?"

Hannah ignored his words, because the next thing I knew she was hovering over me in the gloom, hissing words like a kettle releasing steam.

"You were too drunk to drive, weren't you? I expected you and Zane to be home when I got there! Do you know how embarrassing it was to have my friends with me and find you gone? Not like I even need to explain; they all know you're an alcoholic anyway."

I muttered, "Don't fucking *call me that*."

From somewhere beyond my sight, Dad said, "It's late. Maybe now isn't a good time."

Hannah rounded on him. "Stay out of this, Clark. This is between *Wy and me*."

I sat up in a rush. "Don't you *dare* talk to my father that way."

Dad cautioned, "Wy . . ."

Hannah hollered, "How about the way your family talks to *me?* I'm your wife and you let them say whatever they want about me!"

"You know that is not true." My teeth were on edge; we had wasted so many hours fighting over this same issue, never resolving it.

Never resolving anything.

"They try to control Zane's life!"

I exploded, "My family loves Zane! He loves them! They have never tried to control him. Are you so goddamn blind that you can't fucking see that?!"

"Don't swear at me!" she screamed.

I choked back all the additional venomous words burning holes in my throat, well aware that my father stood observing. I sensed his shock even without seeing his face. Maybe it really had never occurred to him that my wife and I fought this way; to be fair, I'd always done my best to hide it. I was grateful that Zane was over at Marshall and Ruthie's house just now, with his cousins.

Hannah cried, "Where's Zane? I'm bringing him home!"

"He's asleep at Marshall's, it's the middle of the—"

But she was already out the door. I stood to follow, but Dad caught my right arm in an unyielding grip.

"Son, let her go. She's too angry to be reasonable right now."

"She'll scare Zane if she's acting like this." I tugged free and hurried outside.

Hannah stood pounding on my brother's front door. The porch light clicked to existence and Marsh answered just as I jogged up the steps behind my wife. Marshall registered surprise, forehead wrinkling with concern; his gaze moved between the two of us, at last settling on me for an explanation.

"Where's Zane?" Hannah sounded as though he was being held here against his will.

"I got this," I assured my brother, hustling past him and up the stairs to their second floor.

Ruthie stood at the top of the steps, bundled in her robe.

"What's wrong?" she asked in an undertone.

"Nothing." There was no time to explain the obvious lie, but I knew Ruthie would understand.

I slipped into the boys' room, where Zane was curled on the top bunk along with Luke, the two of them snoring. Colin, who had the lower bunk all to himself, propped on an elbow, knuckling his eyes in the glare of the hall light.

"Uncle Wy?" he whispered, confused.

"Go back to sleep," I whispered. "I'm just getting Zane."

I carried my sleeping son down the stairs, feeling the weight of Ruthie's concerned gaze. Hannah took Zane from me the second I stepped onto the porch, shifting him over her shoulder, and to my relief she murmured softly in his ear and he remained mostly asleep. He popped a thumb in his mouth as she headed for her car without another word; her angry wrath having fizzled out, she now ignored all of us. I saw my dad observing from behind his screen door and resolved to talk to him tomorrow. My poor father; I'd caused him so much worry in the past years.

My brother muttered, "What in the hell?"

I sank to the top step, watching Hannah's taillights flicker as she braked before turning from the driveway. And then I hung my head and gripped it hard with one hand.

Marsh knelt beside me and rested a hand on my spine. "What is going on?"

I honestly didn't know how to answer. I'd fallen asleep on the couch thinking of Millie, and she had appeared in a dream, both of us running through golden beams of fractured sunlight, barefoot in a forest that resembled Itasca State Park, all towering white pines and old-growth birch. Millie was laughing, a few paces ahead and calling to me, and I tried desperately to catch up with her, running as fast as I could, unable to draw a full breath. No matter how hard I tried, I couldn't gain ground. My feet were bleeding. Branches scraped my face and tore at my shirt. Somehow, I could see what Millie could not—she was running headlong toward a sharp cliff, a sudden drop, and I couldn't warn her—

I woke in a cold sweat, only to have Hannah appear a moment later. I was nauseous and disoriented from both experiences.

Ruthie knelt on my other side, cupping the nape of my neck as I bowed forward. My shoulders heaved as I restrained the need to sob, embarrassed.

"What's happened?" she asked softly.

"Hannah happened, that's what," Marshall said before I could answer. "I'm sorry, Wy, I try to be nice to that woman, but she makes it impossible."

"It doesn't matter," I mumbled.

"It matters, Wy, don't say that," Ruthie scolded. I sensed more than saw her and my brother exchange a look over my bent head. At last she admitted, "Your marriage was a mistake. We all know it and if I could go back and prevent it from happening, I would, I swear to you."

I appreciated the acknowledgment, at last, but I'd had a long time to think this over.

Staring into the distance, I said quietly, "It was meant to happen. If I hadn't married Hannah, if I'd tried to make it work with Millie back then, a part of me would always have wondered if I'd done wrong by my child. You think I don't know my marriage is shit, that it was shit before it started? But there was no other choice. What would Zane do if I wasn't there every day?"

Ruthie persisted, "He would be just fine. It's time to seriously consider divorce."

I leaned back, sitting upright and displacing their kind touches. Frustration won the upper hand. "You think I haven't thought of that a thousand fucking times?"

"Well, then . . ." Marshall let the sentence trail to silence, hoping I'd finish it.

"You know she'd get custody of Zane." The ashes had returned to my voice. I thought of Celia's words from earlier this evening, about Millie being home in Landon this week, and longing filled me until I thought my skin would peel away with its force. "I wouldn't see my son every day; he would live in a separate house. I've done what I *have to do* to prevent that, don't you understand?"

Marshall picked up their shared gauntlet, with his usual blunt fashion. "But think about the house he's living in right *now*, little bro. You think that's a great place for a kid, when his parents fight like that?"

And they didn't even know the worst of it.

"It's not that easy. I can't just abandon Zane. He's so little; he needs me."

"Don't look at it like that," Marshall insisted. "It's not like you'd move to another state and disappear. And Hannah's family is here, she's not going anywhere. The only thing that would change is that you could *move on* from her."

More gently, Ruthie said, "What you've done these past years, staying married to her for Zane's sake, is honorable. You've tried to make an impossible situation work for a long time now and it's killing you."

When I didn't respond, she added, "I saw your eyes when I told you Millie was on the phone in the hospital that night. Your happiness is worth something. Don't forget that."

If only it was that simple. Hopelessness choked me all over again and I hid my face, muttering, "*Fuck . . .*"

Ruthie issued a small sound of concern and hugged me, taking care not to touch my shoulder, rocking side to side as if I were her son; and in some ways, I really was. I sagged against the warm, familiar solace of her, wishing I could relent to weeping, ashamed to lose control in that way, as I had too many times in the past. Marshall rubbed a path along my spine, slow and comforting.

He said, "We're here for you, Wy, you know that."

At last Ruthie whispered, "It's not too late."

I muttered, "What do you mean?"

"Millie and Russ haven't been together for a long time, that's what I mean. Camille told me they broke up last year."

I stared at her, trying to process this news with what I knew; if they weren't together, then why had Russ been there with Millie in the middle of the night less than a month ago?

Something clicked in my memory—

*I did something really stupid tonight*, Millie had said.

"It's not too late," Ruthie repeated. "I truly believe that."

I had no words, my insides churning.

"C'mon inside," Marshall invited. "You're not going to solve anything tonight."

But he was wrong.

# CHAPTER FORTY

I ASSURED THEM I WAS FINE TO DRIVE HOME, stone-cold sober at this point. There was no point putting off the inevitable return to the house on Front Street. I would rather try to steal a few hours' worth of sleep in my own living room than toss and turn on Marshall's couch until dawn. A low-lying cloud belly obscured the stars as I drove through the quiet streets of my hometown. The moon had long since set behind the mountains, swift and silent, as though dragged to drown beyond the horizon line. I parked on the curb rather than risk waking Hannah or Zane with the garage door and strode across the lawn, unlocking the front door only to find myself hesitating to enter.

As illogical as it sounded, I suddenly imagined Hannah poised on the other side of the door, holding a bat above her head.

My next breath became a hard ball in my lungs. Locked momentarily in place, I forced a slow inhalation through my nose, recognizing the signs of a panic attack. I'd suffered them periodically during my various residencies, in the long, difficult year following Zane's birth.

*You're all right. No one is going to attack you.*

I slipped inside the dark house with caution all the same, leaning backward against the door after closing it.

"Sneaking in?"

I lurched as though jabbed with a cattle prod. I could just barely discern Hannah's outline in the shadowy space. She stood in the archway between the living room and kitchen, a thin silhouette with a disembodied voice.

"Why are you always on the goddamn attack?" I asked hoarsely.

She was primed to lock horns, as always. "That's what they all think, isn't it? They have no idea how you treat *me*. I bet your brother and Ruthie had plenty to say once I left." She adopted a higher pitch, cruelly and ineptly mimicking Ruthie's voice. "'Poor Wy, Hannah is so *mean* to him. What's wrong, honey, do you need to spend the night at our house? I'll tell Marshall to leave.'"

I had no words to confront her delusions.

Hannah carried on, "You and your stupid degree, you think you're so much smarter than me. You always have."

Truly stunned, I whispered, "What are you *talking* about?"

"I wanted to go to college too, you know!"

Bombarded by increasing unease and the smothering darkness, I clicked on the nearby table lamp, squinting at the sudden brightness. Hannah stood ten feet away, still wearing her clothes from earlier.

I gained a small handhold on my composure and challenged, "If that was in any way true, you would have graduated years ago. You could have gone to school anytime in these past years; I would have supported that."

Hannah was red-faced. "I got *pregnant!* How could I go to college? I've been a mother; I've dedicated my life to *my child.*"

"I did it." I kept my voice low, glancing down the hallway, toward Zane's room.

Hannah pounced almost joyfully on this statement. "Oh, yeah, throw that in my face too. I lived here without you for months at a time, doing everything alone."

"You knew it would be that way, don't pretend like you didn't. I was finishing school. And I was home every weekend."

"What about during your residencies?!"

"Would you keep your voice down?"

She hissed, "How typical. Avoid everything like you always do, avoid all your responsibility!"

She knew just how to come at me, every time. I should have kept my mouth shut, but I stupidly confronted this statement. "I have never avoided a single responsibility! I provide for you and my son and I have since the *day we were married!*"

"Do you want me to *thank* you for that?" Her caustic tone scorched the air between us, her hands in tight fists, punctuating her furious words. "You think I *owe* you something? I owe you *nothing!* I've done my best to be a good wife to you and you've been screwing around for *years.* I'm not as stupid as you think; I've known all along! Who is she? I deserve to know the truth!"

Something inside me cracked with a violent sound, like an ax blade splitting dry wood.

"You want to discuss the truth?" I hardly recognized my own voice, tight with restrained hostility. "Fine, let's discuss it. You tried to get pregnant that night, didn't you?"

Hannah's lips compressed to a tight black line; a cartoon mouth, grim and defensive.

"Didn't you?" I repeated.

I sensed her composure was at breaking point as we stared each other down.

"Yes!" she cried at last. "Yes, I did! You're right, Wy, *you fucking asshole*, does that finally make you happy?"

I had always known, but somehow hearing it confessed aloud spread the truth like a toxin through the air.

"You ruined my life," I rasped—a statement I regretted the second it cleared my mouth.

She was already sobbing. "*I loved you.* I wanted to be your wife and you wouldn't give us a chance!"

"So you forced it to happen? What the hell is the matter with you?!"

"You don't think I've paid for that mistake a hundred times over?" Tears streamed over her face faster than a leaking faucet, but I was beyond being moved by displays of drama.

"*You've* paid for it?!"

"I'll never have another child!"

Her words gave me pause, draining some of my anger. I said quietly, "I am truly sorry about that, but you can't blame me for it. That's not fair."

"You could have stopped it!" Her eyes were wide, shiny with tears and frightening in their intensity; she truly believed her words.

"I couldn't, Hannah. It was a medical necessity beyond anyone's control."

"I *hate* you," she whispered.

"I want a divorce."

In the resultant silence the words became a mushroom cloud, swelling to fill the entire house. Hannah appeared outright shocked, mouth falling open, brows lifting; as though it had never actually occurred to her that I would admit such a thing.

I could hardly believe I'd done it either, and the truth lent me courage. Making fists to control the trembling in my hands, I added, "And I want shared custody of Zane."

She seethed, "Who is she?!"

"I want a divorce because you and I are miserable. You know it as well as I do."

She lunged forward and clutched my right arm, gripping hard. "You won't leave. If you do, I'll keep Zane away from you, I swear to God I will. No judge is going to award custody to an alcoholic."

My vision swam; I despised her more in that moment than I ever had. "That's an empty threat and *you know it.*"

"You think so?" She turned and stalked to the kitchen.

I followed, entering just in time to spy her digging through the cupboard alongside the dishwasher. She found what she was seeking, triumphantly brandishing the slender green bottle.

"You're an alcoholic who hides booze all over our house. You're a cheater and a liar. You don't deserve custody of a child."

Wrath rose like bile; I could not stop the hot flood from erupting. "You *evil bitch*. You know goddamn well I am no alcoholic. You will take my son away from me over *my dead body*, do you hear me?"

"Don't you dare call me names, not when you're the one sneaking around behind my back! You've never loved me!"

I bit back all possible responses and turned away, intending to wake Zane and take him to Dad's, but of course it wasn't that easy. Before I guessed her intent, Hannah chucked the whiskey bottle like someone hurling a hatchet. She missed, but only by a few inches—I watched it sail past the left side of my head and smash against the kitchen counter.

"You *rotten son of a bitch!*" she wailed.

*Fuck, fuck, fuck.*

But it was already too late; from down the hall, likely standing in his bedroom door, Zane's small, scared voice questioned, "Daddy?"

I changed course, immediately heading for him, but Hannah screamed, "Your dad threw a bottle at me, Zane! He tried to hit me!"

My heart plummeted like a rock chucked into a cold lake.

Zane stared up at me, my boy in his flannel footie pajamas, his brows crooked like question marks as he wondered what to believe; which parent to trust.

"I did no such thing." I dropped to my knees and engulfed him in the curve of my right arm. I felt as broken as the stupid bottle, a failure in too many ways to count. I'd messed up so many aspects of my goddamn life, burned so many bridges, there was no way to ever return to what had been. I sheltered Zane against my chest.

"It's okay, buddy," I whispered against his downy hair. "It's all right."

Hannah was on my heels, burning up with rage. She ordered, "Get dressed, Zane, we're going to Grandma's house. We're not safe here!"

"You know that is *not true*." My heart was churning with true fear, my pulse gurgling like water vanishing down an industrial-sized drain, but I kept my voice level for Zane's sake, not about to relinquish my hold on him.

Hannah's eyes appeared feral as she grabbed Zane's arm.

"*Let go*," I warned; my pupils felt like daggers as I held her gaze.

She yanked, attempting to free him from my grasp, and Zane began crying. I tightened my hold, drawn into an unwilling tug-of-war with my child.

"We're leaving," she insisted, teeth bared as we faced off over our son's head.

"You can leave, go right ahead, but Zane is staying here."

Hannah gripped my shoulder, digging her nails, and put her mouth to my ear, her voice like a train jumping the tracks. "I will call the cops if you try to stop us. I'll tell them you're drunk and that you threw a bottle at me. I'll tell them you tried to hurt us and that *I don't feel safe.*"

I wanted in that moment to deck her in the mouth, to put every ounce of my strength behind the punch; I would never lay a hand on her, but a sick, bile-green urge came close to overpowering my better judgment. Zane clung to me, crying hard, and I cupped his small shoulders, easing away so I could see his face. I clamped down on a thick, scalding panic and said, "Buddy, you and Mommy are going to Grandma's for a little while, okay? Can you go get dressed?"

He shook his head, wide-eyed, nose running. "No, Daddy, I don't want to go."

Hannah jabbed an outstretched finger in the direction of his closet and hollered, "Go get dressed!"

I stood and lifted Zane, carrying him into his bedroom while Hannah scurried down the hall. I heard her flinging open the closet and slamming drawers. Zane would not release his hold on my neck and I had never felt more terrified, not even the morning I knew I was losing Millie Jo. I thought I'd been prepared for facing the reality of separating from Hannah, but I'd been sorely mistaken.

*It will be all right.* I tried desperately to reassure myself. *Hannah is just going to her mother's, she's not taking Zane anywhere you can't follow. It's all right.*

But I felt like dying at the thought of my son in a different house, listening to her lies. What if he believed her? She was his mother. He trusted her.

Zane buried his face in my neck. "Why is Mommy so mad? Why were you yelling?"

I steadied my voice so I could answer. "We were just upset, honey, that sometimes happens. You go with Mommy now, okay? I'll see you in the morning, I promise."

He gulped; my shirt was wet with his tears.

I felt gutted but I could not let him see it. I kissed the top of his head. "Should we pack up some stuff? Like for a sleepover?"

Zane nodded, slowly warming to the idea, and I set him down.

"How about doggie, does he want to come?" I asked, grabbing Zane's backpack from the hook on his door. I unzipped the small blue pack. "You want to put him in?"

A hint of a smile broke through his tears and he nodded again. We packed him clothes for tomorrow, two pairs of underwear and socks, while Zane chose and added several toys; by that point, Hannah had appeared in the doorway, carrying her purse. An armload of clothes hung like skinned animals over her forearm.

"Let's go," she ordered, jingling her keys on their metal ring. "Get your shoes, Zane."

He didn't move, staring up at me.

I cupped his shoulder and gently squeezed. "It's all right, buddy, go put on your shoes."

Zane asked, "Daddy, can't you come too?"

My chest ached. "Not right now. I'll see you tomorrow morning like I said, I promise. Now, go get your shoes like Mommy asked, all right?"

He collected his backpack without another word. Hannah stepped to the side to allow him through the door, and we listened as his footsteps continued on to the kitchen and out of direct sight. In the wake of our son's absence, I said, "You can't keep him from me, no matter what you say, no matter what lies you tell."

Hatred oozed between us; no more pretense of trying.

"Fuck you, Wy."

I leaned deliberately into her space. "I will fight for Zane to the *fucking end of the earth*. You will not keep him from me. No one in this town will believe your bullshit. I have never laid a hand on you and you know it."

"Try me," she challenged, upper lip curling. "Just try."

I shifted, intending to follow Zane to the kitchen, but Hannah cringed, ducking away as though I'd raised my fists. Shocked anew, I froze.

She slowly straightened, flicking hair from her eyes with a small movement of her head.

"See how easy it is?" Satisfaction radiated from her. "*Everyone* will believe me."

"You're right about one thing." I looked hard into her eyes. "I've never loved you. Not for one single day of my life."

Fresh tears rolled over her cheeks, but I was hell-and-gone past any residual compassion. I wanted Hannah out of my life, for good—but for the sake of my son. Her partial control over his life was a spear staking my heart.

"Fuck you," she repeated, swiping at her nose.

"Please get out of my way so I can tell my son good-bye."

She stood her ground.

"*Get out of my way*," I ordered again.

She hit me across the face with the hand holding the keys and then bolted, racing down the hallway as though I'd chased after her. I sank to a crouch, unwilling to confront her regarding anything else in this moment, realizing somewhere in the back of my churning mind that it would only make things worse. I listened as she hustled Zane outside; I heard the garage door open and her car growl to life. And only then did I stand and head for the bathroom.

# CHAPTER FORTY-ONE

IT WAS EDGING TOWARD TWO IN THE MORNING when I heard the muted beep of a text message. I rolled to my right side, toward the nightstand on my side of the bed, and fumbled for my phone before it woke Rae. She had drifted off about an hour ago, leaving me at the mercy of my spinning thoughts. As I'd been unable to shut my eyes for longer than a blink, the text had interrupted nothing but my fixed stare, directed at the dim ceiling beams above Rae's bed. My underwear bore no telltale dampness of blood stains to indicate that my period had started, no relief from the death grip in which I'd been enclosed since earlier this evening. I'd grown numb with certainty, picturing the tiny collection of cells multiplying within my womb and forging a connection between her father and me, a connection I would be incapable of severing.

*My period isn't always on time; this could mean nothing . . .*

But Rae had seen my daughter, and her notions were not to be doubted.

*My daughter.*

The two words swam through my mind like small, shining fish. Just words, not yet reality.

All too soon that would change, I knew.

My daughter, a little girl who would belong equally to her father and me, a daughter who would bind me inexorably to Russ Morgan for the foreseeable future and well beyond.

*Oh God oh God, please no . . .*

*This can't be . . .*

*This is how you felt, Wy, wasn't it?*

*This is how you felt that day, riding home to Jalesville with your dad, knowing you had no more control over your own life.*

I tapped my phone's screen to life at the sound of the message, figuring maybe Mom had texted. I couldn't imagine who else could be attempting to reach me this late, and prayed it wasn't Russ; we hadn't spoken since that night in my dorm. He had no idea what I suspected, and I intended to keep it that way for now. I rolled to one elbow and saw that the message was from Aunt Ruthie.

She had written, *Are you up? Do you have a minute to talk?*

My aunt's words didn't suggest an emergency, but my heart accelerated all the same. I wondered wildly if she'd somehow guessed what I suspected. While I'd never known her to possess the second sight, Ruthie was incredibly intuitive. I rose from bed and then crept downstairs and outside, easing the front door shut. I ran for the screen tent set up at the outer edge of Aunt Jilly and Uncle Justin's big yard, a space that served as a playhouse for the little kids, unzipping the entrance flap and hurrying within. I sat on the picnic table, propping my bare feet on the bench, and then called Aunt Ruthie's number.

She answered almost immediately. "Millie? I didn't wake you, did I, honey?"

"No," I assured her. "I was up. Is everything all right?"

"Well, yes and no," she said enigmatically, while I waited on the sharp points of fishhooks, certain that she was about to tell me she knew I was pregnant.

"What do you mean?" I whispered.

She sighed. "I'm sitting out here on our front porch and I don't exactly know how to say what I want to say."

I sat in mute anxiety, sweat forming along my hairline, staring at the black, impenetrable edge of the pine forest that bordered the yard; by night, it looked like something straight out of an eerie fairy tale.

Aunt Ruthie sighed again, and I pictured her pressing her fingertips against her forehead, just like my mom did when she was overwhelmed or frustrated. At last she said, "I'm sorry. Maybe this is out of line. I know this isn't exactly my business, I'm just so damn worried . . ."

"About what?" My lungs compressed.

"About Wy," she breathed. "Sweet Wy. I *hate* that Hannah Jasper."

"What?" I whispered, slightly shocked by her words. My eyes darted back and forth, as if searching the immediate vicinity for a sign of him. As if he would materialize from the dark wall of trees just as he had the night we made love for the first time.

*Oh God, if only, if only . . .*

Aunt Ruthie continued, "He left our house just a little bit ago. He and Hannah are fighting. She is so awful to him. He's miserable. If I could go back in time and stop their marriage, I would. He wants a divorce, but he's terrified Hannah will get custody of Zane."

"Why are you telling me this?" Lightheaded and trembling in the chill air, I squeezed my free hand into a tight fist and then repeated the gesture again and again, as if the movement would snap me back to a state of reality.

"Because if there's a chance that you still . . . " Aunt Ruthie's voice trailed away; she was obviously troubled.

"Still what?" I whispered faintly, feeling the world rotate on a slow, tipsy axis. I gripped the hard edge of the picnic table beneath me, seeking grounding.

"If you still care for Wy—"

"Then what?" I cried, interrupting her, strung with unbearable tension and disbelief; the shock of this conversation on top of everything else that had taken place this evening was like scalding water splashed across my skin. "Then I should call him and tell him to divorce his wife and come find me? He *chose* Hannah, he chose to be with her. He left me behind years ago." Anguish choked me for the hundred-thousandth time. "He has a son, he's *married!* I belong nowhere in that picture!"

Ruthie spoke with quiet certainty. "He's still in love with you. You think I don't know it? You think I can't see it on his face every time he talks about you? He's done the honorable thing for the past four years, trying to be a good husband and father, but he's dying without you, Millie, a little more every day."

"*Stop,*" I pleaded, pressing hard against my eye sockets, a roaring in my ears.

"The last thing I want to do is hurt you," Aunt Ruthie said intently. "I am trying to make things right. If you still love Wy, you should tell him. I don't believe it's too late."

I lifted my aching eyes upward, seeking answers, seeking absolution from this pain.

"Of course I still love him. *I've never stopped loving him . . .*" My words broke off as I began weeping with no warning, unable to control the aggressive rush of tears. My aunt may have believed it was not too late, but I knew otherwise. The eleventh hour had come and gone, brushing its fingers across my cheek in passing.

"Millie?!"

I curled forward, unable to bear the weight of the secret. I gasped, "Rae had a notion . . . earlier tonight . . ."

"What did she see?" Aunt Ruthie sounded dead serious.

"*My daughter,*" I sobbed.

. . .

My face was bleeding; the goddamn keys had left a welt beneath my left eye, which hurt, but was nowhere near the worst hit I'd ever sustained. I wet a washcloth and pressed it to the wound, trying to ignore my jumping innards so I could think straight. I reminded myself that Hannah was Zane's mother and that she loved him—she would never put him in harm's way, not even to punish me. Try as she might, she would never succeed in keeping him from me. I would fight her to the ends of the earth; there was no exaggeration in the statement. But I prayed it would not come to that.

My guts were twisted in knots, sick at what had occurred in the last thirty minutes. I searched the house for my phone, wanting to call Joey or Marshall, but it was nowhere in sight. My hands and kneecaps were shaking as though equipped with vibrating motors. I paused in the living room to bend forward and inhale, and this posture brought me eye to eye with the broken glass scattered across the kitchen floor; bits had reached the living room carpet. I collected the broom and dustpan; the process was awkward and tedious without the ability to use both arms, but it centered my focus, a welcome distraction. I dragged out the vacuum and was in the middle of using it when someone pounded on the outer door; the vigorous, repetitive sound suggested an angry someone. I switched off the vacuum and peered through the curtains, gritting my teeth at the sight of Hannah's father.

*Goddamn it*, I thought. *Goddamn her to hell.*

"Wyatt, I know you're in there!" Bill yelled.

There was no use pretending otherwise. My truck was front and center at the curb, after all. I opened the door and Bill almost fell inside. We stood assessing each other, Bill out of breath, glaring openly at me. I made no effort to invite him in.

"What the hell is going on?" he demanded.

"Hannah took Zane to your house because I told her I want a divorce." I stared square into Bill's eyes as I spoke. I knew him for a levelheaded man. As long as I didn't appear confrontational, I figured I could handle this situation.

"What happened here? Hannah's all stirred up, said she's scared, that you tried to hit her! I won't stand for this, I'll have you know—"

"Bill, listen to me. I did *no such thing.*" I was stunned; when all was said and done, I couldn't believe Hannah had actually lied to that level.

"What happened to your face?" he demanded next, gesturing at my eye.

"Your daughter hit *me* with her keys. She was angry because I didn't want her leaving with Zane." I paused, aware I was speaking heatedly and ran the risk of sounding unhinged—or worse, like a man who might have been pushed beyond control. More slowly, I said, "Hannah and I are over, Bill, you might as well know. I'm done acting like everything's all right when it's not. I'm sorry you had to find out like this, but there you go."

Bill appeared both skeptical and belligerent, and so I prattled on.

"I would never hit her, I would never hit *any* woman. You've known me most of my life, for Christ's sake. Do you really think I'd do such a heinous thing?"

"What about that Watkins fellow?!"

I struggled hard to maintain calm. "He attacked *me*. My arm is still in a goddamned sling!"

"My daughter wouldn't lie to me." Bill was stuck in a single-minded rut.

"I can't control what you believe, but I'm telling you the truth. All I want is to share custody of my boy. Hannah can't keep him from me with her lies." Tears welled on my lower eyelids, completely without warning, but I was beyond caring. "I won't let her. I will take her to court and fight for all I'm worth. Zane is all I have in this world; he's the only reason I can manage to face each day!"

Silence hung heavy in the air after I shut my mouth. Bill was visibly uncomfortable.

"Shit, Wy," he muttered in a completely different tone.

"Is he at your house?" I demanded, using my thumb to staunch the tears. "Did she bring him there?"

"He's there," Bill finally admitted, shuffling his booted feet, studying the pitted concrete beneath them. He heaved a sigh before adding, "I think it's best if Hannah and Zane stay with us for a while."

"I want to see him tomorrow morning. You can't keep my son from me."

Bill was already halfway down the sidewalk, headed for his idling truck. He said over his shoulder, "I'll talk to Hannah."

I finished cleaning up the broken glass. My shoulder hurt like hell—but that was the least of my worries just now. The clock had ticked past three in the morning and I couldn't bear to remain in this house, this miserable rental house in which I'd lived for years. Intending to drive over to Dad's, I swept clothes and boots from the closet, jamming them into garbage bags, then filled my battered old travel pack with everything of mine from the bathroom. Anything else I would gather in the next week. I loaded up my truck in the predawn darkness, beneath a light rain, and as I slammed shut the tailgate it suddenly hit me and I paused, overcome by a rush of dizzying, half-hysterical elation. I wasn't deluded enough to think it would be simple; I recognized the custody battle that lay ahead would be colossal—but I could be thankful for one monumental truth.

I'd done it.

I was free of Hannah Jasper.

# CHAPTER FORTY-TWO

THERE IS IN EVERYONE'S LIFE A MOMENT OF reckoning, and that day was mine.

Rae had seen my daughter in her mind's eye that summer afternoon sitting beside Flickertail—there was no mistake.

Years later, I would pause for a moment to watch my husband and our little girl as they walked together across the stable, hand in hand, and it would hit me all over again how much I had to be thankful for.

I woke just after dawn that Sunday morning, alone in my own bed, and curled up, drawing my knees tightly to my chest. I didn't remember falling asleep; after talking to Aunt Ruthie I'd walked home, the lake a smooth sheet reflecting the stars in rippling flickers, and crept up the stairs to my old room. Lorie hadn't stirred as I slipped from my clothes and beneath the covers, where I lay as motionless as a wooden carving. Endless pictures swirled in frenzied sequences across my imagination—I saw my daughter as an infant, a toddler, a teenager with dark curls like mine and Mom's; I saw Russ putting a ring on my left hand; Russ holding a child wrapped in a pink blanket.

I saw little Zane Rawley smiling innocently across the space of a waiting room. I saw Wy climb from a pickup, only steps away and yet on the other side of an impassable distance. At some point the images melted to dreams and I dozed—waking to a sharp stab of pain, low on my left side.

*Implantation,* I thought wildly, heart clubbing.

Rae and I had read through every symptom of early pregnancy last night, using her phone, and one of the first signs was the brief, sharp pain of the egg implanting in the uterine lining.

I felt almost beyond emotion in the misty, graying light of dawn. There were a dozen things I needed to do, a dozen things I would force myself to do later this very day, but in this moment I wanted only to die. It was cowardly to the extreme, a nasty thought spawned by desperation and terror, but it seemed a pleasant alternative to confirming what I already knew with a pregnancy test, let alone calling Russ and then divulging the resultant news to our families. I suddenly remembered that Aunt Ruthie and Auntie Tish, along with their families, would be arriving tomorrow, their first summer visit in years. I pictured my mother's face upon hearing my secret. Aunt Ruthie had promised not to tell her before I was able. And then, for the hundredth time, I pictured Wy—any chance of being with him at some future point in time now reduced to ash, once and for all.

*I'm so sorry*, I thought, over and over again, no longer sure to whom or what I was begging forgiveness; maybe it no longer mattered.

*I am so, so sorry.*

...

If my father seemed surprised to find me back on the couch in his living room by morning's first light, he gave no sign. I woke to find him sitting on the adjacent leather chair, coffee mug in hand, studying me with his mustache in a somber droop. I rolled to my good arm, propping on an elbow, and announced quietly, "I'm divorcing Hannah."

"Good," Dad replied. "It's about time."

I told him everything that had taken place just a few hours ago, from Hannah's accusations and the way she'd smacked my face to Bill's appearance at the house on Front Street. By the time I finished explaining, I was seated on my old barstool at the kitchen island while Dad made pancakes and bacon and brewed a second batch of coffee. Potted bitterroot, my mother's favorite flower, adorned the table, same as always, and warm yellow light spilled across the floorboards as the sun inched upward in a clear sky.

Did I dare imagine it was the color of resurrected hope?

Dad had said no less than three times, "I'd like to have a little conversation with Bill Jasper today." He added, "Anyone who knows you, son, knows that Hannah's accusations are false. We are all on your side, unequivocally."

I was still in partial shock at this drastic change to my life. And I wanted badly to collect my son and bring him home to Dad's.

I pushed my plate to the side. "I need to see Zane. I'm scared of what Hannah might be telling him."

"I'll drive you over there," Dad said immediately. "I don't want you facing this alone."

My throat tightened. "Thank you, Dad. I don't know what I would have done without all of you these past years. You have no idea."

Dad rested a hand on my shoulder. "I love you, son. You deserve to find happiness."

The screen door clacked open out in the living room.

"Good morning!" Dad called, figuring it was one of the grandkids. "You must have smelled Sunday breakfast!"

I set down my fork as Ruthie entered the kitchen a second later, appearing serious and unduly pale; no trace of her usual smile.

"Can I have a minute, Wy?" she requested.

I was already on my feet.

"You must have heard," Dad said, drawing the griddle from the burner.

"Heard?" Ruthie repeated.

"I left Hannah last night," I told her, wondering at her continued apparent anxiety. I figured she and Marsh would be nothing but happy for me at the news. I elaborated, "For good, I mean. We're getting divorced."

Ruthie's solemn eyes searched mine, almost as though she hadn't heard my words; she wanted very badly for me to understand something.

"What is it, what's wrong?" I asked, with mounting concern.

"I talked to Millie last night," she finally whispered. "I called to tell her that it's not too late for you two."

Dad sank to a seat at the table, listening wordlessly, while I processed this information with a galloping heart, thinking of the strange dream from last night— Millie running toward a sharp drop—

Ruthie spoke before I could respond. "Millie's still in love with you, Wy. And I told her that we can't bear to see you suffering without her like this."

I said hoarsely, "That wasn't your right. *I* need to be the one telling her those things, not you. It needs to be *me*."

"I know, Wy, I really do. I thought I was doing the right thing." Ruthie's expression was full of unmistakable anguish.

A cinch strap banded my chest, squeezing ever tighter. "What aren't you telling me?"

She closed her eyes. "Millie's pregnant."

. . .

By late afternoon, I was strung out with tension to the point that my consciousness seemed to hover in the air somewhere above my parents' house. I swore I could see for a hundred miles in every direction, transparent sunlight penetrating the hollow spaces of my floating form; my pregnant body pierced by regret and guilt, fear and sinking sun. I drifted without aim over the tops of pines and oaks and observed Flickertail from high above, studying its clamshell shape and glittering agate-blue water, the same cool liquid caress I'd felt since I was a little girl. I interlaced my fingers above my belly and pressed inward, seeking answers. Seeking return pressure; proof of life.

*You can get an abortion.*

*I know, I've thought of that since last night.*

*But Rae saw her, she saw my little girl's eyes.*

*It's not her fault. She didn't ask to be conceived.*
*A child deserves both her parents . . .*

Early this morning I'd told Mom I felt sick and needed to rest; I wasn't ly-ing. I was sick, down to my bones, and huddled on my right side almost without moving, staring at the window as the hours of Sunday waned. I set aside my phone; I did not contact Russ. I ignored Rae's text messages. I refused—however politely—Mom's offers of water and ginger ale and, eventually, lunch. The house was currently empty, everyone having left for an evening pontoon cruise. I imag-ined seeing Aunt Ruthie at some point tomorrow and found comfort in realizing I could wait until then to tell everyone; Aunt Ruthie would help me find a way. Had she told Wy? Even though I'd asked her not to, I couldn't help but wonder, any pathetic hopes I'd harbored now obliterated.

For the second time in our lives, an unborn child had come between us, pry-ing us in separate directions.

The sun finally disappeared beyond the trees outside my window, diffusing the light in the bedroom to the color of whiskey. My limbs felt bloodless and numb; my nerves prickled as I rolled to an elbow. Gray spots danced across my vi-sion and a roaring in my ears momentarily overrode the sound of my phone buzz-ing with an incoming call. I let it go to voicemail, mildly surprised when it rang again, insistent as a hornet. I spied Rae's name on the screen, but answered just a second too late. I knew she was concerned—I hadn't made contact today—and so I dressed in cut-off jean shorts and a faded lavender tank top, one I'd liked back in high school in what seemed like another life, intending to head over to Shore Leave, where Rae was likely just finishing the evening shift.

A quick glance in the bathroom mirror revealed my ice-pale face and de-spairing eyes, smudged by sleepless shadows, but I didn't care how I looked. Rae certainly wouldn't care.

I elected to walk, stowing my phone in my back pocket. The evening was calm, the sky golden and benign, mellow sunbeams dusting my hair and shoul-ders as I made my way along the familiar route. No cars or trucks in sight; all traf-fic was on the lake at this hour. Barefoot, carrying my sandals by their toe straps, my feet were soon covered in soft gray dust. It was humid and the caress of the gentle lake breeze was welcome on my face. Lost in distress and speculation as I'd been all day, I tried now to avoid all thoughts, breathing in and out, in and out. When I heard a vehicle crunching over the gravel around the bend just ahead, I considered ducking into the cover of the trees. The last thing I wanted to do was talk to anyone other than Rae.

For a second I thought I was seeing things—it was approaching dusk after all, twilight, when the edges of things blurred and distorted and melted to the color of ashes—

The dusty blue truck stopped dead in the middle of the road and the driver's side door opened. I saw his name first, stenciled on the door in yellow letters—

And then I saw only him.

...

I burned rubber on the interstate east, the hours slipping by as quickly as the miles, resolve squaring my shoulders as I drove stone-faced and with one purpose, keeping Ruthie's revelation held in a tight clamp. What I was doing was beyond sense, beyond sanity—I knew these things, but they weren't enough to stop me. I'd simply understood what I had to do. If this was my last chance at a future with Millie, I was taking it. I refused to acknowledge any similarities between this day and that terrible morning we parted ways on the side of a northern Minnesota highway, all choices but one stripped away. The undeniable reality of an unborn child forcing us apart—

*Stop it.*

I shut out the remembrance, once and for all. The past was gone; nothing could be done to change it. But I refused to let the same be said of the future. Everything had been out of my hands back then, unfolding beyond my control, but I was no longer a scared kid, not knowing which direction to turn. This time, I would not allow the path of my life to be decided for me.

*You would raise another man's child?*

I knew the answer even before the question.

*I would.*

*If it's the only way to be with Millie, I would. I've lived without her long enough to realize I can't live without her, not anymore.*

I didn't know if there was even the remotest chance, but I was determined to find out. We still loved each other, we belonged together, and I clung to that. If Millie told me to leave, that she could never forgive me for how I'd hurt her, or that she intended to raise her child with Russ Morgan, I would respect her wishes; I would walk away. But I had to know the truth. After all this time, I would not walk away without knowing for certain. I'd left Jalesville late this morning, after driving to Bill and Irene's house; Dad waited in my truck while I knocked on their front door and spoke briefly with Bill. There was no confrontation with Hannah, and I thanked God for small favors that she refused to come to the door; instead, Zane raced from upstairs and straight to my open arms.

I brought him outside to the truck, where he hugged Dad and then sat between us, bare feet braced on the dashboard, as I explained where I intended to be for the next forty-eight hours.

"I'm going to visit an old friend in Minnesota," I explained. "I'll be home by tomorrow evening, buddy, and then you can come to Grandpa's with me."

My son chewed on this information, studying the windshield.

I cupped the back of his head. His hair was overgrown, forming curls along his neck just like mine did when I'd gone too long without a haircut. I added quietly, "You can ask me anything you want, you know that. What are you thinking about?"

"Mommy said you moved out of our house," he finally said.

I met Dad's eyes above Zane's head; my father nodded encouragement, letting me speak.

"I did, she's right. Your mom and I are getting divorced. I know it's a lot to understand, sweetheart, but I'm going to move in with Grandpa Clark for a while, until I find a new place in town. I will see you every day, okay?" Tears stabbed my eyes, hot and sharp.

Zane looked my way and I forced a smile.

"I love you so much," I told him. "Nothing could ever change that."

"I love you, Daddy," he whispered, burrowing close. Against my chest, hiding his face, he confessed, "Mommy said you hit her."

I drew back and looked square into my son's eyes, knowing I must tread with extreme care over this unknown ground; one wrong step risked permanent damage.

"Zane Alexander Rawley, I need you to listen to me. I would never hit her. Mommy said that because she was angry at me last night."

Zane appeared so small and vulnerable I wanted to stow him in my pocket and keep him safe, tucked close to me forever, sheltered from the ugliness of what lay between his mother and me; his wide, innocent eyes looked to me for answers, just as I prayed they always would, and I wanted him not only to know the truth, but to believe it rather than Hannah's lies. I didn't realize I'd been holding my breath until he nodded slowly.

"I didn't think you hit her, Daddy."

My father said, "Zane, when your dad was about your age, he lost his mom."

Zane looked at Dad. "Grandma Faye?"

"That's right. I raised your dad all on my own, you see, after your dear grandma passed. It's not always easy raising a child alone, but I had plenty of help. Who do you think helped me?"

"Aunt Julie and Aunt Ruthie?"

Dad's mustache twitched with fondness. "Well, Aunt Julie helped me, for certain. But Aunt Ruthie was only a little girl back then; she hadn't grown up and married Uncle Marshall yet."

I understood why Zane appeared somewhat perplexed; it was almost impossible to imagine a time when we hadn't known Ruthie. With all the passionate resolve I'd kept buried for so long, I thought, *God willing, someday my boy won't remember a time before he knew Millie.*

Dad continued, "You're a lucky fellow, Zane, to have two parents who love you. Even if they don't live in the same house anymore, they are still your parents."

Zane nodded again, trying hard to absorb this serious, adult-sounding conversation.

"You know who else loves you?" Dad asked.

Zane beamed. "You do, Grampa!"

"You bet I do." Dad leaned to kiss Zane's forehead. "I'm looking forward to seeing you more often, that's for sure."

Good old Dad; when I told him my intention to drive to Minnesota, he said, "You did what we all thought was right at the time, marrying your child's mother and trying to make it work, and I am damn proud of you for that. But it was the wrong decision. It was so wrong on so many levels for us to force you into that situation. Go and find Millie Jo. Don't lose any more time, son."

# CHAPTER FORTY-THREE

HOURS LATER, I TOOK THE EXIT TOWARD LAND-on under a lowering sun, leaning forward to peer through the windshield at the familiar sights along Fisherman's Street—there was Eddie's Bar, where I'd first danced with Millie; there was the Angler's Inn, and just ahead, the curve in the road that led out to Shore Leave. Afire with purpose the entire drive east, I'd kept the bulk of my anxiety submerged, but as I approached Millie's family's café, emotion jammed my lungs and sent my heart into a series of rapid seizures. No one here expected me; I could have waited until tomorrow and ridden along with Marshall and Ruthie like the old days, but I was through waiting. I was determined to find Millie Jo—and the thought that she might be at Shore Leave was almost more than my heart could bear.

I parked in the crowded lot; the sultry Sunday evening attracted a large crowd at the little café. Immediately I saw Rae on the side porch, clearing empty beer mugs from a table, her long hair tied back in a ponytail, same as always, as though I'd only just left this place. A tall blond man leaned against the porch railing nearest the table, grinning at her as they talked. He seemed familiar, but I couldn't think of his name. My internal radar swept the area in continuous arcs, but Millie was nowhere in sight. I walked through the mellow air with my gaze fixed on the screen door to the dining room, from which she could appear at any second, my heart thrusting and white spots flickering across my vision—but nothing could stop me now.

Rae caught sight of me and her cheerful chatter froze mid-word.

The blond man straightened and turned my way, clearly wondering what was wrong.

Rae dropped the mugs on the table, ignoring the clatter, and flew from the porch. "Wy, oh my God! What are you *doing* here? Does Millie know you're here? How did . . . when did . . ."

All bravado faded and I begged hoarsely, "Is she here? Can I see her?"

Rae studied my eyes, her own intent and worried. I knew she was dying to ask and so I admitted, "I know."

She nodded slowly, understanding with no additional explanation as she said, "Millie's at home."

"In Minneapolis?" I was already primed to aim my truck south.

"No, no, she's just around the lake. Everyone else is out on a pontoon ride. Here, we can call her." Rae dug her phone from her server apron.

"Zig Sorenson." The man from the porch had joined us, politely offering his hand.

I shook without introducing myself, unable to focus. I could hear the phone ringing as Rae held it to her ear, chewing her thumbnail with nervous energy.

"Dammit," she muttered. "She's probably sleeping. I'll try again."

I said, "It's all right, I'll head over there," and hustled back to my truck. I knew the way to the homesteader's cabin where Millie had grown up, less than five minutes away. I was shaking so hard I had trouble shifting gears as I left Shore Leave behind, driving through the pine forest along the winding gravel road, and as I drove around a bend I thought at first that I was seeing things, the silvering air playing tricks on my perception. A woman was walking along the side of the road closest to the lake, the last of the sun creating a glowing halo around her long hair and outlining her limbs. She was barefoot, pausing to watch warily as an unknown vehicle approached.

It was her—I had not been imagining it.

I parked and stepped from the truck like someone in a dream, afraid she would disappear between one blink and the next.

Millie dropped her shoes, and her hands flew to her mouth, staring as though I was a ghost, as if I'd go up in smoke if she dared to move. She was pale and drawn, her beautiful face stark with disbelief.

I spoke like someone in a trance. "Holy God, it's good to see you."

...

The man standing before me on the old gravel road to Shore Leave had left all traces of boyishness behind; Wyatt Zane Rawley, whose return I had longed for with such obsessive fervor it seemed almost unreal in this moment—a cruel trick of fate, throwing us into the other's path on the same stretch of road upon which he'd first found me walking all those summers ago. We stared at each other with maybe six steps between our bodies, distance I could have closed in one bound toward him, but I stood rooted, stunned. He was hatless, the sun glinting over his wide shoulders and dark hair, clad in jeans and a gray T-shirt, his left arm held close to his body in a cloth sling.

"It's been so long." Wy sounded as if he was under a spell. "All the things I wanted to say, all the letters I wanted to write to you, all the plans we made. Everything changed so fast, from one second to the next. I destroyed everything we planned. It was all my fault."

I could no longer allow him to take such blame. "It wasn't all your fault, Wy, don't say that."

"I know it's crazy to show up like this, with no warning. I didn't come here because I expect anything from you, Millie Jo, I want you to know that." His deep voice was husky with longing as he added, "I just needed to see you."

My throat was closing fast. "I've missed you so much, you couldn't know how much . . ."

"I've been torn apart with missing you, every day, every night." He stepped slowly closer, as though afraid I might bolt, and asked quietly, "Will you let me hold you?"

In the next moment I was in his arms—he had chucked aside the sling—and he was in mine. He released a low, ragged breath, burying his face in my hair as I clung to him, and the physical contact flung me over the edge. Years' worth of suppressed emotion shattered in my chest and I wilted against the immeasurable relief he provided, shuddering with sobs. He cupped the back of my head, the tender gesture further tearing at my heart, and said not a word as the gloaming crept slowly over our bodies. He let me weep, stroking my hair with a touch simultaneously gentle and passionate, as it had always been.

I babbled, "Your shoulder . . . you're hurt . . . am I hurting your arm?"

"No," he assured, squeezing me closer. "I wouldn't let go for the world."

When my sobs finally ebbed, he put lips to my ear for the space of a heartbeat. "I am so sorry I hurt you. I have never forgiven myself for it. I died that day, knowing what we were losing, knowing I had done that to us, to everything we'd planned."

His pulse beat against my flushed, tear-damp skin, my nose resting at the juncture of his collarbones as he curved protectively over me. I pressed a soft kiss on his neck, inhaling his scent, unable to resist instincts so powerful. Words I'd kept buried rose in my throat.

"I hurt you too, and it's eaten me alive ever since. I know you were in shock that morning. I lashed out at you because I couldn't deal with it, I couldn't think beyond protecting myself from the pain. I knew I was losing you and I didn't want to acknowledge it . . ." New grief welled in my chest, but I forced it down, determined to finish. "You couldn't have made any other choice, I realize that now."

He lifted my chin, and my heart jolted all over again at the sight of his expression, severe with sincerity; I had never doubted Wy's sincerity and I would not start now. He said softly, "The night we spent at Itasca was the most beautiful of my life. Just the memory of it has sustained me through all these years, you have no idea."

"I have *every* idea. It was the most beautiful night of my life too." I faltered, feeling as though I would sink to the ground if not for his embrace. "Do you . . . did Ruthie tell you . . ."

He held my gaze as he slowly nodded, and hot orange hope blazed in my chest, momentarily overriding all else. It was foolish, I knew, hell and gone past foolish. I couldn't relinquish control and free fall as I had once before with this man. I still hadn't recovered from that impact. And yet—he was here. Wy had come to me. He was still married and I was carrying another man's child, and still he had come. His hands rested on the sides of my waist, his long thumbs making slow, sweeping arcs along the soft material covering my belly; the touch I had longed for with a palpable ache ever since the morning I last felt it upon my skin.

"Is there someplace we could go to talk?" he requested gently. "There are so many things I need to tell you."

We couldn't continue to stand here on the side of the road in the gathering darkness, Wy's truck blocking both narrow lanes.

I nodded, swiping at the last of my tears. "There's a little clearing in the woods near here; it's not far."

Wy moved to open the passenger door for me, exactly as he had the night when we danced at Eddie's Bar, but I stopped him by reaching to trace my fingers over the letters of his name and title painted on the door panel.

"*Doctor* Rawley," I marveled softly.

"It took me a long time to get used to the whole 'doctor' bit," he admitted, standing with his fingertips on the door handle, studying me. "But it feels natural now."

"I'm so proud of you, Wy. You've worked so hard for this."

"Thank you," he said solemnly, resting a hand lightly on my lower back as I climbed inside his truck.

I ran my fingertips over the dash, this space that belonged wholly to Wy, that spoke so clearly of his veterinary career. I breathed in the familiar scents—horse and hay and man. There was his same old gray hat, waiting for him in the middle of the bench seat. A pair of worn leather work gloves lay alongside it; how powerfully these simple things moved me, because they belonged to him. I resisted the urge to pick up his hat and cradle it to my chest.

"Where to?" he asked as he joined me in the truck.

A mere eighteen inches separated us as we sat staring at each other, and it felt so unnatural to keep from reaching for him. I noticed again the small, jagged welt beneath his left eye.

I slipped my hands under my thighs as I said, "Straight ahead, the first right."

We drove the short distance in semi-tense silence, Wy taking the truck through the forest at my directions, to the small clearing where high school kids met to drink on summer weekends; on this Sunday evening, it was empty but for us. Evening had advanced, and only the dash lights illuminated us as he parked and killed the engine. The front seat of his truck was one long, smooth leather bench, and we turned toward each other, awareness thrumming between us in heated waves.

We both spoke at once.

"When did—"

"I—"

"You first," I invited, tensing my thigh muscles to still their trembling.

He said without preamble, "Hannah and I are over, for good. We're getting divorced."

This news was like a bolt of pure energy delivered directly to my heart; I stared speechlessly at him.

"I thought the only choice I had back then was to marry her and start a family. I thought it was what was right, my responsibility as a man, you have to understand that. It was my child she was carrying, and I couldn't leave her in the lurch, no matter how goddamn scared and immature I was, no matter how much I rebelled against the reality of it. But our marriage has been one unending hell. The only good that came of it is Zane. I can't imagine my life without my boy. He means the world to me, Millie; I love him more than I ever thought possible."

I found my voice. "You love with your whole heart, Wy. I've never doubted that."

"I try my damnedest to believe things happen for a reason. Zane was meant to be, I know that now, and I have done my best to be a good father to him. I always will. But Hannah and I were miserable from the start, even before our wedding. I would have left her years ago, but I couldn't handle the thought of not seeing Zane every day, of living in a separate house. I was prepared to stay married to his mother for his sake."

"What changed?" I whispered, overwhelmed by this version of him I had never before witnessed: protective, caring father, a man who loved his child and would do anything for him. Wy was all man, any last hints of boyish uncertainty forever tucked away.

He studied me for the space of a heartbeat—an eternity—until the air between us seemed to pulse, as though the earth itself exhaled a soft breath, begging for release . . .

To my surprise he suddenly shifted position, exiting the truck and striding around the hood to my side. Before I could blink, he opened the passenger door and caught my knees in his hands, turning me to face him as he stood on the ground outside. I stared at him in astonishment, burning alive in the heated intensity of his gaze.

"You are the woman I love, the woman I will love until I die, and I don't want to spend another day of my life without you."

Such admissions struck hard, leveling all hope of salvaging control.

Wy continued in a passionate rush of words. "If you tell me to walk away, I will, but not until you hear me out. I've lived without you long enough to know I can't. If there's a chance in hell you will share your life with me from this day forth, I'm taking it. When we talked that night when I was in the hospital, I knew then you still loved me. I'd convinced myself otherwise these past years, but I knew that night. We belong together, Millie Jo. If that means raising another man's child at your side, I accept this with all my heart."

Trembling, tears stinging my eyes and throat, I clutched the front of his T-shirt, fisting my hands around the warm material, feeling the thrust of his heart beneath my touch.

"Tell me," he demanded, harsh with need, his touch gliding higher, anchoring around my hips.

Had I known, somehow, what would happen once we were completely alone? *Of course I'd known.*

I said roughly, "You know I love you, oh God, Wy, I've never loved anyone *but you—*"

He took my face in his hands, any further words lost between our hungry kisses—our bodies racing headlong toward the destination for which they'd been bound since the moment we set eyes on each other. There was no hesitation, only the force of our need; recognizing no other option than to possess each other fully. Without breaking the contact of our mouths, I frantically unzipped his jeans and he tore both shorts and panties down my legs, clamping a two-handed grip on my ass. My thighs spread wide and he drove deep inside with a low, harsh breath, matching the gasp that rose from my throat—*at last, oh God, at last.* I returned each vigorous thrust, gripping the hard, warm curves of his upper arms, loving the sound of his throaty groans. Shuddering and gasping, I locked my ankles at the base of his spine just as I felt his hot, jetting release.

"Come here," I begged, tugging him as I scooted backward on the bench seat of his truck. "I need you so much, *don't stop* . . . "

"I'll never stop, oh God, Millie, *I love you so fucking much* . . ."

Enough could never be enough, now that we'd tumbled together over this cliff.

"Get this shirt off . . . " I yanked it over his head. His jeans bunched around his ankles, which only slightly hampered his movements as he stepped out of his boots and shed his pants. My legs were blessedly free and I wrapped them straightaway around his waist, squeezing before I glided my calves up and down along his bare torso, reveling in his lean strength.

"My sweet, sweet Millie Jo," he murmured in a husky tone of rejoicing, biting my chin, holding himself deep and momentarily still within me.

I shivered, lightly raking my fingernails along his scalp, following the path to his facial hair, caressing the shape it made around his sexy, familiar mouth; he bit the tip of my exploring finger. Remembering his long-ago words, I murmured, "I swear I could come just looking at you."

His eyelids lowered slightly and my entire body throbbed in response as he whispered, "I want to eat you alive, woman."

I tightened my grip on him at all points of contact.

Wy dug his hands in my tangled hair, tipping my head to kiss my neck, my collarbones, releasing hold only to sweep both shirt and bra from my flushed, sweating body. He opened his lips over my breasts, lavishing each by turn, continuing to pump deeply inside me, each thrust inspiring a new swell of intense pleasure, our bodies starving for each other. I clutched his ass, pulling him tighter, begging for more even as he filled me to bursting. I licked sweat from his skin, took his earlobes between my teeth, sought his mouth yet again and reveled in it, in his taste and textures, the intimate familiarity of this man—the only one I had ever wanted to share these sacred, beautiful things with.

The expanse of heavens arcing over the forest grew electric with stars that blazed down upon us as we made love. Lost in each other, we refused to surrender hold, shifting so that at times I straddled him on the bench seat, our hands clasped, fingers linked as I moved rhythmically atop him; at times Wy's shoulders curved wide above me as we joined full-length on the long front seat, his strong, lithe hands guiding my hips, lifting me ever higher, taking both of us beyond all reason, beyond any hope of ever returning. Time melted, flew, stalled out. At long last we fell still, my thighs cradling his hips, his right arm holding me secure; he lay so that his left shoulder supported none of his weight. Overcome by tenderness, I cupped his bicep and caressed the dips in his muscles, smoothing a thumb over his tattoo, nuzzling my face against his neck.

"Is your shoulder hurting?" I whispered, knowing he'd minimized the pain for my sake.

He kissed my temple, lingering against my skin. "It's not, I promise."

The darkness robbed us of color, but I saw his eyes all the same, at close range as he touched his forehead sweetly to mine. How I longed to remain in this moment, alone together, sheltered against his chest. Movement meant the inevitable parting of ways, no matter how much we wished otherwise; it meant facing the reality that waited for us out there in the world, only miles away.

I sensed the same feelings rising in Wy. He traced his thumb over my lips as he whispered, "Tonight has been so beautiful. It's more than I could have dreamed in a hundred years. I didn't come here expecting this, I want you to know that."

I cupped his face, struck all over again by possessive passion. "I know, I really do. I'm so glad you were brave enough to find me."

"You've never left my heart, baby, not for one second. When Ruthie told me you were pregnant this morning, it was like a bomb went off in my chest. I knew what I had to do and I prayed the entire way here that it wasn't too late. I was afraid if I didn't take this chance I'd never see you again, that I'd spend the rest of my life destroyed by what might have been."

My next breath stuck in my lungs and I saw his eyebrows draw together in concern. I admitted on a quivery exhale, "I'm so scared, Wy. Nothing about this is going to be easy."

He shifted just slightly, smoothing hair from the sides of my face, pressing a soft kiss to my parted lips. "It won't be easy, but it's going to be all right. Don't be scared. We're together now, and I will never let anyone separate us again, you have my word."

Doubt and fear crowded close all the same, tugging at my hair, whispering in my ears; we both knew countless obstacles lay across the path between tonight and some future day when we could be together. Wy saw the change in my expression and turned us sideways so he could hold me closer, cupping the nape of my neck, glossy with sweat beneath the thick mass of my tangled curls. The passenger door remained open, his long legs hanging off the bench seat, our clothes crumpled in small piles on the grass near the truck tires. The night air was perfectly motionless, rife with the tuneless chirping of crickets, the stars alive in the black vault of sky stretching above. I rested my nose against him and inhaled, storing up for later.

I felt his chest rumbling with the words as he invited, "Tell me," but it was a gentle request this time, a need to know more.

I was quiet for a moment, unsure how to begin, how to sort through the complexity of emotion in my chest—fear, and a strange, bright reverence, and aching dismay, all tangled in knots at the thought of my daughter. I whispered, "Rae and I were sitting on the dock yesterday afternoon and she had one of her visions."

"Like Jilly's, right?" Wy asked, and I loved that he understood without explanation, that he recognized the seriousness of my statement.

"Exactly like that. And she saw . . ." I gulped, losing steam, but I was determined to tell him. "She saw my daughter. She saw the baby in my arms looking back at her." A shiver scoured a cold line along my spine. "I don't doubt it, Wy.

Rae is never wrong. She saw my little girl."

"What about Russ? Have you talked to him? Does he know what you suspect?" Wy's tone betrayed nothing but the quiet desire to know more. He used his knuckles to smooth a tender, repetitive path up and down along my spine as he waited for a response, and I was reminded of the ways I'd soothed horses.

"No," I whispered. "On all counts, no. The last time I saw him was the same night we talked when you were in the hospital. I broke up with Russ last summer, over a year ago. We hadn't been together since then, until that night. It was a mistake, I knew it was a mistake even *while* it was happening."

Wy didn't immediately respond, and I searched his eyes with an unexpected flash of anger.

"You're not *upset*, are you?" I cried.

He said tightly, "If I'm completely honest, the fact that he's touched you, that he's had your time and attention, makes me want to hunt him down and rip him limb from limb. I've pretty much hated him since I first heard about him."

I fired right back. "You think I don't understand?! You've been married for four years. *Four years*, Wy, of picturing you touching Hannah, of picturing you *making love to her*. I could barely function that first year after your wedding, imagining those things. I've lived with it *all this time!* How do you think that feels?!"

"It feels like fucking hell," he said heatedly. "Don't think I don't know. I've tortured myself with the thought of you and another man. Hannah and I barely touched. Clearly that's not the case with you and *him*."

I swung my legs to the floor of the truck, displacing the contact of our skin. "How *dare* you throw that in my face?! You've been *married!* As though *I* knew those things about you and Hannah! It's not like you told me when we talked! Did you expect me to sit around in Landon forever, waiting for you to come back?"

Consternation radiated from him; he sat and ran a hand over his face before saying quietly, "I'm sorry. I'm way out of line and I know it. But I can't pretend it doesn't slaughter me, thinking of you with someone else."

I released a slow sigh, letting his apology sink in; at last I said, "If you think it was any easier for me, you're wrong." I paused to collect my thoughts. "You told me once that the last time you'd had sex with Hannah, it 'just happened.' I only pretended to understand what you meant by that. I never actually did, not until this past year or so with Russ. When he and I had sex last month it just *happened*, exactly like you said. It was so stupid. I felt nothing but resentment and guilt. I told him it was a mistake that very night. My motives were such shit, Wy. Do you think for a second I thought that mistake was going to lead to a baby?"

He curved a hand over my thigh; my tone had escalated with desperation.

He whispered, "I understand better than anyone, believe me."

"I haven't talked to Russ since. He was furious and I don't blame him. When he left that night, I was nothing but relieved. I figured I'd never see him again. And now . . ." I closed my eyes, pressing hard against my forehead.

"Now your life feels out of your own hands," Wy finished somberly.

I sat straight and met his gaze.

"It feels that way, but it doesn't have to be that way, Mill." He spoke with calm reassurance, and it struck me then, in entirely new ways, how much he'd changed. No longer inhibited by doubt, he was possessed of a deep understanding of the pain caused by someone else dictating the path of his life. He had come full circle.

He continued, "I don't mean to imply that I would make any decisions for you. But if I've learned anything from the last four years, it's that staying together for the sake of a child doesn't help anything, or anyone. Zane has never seen genuine affection or love between his mother and me, and I hate myself for it. I fooled myself thinking that he always slept through our fights. It's something I can never take back, never change, and I have to live with that."

"Don't say that, don't run yourself down. You have done your best by your son since the moment you knew he existed. I know, I was *there*. And I know you've tried with Hannah over these years because that's the kind of man you are: a good, honest, honorable man."

"There's been plenty of times I haven't felt like a good man, believe me. Things I've felt, and said . . . it was so ugly between Hannah and me, especially at the end."

"You can tell me those things, Wy, it won't shock me if that's what you think."

He was silent for a beat before saying quietly, "I hid booze in our house; for a long time I drank every night once Hannah went to bed. It's so easy to blame her for everything that was wrong between us, but I can't do that, not when she never stood a chance. I never loved her, not the way I should, and she realized it. And there were things about her I never knew, could never have guessed before I lived in the same house with her. The way she screamed and cried to get her way, and constantly manipulated people. She tried her best to drive a wedge between me and my family, from the first week we were married. I thought things might get better once Zane was born, but they only got worse."

I whispered, "I spent so many nights imagining the complete opposite."

"Just like I imagined when I first heard you were seeing someone."

"I couldn't bear to think of you loving her the way you loved me."

"I know, baby, I really do. I felt exactly the same thinking of you and Russ, even knowing it was none of my damn business. But I died a little more every day."

"I tried to stop loving you, but I couldn't. Loving you is part of who I am."

He pulled me onto his lap and encircled my ribcage with both arms, his eyes luminous even in the darkness. "Once you've been loved like that, nothing can touch it, nothing else can suffice. You sure as hell can't live with a substitute for it. Those days with you that summer were the happiest of my life."

I held his face, the better to study it, tracing the path of his eyebrows, his long and stubborn nose, as I whispered, "There's plenty of ugly things I wish no one ever had to know, like the way I've treated Russ, using him these past few years to try to get over you, when I always knew in my heart there was no getting over you. Russ looks a little like you when he smiles. When he touched me, I pictured you. *You*, do you hear me? It's so sick, but I craved even that little bit. What kind of person does that make me?"

"You're too hard on yourself. It's no wonder we looked for glimpses of each other in all this time. It was never supposed to *end* between us, we both knew it." He paused for a second. "I saw you last year. I drove from Montana and saw you at Lake View."

Awareness slowly dawned. "It *was* you that day, I *knew* it. I thought I was going crazy! Wait, who—"

"Joey," he said at once, knowing what I meant. "My best friend, Joe Quick. He works with me at Bitterroot. He went inside and asked about you because I was losing it, out in the parking lot. And then you showed up with Russ, and I felt like a criminal, like I was stalking you . . ."

I was shaking my head, laughing, before he finished speaking. "If that makes you a stalker, then so am I. Oh my God, Wy, I drove out to Jalesville only a few *days* after that, once my last final was over."

"You did?" He sounded stunned.

"I drove through town, and then to the road out to your dad's, and then I drove up to Bitterroot. I was in the waiting room with Netta when you pulled up outside that day. You want to talk about losing it . . ."

"Hold on. You've been at Bitterroot? You were there a year ago?!"

"I saw Zane that day. I almost crashed into him when he ran inside. I hid in the bathroom until I was sure you'd left. I heard you talking to Netta, only a few steps away. Seeing you with your son made me feel like I was somewhere I didn't belong, like I was forcing myself into your life . . ."

"Millie *Jo*. You mean to tell me you were in the bathroom, you were right there? I wish to God I would have known it that day. I would have kicked down that door!"

I giggled at his continued shocked tone. "I don't think it was locked."

He aligned his hands with my shoulder blades, caressing my skin as he demanded, "Did you talk to Netta? Didn't she know who you were? Why didn't she stop you from leaving?!"

"She hadn't seen me since I was fifteen," I reminded him, picturing the beautiful rehabilitation center. "It was so amazing to see Bitterroot, after seeing it so many times online. And driving through Jalesville was like coming home. I've missed being there with you, so much."

"You can't begin to know how much I've wished you were there with me. But that's changing, starting right now."

"It's not that easy. You're still married, I still have to face Russ . . . we can't just magically change those things."

"Maybe not tonight, but we will. I'm married as of this second, at least legally, and cheating on my wife as we speak, but I don't give a goddamn. I've grown to hate the woman I married. How's that for an ugly truth?"

"I found her online once, not long after you were married. Just seeing her face and thinking of her with you was worse than a beating. I would *rather* have been beaten."

"I know how you feel, believe me."

I leaned closer to gently kiss the wound beneath his eye. "How'd you get this? I saw this earlier. Is it from the night with Jarred Watkins?"

He hesitated, as though waiting for permission to continue.

"Tell me," I insisted. "Tell me everything. I don't want secrets between us, now or ever."

"I don't want secrets between us either; I've lived with that for too long." His gaze moved upward, as though searching through time, before returning to mine. "Hannah smacked me with her keys."

"She *hit* you?" I cried, my entire body tensing.

"It's more complicated than that," he said, and sighed, his jaw jutting to the side. "It sounds terrible, I know. It wasn't even the first time she hit me. It took me a long time to tell anyone the truth, I was so ashamed and embarrassed. I finally told Joey. Well, actually he guessed . . . "

"You've been living like that? Oh, my God . . . " I wrapped him all the more securely in my embrace. Something else occurred to me. "Does she hit Zane?!"

"No, no, she saves all her wrath for me, believe me. She always thought I was cheating on her, and flinging that in my face. I've made so many mistakes, Mill, but the worst was trying to convince myself that Zane needed his parents in the same house. I've paid for that a hundred times over. Instead of solving anything, I just made everything worse."

I curled my fingers in his hair, stroking its softness, and he shivered.

"That feels so good, you can't know how good," he murmured, resettling his warm hands around my backside, not an inch to spare between our naked bodies. "After the wedding, I spent almost all my energy and effort living in a fantasy world. I'd pretend that when I got home from Pullman on Friday nights, *you* would be there waiting for me, that you were carrying my baby. I wished every night that I could call you and tell you about my day, and hear about yours."

I had an admission of my own. "I lived in a fantasy world too. I refused to believe it was over between us, just like you did. I pretended that you'd eventually send me a letter, or call. I imagined so often that you'd show up at my high school graduation that I almost convinced myself you would, and then we'd drive out to Montana together, like we planned."

"I would have been there in a heartbeat if I could have."

A ray of pure joy beamed in my heart, despite everything; if someone had told me this morning that by tonight, I'd be in Wy's arms, I would have called them crazy.

"You're here now," I whispered.

# CHAPTER FORTY-FOUR

MY KNEES WERE STILL WEAK.

Millie sat to my right, her hand engulfed in mine on the seat between us, and I could hardly keep my gaze on the lake road as I navigated the truck in the direction of downtown Landon. If I looked away from her too long, I might wake up alone on the couch in the living room on Front Street. I lifted her hand to my lips and kissed her knuckles, resettling our threaded fingers on my right thigh. Millie scooted across the seat, and I tucked her close and grinned—wide and warm, my real smile, the one I'd left behind for so goddamn long. She melted against my side, her cheek on my chest, her hair tickling my nose and chin. The wealth of feelings she inspired, the gift of the past few hours together, was probably more than I deserved.

But immediately I thought, *Stop that. You deserve to be happy. Life is giving you another chance. Life is giving both of you another chance.*

We'd cleaned up as best we could in the dark truck after two hours of intense lovemaking, having retrieved Millie's shoes and my sling from the side of the road, and were headed now toward the apartment complex where Rae lived with her boyfriend. Millie had just talked to Rae, who was upset and irritated that Millie hadn't responded to her multiple texts. I'd arrived in Landon with no plans other than to find Millie; now, having no place to spend the night, Rae and Zig had offered me the couch in their apartment. I also wanted to talk to Millie's parents, but it was past midnight.

"In the morning," I decided. "Right away. I've wanted to talk to them for a long time now."

"I haven't told anyone yet," Millie said. "Except Aunt Ruthie."

"Tomorrow?" I asked with care, not wanting to push her. "I'll tell them with you, if that's what you want. And I owe Camille and Mathias an apology. I want to make things right with them, I want their blessing. I want your family to know I love you and that I intend to be at your side from here on out."

"Say that one more time," she requested in a whisper, rubbing her jaw softly up and down against my shirt. "I can't hear it enough."

I squeezed her closer, resting my chin on the top of her head. "I love you, Millie Joelle Gordon. God, how I love you."

"I know you can't stay here, you have to get home to Zane, but I don't want you to go. I can't bear it. And I have classes starting in Minneapolis next week . . ."

The thought of returning to Montana without her, as I would surely have to do as soon as tomorrow, made my chest feel like a punching bag, but I intended to be strong for her. For us. "I can't stay away from Jalesville for too long, you're right, but it's not the same this time. We have our future to build, and our lives are in our own hands. This time no one can take that away from us."

She lifted her head. "We don't want to admit it, but we're still living in a fantasy world. I have to face Russ, no matter what I want. And once his shock wears off, he'll want to be in my life. He'll want shared custody. I know his family; I worked with his mother for years. They'll want to be close to their granddaughter." Panic crept into her voice. "Russ won't let me move to Montana. He won't want to be that far away from his child."

"He'll be a part of his daughter's life wherever we live." I battled a sudden rush of dread; I had to be stronger than this. I had to accept that Russ Morgan would be in our lives for a long damn time.

Millie would not be comforted. "And what about Zane? What if he doesn't like me? How could I blame him? What if he sees me as the woman who came between his parents?"

I didn't want to say something that would seem patronizing, and an assurance that my son would love and adore her was exactly that. In my heart, I was sure he would—but Millie wouldn't buy such an answer just now. I thought for a second before saying, "We can't solve everything tonight. The point is we'll solve everything *together*, no matter what comes our way."

She was silent, letting these words sink in. At last she whispered, "We survived all this time without each other. We can face this. *All* of this."

"Damn right," I murmured, resting my cheek against her hair, grateful beyond words for the feeling of her sweet, familiar body aligned with mine, as it should have been all along.

. . .

Rae and Zig were waiting up for us when we reached the small apartment building on the south side of Landon; their unit was on the second floor, and Rae had made up the couch with blankets and a pillow. She hugged Millie, then me, offering pajamas and food and extra blankets, bustling around the crowded space and making small talk in an obvious effort to mask her concern.

"You guys want a beer?" Zig inquired, rooting in the fridge. Millie had given me a few details about his relationship with Rae, and he surely knew everything Rae knew. He didn't ask any questions, though, striking me as a person who took things in stride. He called, "Maybe a whiskey instead?"

"Hon, let's give them some privacy," Rae insisted, tugging him toward the bedroom. "Help yourselves, you guys, to anything."

Their door clicked shut moments later, leaving us in the glow of a solo table lamp. I sank to a seat on my makeshift bed while Millie remained standing, holding a bundle of flannel pajamas against her belly.

"I'll go change quick," she said, a soft smile bowing her lips as she added, "Your hair is all messy."

I grinned at her tone. "Yeah, I don't think we were fooling anyone about where we've been all evening."

"I know that couch is barely big enough for you—"

I reached for her. "Don't even think of spending the night anywhere else."

Her smile deepened, the lamplight catching the glints of gold in her hazel eyes. "I was about to say we could make a bed on the floor instead."

We attempted to condense four years into a span of hours, talking in hushed voices, sometimes laughing, our legs intertwined, never removing our hands from each other. Already I felt the pull of time like water flowing between my clenched fingers, unable to prevent it from slipping away. Millie told me about her years at college, and her Parelli certification, and Wallace the mule's abrupt departure from the stable, one of the many animals she had come to love in her time at Lake View. She told me about Russ's mother, Dee, and how much she'd learned from her. She told me about things she'd done last summer, in the company of Rae and Zig and a guy named Jere; she was hesitant at first to mention certain parts, and I couldn't deny it hurt to hear them, but she was right—I wanted no secrets between us, now or ever. At last she told me about her acceptance to grad school in Billings.

In turn, I told her about the long, stressful night of Zane's birth, and Hannah's emergency operation, and how she had blamed me for it ever since; deadweights of pain were shed, burdens released, as I spoke openly with Millie, her listening a gift for which I would forever be thankful. I talked about Zane growing from a sweet, chubby baby to a busy toddler in constant motion. I talked about how much I truly loved being a father, how the love for a child is its own separate, untouchable entity in your heart. I told her about my work at Bitterroot and surrounding ranches, and how much joy I found in the practicing of medicine.

"I've imagined you at my side so many times, riding along with me in the truck through all those miles and sunrises and long-ass days, helping me with horses and mules and every other kind of animal. You, just *being* there. Oh God, Mill, just being there with me." My right hand was buried in her curls, our noses only a few inches apart; our eyes had long since adjusted to the darkness of the little living room.

"I've imagined all those same things, being at your side, working at Bitterroot, sharing our lives," she whispered, her hands resting softly on my chest as we snuggled beneath two quilts, on the floor in front of the couch; I'd moved the coffee table to give us more room. "I've wanted to work at the center since that first night we talked about it!"

"You will." I would make it happen as soon as humanly possible.

"I can't wait to see Scout. I know he's full-grown now, but I still picture him as that beautiful little foal. And Shadow! How's Shadow?"

On and on we talked. I told her about Joey and how his friendship had helped sustain me these past years; I told her about his relationship with Quinn, how happy I was that it meant both of them would stick around Jalesville for the time being. I talked about how much I'd loved Lucky the pit bull and still missed his presence at Bitterroot.

"In the end, though, Jarred Watkins did me a favor," I concluded. "If not for him, we'd never have talked that night I was in the hospital. Hearing your voice was like being granted a wish. I prayed that somehow you'd show up in Montana and be there when I woke up in the morning."

Millie leaned closer, letting our lips brush; I inhaled the scent of her breath like a drug I could not live without as she whispered, "I want to be there when you wake up for the rest of our lives, Wyatt."

I kissed her sweet mouth, gripping the notches of her waist, her skin like warm satin under my greedy touch. "I thought I would never see you again. I thought I had to live with that . . ."

"Come here," she insisted in a whisper, working one-handed to unbutton her flannel pajama shirt.

Unable to resist, I finished the task for her, tasting every inch of her bared flesh. Hard as a rock, lightheaded, I managed to whisper, "I don't want you to think sex is all I think about . . ."

"I don't think that," she assured me, tugging down my pajama pants and shifting on top, taking me inside her body with a soft exhalation of breath.

I muffled a groaning cry against her neck, almost done for right there, she felt so good. So right. Safe beneath the quilts in the deep of the night, we made love slow and sweet, lingering over every touch and taste, taking each other somewhere beyond—to a sacred, nameless place we created together. No words were necessary in those moments, muted sounds of love and pleasure caught between our kisses, colors swirling on the backs of my eyelids in the surrounding darkness, my every sense inundated by the woman in my arms.

Though I didn't want to waste a minute of this night, sometime later I was on the edge of sleep, Millie's head on my chest. Then she made a small sound.

Nothing suggested an emergency, but I was instantly alert, whispering, "What's wrong?"

I felt her shift to sit up, drawing a quilt with her. The tone in her voice was unreadable as she murmured, "Nothing, exactly . . . I just . . ."

"Just what, love?"

Instead of answering, she rolled to her knees and whispered, "I'll be right back."

She rose and headed for the bathroom. I sat and clicked on the lamp; no more than five seconds later, I heard Millie's voice through the closed door.

"Wy, come here, quick . . ."

I flew to her, entering the bathroom with my heart clunking, all at once realizing what Millie already had; struck by a sudden and potent rush of déjà vu, it seemed we were back in that little orange tent in the state park, the very first night we'd made love.

Millie had slipped down her pajamas, a puddle of flannel around her ankles as she stood facing me, both palms braced on her belly.

"It's my period. Oh my God, it's my *period*. Oh, Wy, it's all right now, *everything's all right* . . ."

I took her by both shoulders, my gaze roving over her lower body, on the lookout for any hint of a problem. To my extreme relief, the blood staining her underwear and inner thighs was dark in color, not the bright red of hemorrhage. "Are you in any pain? What about cramping?"

"No, no, I'm not in pain," she assured, tipping forward. "It's just my period, not a miscarriage. It was just late." A half-sobbing laugh burst from her lips as she clutched my forearms. "Thank God, oh thank God, Wy, *it's okay now*. I have to tell Rae . . ."

When it was apparent Millie was about to race to her cousin's bedroom half-naked, I said gently, "Hang on, love, you're not dressed."

Overcome, she wilted back into my open arms. Weeping and laughing and hiccupping, she clung to my bare torso, moisture pouring from her eyes and nose, and relief pelted me in great, swinging bursts. I kissed the hollow beneath her ear, feeling the steady beat of her pulse; she seemed at once invincible and unimaginably vulnerable, and I held her all the harder.

"You're sure you're not hurting?"

"I'm not hurting, I promise. I'm so relieved I can't think straight. I was so scared, I felt like dark water was closing over my head every time I thought about telling Russ. Now we don't have to face that; we're *free*, Wy, I can't believe it."

"I feel bad admitting I'm relieved," I whispered against her hair. "I was prepared to face this, no matter what."

"Are you kidding?! I've never been so relieved in my life." Laughter won out and she drew back, the two of us grinning at each other in the glow of the bathroom fixture, our eyes sleep-smudged and brimming with our mutual joy at this unexpected reprieve; Millie's curls were in snarls and my hair stood on end. She reached up and took me by the ears, tugging me close for a quick kiss. "Here, let me clean up and I'll be right out."

There was no more than an hour before dawn as I sank to a seat on the couch and turned off the table lamp; the microwave clock read 4:42. I thought of how many nights in the past four years I'd retreated alone to a living room couch in a haze induced by whiskey. I thought of how I'd tucked my son to bed every one of those nights, and how, some day in the near future, Millie and I would tuck him in together. Overwhelmed by gratitude, I bent forward and covered my face with both hands, taking a moment to simply absorb the past few minutes. I'd been unwilling to admit to Millie the primal fear that stabbed through my heart at the thought of what might have happened—Russ could very well have insisted that she remain in Minnesota, perhaps even convinced her that they should try to be together for the child's sake. And losing her again would do me in, for good this time.

I didn't hear Millie slip across the carpet on her return from the bathroom. Instead of sitting, she took my head against her belly and hugged me close. With a choked breath, I wrapped my arms around her hips, my forehead on her stomach, inhaling in gulps as she stroked my hair in a gentle, repetitive motion.

"It's all right," she murmured. "It's all right now."

I pulled her onto my lap and we curled together on the couch, talking softly, watching dawn paint the sky yellow one stripe at a time through the east-facing window.

Millie whispered, "There's just one thing I can't figure out. Rae is *never* wrong."

As she spoke, sun crested the trees, spilling golden light over us. And in my heart, I knew the answer; maybe I'd known all along, certainty rooted in a place even deeper than instinct.

I lifted her chin so I could see her beautiful topaz eyes. "You know what? I think Rae just saw farther into the future than she realized."

# EPILOGUE

IT WAS MY DAUGHTER RAE SAW IN HER VISION that afternoon. Millie could not have known in that moment on the dock outside Shore Leave that the baby she held in Rae's brief glimpse of the future belonged to the both of us. Clae Louisa Rawley, our first little girl, joined our family approximately two and a half years after our wedding, arriving on a humid summer afternoon during which a ferocious thunderstorm knocked out power to half the town, including our home. We had built a cabin in the foothills the spring after our wedding, on land we purchased from Tuck and Netta. Bitterroot was only a few miles away, where Millie and I had worked together since the month she returned with me to Montana, the very same June we discovered she would not be expecting Russ Morgan's child.

People sometimes asked us if we grew tired of each other—married and working together, they meant—to which Millie would reply, "I can't imagine *not* working with my husband every day."

But Joey, who once overheard the question, said it best—"I've never known anyone who loves his wife the way Wy does."

That first summer, Millie transferred to Montana State in Billings, and we lived with Dad. He, Millie, and I spent hours clearing out the basement bedroom and living area for our use. At her insistence, Millie stayed at Tish and Case's house on the weekends when Zane was over; she was wary of rushing anything with him. I introduced my son to Millie out at Bitterroot during the first Saturday of July. By contrast, I was full of excitement for them to officially meet. Zane was a child who took things at face value. I introduced Millie as my friend, and Zane had not pressed for more specific details as he might have if he'd been older—or, as Millie pointed out, if he'd been a girl. Any minor concerns I harbored about my son's reactions immediately melted when he peered up at Millie, who I could tell was waiting on tenterhooks, and asked, "You want to meet my horse? Her name is Sage."

Her answering smile was of genuine relief. "I'd love to meet her."

The following Monday, I received an acerbic phone call from Hannah, which prompted a subsequent conversation with Millie about perhaps buying land for our future home somewhere outside Jalesville. Late afternoon sunlight fell over us as we rode alongside each other through the foothills astride Scout and Shadow, as we did almost every day after work.

"Wy, absolutely not. Jalesville is your hometown. Do you know how long I've imagined it being mine too? Hannah doesn't bother me; I won't *let* her bother me."

"But it's such a small town. Hannah is already spewing a bunch of garbage about us to anyone who will listen, damn her to hell. I can handle what she says about me, even the lies about me not paying her child support, but I draw the line at what she says about you."

"The people who matter most won't listen to that junk," Millie insisted. After a pause, she added quietly, "Except maybe Zane. I hate to think of the ugly things she might say to him, about me. About us. I'm sorry, Wy."

"You have nothing to be sorry for. Hannah is her own problem now; she can cry and carry on all she wants. Jesus, I just hope she doesn't act that way in front of Zane." The thought filled me with a sense of momentary defeat. "Goddamn her."

"Then whenever he's with us we'll do our best to show Zane what it means to be a happy and loving couple," Millie insisted, not about to let me sink low. "He deserves to see you happy. *You* deserve to be happy, honey; don't let guilt make you think otherwise." And then she sent me the sweet, half-teasing smile that belonged to me alone, the one that knocked the breath from my lungs every damn time. Heeling Scout, she called, "Come on, race you to the rock!"

That first Thanksgiving, as we were all sitting around the tree after dinner, Zane on my lap, he turned to me and asked, "Daddy, do you love Millie?"

There could not have been a more beautiful moment to admit the truth to my son. I studied his precious face in the glow of Christmas lights, the two of us surrounded by family and love. Nearby, Millie knelt at the base of the tree with Ruthie, Becky, Jessie, and Joey, the five of them passing out ornaments for the kids to hang. The warm, glowing colors of the lights spangled Millie's hair and skin, and even though it was far too noisy in the living room for her to have heard Zane's question, she beamed in our direction. My heart swelled with love and gratitude. I would never take a single day of our lives for granted, so help me.

"Yes," I said softly to Zane. "I love Millie."